A Scattering of Jades

ALEXANDER C. IRVINE

TOR®
fantasy

A TOM DOHERTY ASSOCIATES BOOK
NEW YORK

This is a work of fiction. All the characters and events portrayed in this book are either products of the author's imagination or are used fictitiously.

A SCATTERING OF JADES

Copyright © 2002 by Alexander C. Irvine

Edited by John Klima

A Tor Book
Published by Tom Doherty Associates, LLC
175 Fifth Avenue
New York, NY 10010

www.tor.com

Tor® is a registered trademark of Tom Doherty Associates, LLC.

ISBN: 0-765-34098-4

First edition: July 2002
First mass market edition: July 2003

Printed in the United States of America

0 9 8 7 6 5 4 3 2 1

To Elizabeth, Emma, and Ian

Acknowledgments

Thanks to Beth, for deciding that we should go south instead of north on her birthday camping trip; to the rangers at Mammoth Cave National Park, especially Jim Norris and Chuck (whose last name I wrote down but can't find); to Drew Frady, for the Battleaxe Notebook; to Sean Stewart for encouragement and careful reading; to Tim Powers and Karen Joy Fowler for examples; to Anna Genoese, Patrick Nielsen Hayden, and especially John Klima at Tor; to Jenna Felice, gone much too soon; and to Thom Davidsohn, for beers and conversation.

And many thanks to Wes and Donna at Dom Bakeries in Ypsilanti, Michigan; Pam and Chad at Pat's Pizza in Orono, Maine; and Josh, Casey, and the rest of the baristas at Stella's Coffee Haus in Denver, Colorado.

And when a great wise man had spoken well, and taught the people wisdom, they would say *on tetepeoac, on chachayaoac;* there has been a sowing, there has been a scattering of jades.

—Fray Bernardino de Sahagun,
Historia General de las Casas de Nueva España

Prologue

❖

It was midnight. And the gods all took their places around the *teotexcalli*, the divine hearth. At this place the fire burned for four days . . . then the gods spoke; they said to Tecuciztecatl, "Now, Tecuciztecatl, enter the fire!" Then he prepared to throw himself into the enormous fire. He felt the great heat and he was afraid. Being afraid, he dared not hurl himself in, but turned back instead. . . . Four times he tried, four times he failed. After these failures, the gods then spoke to Nanahuatzin, the Scabby One, and they said to him: "You, Nanahuatzin, you try!" And as the gods had spoken, he braced himself, closed his eyes, stepped forward, and hurled himself into the fire. The sound of roasting was heard, his body crackled noisily. Seeing him burn thus in the blazing fire, Tecuciztecatl also leaped into the fire. When both of them had been consumed by this great fire, the gods sat down to await the reappearance of Nanahuatzin; where, they wondered, would he appear? Their waiting was long. Suddenly the sky turned red; everywhere the light of dawn appeared. It is said that the gods then knelt to await the rising of Nanahuatzin as the Sun. All about them they looked, but they were unable to guess where he would appear.

—Fray Bernardino de Sahagun,
  "The Creation of the Fifth Sun"

❖

A bitter wind gusted through the courtyard that separated the sister buildings of the crumbling tenement, animating strips of newspaper and swirls of powdery snow. Lupita shivered, clutching her woolen serape around her as she squatted on her bony haunches and peered into a cracked basement window.

Through the soles of her shoes Lupita felt the earth trembling, as if in anticipation, and shapes rose up in the snow around the courtyard. The ground she stood on had been a swampy pond not so very long ago, and she wondered what the ghosts of that water felt about the magic she'd laid in the earthen floor of the tenement's cellar. Ghosts hated *nahualli* like Lupita, even though sorcery was the only way the dead could ever experience the world of the living; their irrationality was their power and Lupita's danger.

"Shush, Rabbit," Lupita hissed. The *Tochtli*, the Rabbit in the Moon, was angry tonight, and jealous, agitated because Xiuhtecuhtli had roused himself to keep watch over Lupita's magic. Whenever the Old God stirred, the Rabbit chattered. Lupita looked up at the moon, then away again. She felt the Old God's gaze upon her, and it made her afraid as only *nahualli* using one god's magic in the service of another could be.

A little girl toddled into the dirt-floored cellar bathroom. Her mother followed, carrying a bucket of steaming water, a ragged towel, and a sliver of coarse soap. Lupita watched both of their feet carefully, breathing a sigh of relief when neither stepped on the patch of dirt inside the curtained doorway where Lupita had buried the little girl's umbilical cord four years before.

As the woman had approached her time, Wide Hat had instructed Lupita to stay near, and had forbidden her on pain of death to use any potion to speed the birth. The woman's labor, he said, would be short; if Lupita was not ready to deliver the infant and speak the benediction, the sun would pass five hundred twenty times before the signs fell properly into place again. Lupita had prepared herself, and when the woman's time came, the old midwife was there. The girl had crowned less than an hour before the awakening of the sun, during the time most holy to Tlaloc, and Lupita realized that Wide Hat's excessive precautions had been justified. If he truly knew where the chacmool had buried itself . . . she had whispered the required prayers and slunk to the basement with the umbilicus.

It had not been a task she wanted to perform. Lupita had felt the eyes of the Tlaloques, Tlaloc's children, on her the entire time as she curled the gnarled cord and laid the scarlet-and-black pattern of sand around it. Xiuhte-cuhtli watched as well, and the Old God was powerful even on a day sacred to his enemy Tlaloc. A balance existed between them, as between the two poles of a magnet, and what strengthened one also revitalized the other; if this was not true, the world would long since have flown apart into dust and its people been eaten by monkeys. The Old God kept fires, Tlaloc brought forth water from the sky and earth. In their opposition they made the world complete.

Never get between gods, Lupita thought. Yet here she was, turning fire magic to Tlaloc's gain. She tried to keep her mind on her task. The girl was consecrated by birth to Tlaloc, and Lupita had only to collect her and make sure her father thought she was dead.

The charm would keep for four years, she had told Wide Hat after it was buried; beyond that, if she did not dig it up and replenish it, it would weaken. The little girl might be moved, or someone else—another young girl, perhaps, especially one born on a sacred day—could step on the charm and trigger the release of the *mocihuaquetz-qui*, the fiery spirits of women who died in childbirth. They always hungered to add to their number, which was why pregnant women had to be kept from fire.

Wide Hat had not bothered to placate her. Keep an eye on things, he had said, and set out on another of his frequent journeys west and south, looking always for the chacmool. Lupita knew that he would never find it. If her charm worked tonight, and the *mocihuaquetzqui* burned the child correctly, the chacmool would find him.

The little girl stepped into the washtub. It was mad to bathe in the dead of winter, as the woman insisted they do every Tuesday; her god, whose name was Miller, demanded it.

And the madness might not end there. Xiuhtecuhtli's hand would be in the events of this night, and might yet turn them in unexpected directions; he might well prevent his *mocihuaquetzqui* being used in Tlaloc's service. And, as if the Rabbit was playing one of his jokes, the girl's mother—although neither she nor her husband knew it—was carrying a second child.

A parade of human figurines formed from the snow and danced along the sash of the basement window. *Snow is water,* Lupita thought. *Tlaloc knows what is happening here.* She spat into the figures and they fell into powder.

Jane, that was the girl's name. Jane Prescott, born on the day 1-Rain in the month of the beginning of the rainy season Toxcatl, in the last hour before the dawn during the eleventh year before the end of the cycle. Four times consecrated to Tlaloc, to He Who Makes Things Grow. The mother's name was Helen.

Nanahuatzin who will make the sun rise, Lupita droned under her breath as she watched Jane step into the washtub and lift her arms over her head. Her mother swept Jane's dress off and Lupita saw that she was a big healthy girl, as befit one so closely bound to He Who Makes Things Grow. Jane stood shivering and dancing from foot to foot until her mother poured the water over her head. Then she sat down and began scrubbing herself as her mother stood before a mirror brushing out her hair.

Lupita looked again at the foot-square patch of recently turned dirt inside the doorway. She had tried to pack it down and scatter dust to disguise it, but to her eyes it stood out like a fresh grave. Not that it should have made any difference, as she had dug the charm up and reburied it properly with a new pattern of vermilion and charcoal, but this chance would only come once. Wide Hat would be furious if it was botched, and the *mocihuaquetzqui* were unreliable even when correctly confined. They could smell weakness in any magic and they bred like rabbits, and who knew what the Old God would do?

She turned her face up to the moon, which hung like a round white jade in the frigid night. *Do you hear me speak of you, Rabbit?* she thought. *I mean no offense.*

English was ruining her, and Spanish too; she must remember to speak the charm in the old language. As soon as the woman stepped near the patch of earth where her daughter's umbilicus lay buried, the time would be perfect. *Do not fear, woman*, Lupita thought, laying a hand on the satchel between her feet. The warmth radiating from it brought a sting of returning circulation to her frozen fingers. The woman took a step away from the mirror, toward the curtain that hung swaying in the doorway. *Tonight you die as if in childbirth, and in the afternoon you go on to the House of the Sun.*

Then, disaster. The curtain was slashed aside and a Negro girl about Jane's age dashed in, her huge dark eyes fixed on the privy, and planted one bare foot squarely in the center of the reburied charm.

The floor exploded away from the girl's planted foot, and she was incinerated in a pillar of fire that mushroomed out across the ceiling and rained in fat droplets around Jane and on her mother. The woman screamed and tore off her burning scarf, batting at the embers that crawled across her back and scalp. As she fell to her knees, her boots and the hem of her dress bursting into flame, she threw the towel toward Jane. A swarm of the pinpoint-sized *mocihuaquetzqui* swirled around it, charring it to smoldering flakes that hung in the turbulent air.

Jane stood paralyzed in the tub, her screams forming an awful harmony with her mother's. The water in the tub began to boil over the sides of the tub to hiss and jitter on the churning floor. Although none of the *mocihua-quetzqui* touched the girl, patches of skin blackened on her back and face.

Lupita fell back from the window, dizzy with fear and the sudden rush of petulant voices buzzing in her head. At least the charm was doing what it was supposed to, she thought absently; already the burns on the girl's skin had taken on a pattern.

But the *mocihuaquetzqui* were also ferociously out of control. Apparently Xiuhtecuhtli had his own ideas about the girl's destiny.

The young black girl had provided just the stimulus that the *mocihuaquetzqui* needed, bare flesh in contact with the earth that bound them. Now, loosed from the limits of the spell Lupita had pronounced, they shouted and whistled with malevolent joy. Already flames had begun to glow in the tenement's ground-floor windows. People in the building across the narrow courtyard began to take note of the fire; soon a crowd would gather.

Panicked by the thought of losing the girl, Lupita punched through the window and grasped the wooden frame, ignoring the glass that slashed her fingers. She hauled back with all her weight and jerked the window open.

A blast of heat dried her eyes and cracked her lips. "Jane!" Lupita screamed against the throaty crackle of the flames.

The woman, her hair and dress aflame, hoisted the wail-ing girl out of the washtub and turned toward Lupita's voice. She took a step toward the window as her bootlaces flared simultaneously into latticed pale flame.

Lupita stretched her arms toward the panicked woman. "Give me Jane!"

Mocihuaquetzqui raced around Helen's head, burning off the rest of her hair and alighting on the back of her neck. Hot wind howled out through the window now, louder than the child's ragged shrieks, and the sprites rode it in clusters, dancing in an updraft to the roof of the tenement, some catching in clotheslines and on windows-ills, the rest swept away south with the main flow of the wind.

Helen thrust Jane up to the window, and Lupita saw that the *mocihuaquetzqui* had forgotten the pattern she'd carefully laid in the sand. The girl's body was blotched with black and red, the hair burned from her head and one ear melted to a lump.

"Find Archie!" Helen shouted, one of her eyebrows vanishing in a tiny curl of smoke. A string of *mocihua-quetzqui* streaked out the window close enough to singe Lupita's hair. "Find my husband!"

Blisters bloomed on Helen's hands and arms as Lupita gripped Jane under the arms and pulled her through the window. Only a few of the *mocihuaquetzqui* remained in the cellar; Lupita could hear their questions in her head as they burned black streaks across Helen's body—*Is she? Is she? I think—another girl—she'll come with us!*

Helen's eyes widened as they met Lupita's. She can hear them too, Lupita realized, as Helen's mouth opened— what beautiful strong teeth she had—and the last of the *mocihuaquetzqui* dove gleefully down her throat.

Lupita turned with the screaming child and wove her way through the gathering crowd, hearing the futile squeak of a pump handle in the courtyard behind her and seeing the mother's doomed gaze every time she blinked wind-driven snow from her eyes.

———

Her lungs raw from the frigid air, Lupita crouched in a sheltered doorway off Mulberry Street, murmuring a soothing chant until the child's screams subsided into quaking sobs. *You have wearied yourself, you have fatigued yourself, my little one, precious necklace, quetzal feather. You may rest, you may repose.* She rocked Jane gently, searching the street for any sign of Maskansisil or his tribe. As out of control as the *mocihuaquetzqui* had gotten, any of the Pathfinders within a hundred miles would have been aware of the charm. Maskansisil himself would certainly know of it; she would have to leave the city as soon as she concluded her business with Wide Hat.

Lupita finished the midwives' blessing, giving her ancient legs a chance to recover before she set off to meet Wide Hat. *Perhaps, wee as you are, the Maker, He Who Makes Things Grow, shall summon you, shall call to you. Perhaps you shall merely pass before our eyes.*

The *mocihuaquetzqui* still chittered in her head, away to the south. They would have to be reined in before they burned the entire island to the ground, or brought the Pathfinders to her, but she had to get the girl to Wide Hat first. The sprites couldn't move against the wind, anyway, and it wasn't likely that any of the Pathfinders were near. Maskansisil was probably, in fact, the last of them; the whites had destroyed them as surely as they had the rest of the Lenni Lenape, using smallpox and whiskey where bullets and treaties failed.

A crowd, mostly men, materialized from farther north on Mulberry. Lupita tucked the naked girl under her serape and buried the child's face between her scrawny breasts as she scurried out of the doorway and melted into the flow of people. Just as quickly she ducked away from them, though, like a fleeing slave who crosses water just to reverse direction on the other side.

The mob grew more boisterous as it flowed east onto Chatham and then south. The men around her were practically celebrating, some carrying crowbars and large sacks as they skipped along the snowy cobbled streets trailing a wreath of condensation and discordant song.

After the disastrous release of the *mocihuaquetzqui*, the appearance of the crowd struck Lupita as extremely lucky. She looked up and wasn't surprised to see the Rabbit grinning in the Moon. Fickle, *Tochtli*, she thought. Next you will turn them all into turkeys. She let the crowd sweep her south, the press of bodies warming her a bit, until they came to Beekman. By then, her look up at the *Tochtli* had shown her something else, and she ducked away into the narrow quiet of the side street.

The southern end of the island was aglow like the horizon before sunrise, slowly brightening in the clear, terrible cold. Between that, the riotous buzzing in her head, and the mob's fierce elation, Lupita guessed that her fears had been justified. The *mocihuaquetzqui* had ridden south until their progress was arrested by the crosswind that swept the Upper Bay. Then they had fluttered down to burn wherever they fell.

She crept into the overhung gap between Tammany Hall and its nearest neighbor. Pigs snuffled in horse manure shoveled into the alley by shopkeepers, and grunted as they wallowed deeper to keep away the cold.

At the rear of the Hall, a stair led down to a locked basement entrance. Lupita stopped under the alcove at the top of the stairs, relaxing for a moment until she realized how cold she was. She cut that thought off at the root; it would only excite the attentions of the sprites, and she had let her protections lapse. She stripped off her serape and wrapped Jane in it. The girl's eyes were wide and unblinking, and she didn't react when Lupita's fingers, searching for a heartbeat, stuck to the blistered skin of her breast.

Good, Lupita thought. Maybe the pain would keep the girl stunned long enough that she could finish her business with Wide Hat and be gone.

As soon as she had the thought, she chided herself for being harsh. *My apologies, Nanahuatzin; I grow thoughtless when I'm frightened.*

Lupita rummaged in her satchel, bringing out a clay pot heavily wrapped in coarse cotton. She pulled the lid off, her slashed fingers flinching from the heat, and saw that the charcoal-and-vermilion pattern she'd duplicated in the basement floor was undisturbed, pressed flat onto a second lid. The cold made her clumsy, and she wished she could just break the pot and scatter the shards among the rubbish. But that would release the *mocihuaquetzqui*; what she needed was to dispel them.

"Xiuhtecuhtli," she murmured, "call your children back. I have done with them. They drown. They drown."

She flicked blood from her index finger onto the pattern of sand. The wind changed direction and blew more fiercely, howling now out of the west, and Lupita huddled over the pot, protecting it from the angry god. If the pattern was blown away before the banishment was complete, the *mocihuaquetzqui* would level the city. They could not cross water, but that would do her and the girl very little good.

"They drown!" she shouted over the screaming wind. Another drop of blood fell onto the sand, and she took a deep breath against the wind that sucked the air from her lungs. The buzzing in her head grew angry and frantic and her eyes began to water, the tears freezing on her lined cheeks. Lupita gasped and, black spots dancing in her vision, blew the sand out of the pot.

The pot glowed with sudden heat and the sand exploded upward, scouring the skin of her face and stinging in her eyes. She tottered upright and upended the pot, tossing its contents out into the alley. Through streaming tears she saw the second lid shatter on the ground. Where the embers fell, snowy dancers sprang up to stamp them out.

The wind subsided. After a pause, the Old God's held breath blew out, now just a normal December gust and swirl. Powdery snow covered the ashes and drifted over the dead fragments of clay. Wiping sand out of her eyes, Lupita stooped to pick up the catatonic child as she heard the clatter of a wagon approaching down the narrow alley.

The wagon was painted canary yellow and festooned with brightly colored banners and flags that snapped in the blustery wind, advertising dentistry, puppet shows, and other things Lupita didn't have the English to read. Its driver was a sober contrast, dressed entirely in formal black save for a battered rosebud at the left lapel of his woolen greatcoat. Muttonchop sideburns framed a round, heavy-boned face hidden from the nose up by a broad-brimmed hat that he held against the wind as he stepped down amid the broken pottery. He kicked at the fragments, covering first one eye and then the other as they skittered across the earth and packed snow. The two horses, tall spotted grays, tossed their heads and stamped, trying to back away from the spot where the ashes lay covered. A whistle set on the wagon's buckboard keened a note that rose and fell with every gust.

"I've got a thermometer in the back," Wide Hat said. "Fourteen degrees below zero and falling. Fourteen below, and you've nearly burned the city."

"You should know better than to trust mercury tonight," Lupita said.

He shook his head, then looked at her, his eyes still shadowed. "Did you get the girl?"

She tilted her head at the bundle in her arms.

"And you've brought the Pathfinders running, too, I'll wager. Trouble like that could be worth my life. It ought to be worth yours," he said.

Lupita kicked a shard of clay at the horses, a rough triangle with the drop of her blood still frozen to it. The animals whinnied and shivered, rearing into their yoke. "Try to flay me, Wide Hat, and we'll see who wears the other's skin."

Jane thrashed suddenly in Lupita's grip, nearly wrenching herself free. Wide Hat watched intently, covering his right eye. After Jane relaxed again, he stepped forward. "Did it work?"

Lupita held the girl out to him. "See for yourself." He hesitated for just the barest moment before taking her and

peeling the wool serape away from her seared skin. She
wailed as the fabric tore away and Wide Hat clapped a
hand roughly over her mouth. Jane quieted and he
squinted his left eye shut to give her burns a cursory
glance, then nodded as he rewrapped her in the serape.

"There's one more thing you agreed to do, am I correct?"

Lupita nodded, shivering again at the bite of the wind.

"Good," Wide Hat said. He tossed a leather purse at
her feet. She scooped it up and was gone down the alley
before he had remounted the wagon.

The girl wriggled in Riley Steen's grasp again. He shifted
her into the crook of his arm and climbed back onto the
wagon. She cried out, and he fished a plug of leaves from
his pocket and worked it into her cheek before flicking
the reins to move back out onto Broadway. The drug,
together with the wagon's creak, seemed to soothe her a
bit, and he caught himself rocking her as he turned south.
Don't get sentimental, Riley, he told himself. You know
how this ends. You've been waiting nearly thirty years to
have her.

Steen looked to his left, in the direction of Richmond
Hill: General Washington's quarters during the Revolu-
tion, John Adams's home when New York had been the
nation's capital, and later home of Aaron Burr. The Richmond Hill mansion had been the site of the first meeting
between Burr and General James Wilkinson, governor of
the Louisiana Territory and consul to Spain who had first
hinted to Burr that his political ambitions did not have to
end with the killing of Alexander Hamilton. The Florida
question might lead to war with Spain, Wilkinson said. In
the event of such a war, a certain kind of man might be
able to lead an army into Mexico, and once there, might
be able to keep it. Might, indeed, be able to claim everything between the Rockies and the Alleghenies, the Isth-

mus of Darien and the Ohio River. Was Burr that sort of man?

Burr thought he was, and he had in fact raised support from such luminaries as Andrew Jackson to equip his nonexistent army. On several trips through the West and south to New Orleans, Burr incited idle young men with talk of oppressed peasants and border incursions. Merchants built him boats and bought him guns. In the fall of 1806, he actually embarked on the enterprise, gathering an army of roughly one thousand men on an island in the Ohio River belonging to one Harman Blennerhassett.

Blennerhassett had money, and revolutionary fervor—he'd once been involved in Irish terrorism before fleeing to the United States under suspicion of an incestuous marriage. He also had an interest in the sciences, particularly those of an occult flavor, and in the history of Mexico Blennerhassett had discovered the Holy Grail of both his learning and his ambition. "The Aztecs," he said, "were once the most powerful people on this earth. Now they are forgotten, but the power they wielded may yet be ours."

With those words, Blennerhassett had sent the young Riley Steen to Mexico. Steen had spent a full year there, absorbing what lore he could and crating artifacts for shipping to Blennerhassett. At some point during that year, Steen had discovered he had a minor talent for magic, and when he returned to Blennerhassett's Island in August of 1806, he held more power over the Burr Conspiracy than either Burr or Blennerhassett knew.

Burr was visiting when Steen returned, and the three of them gathered in Blennerhassett's magnificent library on the mansion's upper floor. "So at last it begins," said Blennerhassett, and Burr nodded. "We go south in December," he said. "The men will gather and provision here before setting out for New Orleans."

"And if you have not discovered the chacmool by then," Blennerhassett asked nervously, "then what?"

"Then we go ahead," Burr snapped. "I have read the

codices just as you have, Harman. April is the critical month. We must be prepared by then. But this is August, and I am certain that the chacmool lies buried somewhere in Kentucky. I will find it."

"Steen here has something that might help," Blennerhassett said, and Riley Steen uncovered an obsidian bowl in the middle of Blennerhassett's desk. It was nearly brimful of mercury. Blennerhassett gestured to Burr. "Look inside."

"I should think your study would be a better place for this, Harman." Blennerhassett's study, at the end of a long, curving hall leading away from the main house, contained a fairly sophisticated chemical laboratory and a fine selection of scientific and medical books.

Why, Steen had wondered, is Burr hesitating? He has brought us to this point. Is he afraid to go through with it?

Blennerhassett grew impatient. "It's here, Aaron. We're here. Look into it."

For a long moment Burr looked tempted. Then he held up a hand. "I don't believe I should," he said. "Leave sorcery to the sorcerers; if this works as you say it will, that will be proof enough. Who would I see? Wilkinson?"

Burr had laughed then, and looking back on the evening, Steen laughed now, because even at that moment General Wilkinson had been drafting the letter that led to the collapse of the Burr Conspiracy, the exile of Harman Blennerhassett, and the slow, unnoticed ascent of Riley Steen. Whether out of belated loyalty to Spain or fear of his own life, Wilkinson had alerted Thomas Jefferson to the conspiracy. Jefferson had been hearing rumors of it for at least a year but acted only in November of 1806, commanding the arrest of Burr and Blennerhassett. On December 10, the Wood County militia arrived on Blennerhassett's Island just as the expedition force—and Blennerhassett himself—were escaping by boat. Before pursuing the traitors, the militia depleted the estate wine cellar, and Aaron Burr's supposed army escaped down the river. Burr himself was in Frankfort, Kentucky, answering charges of inciting war.

But of course none of them had known that at the time, when it seemed that they might really be able to bring it off. This had all been before the battle of Trafalgar had broken the Spanish navy and inclined Spain to sell Florida rather than fight over it, before Wilkinson had realized that supporting Burr endangered his lucrative spying arrangement with the Spanish government. Absent a war with Spain, Burr's army of disaffected young men broke apart, providing the western territories—it would later be said—with an abundance of dance and penmanship instructors.

Steen remembered that night as a lesson. The contrast between Burr and Blennerhassett had struck him at the time: Burr diminutive but fiercely handsome, charismatic, immersed in the pragmatic world of political ambition and personal advancement, and Blennerhassett tall, stooped, myopic and homely, his head full of ideals, concocting magical schemes while a thousand miles away a man wrote a letter that would bring all of his fantasies crashing down around him. If this goes wrong, Steen had told himself at the time, Burr will survive it. Blennerhassett will not. And Riley Steen? He would keep the power of his knowledge and his anonymity, and when the moment came, his moment, he would not hesitate to commit himself.

"Well," Blennerhassett had said when Burr refused to look into the *tezcatlipoca*, the Smoking Mirror. "Perhaps not. But perhaps it might assist you in locating the chacmool. April, as you said, approaches."

"Sorcery to sorcerers," Burr repeated. "You and your man here can be trusted with it. And, I hope, with this." He removed a leather-bound journal from his coat pocket. "The location of the chacmool is hinted at in this book, but I have spent a good part of the spring and summer scouring Kentucky and cannot find it, and I believe there is no longer time to look. April will have to take care of itself; I must concern myself with munitions, men, and statecraft." He tapped the journal. "It is no longer safe for me to keep this. Can I trust your man here to return it to the correct parties in New York?"

"Steen has never failed me," Blennerhassett said. Burr's uncertainty seemed to settle over him like an invisible weight. His stoop grew more pronounced, and he removed his spectacles to rub at the hooked bridge of his nose.

"Never?" Burr said. "A remarkable record. Pray extend it, Mister Steen."

Steen took the journal and slipped it into his own coat pocket. "I will get it where it needs to go," he said.

"Excellent," Burr had said, and fixed Steen with his commanding gaze. "Very good. And now, Harman, I must to Pennsylvania—after, of course, one last errand in Kentucky."

Steen had indeed gotten the journal where it needed to go: into the hollow of a great sycamore tree on Blennerhassett's Island until December, after the militia had sacked Blennerhassett's mansion, threatened his wife, and run off his slaves. Rumor had it that the great tree had sheltered (among other things) runaway slaves on their way across the Ohio River and love letters between Aaron Burr and Mrs. Blennerhassett, but all Steen found at his return was the journal, wrapped in canvas and jammed into a crevice above the height of a man's head. It hadn't been safe for him to take it to New York, not until he was more certain of how Burr's escapades would turn out; the Tammany Society, then in its infancy, might have misused the information the journal contained. Once he had known the conspiracy to be doomed, known that he no longer had anything to fear from Aaron Burr, Steen had kept the journal himself. He had spent the intervening twenty-nine years puzzling out its contents and pursuing the possibilities he had discovered there- in . . . with a little unsuspecting help from one Phineas Taylor Barnum.

Twenty-nine years, Steen thought as he turned the horses toward a house he kept near the Hudson River docks. I was an Indian fighter then, with magic skulking into my soul, and I may yet be an Indian fighter again if this damned fire brings Maskansisil and the other Path-finders—if any survive—sniffing about.

When morning came, he would be gone from New York. In the back of the wagon he had surgical instruments, tinker's tools, bottles of elixirs and emollients, and a complete set of hand-carved puppets rattling like the teeth of the girl tucked under his coat. He knew ways to get along, and he had been thinking about going into the carnival business. The girl would be his assistant, and he would travel into the West, continuing the search for the chacmool. Burr had been right about Kentucky. The chac-mool was there, and now that Steen had a girl born at the right time and properly disfigured, he had seven years to set things in motion.

In April 1843, the dream of Burr and Blennerhassett would come true. Sad that neither of them would live to see it. Blennerhassett was already dead, in February of 1831 somewhere in the British Isles—two months before Jane Prescott's birth. Burr, nearly eighty years old and in poor health, was likely watching the fire from the window of his grimy hotel room in Staten Island. He would be lucky to survive the winter.

For my part, thought Riley Steen as he guided his wagon into a darkened warehouse, I am going to do my damned level best to keep luck out of it.

A frigid gust brought Archie up short as he rounded the corner onto Roosevelt. He hunched deeper into his up-turned collar and shoved his hands deeper into the torn-out pockets of his tattered greatcoat, but he could escape neither the wind nor the sick embarrassed shame that crept along his skin like a fever. Udo would come through for him if he could, Archie didn't doubt that. He knew James Gordon Bennett, and could probably get Archie on at the *Herald*. The real problem was whether, with or without

Udo's help, Archie would have anything left of his self-respect by the time the first of the year came around. This was all supposed to be different, he thought. My in-laws were supposed to think highly of my prospects, my neighborhood was not supposed to turn into a slum, my wife wasn't supposed to find a church whose leader believes we have to bathe on Tuesdays during the winter. Nevertheless, all of that had happened, and Archie hadn't held down steady work, and he hadn't started a business, and his wife and little girl were living in a slum.

God, it was easy to loathe oneself after drinking with a prosperous German like Udo. Archie shook his head ruefully. *Your last three dollars and you're out drinking.* But that sort of guilt was cheap and easy to come by. It was also ultimately meaningless; if he wasn't able to pay the rent come January, the twenty cents he'd spent tonight would make very little difference.

What would make a difference tonight—or tomorrow, since it was after twelve and the only shops open were groceries—was a little gift. Something unexpected. Candy canes would be good, or a little top for Jane and perhaps a book for Helen. Three dollars would cover it easily, and there was plenty of day work to be had with Yuletide just around the corner.

A little something to say things will get better, Archie thought, and I love you, and even if you want to bathe our daughter when the cold would freeze the balls off a wooden Indian because crazy William Miller says the world's going to end in 1843, I look forward to rowing across Lake Champlain with you when we're seventy.

Ahead, through the blowing snow and skipping bits of rubbish, he could see the broad intersection where Chatham Street widened and split into East Broadway and the Bowery. Almost home, he thought. Home to a warm wife and a sleeping child and never mind the filth and the looming rent and the who-knows-how-many neighbors coughing and screaming at each other all night. Udo would help him out. Bennett would give in, he was expanding after all, and Archie had schooling. There would be a job on the *Herald* for him. He'd start as a pressman perhaps, show Bennett he had a willingness to work, then start asking after assignments. It would all lead to a real house, around Madison Square would be perfect. Room to breathe and no stink of urine and disease choking them on their doorstep.

The clattering din of horses and wagons at full gallop reached Archie as he stepped out onto Chatham. To his left a fire wagon loaded with a dozen men sped south, disappearing down Pearl Street. Looking over the tops of the buildings lining the broad avenue, he saw the hungry glow of fire, a huge one from the look of it, some distance to the south. A ship off the Battery, perhaps? He heard one of the new steam fire engines, its bell ringing and crew shouting, farther down toward City Hall, where Broadway and Chatham angled together. The fire had to be near the financial district.

What a story that would be, he thought excitedly. Shouts were all around him now, scattered small groups of people running past him as he stood in the middle of the street. Firebugs, obviously, but what kind of a conflagration would get even a pyromaniac out in this weather? Bennett wouldn't be able to turn down a firsthand account.

I should be home, though, Archie thought. Should have been hours ago.

Archie weighed the freezing night, the distance to Wall Street, and the thought of Helen warm in bed against the vision of the house on Madison Square. Devil take the cold, he decided. I won't freeze.

As he turned to follow the ringing fire bells, a group of people swept past, carrying bags, pillowcases, buckets, even washtubs. They continued on past him as if he wasn't there, and behind them he could see the tenements of Mulberry and Mott Streets disgorging their dwellers, a flow of people swelling into a mob as if some signal had gone out. Archie recognized some of them, people he had worked with or bought fruit from or had sharpen Helen's knives, and finally managed to catch hold of Mike Dunn, a rail-thin Irishman he knew from the neighborhood.

"Mike!" he shouted over the din. "What's going on here?" As he let go of Mike's coat, his hand came away black.

"You haven't heard?" Mike's eyes gleamed in his stubbled face and a frantic grin bared all of his teeth. "We're headed for Wall Street. Tonight we make a haul."

"What, from a fire? Taking bets on what burns, are you, Mikey?"

Mike shifted his weight impatiently. "Not just *any* fire, Archie. The whole bloody First Ward's gone up. Situation like that, it's every man for himself, know what I mean? Police won't do nothin'."

The black on Archie's hand started to make more sense. "You've been there already?" he asked wanly. If Mike had, it was certain that Bennett had as well.

Mike had started to run again, but he stopped long enough to shake his head. "No, this is from a little blaze we have going right at home. Pickings are better down south, though." He jerked a thumb over his shoulder. "See you there." Mike shouted a laugh and sprinted off after the mob.

A police wagon careened around the corner at Mulberry, and bells rang distantly over the clamor as more and more rival fire crews converged on the blaze. They would do more brawling than firefighting, and then the police would arrest them, but come morning they'd boast about having been there all the same. The racket had also roused a few of New York's ubiquitous pigs, who braved the numbing cold to nose among frozen garbage and mutter porcine threats over fresh horse manure. Mules and dray horses, even a few oxen pulling carts, pushed through ragged clots of people on foot, and standing in the middle of the street was getting dangerous. Getting in these people's way down on Wall Street would be dangerous, too, Archie decided. Not a night to be a policeman.

Fire bells sounded again, nearer this time. Looking back to the west, Archie saw bright flames leaping over the jumbled rooftops of the Five Points. There were always bonfires going in the courtyards of the shabbier tenements, but this was much too large for a barrel fire.

A little blaze we have going right at home, Mike had said; it was on Orange, from the looks of it. The thought got Archie walking again, peering intently at the peculiar shapes brought into vivid relief by the flames. For a moment, they'd seemed oddly like faces. Women's faces.

In a few steps, he broke into a trot, and then he was running, fighting against the tide that flowed from the slums down toward Wall Street.

The four-story building on the corner of Orange and Franklin Streets had been one of the first tenements constructed in the city of New York. Archie had watched it being built in four frenzied days during February of 1832, knowing that when it was finished, he and Helen would finally be able to leave her parents' house and begin a life of their own after six months in the stifling Brooklyn gentry. They had rented a corner apartment on the third floor before the building was completed and moved on the first of March, meeting Udo when they hired him to move their things from the Brooklyn ferry docks to their new home. Jane was born on April third, midwifed by an old Mexican woman who lived alone in the attic.

Originally the ground floor had been home to small merchants, but they were gone and their place taken by starving, cholera-ravaged squatters. Before being built over, the area had been a swampy pond called the Collect, drained because of its threat to public health. But even with the Collect Pond gone, disease persisted in the Five Points. Its victims lay in courtyards until city crews removed them for burial.

Now Archie stood rooted to the cobblestones of Orange Street, helplessly gaping at the burning, blackened ghost of his home. The roof of the Destiny tenement, called by its tenants the Destitute, tilted and collapsed, crushing the rest of the building beneath it and uncoiling a flattened mushroom of fire into the icy December night. Showers of sparks and embers twisted and danced on the frigid currents of the north wind, whirling away south as the gathered crowd scattered to the other side of the street, away from the building's roughly carved cornices shattering on the frozen ground. The piles of refuse choking the gutters ignited in the spill of wreckage, and the few fire companies not gone to the financial district gave up, removing their wagons and horses to safety.

As the street cleared, Archie saw a line of bodies laid in a row on the stones of Franklin Street, scarcely six feet from the mounds of burning rubbish and the collapsed innards of the tenement's rooms. He walked slowly toward them.

Behind him, firemen shouted warnings and someone called out "Suicide!" Archie moved from body to body, peeling back the threadbare coats and blankets covering dead faces. The heat from the fire hung on him like a living thing, steaming the blown snow from his back and shoulders. He lifted the next makeshift shroud, glanced at the tiny form huddled next to it, and sank to his knees.

Helen's dress was nearly gone, a bit of its high collar and bodice all that remained other than a cuff on one blistered arm, and the laces had burned out of the boots he'd bought her the Christmas past. Her hair was burned away, the skin of her neck and scalp split and blackened, but her face was marred only by singed-away eyebrows and its expression; there was no real fear in it, or pain, but a deep and searching shock, as if something at the very end had surprised her more than burning to death in a dirt-floored tenement privy. Whoever had laid her out had tried to cross her arms over her breasts, but one hand still clutched at the singed collar of her dress as if she'd been choking on something.

Archie stood, wanting to touch her but horribly afraid

that she would *feel* dead, that a single touch would strip away the last veneer of disbelief that kept him from walking straight into the firestorm. He couldn't look again at the little girl, at his little girl.

He turned to the fire, feeling his skin redden under the blast, wanting absurdly to say something to it. I could have been here tonight, he thought. I could have been bathing my daughter instead of swilling beer and handicapping faro. He swiped a sooty hand across his eyes, tears streaking black on his face. Now she's lying naked in the street with ashes falling in her eyes.

The wreckage that had fallen farther away from the main hulk of the building was burning down, settling into sullen embers, and among them Archie could pick out debris of peoples' lives—a teapot, the charred rectangle of a box spring, the base of a kerosene lamp, a knife.

As if borne by the fire, the smell of lavender washed over Archie, the smell of Helen's parents' home and the goose they had eaten the Christmas before, when he had given Helen the boots she died in. Helen's mother had given her a set of flatware, and a companion set of knives.

With a hoarse cry Archie ran toward the fire, leaping over the piles of smoking rubbish. A few shouts went up from the crowd, sounds without words. What were the firemen *doing* with their fancy new steam engines?

He kicked the knife out of a pile of glowing ashes, and sparks flared up, caught in the fire's insistent updraft until the north wind bore them away. Archie's hair singed, curling white over his forehead as tears evaporated from his cheeks. Wrapping the hem of his coat around both hands, he picked up the knife and dashed back to the opposite side of the street. Another cheer went up from the crowd.

Archie dropped the burning knife and crouched there sobbing, his gaze drifting through the fog of his breath until it came to rest again on the dancing sparks. They seemed to be flying, not just drifting but dipping and weaving amongst themselves like playful birds, all eventually shooting away on the steady howl of the wind.

Women's faces, he thought. Earlier the flames looked like women's faces. Helen's face, saying goodbye, and I didn't know to look.

The wind shifted and gusted violently, the sparks diving at once back into the roaring flames as if suddenly fleeing the cold night. A soft rain of tiny cinders fell around Archie, and with a booming rumble the rest of the Destiny tenement collapsed into its foundation, timbers falling outward to crush the row of covered bodies. A blast of scorching air knocked Archie off balance; he sat hard in the packed snow, the knife between his feet.

Nothing even to bury, he thought numbly. At least they aren't naked in the street.

Then the bone-chilling northerly gale returned, and he huddled over the knife, his eyes blank as he stared at burning timbers like shadows in the depths of the blaze.

"I thought you would run straight in." The voice had a Spanish inflection. Archie nodded dully, then started as he realized who was speaking. The fire had died down, and when he shifted his weight, the cold groaned in his knees. How long had he stared into the flames? The crowds has dispersed, the firemen gone south. The knife at his feet was dark with soot and cold to the touch.

He gathered it up as the old midwife spoke again. "It would not have helped, you would only have damned yourself," she said quietly, and Archie heard the click of rosary beads flicking through her fingers. "Everyone you lost tonight, you will see again if God wills it." She paused, hitching her breath in the middle of a sigh. "Helen and little Nana—Jane, too."

Archie stared at bare cobblestones where the hot knife blade had melted away the snow. "It *was* Jane, wasn't it?" he said. He thought he was crying, but the fire had dried his eyes. "I couldn't tell for certain, she—she was too—" He waved one hand limply in the direction of the fire.

The wooden beads clicked again as she laid a gnarled

hand on his shoulder. "Tuesday, Señor Archie," she said softly, the lines in her craggy face deepened in the dying fire's glow. "You know the day of the week. She waited a time for you, and they go downstairs and people outside shout fire. Those who got out were running, and she wouldn't leave the little girl. Three men drag her through the window and her still holding your daughter. The firemen laid them together."

He stood, scuffing snow across the bare wedge of stone between his feet. "*Lo siento,* Señor Prescott. A beautiful child," the old woman said, and then Archie stumbled away from her, the knife heavy in his pocket next to his last three dollars as he fled the crowd, fled the noise, the smoke, and the unbearable sorrow.

Sun has already left me,
  has slithered away like a snake.
My heart is like an emerald.
  I must see the gold
My heart will be refreshed,
  man will grow ripe,
and the lord of war will be born.
You are my god,
  let there be an abundance of corn.
The tender tassle of corn
  is shivering in the wind before you
has fixed its sight on you,
  toward your mountains,
worships you.
My heart will be refreshed,
  man will grow ripe
and the lord of war will be born.

—Poem to Xipe Totec

Book I

❖

The light from Stephen Bishop's oil lamp seemed to fade as soon as it left the flame, swallowed by the domed ceiling, the pit that yawned at his feet, and his own black skin. He knew that it dimmed only because there was less surface reflection when he held it over the Pit, but it was always a good effect for visitors to the cave. The elderly Englishman behind him took a stealthy step back, his breath quickening into a shallow pant.

"Bottomless Pit," Mr. Tattersfield said to himself. He leaned forward, resting a hand on Stephen's shoulder, and peered into the depths. "How deep is it?"

"Never been to the bottom," Stephen said. He pulled the light back and turned to face Tattersfield, aware of the emptiness that fell away just a step or two behind his booted heels. "Just from dropping rocks, I'd guess two hundred feet. Maybe more." He knew it was an inch shy of two hundred twelve feet on the opposite side, to the right; he had plumbed it himself the week before. But it wouldn't do for that to get out. Dr. Croghan was not as forgiving of unplanned excursions by his slaves as Mr. Gorin, the previous owner of the Mammoth Cave and of Stephen himself. Gorin had recognized that while people came from all over the world to see the cave, many of them specifically came to be escorted through by Stephen Bishop. And one of the biggest attractions to being escorted by Stephen was the chance of coming upon virgin cave; dozens of rocks and rooms and stifling crawls already bore the names of visitors from the past two or three years. So Gorin had let Stephen explore when the tours were finished and the money made, let him seek out the next place that a tourist would make famous.

Dr. Croghan, on the other hand, demanded that he be informed of every discovery as soon as it was made, and if there was any significance to it, he'd have signs put up all along the road to Louisville and Bowling Green. This brought people to the cave, but Dr. Croghan was slowly stripping the sense of mystery away from it: improving the hotel, hiring an orchestra, building a new road. Stephen shook his head; half the reward of experiencing the cave was that it was difficult to get to the truly magnificent places. Soon Croghan would want to blast entrances straight to anything he thought people would pay money to see.

"How do you figure the depth by dropping rocks? I wouldn't have guessed that a Negro boy in Kentucky would have had much of a chance to read physics." Tattersfield was looking past Stephen and over his head, leaning his liver-spotted hands on the guideposts Mr. Gorin had sunk after someone nearly fell in the pit in 1839.

Biting back a hasty reply, Stephen calmed himself by thinking of what the bewhiskered Englishman would be seeing: the wide passage curving ahead of them to the left, its floor fallen away into the sepulchral black of Bottomless Pit, the shadows growing and twitching on the walls as the lamplight reached its outermost limit, the grooved limestone roof barely visible in the glow of the overmatched flame.

"Mr. Tattersfield," he said evenly, "my name is Stephen. It is not 'boy'; boys tend to get lost in caves this deep." *If you take my meaning*, he added to himself.

He knew he'd spoken too harshly. Croghan might hear of it when they returned to the hotel, but the only consequence would be a verbal reprimand and slight loss of goodwill. Stephen knew he was too valuable to whip, and—to give Croghan his due—he wasn't inclined that way in any case.

Tattersfield blinked, clearly affronted, and looked Stephen squarely in the eye for a moment. But his gaze fell to the dust and mud on his shoes as Stephen looked calmly back at him. The doctor cleared his throat and stood up straighter, brushing at his herringbone trousers, and Stephen felt himself relax; the man was a kindred spirit, after all. Not many sixty-eight-year-old academics cared enough about their studies to hike and crawl more than a mile underground for an observation.

"I read the physics in Mr. Gorin's library, up in Glasgow Junction," Stephen said. The silence had gone on long enough, and he had gotten what he wanted.

Beckoning Tattersfield to follow, he walked out onto the bridge he'd helped build across the neck of the Pit. "He owned the cave up until three years ago. I picked up some Latin and a bit of Greek there, too, but you don't need to tell anyone that." He caught Tattersfield's eye and winked. "Mr. Gorin's a good man."

Seeing Tattersfield was still uncomfortable, Stephen stopped. "They say that wishing on a coin you chunk into the pit is good luck," he said. It wasn't true, but it sounded good, and he had something in mind. He turned out his jacket pocket and shrugged. "Want to make a wish?"

A sheepish smile broke across the old professor's face, the expression of a man caught in a guilty pleasure who secretly can't bring himself to feel guilty. He drew a gold coin from his vest pocket.

"Turn your back on the pit and toss it over your left shoulder," Stephen instructed. "Whoa—make your wish first."

Tattersfield closed his eyes and thought a moment, then flipped the coin over his shoulder. Both men imagined they could hear it spinning through the darkness, then came a sharp *ping*. After another few seconds, a series of more distant *pings* echoed off the walls and roof.

"May your wish be granted," Stephen said grandly.

"There it lies until someone finds the bottom," Tattersfield said, still wearing the embarrassed smile. "I do hope my wish is granted first."

Turning back, they skirted the edge of Sidesaddle Pit, climbing and walking in silence until they reached the narrow crack behind the leaning rectangular stone known as Giant's Coffin. Stephen paused to adjust his satchel before slipping through.

"Stephen," Tattersfield began, "let me—"

Stephen waved the apology away. "No, never mind," he said. "I'm snappish today." He dug in his hip pocket and pulled out a pint flask that still held a few swallows of refreshment. Even in the near-darkness, Stephen could see that Tattersfield could use a rest; he was shuffling and using his hands more, and his breathing had taken on a forced slowness as he tried not to pant. "Nip of good cheer," Stephen said, uncorking the bottle, "and all's forgotten."

Tattersfield accepted the flask, sniffed it, took a drink. His face screwed into a puckered grimace and he shook his head, sputtering violently. "Whew!" he gasped. "God, what is that?"

Stephen drained the rest of the pint in a long openthroated swallow. "Mmm, white lightning," he said, grinning. "Grandma's special." He stoppered the flask and tucked it away as Tattersfield wiped tears from his eyes. "You take the light and go on through. I can do it blind."

Croghan was there to greet them as they walked under the out-thrust slab of limestone that overhung the cave's entrance. He fell into step with them as they trudged up the broad path to the Mammoth Cave Hotel.

"Professor Tattersfield!" he said expansively, vigorously shaking the academic's hand as they walked. "I trust Stephen did not lead you astray or play any of the pranks he is known for." Stephen walked a step behind the two, casually eavesdropping; here was where he would find out if Tattersfield was easily offended.

"Not at all," Tattersfield replied. He threw Stephen a wink over his shoulder, and Stephen's opinion of him went up a peg; if he wasn't taking the stage for Louisville the next day, Stephen determined to take him back to the Snowball Room. He and Nick Bransford had discovered it just a few days ago, and they hadn't told Croghan about it. Tattersfield could take news of a new discovery back with him to England.

"I found the excursion marvelously informative," Tattersfield continued. "The cave is extraordinary and Stephen himself deserves every accolade." He stopped in the middle of the trail. "I believe I'll stay another day or so, have a look at that River Styx if I may. After breakfast?" Stephen nodded, thinking he would have to make sure Nick and his brother Mat had brought the boat back from the far beach on Lake Lethe.

"Splendid." Tattersfield touched the brim of his crumpled hat, nodded to Croghan, and went on up to the hotel.

"Well done, Stephen, although I hardly need to tell you that, do I?" Croghan dropped a fatherly hand over Stephen's shoulder. Stephen tried not to stiffen. His stature—four inches over five feet—and wiry build were perfect for navigating tight seams and turns in the cave, but the drawback to his size was that it seemed to encourage Croghan to treat him like a boy—or like a gifted and loyal dog.

"Are you done for the day?" Croghan said. "Any more tours?"

"I thought I might head back to Gorin's Dome," Stephen said. "I saw a little hole on the way I'd like to look into."

"Think it goes to the bottom, do you? Well, if it does, you take Professor Tattersfield there tomorrow, show him something he can tell his friends in England about."

You know you don't have to tell me that. At least you should. "Yes, sir."

"Well then, all right, get another lamp and have a look around. Come and tell me what you've found in the morning." Croghan slapped Stephen on the back and strode on up the path.

I do think *it goes to the bottom*, Stephen thought as he stood in River Hall, about on a level with where he imagined the bottom of Bottomless Pit to be. A narrow L-shaped seam opened in front of him, at the base of the wall across from the pool called Lake Lethe. He'd noticed the crack weeks before, but this was the first chance he'd had to look into it.

But he didn't think it meandered its way to the bottom of Gorin's Dome, and if for some reason Croghan went looking for him there, Stephen would have to pretend he'd gotten lost. The crack in front of him, if his hunch was right, backtracked and snaked right to the floor of Bottomless Pit. Gorin's Dome could wait; tonight Stephen was after bigger game.

He shifted the scuffed leather satchel on his shoulder and, out of habit, tapped the flask in his hip pocket. The trip was likely to be strenuous, and he'd replenished his supplies before reentering the cave. Apples and cheese, water and a nip of good cheer; that was food for exploring.

Stephen stood still for a moment, listening to the workings of his own mind and the barely audible echoes of the ghosts. The cave was full of them, thoughts and impressions left behind by every man and woman who had ever died there. Mat and Nick heard them too sometimes, but the voices scared the Bransford boys. Stephen found them reassuring, knowing that the ghosts trusted him, that they felt as he did. The cave was awesome and magnificent because of its vastness and its age; it had seen people come and go since long before old Farmer Houchins had chased a bear into it fifty years before, and there were parts of it, Stephen was sure, that no man would ever see.

Croghan was deaf to the ghosts. All he saw in the cave was prestige and money. He admired it while he sucked out its marrow, blasting new entrances, bankrolling schemes like the tuberculosis sanatorium that took up part of the main hall. The man did nothing for the love of it, and his grand plans were turning the cave into just another sideshow attraction.

Stephen listened to the ghosts chuckle and plead. Then he shook off the reverie and squatted in front of the crooked crevice, pushing the satchel in ahead of him.

Just as he'd thought, it turned around a bit before rising gently away from River Hall. He belly-crawled for the first hundred feet or so, pushing the satchel ahead, careful not to knock the lamp against the knobby walls as he pulled himself forward. Then the passage opened enough that he could bearwalk, clambering ahead on his hands and the balls of his feet, ducking his head to avoid spines and ledges projecting from the ceiling. He scanned the walls and ceiling of the tunnel as he moved, seeing no smudges of soot, no charred bits of reed torch that would indicate that someone had been there before him. Most of the cave Stephen had been given credit for discovering had been traveled centuries before by barefoot Indians with cane torches; but there were no footprints here, no seeds, no bits of clay. Nothing but water-smoothed limestone and the occasional outcropping of calcite, gleaming milky in the lamplight. *Virgin cave*, he thought, his pulse quickening.

The passage broadened even more, to the point where Stephen could stand upright, then ended abruptly in a ledge thrust out into a huge dome. A breakdown slide sloped from his right down to his left, fading beyond the range of his finger-ring lamp.

Climbing breakdown was tricky work. Until you found a good path, it slipped a lot, and a long tumble was always a possibility. Stephen had already led two long tours since dawn, and now he at least knew that the branch from

River Hall came out in a big dome. Why wasn't that enough to take back for one day?

Because, he answered himself, *you know it goes. You know it drops to the floor of Bottomless Pit, just like you knew what was on the other side of Giant's Coffin when you dug it out two summers ago.*

Stephen shut his eyes. That was the ghosts talking. He thought of the Allegory of the Cave, one of the first Greek things he'd read, when he was a boy overwhelmed by the dark musty promise of Franklin Gorin's library. People chained in darkness, seeing only shadows of what was outside and thinking that what they saw was all there was; it was an idea he'd never been able to get out of his head. But down this far, the shadows had substance. There was no outside, and when they spoke, that was all there was.

He opened his eyes and looked out into the dome again. From here, it sure looked like Bottomless Pit.

"Dammit," he said aloud. He tried to figure how far he'd come. More than a quarter-mile, less than a half. That would put him right in the neighborhood of the pit.

"Too close not to find out," he said, and swung his legs out into the dome.

The light from the handheld lamp was only good for twenty feet or so, and Stephen kept track of how far he'd come by counting twenty feet when the ceiling of the shaft faded beyond range of the light and marking a discoloration on the wall at his level. When the stain was swallowed by darkness, he added another twenty feet, and so on. After four marks, he could see open ground below him, but it seemed like he'd climbed down farther than he should have. Had he found something else, another pit that dropped parallel to Bottomless? If this passage didn't connect—

He pushed the thought away. It did connect. He knew it and the ghosts knew it, they were loud in his head, some begging him to find them and others jeering at him, muttering that he'd taken the wrong way. He had to be close; they had never been this loud before.

But close to what?

He finished the climb down, dropping off a ledge formed by a fallen rock the size of one of the rooms in Croghan's hotel. His knees nearly buckled when he landed, and Stephen realized he didn't have much caving left in him today. But there was nearly level ground under his feet, and walls winding around him in a rough kidney shape and rising unbroken out of sight. His heart beating fast, Stephen raised the lamp and turned a complete circle.

Something clinked on the floor. Lowering the lamp, he saw Dr. Tattersfield's gold piece winking up at him, not three inches from his right foot.

Bottomless Pit has a bottom, Stephen thought. *And I found it*.

He sat on the floor and basked in the glow of new discovery for a few minutes, digging an apple and a wedge of cheese out of the satchel and chasing them down with a long drink of water. Then the flask came out: he stood, holding it up like a communion cup, and toasted the ghosts.

"Always something new to discover."

And may I always be the one to do it, he added to himself, taking a long swallow and reveling in the liquor's clear burn.

Putting the flask away, Stephen held his watch up to the lamp. It was just after nine o'clock. He'd spent nights in the cave before, but it was not something he enjoyed; besides, Tattersfield would be ready to go at the crack of dawn. Just a quick look around, Stephen thought, and then I can head back before it gets too late.

He walked around the floor of the pit, poking his light into crevices to see if there were any other ways out of the pit. When he got to the narrow end, directly across from the River Hall branch and below the place where the lip of the pit above faded back into the wall, the smoothly grooved walls gave way to a jumble of rocks and gravel. It looked as if part of the ceiling had collapsed sometime after the pit was hollowed out. At the bottom of the deadfall, two huge oblong stones had fallen against each other, leaving a triangular opening between them easily big enough to crawl into. Squatting in front of it, Stephen shone the lamp in. The ghosts, who had been muted since he came out of the chimney, began shrieking and gibbering again, their noise nearly loud enough to drown his thoughts.

It goes, he thought. *I know it goes*.

John Croghan took in a deep lungful of the sharp, rich September air. Fall was a beautiful season in Kentucky, all the better when the people touring the cave were as effusive as Professor Tattersfield had been at supper that night. The Englishman had talked incessantly, paying scant attention to his meal, telling Croghan repeatedly what a marvel the cave was and how excellently Stephen performed his function. Croghan had paid ten thousand dollars for the cave, the hotel, the slaves, everything. In three years he'd made it back five times over.

He tamped tobacco into his pipe and stood at the railing of the hotel porch, thinking of all he had done to make Mammoth Cave the attraction it was. The hotel itself had been little more than a blockhouse when he'd purchased it; now it had been improved and refined into a facility that, if not luxurious, was—notwithstanding the reputation of Bell's Tavern—certainly the best between Louisville and Bowling Green. A fine dining hall, private rooms, a covered wraparound porch, all had been added at his expense. He'd even hired a seasonal orchestra.

Croghan struck a match, careful to avoid singeing his drooping mustache, and savored the smell of good tobacco mingling with the forest air.

The clop and creak of a horse-drawn wagon came from around the corner of the hotel, where the road (another thing Croghan had built himself) led out to the state highway. Croghan checked his watch, replaced it in his vest pocket. It was after nine; where was Stephen? Gone straight home and to bed after his excursion, Croghan decided. He wouldn't have had to pass the hotel to reach the slave quarters overlooking the cave trail.

The wagon clattered into view, and Croghan cocked an eyebrow in mild surprise. He'd seen itinerant tinkers and traveling salesmen, country doctors, carnival wagons, and even wandering dentists, but never had he seen a drummer-wagon that proclaimed its driver to be all of those. RILEY STEEN, read the banners draped along the sideboards. EXTRAORDINARY ELIXIRS FOR EVERY MALADY, PAINLESS DENTISTRY. Below this ran PUPPET SHOWS—HOUSEHOLD GOODS BOUGHT, SOLD, REPAIRED, and a third line said MEDICINES FOR LIFE, LOVE, PROSPERITY. OTHER SERVICES AVAILABLE—INQUIRE!

Croghan squinted at a line of smaller script running along the bottom of the banner nearest him, but the oil lamps hung from the posts of the porch flickered, distracting him as the wagon creaked to a stop. The driver appeared to be peering in the direction of the cave mouth, one hand covering the right side of his face. He grunted in satisfaction, dropped the reins, and faced Croghan. *And this must be Mr. Steen*, Croghan thought. He was glad he didn't have a toothache.

Steen wore a broad-brimmed black hat of indeterminate fabric, pulled down nearly to the bridge of his nose. In the failing light of the lamps, Croghan decided he looked like a man with a toadstool for a head. His topcoat was black as well, and bore a single rose in its left lapel. Croghan caught the odor of myrrh on the breeze, dimly remembered from childhood funerals. He glanced at his pipe. It had gone out.

Steen dropped the reins and pushed his hat up an inch. Croghan noted a squashed cauliflower of a nose and three silver finger rings, set with stones of bright blue and smoky green. For no reason at all, the rings disconcerted Croghan. Nervously he rummaged for a match.

"Dr. John Croghan, if I am not mistaken?" Steen's voice carried the depth and richness one would expect of a salesman, the self-assurance of a actor or medical man, but something else was there as well, a quiet smirk that went well beyond self-assurance. It was the unspoken assertion that *if I am not mistaken* had been a formality, nothing more. This man very rarely found himself mistaken, if that tone was any indication.

Croghan found himself irritated, again for no good reason. What had the man done but offer him a greeting? He was not exactly anonymous in this part of the state.

"I am," he said, more brusquely than he'd intended.

"A pleasure to make your acquaintance," Steen said smoothly. Croghan never doubted that the man had noticed the shortness of his response and chosen to ignore it.

"Likewise," he replied, recovering his civility. "If you've come to see the cave, there's certainly room at the hotel. Professor Tattersfield of Westfield College was through today, and I'm sure he would be happy to share some of his experiences with you if he hasn't retired."

Croghan indicated the hotel's front door with the stem of his pipe. "If you would like to go inside and register . . . ?"

Steen cocked his head suddenly, as if he'd heard a voice he couldn't quite place. He slid out of the wagon seat and bent over. When he stood again, Croghan saw that he had plucked a tuft of grass from the narrow lawn bordering the hotel. Covering one half of his face again, he studied the grass, murmuring under his breath, and Croghan looked up at the night sky. It was clear, but for a moment he could have sworn he'd smelled rain. And the damned lamps were flickering out; someone obviously hadn't filled them properly.

When he looked back to Steen, the salesman was brushing the grass off his hands. "Perhaps I will," he said.

"Pardon me?" Croghan was distracted again. Narrow lines of ants were working their way methodically up the railing. They crawled in sinuous curves around the support posts and onto the lamp fixtures, where they circled the glass rims. Those who fell into the floating wicks were immediately replaced by others from below.

"Perhaps I will. Register." Steen's eyes narrowed as he too took note of the ants. He looked again at the clear autumn sky. "Would it be too late to first have a word with your man Stephen?"

"Ah, so you've heard of Stephen," Croghan said expansively. He stowed his pipe again. "No, I'm afraid Stephen has already retired for the evening," he added, wondering if it was true. "He has a tour scheduled for early tomorrow morning, but when he returns I'll certainly see that you get to speak to him. We offer quite a variety of tours—"

"I suppose I will stay the night then," Steen said. "Could someone see to my horses?"

"Of course," Croghan said, escaping with relief into the hotel to roust a stable hand. That man Steen certainly threw him off balance.

❖

Croghan rose promptly at six the next morning, as was his custom whether at his estate in Louisville or in the room kept for him at the hotel. He was dressing for breakfast when someone knocked on his door.

"Who is it?"

"It's Mat, Dr. Croghan." Even without seeing him, Croghan could tell that the boy was upset. "Come in," he called.

The door opened and the skinny slave rushed in, twisting his cap between long-fingered hands. Croghan saw the expression on Mat's face and stopped fiddling with his cravat. "Well, boy? Out with it."

"It's Stephen, sir," Mat began, the words coming in a trembling rush, "he ain't come out of the cave near as anyone can tell. We was wondering if he talked to you, since Charlotte ain't seen him, nobody seen him, he musta had an accident in the cave since he didn't say nothing about staying the night and he hates—"

"Get Nick and Alfred!" Croghan snapped, flinging the cravat onto his bed. "Right now. He was supposed to be near Gorin's Dome. Hurry!" Mat dashed off to the slaves' quarters near the river.

By the time he returned with Nick and Alfred, Croghan was fully dressed and waiting at the head of the trail that led to the cave mouth. He looked them over quickly. Three young Negroes, eighteen, twenty, and thirty-one years of age; healthy, capable guides, worth perhaps a thousand dollars apiece. Stephen's reputation alone, to say nothing of his skills, was worth more than all three together.

"As soon as you find him," Croghan said as they reached the entrance, heavily shadowed in the thick purple predawn darkness, "send Nick out to tell me." Nick was the least experienced caver of the three, but he was also the fastest. "Do you have rope? Bandages and splints?" They nodded, their faces harshly lit by the glaring lamps.

"Won't need them," called a voice from just under the looming overhang.

Mat, Nick, and Alfred dropped their packs simultaneously and ran into the cave. Croghan started to follow, then remembered his position. A man of his stature couldn't be running around like a schoolboy simply because a slave had gotten himself lost, but still, he barely checked himself. Stephen represented a lot of money and no little prestige.

An excited jumble of voices rolled from the cave, so riddled with echoes that they might have been speaking any language in the world. Dignity be damned, what was going on? He took a step under the overhang and nearly collided with Nick. "Mr. Croghan—"

Croghan cut him off. "Stephen is there? He's uninjured?"

"He look like somethin' the cat drug in, but he okay," Nick panted. He was lighter than Croghan's other slaves—even Stephen, whose father had been white—and a flush was visible under his caramel skin. The phenomenon piqued Croghan's medical interests, but he shoved the thought away.

"What's all the jabbering about, then? Bring him out."

"He'll come in a minute," Nick said. "He found a mummy, just makin' sure Mat and Fred don't bust it up none." Before Croghan could frame a reply, the rangy youth turned and loped back into the cave.

———

Stephen sat on a rock just off the path and watched Alfred and Mat carry the carefully wrapped mummy to the hotel. They disappeared around the corner of the building, and Stephen slid gingerly to the ground, trying to ignore the throbbing in his right ankle and the high, persistent whine of fatigue keening at the base of his skull. Every muscle in his body twitched and trembled, and his hand shook as he drank from his flask.

He tried to remember how he'd gotten the mummy up out of the cave, but his memory of the trip back was gone, lost somewhere in the exhausted maze last night's excursion had become in his mind. Stephen heard Dr. Croghan's apologetic voice explaining to Professor Tattersfield that all tours would be postponed a day, the professor graciously accepting the delay. He rubbed his hands across his face and walked himself step by step through the previous night. The lead away from River Hall, the winding crawl, the gold coin and the rush of exhilaration at having conquered Bottomless Pit, the triangular opening that looked too regular, too *made*. Reaching the lamp in and hearing the cacophony of the ghosts, feeling certain that it led somewhere, scrambling through the short tunnel into the domed chamber beyond . . .

The room. Everything became confused in the room. Stephen placed his palms flat against his temples and massaged gently, trying to paint a coherent picture of the room in his mind. It wouldn't come. Disconnected images thrashed in his head, fragments of odor and sight and sound, but he could make nothing of them.

He remembered walls, squared off into terraces rising beyond the range of the lamp, the wall opposite him completely lost in the darkness. A stone block, its top face slanted with the high edge toward the invisible far wall. A dead man, a mummy, reclining on its slanted top, head sunk into its chest and hands cupped over its stomach, bare feet dangling over the block's lower edge. Feathers, he remembered feathers. Long and green, they sprouted from the mummy's shoulders and flowed over the stone's sides. Its skin was tautly drawn over the bones of its face, strong teeth bared to the silent gloom. Deeply set stains on the stone's carved sides and at its base seemed to trickle as the lamp's flame guttered in the still air. Figures of snakes and birds, of men in bizarre masks, undulated under the wetly gleaming stains, their strange movements leaping out at him as the rest of the room faded into a shadowy indistinct mist. He smelled rain, felt it cool on his cheeks, heard it sizzle as if falling into a fire. An immense growl rumbled through the chamber as Stephen caught the hot meaty stink of charring flesh, and then the darkness consumed the weakly flickering lamp.

Tlaloc.

He heard the word as clearly as if it had been spoken, and the chamber began slowly to fill with a murky orange light, the struggling radiance of twilight or the last hour before dawn. The clean smell of falling rain warred in his nostrils with the wicked burning stench as the far wall resolved into a giant bas-relief of a masked and cloaked figure holding what looked like a lightning bolt in one hand. A line of human skulls trailed from the other, weaving between the figure's dancing feet. Its slanted eyes were starkly outlined in red, its lips drawn back in a fanged snarl and split by some kind of bar. Feline ears lay flat on either side of a headdress worked with feathers and a repeated pattern of a crescent moon inside a setting sun.

Tlaloc, macehuales imacpal iyoloco. The words tolled silently through the chamber, and Stephen understood them now: *Tlaloc, He Who Makes Things Grow, he holds men in the palm of his hand.*

The figure on the wall grew indistinct again, the light falling only on the line of grinning skulls. One of the skulls spoke: *Yollotl, chalchihuitl, in nelli teotl.* The words echoed from the mummy on the stone: *The heart, the precious blood, the one true god.* The reclining figure turned toward Stephen with a grating creak of dry bones. He saw that its rictus grin had grown fangs, and its skull seemed flatter and broader, its legs drawn up and crooked, its cupped hands thickened into paws. It lifted its arms, and Stephen saw a human heart beating in the shadowed cavity of its belly.

"Stephen."

Stephen looked up, squinting in the morning sun as if he'd just come from the cave. "Dr. Croghan?"

Croghan looked disturbed and uncertain as he inspected the bowl of his pipe, turning it this way and that before he finally spoke. "How's the leg?"

Stephen noticed he was rubbing at his right ankle. Trying not to wince as he stood and tested it, he shrugged. "It's fine. Good as new in a day or so." In truth, his ankle throbbed fiercely. He wouldn't be much good in the cave for a week.

"Good." Croghan paused a moment. "I'm afraid there won't be any more of these solitary excursions into the cave. From now on, you take one of the others with you." Croghan mouthed the stem of the pipe, working it from one corner to the other. "Paying guests not included. If you want to chart new cave, there has to be someone with you to get you out of any trouble."

"Wasn't no trouble last night. It just took longer than I expected."

Croghan's jaw tightened, his lips compressing into a thin line around the pipe stem. "I will brook no argument on this point, Stephen. You would be difficult, I daresay impossible to replace, both in terms of skill and reputation. Shenanigans like your jaunt last night are far too great a risk to my investment. Understood?"

Stephen stared at his feet, not trusting himself to respond.

"Fine," Croghan said. Stephen watched an ant scramble between blades of grass as the doctor turned back up the trail.

Riley Steen examined the artifact he had placed on the windowsill of his room. It was a carved obsidian bowl approximately a foot across with a flattened bottom that allowed it to sit without rocking. The Aztecs had called it *tezcatlipoca*, smoking mirror, and Steen had liberated it from Harman Blennerhassett's library after the Wood County Militia had finished in the wine cellar and gone off chasing after Aaron Burr. The glossy surface of the mercury filling the bowl cast a perfectly circular reflection of the sun on the ceiling, a good sign. It would cast no reflection of Steen at all, though; he tried not to think of that and returned instead to the delicate task that awaited him.

Perhaps he had calculated correctly from Burr's garbled commentary. Steen looked out the window, watching the two slaves carry the wrapped figure of the chacmool up the trail and around to the back of the hotel. He chuckled softly as he imagined what Croghan must be thinking: another desiccated savage, more free publicity for his precious investment. *Mr. Croghan*, he thought, *you'll never know the debt I owe you. You and your crew of cave-crawling niggers have made this easier than I ever dreamed possible.* Burr had spent years fruitlessly searching for the chacmool, and now Steen had simply waited for it to show itself. Now he would take hold of the moment. Croghan needed money, Steen needed the chacmool: a mutually beneficial exchange. After conducting necessary business, Steen would take the chacmool back East and safeguard it until it reanimated in December.

The only problem now was the girl. He had underestimated her, and she had escaped from him in Richmond almost eighteen months ago. But how many places could an eleven-year-old girl with disfiguring burns hide? He would find her.

She knew, after all, that her father hadn't died in the Great Fire seven years before. Therefore she had most likely returned to New York in search of him, and if she had, the Rabbits would soon enough locate her and return her to him.

But back to the task. Steen stepped back, closing his eyes and moving from side to side until he felt the reflected sun shining directly into his face. Opening his eyes, he gazed steadily into the blinding glare for a full second. When he closed them again, the afterimage was bright and sharp, a perfect sphere with no darkened spot within. Definitely an auspicious sign, but he wished he'd had a chance to look at the moon last night around nine-twenty, when the ants on the porch had so shaken Croghan. The chacmool must have awakened, if only briefly; it would be useful to know how long it had been able to sustain itself.

But now, in the morning sun, it was dormant, and if Steen had any luck at all, it would remain so until he had it safely in New York. He ran through Burr's figures again in his head, remembering the feel of the moldering book in his hands. Phineas Taylor Barnum, there was another man he owed a debt. If Barnum had not bought his American Museum's collection whole from John Scudder, who previously had come into possession of the Tammany Society's early archives and with them Aaron Burr's other journals, Steen would never have been able to find his way to Kentucky.

The journal Steen had taken from Burr back in 1806 held a partial solution to the puzzle of the chacmool, but Steen hadn't put the rest of it together until he had gone through Burr's papers in the basement of the American Museum—before he and Barnum had fallen out. Burr had dated the *xiuhpohualli*, the Aztec year-count, from A.D. 1011. Steen had been puzzled by the figure until he researched other accounts from Mexico and Pennsylvania, whereupon he discovered that A.D. 1011 was the year when Aztec records and those of the Lenni Lenape, the Delaware tribe of North America, coincided. The Red Record of the Lenni Lenape gave that as the year they had driven the people they called the Snake down into the "land of swamps." Steen had been to Mexico and seen the ruins of Teotihuacan on Lake Texcoco, all but obliterated by the bustling squalor of the City of Mexico. Land of swamps; it was an apt description.

The Aztecs recorded the date as the year in which they left the "northern paradise" and wandered until their hummingbird god, Huitzilopochtli, showed them the sign: an eagle perched on a cactus eating a snake. There they settled and lived until Cortés destroyed them. The Aztecs, believing him to be Quetzalcoatl himself returning from over the sea, had been betrayed by their own myths.

Living amid a clutter of gods and ceremonies borrowed from the peoples they conquered, the Aztecs had blurred the distinction between those that were merely empty ritual and the few that had any real potency. Their Achilles' heel had been losing sight of the old gods, the elemental deities whose worship began in the faded mists of Mesoamerican antiquity. And if Steen had read the old account correctly, the swathed figure lying amid wine racks in the hotel storeroom was one of those few, the very avatar of the ancient god of earth and rain whom the Aztecs had named Tlaloc. The god's true name was lost, as was the name of its avatar; the Quiche Maya, hoping to tame it, had named the avatar Chacmool, or Red Jaguar.

Steen was reluctant to accept Aztec history at face value. Their recordkeeping tended to be metaphorical, on the order of the Seven Days that began the Book of Genesis, and Burr himself was hardly more reliable. But even if the date 1011 was not accurate (and the appearance of the chacmool at this time strongly argued that it was), the fact that the same date appeared in both histories was definitely significant. Aztec and Lenape history agreed that the date was sacred, the beginning of a new cycle of fifty-two years.

Such cycles were the basic unit of chronology in ancient Mesoamerica. At the end of every one, the gods grew fickle and great sacrifice was required to prevent them from destroying the world. Counting forward from

A.D. 1011, one came forward fifteen cycles to 1791, the date of the American Museum's founding with the Tammany collection and of the white man's discovery of Mammoth Cave. The Tammany Society had been founded a few decades earlier, in honor of the Lenape chief Tamanend, and early Tammany braves had been the first Pathfinders, assisting the Lenape in their task of keeping watch over the threat of the Snake.

Later, of course, the Tammany Society's more immediate political goals had gotten in the way of such mystical altruism. Aaron Burr's search for the chacmool had been every bit as perfidious to Tammany ideals as his attempt to splinter the Republic had been to the Founders' idea of America. After Burr, Tammany Hall had forgotten its origins. Steen, however, had not.

The next cycle would begin in 1843, April third to be precise. Jane Prescott's twelfth birthday. It was a time when new gods could be created and old ones resurrected from the oblivion of forgotten worship. A time when the Pathfinders could be eradicated once and for all. A time when history could be written, when anything was possible for the man who knew how to avoid the errors of his predecessors.

There was a respectful knock at the door. Steen turned to stand in front of the mercury mirror. "Who is it?"

"Nick Bransford, Mister Steen."

Steen recognized the name after a moment; one of the slaves who worked as guides to the cave. "Come in," he said.

The door opened and Nick stepped into the room, keeping one hand on the doorknob. "There's a visitor for you, sir," he said. "Colored man."

"A colored man?" Steen's brow furrowed. What Negro would know he was here? "What's his name?"

"He called himself John Diamond, say he come from New Orleans. You forgive my saying, sir, he look like a drunk."

It took Steen a full ten seconds of gaping astonishment

before he could gather himself to speak. "Send him up," he finally murmured.

As the door closed, Steen found himself fingering the chipped edge of the obsidian bowl. "John Diamond," he murmured to himself. He hadn't spoken the name in over a year, since he had drowned Diamond in a nameless tributary of the Mississippi River near Natchez Under the Hill.

Steen replaced the carved lid on the *tezcatlipoca*; a chat with Lupita would have to wait. Portent after portent, he thought. Eighteen forty-three was going to be a very big year indeed.

The morning sun was welcoming, and Archie Prescott left his room a good two hours before he had to be at the *Herald* to clean the presses and begin setting type. It did him good to walk the city on sunny days. The light banished the worst of the morbid affectations to which he found himself susceptible during the night. When he got out into the streets, amid the shouts and clangor of New York commerce, he was able to see beyond himself a little. Or perhaps he was just able to distract his mind from the enduring pain of loss.

He considered himself a broken man. Not one of the poor raving wretches who limped aimlessly through the Whiskey Wards in search of some lost vision of themselves they'd lost through gambling or drunkenness, no. Just a man unable to make peace with the losses life had inflicted upon him. Archie had spent years trying to deny this to himself, but in the end he had to admit that something inside him had died along with Helen and Jane in the fire seven years before. It was better, he believed, to appraise oneself honestly.

Sunlit days and the bustle of the city helped him, though, and Archie was not so self-pitying as to deny himself what pleasures he could still take. Walking was one such pleasure. Drink was another, chiefly nocturnal, indulgence.

From inside the door of his rooming house, Archie peered into the street, resting his hand on the doorknob until he'd satisfied himself that the mad little street urchin who thought she was his daughter was nowhere in sight. This determined, he opened the door and walked quickly out of the Five Points. Out on Broadway, he felt better. He nodded at shopkeepers and pedestrians, bought a loaf of bread for his lunch, wandered south and west for a while before eventually doubling back and finding himself on Nassau Street.

A young, balding man in a clerical collar thrust a handbill in front of Archie. "Are you familiar with *Prigg versus Pennsylvania*?" he asked.

Archie's first instinct was to brush the paper aside, but he checked the impulse. A journalist had to pay attention to voices in the streets. "*Prigg versus Pennsylvania*," he echoed the clergyman. A Supreme Court decision. He remembered reading about it somewhere, in one of the papers, but couldn't recall the substance of it.

"I'm not," he said, and accepted the handbill.

"Imagine being born to slavery," the divine said. "Reaching your majority amid the crack of the whip and the groaning songs of Africans yearning for the freedom God ordains for every man. Imagine, then, that you steal away one night. You elude the searchers with their rifles and hounds, you survive a barefoot sojourn through the mountains of the Cumberland or the Tidewater swamps of the Carolinas. You avoid the pickets at the Ohio River, or the slave-catchers at the ports of Baltimore, Savannah, Charleston. You voyage north toward freedom and encounter kindness, sup for the first time at the table of dignity. You build a life for yourself, working and living as a free man in Philadelphia or Boston or here in New York, becoming the full soul that God intended. Would you not say, sir, that a man of such strength, of such fortitude, deserves the reward of freedom?"

"Yes," Archie said before he'd had a chance to think about it.

"Then you must join us in protesting this outrage of *Prigg versus Pennsylvania*!" the divine cried. "The Supreme Court of this land, charged with upholding our constitutional and God-given rights, has sunk instead to the basest, most scurrilous pandering to those who value dollars more than souls. After *Prigg versus Pennsylvania*, those brave Negroes who survive the awful rigors of their boreal flight to freedom may be brutally snapped up and returned at any moment during the rest of their lives. When they've married, had children, become churchgoers and pillars of the Negro community, they must suffer the constant fear that a bounty hunter may lay vile hands upon them and spirit them away from home and family to the living death that is chattel slavery! Can such a thing be tolerated? Can we suffer such a gross abridgment of liberty in this, a free country under the eyes of God?"

"But *Prigg versus Pennsylvania* was decided in March," Archie said, remembering more about its specifics, "and the Fugitive Slave Act—"

"Is an abomination in the sight of the Lord!" the divine interrupted thunderously. "The most execrable obtrusion of evil ever to afflict this continent! This was the test of *Prigg versus Pennsylvania*, and seven justices unfit to bear the appellation failed it. Are slaveholders pursuing their human chattel to be treated in the same fashion as banks, amassing their resources unimpeded by any but corrupt federal oversight? Are slaves so many gold bars, to be hoarded for the enrichment of a few wealthy men? *Prigg versus Pennsylvania* says yes. The Supreme Court has ruled that the right of a slaveholder to recover his property—*property*!—outweighs the inalienable right of that property to life, liberty, and the pursuit of happiness. No Negro is safe when a slave-catcher can contest his citizenship, can call into question his very status as a human being. And no right-thinking citizen of the Republic can be safe when such injustices can be freely perpetrated upon our most helpless brethren. Have you, sir, ever heard the term *blackbirders*?"

Archie had. He had seen quite a few of them, in fact, haunting the Five Points, which as New York's poorest neighborhood was also its most racially mixed. Blackbirders purportedly hunted fugitive slaves, but their actual activities consisted mostly of hunting for opportunities to accuse Negroes of being fugitives. Each blackbirder had a group of ready witnesses and a preferred magistrate, and they did a steady business in removing unlucky Negroes from New York to (the clergyman's words rang in Archie's head) Baltimore, Savannah, or Charleston.

"Then you know," the clergyman said, "the depredations these blots on humanity visit upon the liberty of your black brothers."

Archie nodded. An exposé on blackbirders, he thought. Bennett might take an interest in that. The publisher didn't like Negroes, and he hated abolitionists, but he was a very bloodhound after judicial corruption.

"Did you know that these abominable men even steal children?" the divine went on. "Just this past Sunday— Sunday, sir!—a Negro girl, eleven or twelve years old, skipped down Anthony Street to get water from a pump in the tenement adjacent to hers. Fifteen minutes later her father went to look for her, and found the bucket she'd taken, half-filled next to the pump. In a frenzy of worry he searched for the girl, and at last—O heartbreak!—he discovered her fate. Can you imagine, sir? An eleven-year-old girl whisked away in the foul hands of a trader in human souls? And her *father* . . . ?" The clergyman paused, seeing something in Archie's face. "Now you see," he said. "You are of an age to have such a daughter, aren't you? And you possess a sensitive soul. You can see yourself in this poor girl's father, running through the streets in a futile desire to recapture your child, to see your flesh and blood safe again. With you again."

Archie took a step away from the clergyman, bumping into someone behind him. The clergyman closed the distance between them again, and a softer expression banked the zealous fire in his eyes. "If I have caused you pain," he said, "it is to my regret. But we all must begin to share the pain of the oppressed."

He started to go on, but a chorus of vulgar shouts from the other side of the street cut him off. Archie turned in time to see a volley of eggs and rotten vegetables splatter across the cluster of agitators. A window shattered behind him, and as he flinched he caught a glimpse of the plaque next to the building's doorway: AMERICAN ANTI-SLAVERY SOCIETY. Ah, he thought. William Lloyd Garrison's band of Baptists. No surprise there. But who's breaking it up?

Across Nassau Street, a group of young Irishmen readied another vegetable salvo. That made sense too. Irish and blacks competed for the same housing, the same jobs, so naturally the Irish were violently proslavery. Slaves had no influence on wages; free Negroes did.

Each of these b'hoys wore red piping on his trousers, though. That was the uniform of the Dead Rabbits, one of New York's more organized and dangerous gangs. The Rabbits were Tammany muscle, too. This was no random act, then, but what interest did Tammany Hall have in abolitionism?

The clergyman who had first arrested Archie's stroll around lower Manhattan now strode across the street, his head thrust forward and right index finger jabbing at the Irish gang. "You!" he shouted, and his voice cracked. The Dead Rabbits laughed and echoed "You!" in sarcastic falsetto.

"You of all nations," the clergyman went on, "who have known tenant slavery under the English crown, who are beaten in the streets by nativists, despised and kept from common society just as Negroes are. Of all living souls, you should understand the justice of our cause!"

One of the Rabbits stepped forward and knocked the clergyman down with a slashing right cross. "Never compare an Irishman to a nigger," he said, and broke an egg over the clergyman's head.

Several women, their black dresses and severe braids speckled with eggshell and tomato seeds, rushed to the clergyman's aid. "Shame!" one of them cried. "Is this what your pope teaches you?"

"Enough, Margaret," the clergyman said. He wiped blood and yolk from his face. "We will not," he said, standing with a hand on her arm, "answer their vitriol with our own."

Together the abolitionists recrossed Nassau Street and went into the headquarters of the American Anti-Slavery Society, followed by jeers from the red-piped b'hoys. The protest had dissipated, and Nassau Street slowly began to refill with traffic that crushed beneath wheels and feet the broken rinds and rotted pulp of the hatred (Archie thought, already composing the article in his head) that the poor reserve for each other.

Archie was distracted and clumsy at work that afternoon, spilling boxes of type and once dumping a bottle of ink over the imposing table next to the press. Luckily Bennett hadn't come out of his office all day, and Archie's misdeeds cost him only a little joking from the other pressmen. Blackbirders, he thought over and over again, trying to focus on the angle for the article he wanted to write. The clergyman's words to him, though, kept repeating themselves in Archie's head: *You are of an age to have such a daughter, aren't you? And you possess a sensitive soul.* Archie's hands shook whenever he thought of that poor Negro shouting through the Five Points in futile pursuit of his daughter who was gone to bear chains and cry out at the crack of the overseer's whip. Better, almost, to know that one's daughter had died. At least then a man could mourn and go on.

As you, Archie said sardonically to himself, have done so admirably.

Udo arrived with fresh paper as Archie was munching his bread around sunset. Looking at his old friend, Archie could not help a spasm of jealousy. Udo had prospered in the years they had known each other. He delivered personally only to Bennett and one or two other important customers; others received their goods from one of Udo's growing staff of drivers. His success showed around Udo's waistline, and he had become a sort of avuncular pillar of *biergarten* society. His wife was fertile as a flowerbed, his children learned French from tutors, his house had stained glass in its parlor windows. And through all of his success, Udo had not forgotten his friendship with Archie. He still took his own stein when he met Archie for beer and conversation.

"I saw an abolitionist rally today," Archie said as they rolled paper through the *Herald*'s loading door. "The Dead Rabbits broke it up."

Udo shook his head and paused to mop his scalp with a handkerchief. "Troublemakers, all of them," he said. "Abolitionists and Rabbits."

Archie knew Udo hated to discuss politics with friends, but he couldn't forget his mental image of the bereft Negro father discovering the bucket of water and knowing. He must have known what had happened. "Blackbirders are stealing children off the streets," he said. "Children. How must that feel?"

Udo looked Archie in the eye. "You have sorrow enough, Archie. Don't go looking for more."

That wasn't good enough. "Children, Udo."

"Archie, I hire blacks. I pay them like I pay whites. This is what I can do." Udo looked as if he might say something more, but instead he pocketed his handkerchief and walked toward the door. "Let's finish up."

Sometime after midnight, Archie rounded the corner onto Orange Street, his fingers sore and purpled with ink that never quite washed away. Music played from a basement grocery somewhere, accompanied by yells in a language Archie didn't understand. He looked up and down the street. An oyster vendor hitched up his horse and left for more comfortable parts of the city, or maybe just went home. Sailors swaggered, whores beckoned, the destitute watched it all from windows or shadowed corners. Archie was exhausted.

On the steps of his rooming house sat a child-sized figure wearing a hat and heavy coat. Archie stopped in his tracks.

No, he thought. I can't face her tonight. Not with that damned weeping Negro chasing after his daughter in my head. Tonight I need to be able to remember my daughter as she was. That maniacal, horrible shambles of a girl has no right to stalk me the way she does, no right to claim my daughter's name.

Better to have lost one's daughter, Archie thought for the second time that day. He backtracked around the corner and found his way into a grog shop on Leonard Street. Better to mourn and go on.

Quecholli, 11–Deer—September 29, 1842

❖

Steen watched the lithe figure of John Diamond blend quickly into the crowds in front of Independence Hall, then vanish behind a passing cab. Aaron Burr had spent more than a little time conniving in that building; Steen wondered what sort of backstage machinations had been going on during the Constitutional Convention. Because Burr had died disgraced, history had not recorded his true influence. Steen intended to leave a more distinctive mark. He would capture history in his hands and make it speak.

The clock on the Independence Hall tower read eleven twenty-eight as Steen flicked the reins over the horses. They started slowly, tired from the long journey through the Cumberland Gap and north from Baltimore. New horses were definitely in order upon arriving in New York, but Steen's mind was on other things. He hadn't much time before his surprise appointment with Phineas.

How had Diamond found him? Steen had been worried when informed of the dancer's presence, but not over-much; if Diamond had intended any sort of revenge, he would hardly have advertised his arrival. And he hadn't acted at all hostile on the long trip to Philadelphia; rather, he had supplied Steen with an extremely valuable bit of information.

Why, Steen wasn't sure. There were many things about Diamond that Steen wasn't sure of. The dancer might have been walking and talking, but he was obviously far from normal. He smelled of the swamp he'd drowned in, dark rings encircled his bulging eyes, and he muttered to himself—not always in English—at inopportune times. Noon and immediately before sunrise were times of noticeable peculiarity, which was why Steen had let Diamond off before the meeting he had planned for noon. He wanted all of Barnum's attention focused on the merchandise.

Steen frowned as he guided the horses through Philadelphia's crowded streets. If any man had cause to swear vengeance on him, it was Diamond. He had died hard, drowning faceup with the tip of his nose barely three inches deep in the silted water of a Mississippi River inlet.

A New Orleans native, Diamond had been a dancer in Barnum's Grand Scientific and Musical Theatre when Steen had been the company's puppeteer. Jane Prescott had recently escaped from him, and Steen had discreetly let it be known that he was interested in finding a certain Mexican woman named Lupita, whom he thought was in Louisiana. He had been sure that Lupita would be able to locate Jane, and in the spring of 1841 Diamond had led Steen to her in Natchez. The reunion had quickly turned ugly, and Steen had been forced to kill Diamond when the dancer tried to leave.

Steen had been owing Lupita a debt for nearly six years at the time; after her *mocihuaquetzqui* had gotten out of control the night they had captured the girl, Maskansisil himself had come to New York on her trail and had instead found his. Steen had barely escaped with his life the night the Pathfinder had caught him, and when Lupita refused to assist him in tracking Jane he had let his self-control lapse.

Killing Lupita had been sheer pleasure, revenge for Steen's terror during those weeks when he had been certain that Maskansisil would drop out of every tree, but Steen had regretted having to kill Diamond; generally he didn't like blacks, but the dancer had been a valuable asset.

"Sorry, Johnny," he'd said after the last bubble had

broken on the surface and Diamond's struggles had stopped. "There are only so many people who can know about this, and I'm afraid you're not one of them. And there are far worse places than Tlalocan."

As the water settled into perfect stillness, the reflection of the moon had resolved into a glossy circle over Diamond's dead face. The *Tochtli* had been prominent that night; Steen remembered wondering what portent that held. Perhaps a man drowned under the Rabbit would be drunk when he got to Tlalocan, the afternoon paradise reserved for those who died of water or weather or earth. He had left Diamond's body where it floated in the thigh-deep water; a dead Negro floating in the Mississippi was hardly a noteworthy occurrence.

And now, for reasons Steen couldn't begin to fathom, Diamond had sought him out.

Steen turned south onto Front Street and moved at a trot past Society Hill, preoccupied with the strange signs the sky had been giving in recent weeks. The Rabbit, for one; it had been everywhere lately. Beyond being a symbol of drunkenness, the *Tochtli* was also associated with the south and uncertain fortune; it could mean anything, depending on what other signs it was found in conjunction with. The signs that night in Natchez had maintained a stony indifference, even as he went back up the rotting stairs to the hovel to make sure Lupita's ancient body wouldn't rise of its own accord and follow him.

The signs were no clearer today, especially since the sun was obscured by stubborn clouds. It was the last day of Quecholli, when a feast generally took place, and the sign was Deer—sacred to Tlaloc—and the number was eleven, generally unlucky.

And the month has a bloody R *in it*, Steen thought. None of it meant anything as far as he could tell.

At least he wouldn't have to worry about Maskansisil any more, not if Diamond kept his word and found Tamanend's mask. Tlaloc must have gotten to the dancer when he'd drowned; why else would a man do such a tremendous favor for his murderer?

The late-morning sun was a pale smudge in the lowering sky as Steen brought the wagon to a halt at Penn's Landing. Gulls dipped and swooped in the chill wind that blew off the Delaware River, their shrill cries gnawing at his already-fatigued nerves. He looked anxiously up and down the docks, trying also to keep an eye on the back of the wagon. Any would-be thief would get the surprise of his life, particularly today, but Steen hoped to avoid any disturbance; he wanted to accomplish his goals in Philadelphia and move on to New York with as little distraction as possible.

He checked his watch: eight of twelve. Barnum was supposed to be on the twelve-thirty steamer going up the river to Trenton; he should have arrived by now. Cursing the paleness of the sun and the looming proximity of the Gloria Dei church, Steen walked rapidly in a clockwise circle around the wagon. Diamond had said Barnum would be here, and Johnny certainly had sources that were uncommon to say the least, but the showman was nowhere to be seen. Hundreds of people were boarding and disembarking from steamboats all around Steen; it was possible Barnum had simply passed unnoticed.

Steen caught himself mouthing Nahuatl curses under his breath, and he closed his eyes and leaned against the wagon's ribbed canvas. He counted slowly backward from twenty, breathing deeply and evenly through his nose, feeling the heavy veil of tension lift from his mind. Nothing would be gained by stamping around in circles and cursing the day for being cloudy.

When he opened his eyes again, a group of approximately fifteen children had appeared and formed a semicircle around him. "When's the puppet show?" one of them asked. "Do you do *The Battle of New Orleans*?"

The group was ragged and undernourished, varying in age from seven or eight to perhaps fifteen. Probably runaways and orphans who had banded together for protection; if he had encountered them at night and in a secluded area, they would more likely be demanding his purse than asking for a show. Steen had given hundreds of shows for groups of children when he was younger, purely for the joy of it, and these disheveled urchins looked as much in need of a little diversion as any he'd ever seen. He looked from face to face, wondering which of the old Punch and Judy shows he could remember unrehearsed; then he spotted P. T. Barnum over one of their shoulders.

"No performance today, guppies," he said regretfully, shaking his head. "If you can get to Shackamaxon tonight, you might see a real show." Barnum was gesturing expansively as he spoke to a mustachioed and immensely fat man in a red stovepipe hat.

"Some puppeteer you are," one of the children said, and the rest began complaining boisterously, cursing to shame a sailor as Steen swung up into the driver's seat and spurred the horses in Barnum's direction.

"Ahoy, Phineas!" he called. "Half an hour before your ship leaves, isn't it?"

A look of surprise crossed Barnum's jowled face, but the showman quickly assumed a neutral expression. "I won't inquire as to where you came by that information, Mr. Steen," he said coldly. "In any case it is of no consequence; we have nothing to discuss except reparation for your breach of contract."

"Bygones, Phineas, water under the bridge," Steen said, before Barnum could resume his conversation. "I have something in the back of the wagon here that I believe would be quite a sensation at your museum. It's a good many years older than your Joice Heth, and authentic to boot." He winked broadly at Barnum's companion.

"Perhaps we could resume our discussion on board," said the red-hatted buffoon. "In this chill, I'd like to ensure I get a seat near the boiler." He tipped his silly hat and made his way toward the waiting steamer.

Barnum watched him walk away, then returned his attention to Steen. Steen clicked open his watch and shook his head gravely. "You've only got forty-five seconds to catch the show, Phineas. After that, it's over for the day, you're gone to New York, and I have to search for a buyer here."

"Well, you've certainly queered my negotiation with Pembroke there," Barnum replied, frowning at the wagon's flapping banners. "I hope that this show of yours is worth it."

"After you see this, Phineas, you'll thank me for bringing it to you first." Steen stepped around to the back of the wagon, looking again at the sky as he did so. He was unsure whether the heavy cloud cover would have an effect; if it did, Barnum might well walk away, or—if he was feeling petty—call the police and have Steen arrested.

All over a simple case of answering the door when opportunity knocked, Steen thought. When Diamond had brought Steen information about Lupita, the opportunity for revenge was far too important to be subordinated to a traveling medicine show. Steen had secured advance wages from the company bursar and headed north on the river to see if Diamond's claim was true.

Barnum had been far more angry about the loss of his prized dancer than the trivial amount of money taken; he claimed lost ticket sales in excess of five thousand dollars. And, after the events at Natchez Under the Hill, Steen had thought the chances of Barnum hiring Diamond back very slim indeed.

But now Diamond was back, he thought as he tied open the flaps on the back of the wagon, and it might not be a bad idea at all to have him working for Barnum again. It was something to look into if the demonstration went as he hoped it would, and Barnum bought the chacmool for exhibit at his Museum. The American Museum was safe ground of sorts, a place where Steen knew the chacmool wouldn't be disturbed until it reanimated in December. The old Tammany collection, dating back to the time when Tamanend himself had still walked the earth, would attenuate the avatar's power. Selling the chacmool to Barnum would also net Steen some much-needed cash. Money no longer flowed from the Tammany coffers the way it had before Martin Van Buren's defeat in the 1840 presidential election, and that damned Croghan had driven a ruinous bargain.

"Ten seconds," Steen said, beckoning Barnum to stand beside him. The showman's eyes widened as he looked into the wagon bed.

The chacmool looked none the worse for its arduous trip from Kentucky. It lay on its back, the cloak of green quetzal feathers carefully arranged around it. Its hands were empty, crossed on the fragile skin of its chest; Steen had thought of mocking up some sort of weapon but decided against it. Barnum was an expert at spotting frauds when he cared to be, and Steen wasn't altogether sure he wanted the chacmool armed, not until he was reasonably certain of a few things.

Steen's watch said twelve o'clock. The light seemed to grow brighter in his left eye, while in his right it seemed to bend, as if deforming under some incredible weight. Ants, hundreds of them, appeared from nowhere to crawl across the wagon bed, and then the feathers started to move.

They twitched and swayed, slightly at first. Then the motion became more precise, a rippling that swept up and down the cloak in clearly defined waves. Barnum forced his attention from the phenomenon long enough to look at the sky, and Steen knew he was smelling rain.

A dull creaking sound jerked Barnum's attention back to the wagon. The mummy's hands were moving; they uncrossed, slowly, and slid down its emaciated torso until they formed a crude bony cup over its navel. Its head turned back and forth, and the skin of its cheeks cracked and fell away as its mouth opened and shut. The bald head bent forward until the mummy's chin touched its chest, and over the rustling of the feathers Steen heard a choked whistling in its throat.

Then it shuddered and was silent, its head lolling back

onto the wagon bed. The rippling of the feathers lost its pattern; the cloak twitched and quivered a few seconds longer, then it was still.

Steen let the flaps drop and turned to face Barnum.

"Easily enough done for a man who knows how," Barnum said hoarsely. His eyes remained fixed on the back of the wagon.

"You smelled the rain, Phineas," Steen said, grinning. "You can't tell me you didn't smell the rain. And the fire."

A FEW STARS glittered through the broken clouds and the canopy of leaves spread by the Shackamaxon Elm. John Diamond walked slowly to the base of the tree, trying to step quietly among the fallen leaves. He dropped the shovel from his shoulder and leaned against the cool bark of the old tree, fighting to still the muttering in his head. *"Hue-hueteotl, huehueteotl moyucoyatzin, teteu inan, teteu ita."* Diamond gritted his teeth, but the words forced their way out. *The Old God, he who created himself, mother to the gods, father to the gods.*

He looked around the massive trunk of the elm at the few lights still burning in the city. Had he spoken? The Rabbit alone knew, the Rabbit in the moon; the *huehueteotl*, Xiuhtecuhtli, had thrown the rabbit at the moon. It spoke with his voice.

A kaleidoscope of voices rattled in Diamond's mind, a thousand visions of the world to come and as many memories of lives left behind.

Is he badly wounded?

This is a mortal wound, doctor.

Find Burr.

That voice, the Burr-voice, returned often, speaking to itself, gibbering about lost opportunity until stronger speech drowned it out: *Tlaloc, imacpal iyoloco. He Who Makes Things Grow, he holds us in the palm of his hand.*

"*Imacpal iyoloco,*" Diamond said aloud. "Sorry, Johnny." He shook his head and began to dig.

Rain began to patter in the tree's leaves as soon as the blade of the shovel bit into the soft earth. Diamond wished he could feel the downpour, but the canopy of leaves kept most of the rain off. Thin rivulets streamed from low-hanging branches as the rain fell harder, though, and soon Diamond was as wet as if he'd been standing atop the Second National Bank. The rain made him stronger, even as the growing mound of earth at the base of the elm turned into mud and slid back into the hole he was digging.

He kept doggedly at it, not even certain of what he was supposed to find. Lupita's voice came frequently, but it was always faint and quavering, the words mostly lost among the myriad other voices that competed for Diamond's attention. She had told him to dig here, that something was buried in the roots of the tree that Steen wanted very badly; that was good enough for him.

I never wanted to be dead, Diamond thought, chopping through a root. *And once I was dead, I damn sure didn't want to come back, with no one but the moon to talk to.* He felt like Tecuciztecatl, standing before the hearth that would ignite the sun; he knew what he had to do, but was afraid to do it.

Steen had been right when he said that there were worse places than Tlalocan. But even leaving the paradise of afternoon would have been tolerable, Diamond thought, if he could have left it completely behind. As it was, he had been given a glimpse, and now the voices, the smells and colors of the place followed him.

It was all Steen's fault. Why was he getting the mask for Steen?

But it hadn't been his idea. Other voices were speaking for him, and he couldn't always even move his own body. *Imacpal iyoloco.* Drowning him, Steen had turned him into a puppet.

"Damn Wide Hat to hell," Diamond panted, then he stopped and stood up. Wide Hat? He knew he meant

Steen, but he had never heard the wagoner referred to by that name.

"Sorry, Johnny," he said bitterly. "No telling who's in your head now."

The root snapped under a last thrust and the shovel struck something with a sharp clank. All of the voices immediately fell silent, although Diamond could feel their intent focus.

He realized that he could see better at night than he used to; the scored corner of metal glinted despite the heavy rain and clouds, catching his attention before the rim of the hole collapsed and covered it again. He dropped to his knees, then flat onto his belly, digging in the mud until his arms were buried to the elbows. Water ran down Diamond's neck and dripped off the tip of his nose as he worked one hand through the muck under the flat, heavy box. With the other, he scooped mud away behind him, finally exposing the lid.

He seized the corner, the weight of his body loosening the walls of the shallow hole. Grunting, he pulled the box halfway loose, but the earth under him finally gave way and he slid forward. His head went briefly underwater, and he paused there a moment to rest. It was too hard to be on land all the time.

Then he righted himself, got his feet under him, and jerked the box free. He pushed it up onto solid ground and hoisted himself out of the thigh-deep hole. It was rapidly filling with water, and he shoveled the rest of the mudpile back into it. The quagmire would be noticed in the morning, but Diamond planned to be far away by then.

The pelting rain had cut visibility to a few feet, drowning the scattered lights that still burned in the city. Diamond decided that was a good thing; a black man digging at the base of the Shackamaxon Elm, where William Penn himself had made peace with Tamanend, would be sure to rouse suspicion.

He laughed out loud suddenly. "What could they do to me? Sorry, Johnny—not much." Diamond sat heavily at the base of the tree and inspected the box. Its lid was about twelve by eighteen inches and it measured maybe six inches deep, made of some kind of lacquered wood. Beaten copper, green from long burial, reinforced the corners, and a pattern was carved into the lid. He held the box out into the rain until it was washed clean, then examined the picture.

It was an engraving of a beast that combined features of man and jaguar, adorned in cloak and headdress. Diamond looked closer; its tongue appeared to be forked, and if he wasn't mistaken its eyebrows were upswept feathers, smaller and thinner than those that made up the cloak. It was depicted from the waist up, puzzling Diamond until he turned the box over and saw that its lower half was engraved there.

The box had no lock and appeared to open lengthwise, with the carving split by an invisible hinge. If the box was opened, Diamond realized, the engraving would be made whole. And what would happen then?

It's an engraving of the chacmool, Lupita said. The other voices murmured a nervous assent.

"I know," Diamond said aloud.

You know nothing, Lupita said shrewishly. *No Mexica carved that box, no Toltec or Olmec.*

"Lupita, if you're going to rattle in my head, say something," Diamond groused. He opened the box.

The darkness inside it leaped at him with a snarl. An agonizing cold weight pressed on his forehead, and he reeled back, dropping the box and crying out like a child.

Then, with a light push, the cold was gone. Diamond rolled in the mud, clutching his head until the pain subsided sufficiently for him to sit up and lean against the solid weight of the tree.

Have to get wet again, he thought. Been on land too long.

The rain had stopped. Diamond looked up and saw stars winking again through the elm's dripping leaves, and he saw the Rabbit's head peeking from the shadowed part of the moon. His teeth ached like they were all going to fall out.

Idiot, Lupita said. Her voice was distant, quavering. *Get the mask and go before Maskansisil himself strings your guts around this tree.*

I can go now, Diamond thought. Whatever was in the box freed me, a little bit. I can do what I want.

And Riley Steen, that means you can go to hell.

Diamond looked for the box and saw only a canvas-wrapped bundle, lying amid leaves stripped from the tree by the pelting rain. Then he found the box where he'd dropped it on the filled-in hole. He nodded to himself; seemed like he owed old Wide Hat a bad turn or two, all things considered.

The bundle seemed heavier by itself than it had been in the box, and the canvas wrapping was rotting where it touched his hands. He shouldn't put it back in the box again, he knew that.

Diamond laughed again, thinking of how mad Steen would be when he didn't show up in the morning with the mask. Then he thought of what he was going to have to do, and that wasn't quite so funny.

"Never wanted nothing to do with no magic," Diamond grumbled as he thrust the bundle and box separately under his sodden coat and made his way down to the river. "Sorry, Johnny."

Panquetzaliztli, 13–Wind—October 14, 1842

❖

Archie Prescott awoke to the sound of cannonfire. He sat up in bed and squinted blearily out the window, half convinced he'd heard the sound in a dream. The cannon fired again as he kicked at the pile of blankets and clothing he slept under in the unheated room. His feet caught in the tangle and Archie tumbled onto the rough wooden floor.

"Dammit," he muttered, looking at his elbow. A thick splinter was buried half an inch or more under the skin. He picked at it, ink from his fingers rubbing off on the wood, then drew it loose. It caught for a moment, then slid free, and Archie shuddered as he flicked it into a corner. The feeling of it sliding out from under his skin, the idea of something actually inside him, made him violently nauseous.

The cannon fired a third time, and Archie remembered the occasion. The Croton Aqueduct was complete, and New York was celebrating. After two hundred years of uncertainty, the city finally had a dependable source of water. Archie untangled his feet from the bedding and dug his trousers out of the pile. He stepped into them as he moved to the window, hooking his braces over his shoulders.

He could see two blocks north, to the intersection of Leonard, where Orange slanted away to the right. It was just after dawn, but the street was already alive with wagon and foot traffic. Drunken laborers swayed out of basement grogshops, leering and shouting at the whores who jostled with newsboys for position on the corners. The paperboys thrust their sheets in front of everyone passing, even leaping onto the running boards of passing carts to harangue the drivers for a block or so before dropping off and returning at a trot. They hawked pamphlets and broadsides on temperance, abolition, the Oregon question, anything that would draw attention. And they waved copies of the *Weekly Register*, the *Courier and Enquirer*, and the *Herald*.

Below the window, a group of boys had gotten up a game of town-ball, using shingles as bases and an unripe orange for a ball. As Archie watched, one of the boys connected solidly, splattering pulpy bits of citrus across the front of Emil Kornheiser's grocery. The old shopkeeper ran out into the middle of the street, flailing a broom like one of the boys' bats, and the teams scattered laughing into alleyways. There they would wait until Emil withdrew and they could steal another orange from his produce bin to start the game anew. Nothing ever changed in the Five Points; the beggars, the whores, the strange boy on the corner stroking his pet rabbit and watching the game of town-ball. They would all be there tomorrow and the next day and the day after that.

Archie had other plans. He felt strangely rejuvenated by his experience at the abolitionist rally, the unexpected collision of Protestant and Catholic, native and Irish, rich and poor. The tension of it captivated him. The very air of New York seemed in ferment: Romantic writers, Transcendentalist philosophers, suffragettes and abolitionists, Millerites and Fourierists and Owenites, all churning out visions of utopia. Archie, after nearly seven years of malaise, had once again been infected with desire to live. Today he would join New York in its celebration. He did not intend to waste the rare holiday.

Bennett, in a rare act of generosity, had given employees with more than five years' service the day off to enjoy the festivities. Archie had been a pressman with the paper nearly seven years; his anniversary would be in January, twenty days after the anniversary of the fire that had taken his family from him. Even now, thinking of it brought the meaty stink of charred flesh rushing up from his memory.

I survive it, though, he thought. Every day I survive.

For seven years, anesthetized by grief and liquor, Archie had spent his waking hours running presses and then slept tangled in the sheets of a rooming house scarcely two blocks from where his home had burned the night of the Great Fire. Bennett had asked him, in the weeks following the fire, to write an eyewitness account, and Archie had. Since then, though, nothing he'd written would please the irascible Scot, and until the gang breakup of the American Anti-Slavery Society demonstration, Archie had moved through his toneless days animated only by memories and the fading ghost of ambition.

Like a dog returning to its own vomit, he thought from time to time. He was becoming the subject of a sermon somewhere. Old Man Miller probably published pamphlets about men like Archie. But Millerites were always littering the streets with broadsides and handbills. The last one Archie had seen offered Miller's mathematical proof that the world would end in April.

Thinking of William Miller brought Archie's mind around to Helen and Jane. It was only recently that Archie had been able to quarry his memories of them, chiseling aside grief to find veins of happiness. Lake Champlain was one he kept returning to, and the time Jane had looked at the moon and for no discernible reason said, "Rabbit," in her awed little-girl voice.

"Where's the rabbit?" Helen had said, and Jane had pointed to the full moon's cratered face.

"Well, carrots don't grow on the moon, and I don't think rabbits eat cheese," Archie had said. "He must get awfully hungry."

They were still painful memories, even the ones—especially the ones—that had once been pleasant, but in seven years of looking for stories, Archie had found more than a few that matched his own for horror and pathos. If anything was to be had in New York, it was misfortune; fires, pox and cholera, starvation and murder. Archie sought it out, chasing funeral processions to gain perspective on his own loss. Part of him was convinced that if he saw enough, he might be able to believe that Helen and Jane were just two more corpses pulled from one more fire that rated a paragraph on the *Herald*'s back page.

"*Schadenfreude*," Udo had clucked to himself the one time Archie had been drunkenly honest enough to admit his feelings. But Archie didn't need any Teutonic aphorisms to justify himself. It was all very simple.

You're a bastard, Prescott, he thought, *chasing others' misfortune to forget your own.* That small self-loathing usually disguised itself as ambition, keeping Archie far enough out of the bottle to hold his job.

Today, though, he felt different. He felt hopeful. Somewhere out there was the story that Bennett would not be able to turn down. Maybe something would happen at the Water Celebration, something Archie Prescott alone could suitably commit to paper. Whistling a popular tune whose name he couldn't recall, Archie rummaged in his pockets to see how much money he had and to locate his key. On the street, a wagon loaded with barrels of beer forced its way through the crowd. The driver cracked his whip over the mules, the beggars who ran alongside the wagon, and the pedestrians who blocked his way. As he cursed a knot of women going to market, two men ran to the back of the wagon and made off with a cask. As soon as they had it free, the women strolled on and the driver, none the wiser, resumed his slow progress.

At the corner beneath Archie's window, the troop of paper-sellers converged on the wagon, their high-pitched shouts carrying above the constant din of the intersection. He looked from one to the next until he found the only girl in the group, a pathetic wisp bundled in clothes far too large and a pair of men's brogans, a battered cap pulled low over her face to hide her disfigurement. It was her, the poor lunatic girl who had for some reason fixated on Archie, following him around and calling herself his daughter. He was already dreading the confrontation he knew awaited him on the front steps.

He looked around the room, something nagging at the back of his mind. The tick mattress on its low frame, the battered writing desk and chair rescued from the garbage, the washstand with bowl and ewer; everything he owned was in its place. He had his coat, and his notebook and pencil were in his pocket; his hat hung on a nail by the door.

The knife, that was it. Archie took a short step in the direction of the bed, but he didn't want to look at it and be reminded. Its blade was still streaked from the intense heat of the fire, even though he'd had it polished and sharpened. A new handle had been put on as well, but the blue-brown streaks on the blade could only be removed if it was completely reground.

And memories were hardly the worst of it. Whenever he touched the knife Archie had the uneasy feeling that he was attracting . . . not attention exactly, but some kind of offhand regard. Of what he couldn't say, but the feeling was there nonetheless. Every time he left his room without the knife, he was plagued by the sensation of having forgotten something. With an effort, Archie left it where it was under the bed and went out into the hall, carefully locking the door behind him.

The girl selling the *Herald* was waiting for him on the front stoop when Archie came out onto the porch. He had a few pennies fished from his pocket, hoping that for once he could just buy a paper without having to speak to her. Her addled conceit that she was his daughter brought certain memories a bit too close to the surface, and they were already bubbling dangerously high that morning. He took a deep breath, waiting for the gauntlet to begin.

"Morning, Father," she said, pushing the stained cap up to her hairline. The pale, puckered welts that dominated the right side of her face flushed to an angry red as Archie looked at his feet, the chipped paint covering the porch, anything to avoid having to look back into her hatefully glittering eyes. "Can't you see it's me, Jane?"

She smiled, showing crooked gray teeth, the smile pulled into a leer by streaked ridges of scar tissue that disappeared under her cap. She had taken the cap off once, revealing the bald patches on her head and the twisted knot that had once been an ear; it had been weeks before Archie could sleep again.

"Can't you see it's me, you bastard?" He could see her shoes, toe to toe with his, but he still couldn't look at her. He stood frozen in place on the slanting porch, holding out the handful of pennies and wondering for the thousandth time where she had heard that his daughter's name had been Jane.

"In the circus Mr. Steen told me where to find you," she said. He could smell the rancid tang of her anger, feel the tension as she trembled furiously in front of him. "In the circus they know lots of things, and when they tell you they beat you so's you remember them right."

Archie thought that if he had to look at her, he would simply go insane, join her in raving at passersby and accusing random workmen of being father or lover or long-lost cousin. He knew that in a few seconds, having exacted her tribute of him, she would slump and allow him to pass. As he stepped past her, careful not to brush up against the ragged cutoff overcoat she wore, she would begin to sob. By the time he reached the end of the block, she would be cursing him at the top of her lungs.

He'd written an article for Bennett about her and the multitude of others like her, demented by the savagery of their young lives, fixating on wishes and nurturing fantasies until they believed them to be true. Bennett had read it quickly while slurping oysters in his office, then set it aside. "Mad children are the project of the Ladies' Home Missionary Society," he'd said in his thick burr. "They don't sell papers."

Bennett might have been correct in his observation, but

Archie wished fervently that the society would take this particular girl on as a project. She bedeviled him to the point where he could only banish the memories with gin.

Standing on the porch with his hand held out, eyes closed lest he see her ravaged face, Archie couldn't remember what Helen had looked like. But his memory of Jane had never faded, chubby, laughing little dark-eyed Jane pointing at the moon over Lake Champlain; this wasted creature capering out of the gutter mocked her memory.

He heard her sniff, saw that as he'd expected, she was crying. She picked the pennies off his palm one by one. "The paper's only a penny, but it's always all right to accept a gift from your father, isn't that right, Da?"

Archie didn't answer. He took a paper, folding it under his arm as he walked off down the bustling street. By the time he turned down Worth toward Broadway, she was screeching like a Fury.

Broadway was full of New York's wealthy, promenading slowly north toward the new Croton Reservoir at Forty-second Street. Their carriages were freshly painted in vivid blues and stately black, their horses brushed to a shine and bedecked in bells and ribbons. Archie watched them as the omnibus he'd caught at City Hall Park jostled along, the driver shouting indecipherable Gaelic threats at coachmen, pedestrians, and pigs alike. A long line of similar vehicles streamed north along the thoroughfare, carrying those too poor to afford a carriage of their own. The edges of the street were jammed with families and strutting groups of young men, the men calling to the women who waved and flirted out the windows of the cabs. Serious-faced young children tried to carry themselves like the society folk across the way while avoiding the pigs that rooted in the gutters and dodged nimbly in and out of traffic. The activity was dizzying, too chaotic to be boiled down into prose. Archie leaned back against the hard wooden seat, closed his eyes, and tried again to come up with an angle on the holiday. Persistence was the key.

The omnibus cruised to a halt at the corner of Forty-second Street. This far north, Broadway was a wide dirt track, graded but not yet paved. Away to the north was farmland and the occasional sprawling manse, while to the south Archie could see the city gradually gather itself into the maelstrom of the Lower East Side and Wall Street. Bells rang as wagons moving south with produce or livestock tangled with those carrying dry goods or scrap iron north to the city's growing outskirts. Drivers flung curses at each other and, not infrequently, exchanged lashes.

It was all, somehow, very fine. Mad little girls were a part of living in the Five Points, but New York had much else to divert the mind and engage the senses. Do not dwell, Archie told himself, on misery. Udo is right. Don't go chasing sorrow.

Archie jumped over a wallowing sow to the margins of the torrential human flow, where people stood and meandered in small eddies instead of charging headlong into the current. A breeze came up, and a column of fallen leaves charged down the street until pedestrians crushed them underfoot. Archie walked for a short time among the crowd, getting a sense of them before arriving at the reservoir, where Mayor Morris would give his speech.

The cannonfire that had awakened him would have been the fanfare of the opening ceremonies near the northern end of Manhattan Island. That had been perhaps an hour ago; the parade would be arriving soon to make the situation even more of a mob scene than it already was. Best to find a place to sit and read the paper until the parade arrived. Reactions of the crowd to the mayor's speech would be interesting, although hardly novel, as Bennett had no special affection for Morris and attacked him in the *Herald*'s pages at every opportunity.

No surprise, Archie thought. Ever since Bennett had fallen out with Matty Van Buren, he had savaged Tammany Hall whenever he had the chance. It made little difference; Tammany owned the city, and during Old Kinderhook's presidency, the Society had pulled America's strings as well. Now that Van Buren was out of office, they had retreated from their ambitious national agenda, but within the city Tammany Hall had always run things fairly well the way it wanted. They were far too powerful and entrenched to be bothered by the accusations of a newspaper publisher whose audience was limited to those who could read.

Which by no means meant that they would not take measures to protect their reputation. Archie knew at least a dozen people who bore scars or a limp from having spoken the wrong way about a particular "brave" or "sachem," as Tammany members called themselves. The terms made him snort; he didn't think any Indian had ever been a member of the Society. Shaking his head, he unfolded the paper and found a bench to read it on.

His attention was immediately riveted by a headline below the obligatory blazing paean to the aqueduct. TAMMANY VOTE-FIXING OUTRAGES REVEALED! it read. Below it was the byline: Eye Peeled on Orange.

It was his byline, the one Helen used to tease him with when he dreamed of publishing his own paper some day. He had used it exactly once, when the *Herald* had run the back-page paragraph about the "other" fire of December 15, 1835.

What was Bennett thinking? Archie skimmed the story quickly—the usual collection of allegations that everyone knew to be true but nobody cared to prove, enlivened by Bennett's bombastic editorial asides and eyewink.

Surely he had people covering Tammany Hall, and one of them had just as surely fed him the information in the article. But why publish it under Archie's byline? Restive after Van Buren's failed reelection bid, the Hall was inclined to return to the old days of running the city and throwing their weight around in Albany. Any attempt to shake their hold on the boroughs would bring a swift reprisal, and they doubtless had ways to find out who "Eye Peeled on Orange" was.

So Bennett was intentionally waving Archie in front of the Tammany Society, a red flag in the face of a bull already angered by the banderilla of Van Buren's defeat. What in God's name was in Bennett's head? It was a situation that could get Archie killed.

Archie flinched as the paper was snatched from his hands. He looked up to see a long-legged young Irishman with a soap-locks haircut calmly fold the paper twice and slide it into the pocket of his coat. Following the motion, Archie saw red piping on the sides of the youth's trousers. A Dead Rabbit. Tammany had found him already.

"I agree," the Rabbit said, rubbing the few whiskers on his narrow jaw and looking around, " 'tis a fine day to be admirin' yer handiwork, isn't it? I'm a bit put out myself. All them names and I'm not mentioned once."

Smirking, the b'hoy executed a graceful mock bow, his pale green eyes never leaving Archie's face. "Royce McDougall, Mr. Prescott. I'll thank you to remember that next time you take up your pen."

He moved closer, shifting so the sun came directly over his shoulders. The blinding halo obscured the features of Royce's face.

Archie looked away, blinking, and saw that the crowd was giving his bench a wide berth. Lounging near a pile of uprooted tree stumps were two more Rabbits, and Archie thought he saw another standing behind Royce.

"Archie?" Archie squinted back up at Royce. "I might advise you, though, in the spirit of human kindness, that there are some who might prefer that you direct your attentions elsewhere." Royce stepped aside, and the sudden sunlight blinded Archie completely.

He ducked his head, grimacing in anticipation of the first blow, and flinched again when Royce whispered into his ear, "I'm sure a man of your perceptive qualities will take my meaning."

When Archie could see again, the Rabbits were gone,

melted into the milling crowd as a strident brass march announced the arrival of the parade.

Bennett looked vaguely irritated as he invited Archie into his office. He sat and indicated Archie should do the same.

"You and I both have plenty to do, Archie," he said. "What was it you wanted to say?"

"Mr. Bennett," Archie said, "I noticed this article in the paper today." He flipped open a copy of the day's *Herald* that lay on Bennett's desk and pointed at the article that bore his byline.

Bennett leaned back in his chair and pulled at his bushy red sideburns. Through the window behind him, Archie watched traffic streaming up and down Broadway. "Seven years ago you used that byline once," Bennett said. "It's a clever one, but you can hardly be proprietary about it, can you?"

He picked up an editing pencil as he spoke, doodling a succession of arrowheads across the blotter that covered the desk. "If all you've come to do is complain about trivia, Archie, I don't have time," he said, glancing pointedly at the grandfather clock in the corner near the door.

Archie bristled at the cavalier disrespect in Bennett's voice. "Mr. Bennett," he said tightly, "I don't think this is at all trivial."

"I do," Bennett said without looking up from his doodling. "Come, Archie, what's the point?"

"The Dead Rabbits are the damned point!" Archie shouted. "You've put me squarely in their sights, and right before an election on top of it!"

He shoved the chair back and stood. "You put a piece out there that named people and accused them of vote fraud and graft, and then you put my name on it. What do you think is going to happen?"

Archie stopped short when he saw that Bennett was smiling at him. He felt suddenly foolish, as if he was about to be the butt of some cruel joke.

"You want to be a correspondent, Prescott?" Bennett's grin was predatory as he leaned forward. The question hung in the air.

"Yes, I do."

"Then don't come whining to me about rubbish like who pinched your little pen-name. Of course it wasn't an accident. If you'd walked out of here without mentioning your dance with the Rabbits, I'd have fired you tomorrow." Bennett pointed his pencil at Archie. "You've been here too long to be just a disgruntled typesetter. I'll be frank with you, Prescott; you're never going to amount to anything if you live your life trying to flee your memory." Bennett paused, waiting for Archie to say something. He nodded after a moment and continued.

"What's important in this situation, Archie, your pen-name or the fact that the Dead Rabbits might stomp you flat?" Bennett gestured for Archie to sit. "Rhetorical question. Listen, here's my offer: Bring me something new on those Tammany bastards and the job is yours. Salaried correspondent. And I don't want innuendo or hearsay, I can make that up myself. I expect names, dates, places. Murder, graft, whatever; I want front-page sixty-point revelations. You live in the right place, you've known the right people in the past; the opportunity is yours to take. And the Dead Rabbits and the Tammany sachems will be keeping an eye on you now. That's useful. You watch who's watching you and they'll lead you to what you want to know."

Bennett stood and offered Archie his hand. "Truth be told, Prescott, I've done you a favor. It's up to you now to capitalize. But you'll do it on your own time, and right now you're due on the floor."

❖

Rosetta Peer's, Archie thought as he cut from Houston Street over to the Bowery and turned south. If anyone knew anything, it would be the wharf rats who went to ground there, and Rosie's brew is cheap. He walked fast to keep the cold away, covering the length of the Bowery to East Broadway in a few short minutes and turning down Oliver to pick up Water and follow it down to the dockside slums.

Archie checked his watch, disguising the motion as an elaborate itch to avoid being accosted; he was due at the *Herald* right then. If nothing came of his prowling tonight, he would no longer need to worry about finding a story or anything else for James Gordon Bennett. After two months of obsessive looking over his shoulder at every footstep and equally obsessive searching the Whiskey Wards for people willing to name names about Tammany corruption, he'd reached some sort of threshold. One way or another, he'd resolve things tonight. Either he would have a story for Bennett, and thus a career, or he wouldn't be working for Bennett at all. The second scenario had its drawbacks, but at least it meant the Rabbits wouldn't be stalking him any more.

"Archie, fancy meeting you here." The voice floated from an overhung breezeway on his right. Archie took a step toward the street, suddenly very aware of the knife pressing into the small of his back. Fearing reprisals by the Rabbits or other Tammany thugs, he'd begun carrying it around, and even though nothing had happened since Water Celebration Day, it had become a habit. The feeling the knife gave him of being watched had not abated, but Archie had gotten used to that as well; the vague presence was now comforting by virtue of its familiarity, and he caught himself sometimes in a fit of jealous worry that it was the knife that was being watched instead of him.

It had been weeks since he had stopped to wonder what it was that might be watching, or why it was that the knife made him vulnerable to nervous delusion, but he found himself wondering both as he watched a gaunt shape amble out of the alley shadow. In the clear moonlight, Archie recognized the man.

"Mike Dunn, by Jesus," he said, astonished. "It's been . . . well, years."

"Since the fire, you mean to say," Mike said. He was thinner than when Archie had last seen him, the stubble on his chin graying and patchy, sweat running down his face despite the dry cold. "Aye, seven years. Near impossible to believe it's a coincidence after all this time, isn't it?"

Archie noticed then that Mike's legs and feet were bare under his long coat, and he took an involuntary step back. Footprints led back into the alley, melted through the inch of packed snow covering the ground, and gentle wisps of steam curled away from the soles of the man's feet. "Mikey—"

"Never mind, Archie, you needn't ask. You're searching, and you'll find out soon enough. Got a nip for an old friend?"

Archie dug the bottle out from under his coat and handed it to him. "How do you mean that? Who's heard I'm searching?"

Mike didn't answer until he had drained the entire bottle of whiskey, his Adam's apple bobbing metronomically until he flipped the bottle over his shoulder and wiped a trickle from his chin.

"Ohhhh," he sighed. "Some things a man misses."

Archie kept his voice down with an effort. "Dammit, Mike, who's heard I'm searching?"

"Them as needs to know, does," Mike said, and chuckled, his breath streaming out in a dense cloud that hung in the still air. Archie could feel heat radiating off the man. Mike looked up at the sky, peering at the moon with first one eye closed and then the other. Whatever he saw pleased him, for when he looked back to Archie he was grinning.

"Quite a fire we had that night," he said. "You know, there's some say fire's a living thing, because it breathes, eats, breeds. I could show them a thing or two." He squinted at the sky a moment longer, saying, "Living fire. Damn these city lights."

"Mike, what do you mean about this not being a coincidence?" Archie was desperate to keep the conversation on a footing he could at least pretend to understand. If Mike knew something about Tammany, Archie needed to know it too.

Sweat dripped off Mike's chin as he laughed hoarsely, wreathing his face in thick vapor. His eyes shone through the mist, far too bright to be explained by ordinary fever. "Pardon me, Archie; sometimes I get wrapped up in other things. Forget matters at hand."

He beckoned Archie into the alley, then stood close enough to him that the heat of his body made sweat break out on Archie's forehead. *A fever like this will kill him by morning*, Archie thought. *And he doesn't even notice*.

"Midnight tonight," Mike whispered. "When the Rabbit's out and the stars you can't see are the highest. You go down toward the back of the Tammany Hotel and you'll see something that might interest Mr. Bennett."

He wheezed a laugh again, and Archie flinched at the heat of his breath. Something struck him as unusual, standing out even in the strange circumstances, but he couldn't put his finger on what it was.

"Might be of interest to a great many people," Mike added. "But I think you in particular."

Again the wheezing laugh, and it struck Archie: Mike's breath had absolutely no odor whatsoever, not even a hint of the quart of whiskey he'd put down.

"See you later, Archie." Mike lifted a hand and wandered away down the alley, leaving a perfect trail of melted footprints in the dirty snow.

Back out on the street, Archie looked up at the sky. The moon was fat, not quite full, and the sky was clustered with stars. *When the stars you can't see are the highest*; he wished he knew what Mike was talking about, but he'd never learned constellations beyond being able to recognize Orion, and he'd never heard of any Rabbit. Had Mike meant the Dead Rabbits?

Archie checked his watch again, then stared back into the alley in blank amazement. Nearly an hour had passed while he exchanged a few words with an obviously very ill Mike Dunn. An hour when he should have been walking down to the *Herald*'s offices on Fulton.

He would have to hurry to be in place behind Tammany Hall at midnight; it would be impossible to simply walk right up to the back door off Frankfort Street. He would have to circle around to the south, use the crooked network of breezeways and accidental spaces between buildings that meandered between New York's named streets. Perhaps that way he could get close enough to observe.

Well, an hour late was the same as absent for Bennett; if Archie showed up now with no story, he might as well not show up at all. He glanced up at the moon again before starting off for Tammany Hall; for a moment there, particularly right after Mike drank off the bottle of whiskey, one of the shadows on its face had looked startlingly like a rabbit. Oh, Jane, he thought, and turned up his collar against the wind.

The imposing steeple of Trinity Church loomed on Archie's left as he turned off Broadway and found an alley that cut north parallel to the main avenue. He crossed Fulton, looking nervously around, but this part of the city was almost entirely legitimate businesses; all of the merchants had long since closed up and gone to bed. Tammany Hall was three blocks ahead. This was the cautious part; he had to get close enough to get names and faces without revealing his own.

He slowed when he heard voices ahead, stepping under the shadow of a fire escape behind the milliner's shop that adjoined Barnum's American Museum. The spotlight Barnum had recently installed on the museum's roof swept across Broadway and cast dizzying reflections from every church steeple within a half mile.

Inching forward, Archie saw three figures step into the alley from Ann Street, rustling loudly as they walked. In the moment before they stepped out of the spotlight's glow, Archie glimpsed red piping on the trousers of all three.

Best not to run into the Rabbits right now, he thought, and stepped deeper into the shadows. If they were posting sentries in the alleyways, there were probably other scouts out along Broadway. And the police couldn't be counted on to roust them; most of them had worn the red stripe at one time themselves. He would have to skirt the edge of City Hall Park and approach from the north.

The wind shifted and the rustling grew more agitated. "Christ," one of the Rabbits snorted, "aren't we a lot of idiots, luggin' dead corn down alleys in the middle of bloody winter?"

"Shut it," snapped another voice, and Archie froze, trying to place where he'd heard it before. "Steen says it'll work. And he's bringing something else as well."

Archie remembered the sun shining in his eyes and placed the voice. It belonged to Royce McDougall.

Two months isn't nearly enough for him to have forgotten me, Archie thought. He imagined crawling home in the snow with broken ribs.

The three Rabbits spread themselves fifteen feet apart, unfurling a woven line of wizened cornstalks between them. Royce stood in the center, at the base of the short stair that led to the rear door of the American Museum. The Rabbit to his right was a hunchbacked dwarf, his bare head bald over an explosion of dark beard. The wind picked up, and the snapping of the banners hung from the museum's facade marked a strange counterpoint to the dry whispering of the strung corn.

"Royce." The dwarf spoke impatiently, his voice reedy and nasal. "How come we just don't go in and get it?"

Royce barked a short, humorless laugh. "Charlie, my friend, if it knew we were coming, we wouldn't even be able to see it if it didn't want us to."

Charlie seemed dissatisfied with that answer. He leaned against the wall, not twelve feet from where Archie crouched. *Steen*, Archie thought furiously. *Where have I seen that name before? Or have I heard it recently?*

"Yeah, well, what if it can't get out?"

"Steen's had the night man unlock the door," Royce answered impatiently. "Now will you shut up?"

"Night man?" Charlie seemed unwilling to let the subject drop. The third Rabbit had been watching the conversation disinterestedly, but at the mention of a guard, he frowned into his heavy scarf and looked at Royce.

"Goddamn it!" Royce spat. "I've told you already, he won't be any trouble one way or the other."

"One way or the other," the third Rabbit repeated. He laughed, obviously hoping Royce would join in, but just then a shadow fell across the alley as a garishly decorated yellow wagon turned into it, creaking slowly to a halt next to Royce. The driver surveyed the situation briefly, his face hidden under a broad-brimmed hat.

"Never a moment to spare, Steen," Royce said. Archie saw him sneak a glance at the moon. "Everything set out front?"

"Everything was set before either of us was born," the wagoner said mildly.

He clicked open a pocket watch, glanced at it, and slipped it back into his coat. "What remains to be seen is whether I've deciphered it correctly. If I haven't, then Phineas gets to keep his exhibit."

Archie tried to flatten himself even further into the wall. He remembered where he'd seen the name Riley Steen; he'd set it to type nearly every day for the last seven years, in the advertisements that took up nearly two-thirds of the *Herald*. What was a dentist and snake-oil man doing here? And why had Mike, who had obviously known something was going to happen, told him to go to the back of Tammany Hall? The main event of the evening was evidently happening right here.

"Look here, Steen," Charlie said petulantly. "Royce says we're to wrap it in these cornstalks when it comes out. You mind telling me why we can't just use a rope?"

Steen set the reins down and slid off the wagon's bench to stand next to Royce. "Rope shirts were something of a fashion then," he said absently, his eyes fixed on the museum door.

The dwarf seemed at a loss for a response to that. "Not in this weather, they wouldn't be," he finally muttered.

Archie had to physically fight down the urge to ask the dwarf what was going to come out of the museum's rear door. He had been expecting a meeting of some sort, New York's leading citizens and Tammany sachems gathered to plot some nefarious scheme, not some queer ambush for an animal to be flushed out of Barnum's Museum. He was going to have to do some fast thinking to keep his job.

"You have everyone posted?" Steen asked. "The Pathfinders, if any live, will certainly be out on this night."

Royce's exasperation grew visibly, and his voice took on an aggrieved tone. "Yeah, Steen—"

"Right here," growled a voice from behind Archie. A forearm clamped around his neck and he was jerked out from under the fire escape. "And I've caught something already." The three Rabbits started toward Archie.

"Don't drop the coil!" Steen barked. All three halted and watched Archie as his unseen captor walked him for-

ward. The arm dropped from around his neck and a knife
was pressed into the small of his back.

"You might have picked a more harmless show to
watch, my friend," Steen said.

He looked closely at Archie, then glanced at the moon
and covered his left eye. "Oh, I *see*," he said slowly. After
another appraising look, he spoke over Archie's shoulder.
"Put him in the wagon. Don't kill him if you can avoid
it."

Archie saw Royce grinning at him, the boisterous grin
of a young man on the giving end of a practical joke. "I
told you to stay away from things as didn't concern you,
Mr. Archie Prescott. You should take a hint."

Archie didn't answer.

Knife behind me, wagon in front, he thought. *Only one
place to go; I hope the night man really did take care of
it.* He let his shoulders slump and shuffled a step toward
the wagon, then dove to his left, under the cornstalks between Charlie and Royce. Skidding on the packed snow,
he scrambled to his feet and gained the low porch in two
steps. Before the Rabbits could react, Archie slammed the
door behind him and disappeared into the American Museum.

He took the main stairway three steps at a time, hearing
boots thump on the stairs outside. The door slammed
again as Archie ran the length of the main hall and ducked
into a corner alcove at the front of the gallery.

His pursuers banged through the door and pounded up
the stairs, halting under a sign that read TO THE EGRESS.

"Why'd you stop?" The spotlight swept away, and Archie could only see shadows, but he recognized the voice
of the man who'd captured him. He drew the kitchen knife
from his waistband, thinking *God knows he's likely better
with his than I am with this thing*.

"Place only has two doors," Royce answered. "Steen'll
have us skinned if we let *it* go because we're chasing after
him."

He raised his voice and called out, "Evening there, Archie. I've some more advice for you, if you've a mind to listen this time. Here it is: Stay in there too long and you're going to wish you'd come with us." His words echoed slightly in the domed hall. "Hear me, Mister Paperman? I tell you this as an act of human kindness."

If you knew how far I was from being a newspaperman, Archie thought, *you wouldn't have gone to the trouble in the first place. Perhaps I should have explained that.*

"Go down front and tell the boys there to watch for him and the booger," Royce said to the other Rabbit. "I've got to go hold the damned rope." He paused. "Archie? Last chance."

After a pause, Royce snapped his fingers. "All right then. Good luck, my friend."

Archie relaxed a fraction as they went back downstairs. He wouldn't be able to get out until they caught whatever it was they were looking for, but he could safely hide until then and hope to escape afterward. He looked around, searching for possible escape routes even though he knew as well as Royce did that the museum had only two doors.

The sweeping spotlight reflected in through the leaded windows along the front of the massive building, revealing various pictures and cases, some with banners strung above them. Archie was squatting in an alcove between a glass-topped display case and a window seat. Over his head hung a sign reading AZTEC CAVE MUMMY in bold print, with indistinguishable smaller lettering below. Not a case then; a sarcophagus, laid on top of a gilt-painted wooden frame. Archie stood and looked through the glass, tilting his head to see past the reflections.

The mummy had papery black skin drawn tightly over broad, heavy bones. Its eyes were closed and its hands folded over its chest in an attitude of quiet repose. A crazily patterned cloak of beads and feathers lay over one shoulder and its sunken chest, covering it completely below the waist.

The knife jumped in Archie's hand, and he set it down.

Things were bad enough without him stabbing himself in the bargain.

He bent to take a closer look at the long, curling green feathers, catching a brief glimpse of an odd pattern worked into the beads before the spotlight dimmed and went out, its last flicker making the mummy appear to twitch. *Must be midnight*, Archie thought. *Long past time for me to be away from here*.

Footsteps echoed in the hall, coming across the main hall in his direction. Archie's eyes had not yet adjusted to the dimness, but he didn't think it was the Rabbits. There would be more than one of them. The night watch, then; under the circumstances, a stroke of good fortune. "Right here," Archie stage-whispered.

"Who's there?" The footsteps quickened. "Come out or I'll call the police!"

"No, the Dead Rabbits have chased me in here, I can't—"

The display cover heaved under Archie's hands. He stumbled back, kicking the knife across the floor as the glass shattered against the wall. The mummy *had moved*, had thrown the cover off; it crouched now in the sarcophagus, turning its face to the moon as Archie's senses flooded with the smell and sound of falling rain.

"A vandal, are you, you bastard?" The watchman hadn't seen the mummy. He grabbed Archie's collar and hauled him back another step as it lunged from the case. Archie lost his balance, toppling backward as the mummy landed on him. Its hand thrust inside Archie's coat and he felt its fingers lengthen, fingernails sharpening into claws.

Dry tendons creaked and a rattling noise came from the creature's throat as it scratched furrows in the skin of Archie's chest. He planted both hands in its midriff, his heels scrabbling on the polished wood floor as he tried to push it off.

"Off him, damn you!" The watchman's truncheon cracked into the side of the mummy's head, leaving a dent visible even in the faint moonlight. Is the watchman blind? Archie thought. He thinks it's just a burglar.

Claws grated along Archie's ribs as the beast let go of him and turned to face the guard. Gasping from the pain of the gashes, Archie scrabbled backward, seeing with a shock that it was *changing*.

The mummy's skull flattened, nose and mouth protruding into a blunt snout, patchy ringed fur sprouting across its face and exposed shoulder. Its legs thickened and grew shorter, crooking backward at the knees. The watchman saw it too; his face paled as he drew back for another blow.

Its whispering deepened into a murky growl as the creature ducked under the watchman's second swing and sprang on him, hooking suddenly clawed feet into his belt. Its weight bore him to the floor. He shrieked as it slashed the side of his face open and locked its clawed fingers onto his collarbone, the effort splitting the brittle skin over one stringy bicep. The bones in the guard's wrist crunched as the mummy bit into them, sawing his hand off and flinging it away with a jerk of its skeletal head. Hand and truncheon landed separately against the wall.

Blood spattered thickly to the floor as the mummy crouched over the man and dug its claws into the soft flesh under his ribcage. He flailed weakly at it with the spurting stump, his mouth working silently, then freezing in a perfect O as the beast ripped a gaping hole in his chest. His ribs and sternum cracked like twigs as it tore his heart free.

"Yollotl, eztli," it grated in a voice like dry leaves, holding the heart above its head. Moonlight through the grand windows caught a puff of steam rising off the organ. It pulsed twice, blood pumping onto the watchman's face, and the creature spoke again. *"Ompa onquiza'n tlalticpac."* Archie realized with a shock that he understood what it had said: *The heart, the blood; the world spills out*.

It flicked a forked tongue over the twitching heart, then gulped it whole. It shuddered, and a spotted tail snaked out from under the feathered cloak. The ringed fur on its muzzle and paws thickened and grew more lustrous as it swung its skeletal head toward Archie. Its tongue flicked out again, twice.

Archie felt behind him, unreasonably comforted when his hand fell on the hilt of Helen's kitchen knife. The cloaked monster gazed intently at him and Archie stared back, paralyzed like a rabbit under the force of its steady hooded gaze. He hardly noticed the pain from his gashed chest, or the thin trickle of blood running down his stomach and under his hip.

It's memorizing me, Archie thought, and the mummy blinked under feathered eyebrows and looked from him to the knife. *It knows me. It recognizes me.*

"Jesus, Mary and Joseph."

Royce and the squat dwarf Charlie stood at the head of the stairway, the braided cornstalks bunched between them as if they were about to throw a net. Royce's eyes were huge, and Charlie was making some kind of whining noise deep in his throat. The creature turned its attention to the two Dead Rabbits, and Archie found that he could move again. He scuttled backward, away from the werewolf or werecat or whatever it was. It stood erect and he saw how wasted its frame still was, naked tendon and bone showing where desiccated skin had flaked away.

The feathers of its cloak twitched in the still air and Archie felt a stirring in his left hand. He was clutching a penny sized gold medallion with three feathers beaded onto it in a cluster. Its surface was worked in some sort of pattern, too faint to see in the dimness.

A quiet crackle sounded in the tense stillness of the hall, and Archie saw that the corn the two Dead Rabbits held was growing. Thin white roots sprouted from the stalks' dusty ends, and the leaves and stalks smoothed and swelled. The ears of corn grew fat, hanging pendulously from the braid as they ripened before his eyes. The dwarf jerked one arm up, but it was already tangled in the rejuvenated leaves. They wound around his wrists, preventing him from dropping the woven strand, and crawled up to his shoulders. Royce was entwined as well, the stalks binding his legs to the railing.

Archie heard shouting from the street in front of the museum; the Rabbits stationed there sounded as if the same thing was happening to them.

"Tonacatl, macehuales tonacatl," the creature rumbled, its voice stronger now. Archie heard the words as *our substance, the substance of men.*

It had reassumed a more human form, but its eyebrows were still crescents of tiny feathers, and patches of scale reflected moonlight from its forehead. The skin around its mouth and on the hand that had held the watchman's heart shone a deep ebony as it looked out the window to the moon, murmuring words that echoed in Archie's head. The feathers in his hand renewed their twitching.

There was a series of plops as the swollen ears of corn dropped to the floor. Their shroud of leaves peeled back and tiny human figures wriggled out, their knobby skin mottled yellow and red and white. They swayed as if drunk, bumping into the railing and each other before collapsing into mounds of corn kernels at the feet of the entwined Rabbits. Royce and the Geek stared like sleepwalkers at the rejuvenated mummy.

Archie registered another sound, a faint drumming of rain on the museum roof. *Rain, on a night this cold?* The mummy stood chanting to the moon as the sound slowly grew to a deafening crescendo, and then with a crash of shattering glass it was gone.

And now the Lord of the Region of the Dead takes you . . .
you have gone to the dwelling place of the dead,
the place of the unfleshed,
the place where the journey ends,
a place without a smoke hole, a place without a vent.
Never again shall you return,
never again shall you make your way back.

—Farewell to the dead, recorded by Sahagun

Book II

BOOK III

❖

Riley Steen found himself in an irksome situation. It was difficult enough to gauge the matrix of influences governing the chacmool's reanimation without the sudden intrusion of bloody Archie Prescott, and the mayhem echoing from the museum's upper gallery indicated a plan come partially, perhaps completely, unstrung. He reached into his pocket and extracted a damp paper package. Unwrapping it, he inhaled the calming scent of myrrh: his own strain of roses, one he'd worked obsessively to cultivate. He'd intended to don this tiny bud as a modest celebration of the night's accomplishments. Now, it seemed, he needed it to soothe himself. At least it had been clipped at the proper time, when the afternoon moon had risen to obscure the seeing powers of the *huehueteotl*, Tlaloc's only rival in antiquity and devotion among the Mesoamerican civilizations that predated the Aztec empire. The Old God, He Who Gives Men Faces, had thrown the Rabbit at the moon, and the *Tochtli*'s mischievous revenge was to blind him whenever the sun and moon shared the sky.

Steen hoped to avoid the Old God's attention until the chacmool was safely in his grasp. The avatar of Tlaloc would certainly draw such attention, since one of the *huehueteotl*'s many incarnate aspects was Xiuhtecuhtli, Lord of Fire and Time—the opposed principle to Tlaloc, the god of earth and rain.

The Old God was doubly difficult to understand be-

cause its nature was both male and female. Steen was in
the habit of referring to the god using the masculine pro-
noun, as the Aztec priests had, but that habit could be
dangerous. To ignore Ometeotl's female aspects could result in fatal miscalculation, but the conflict inherent in the
god's duality made some simplification necessary. The
one usual certainty when dealing with the *huehueteotl* was
that the *Tochtli* interfered with its power. Unfortunately,
the presence of the Rabbit brought its own tendency toward unpredictability, the kind of plan-corrupting chaos
that had brought Archie Prescott to the American Museum
tonight.

Steen covered his right eye and looked up at the moon,
which was streaked with thin bright clouds. Even through
this cover, the Rabbit was clear tonight, as he'd expected.
Also clear, though, were other portents whose meaning
for the night's endeavor was uncertain. There was fire in
the moon, a flickering about the Rabbit that could only
mean that Xiuhtecuhtli had been awakened by the events
taking place in the museum. And this on a day sacred to
Tlaloc, when the prominence of He Who Makes Things
Grow should have had dominating influence. *"Mitzayani
in ilhuicatl,"* he muttered—*the heavens split asunder.*
Some vital piece of information was missing, and Steen
had no idea how to begin pursuing it.

He couldn't be certain because of the damned clouds,
but it looked like the Rabbit was holding a knife.

Glass shattered somewhere in the museum, and thicker
clouds blurred the *Tochtli*'s figure. Damn Lupita and her
schemes, he thought. She had argued that using the *mocihuaquetzqui* to scar the child was the only way to lay
the proper groundwork for the coming spring's sacrifice.
Steen had reluctantly agreed, knowing that the use of the
fire sprites would draw Xiuhtecuhtli's interest but hoping
to maintain the integrity of his plans by closely guarding
the girl until she was needed. It seemed now that Lupita's
devotion to Xiuhtecuhtli had corrupted the entire process

from the beginning, opening the Old God's eyes to Steen's plan.

And he hadn't anticipated the girl's escape, thinking her cowed by years of captivity. The fact that he hadn't been able to locate her, despite his certainty that she was in New York, solidified Steen's conviction that the *huehueteotl*, in one of its aspects, had taken an interest in his affairs. Killing the girl's mother had proved to be the most damaging of Steen's (or Lupita's) errors; having died pregnant, she was no doubt a *mocihuaquetzque* herself now. Steen had given up smoking cigars since that thought occurred to him. He was never sure when a flame would acquire a life of its own.

A slight teenager wearing the red piping of the Dead Rabbits ran down the alley from Ann Street, fear etched on his pockmarked face. A living cornstalk was wrapped around his right arm, sprouting a husk that dangled at his wrist. "Jesus, Mr. Steen," he gasped. "It's gone, it—"

"What about the barriers?" Steen snapped, although the greenery adorning the youth's sleeve answered the question for him. "Where did it go?"

"Right through the bleedin' windows—Christ!" The youth had raised his arm to indicate a direction and noticed the cornstalk. He ripped it from his sleeve, shredding the fabric, and flung it away. Its torn end sprouted roots that sought purchase in the packed snow.

"Dammit, boy, where did the chacmool go?" Steen realized he was crushing the rosebud in his fist. He relaxed the tension in his arm.

The museum's rear door banged open and Prescott appeared, his arms pinned by Royce McDougall and the hunchbacked carnival freak Steen knew only as the Geek. Like the frightened sentry, the two Rabbits were draped in snapped-off tendrils of cornstalk. Prescott's coat was shredded and his shirtfront streaked with blood.

"Mr. McDougall!" Steen forgot about the sentry and the fresh rosebud. "Did Mr. Prescott touch the chacmool?" Steen fervently hoped that Prescott's injury was due to an altercation with the two Dead Rabbits. If he had been in physical contact with the chacmool, the consequences would be impossible to predict. Like the *Tochtli*, Nanahuatzin's father was a wild card, a further intrusion of uncertainty into an already tenuous plan.

"It touched him, that's for damn certain," Royce replied. "Nearly ripped his heart out like it did the watchman's, but then it backed away. What the fuck is going on here, Steen?"

"Complications, Mr. McDougall. We must be rid of Prescott at once."

Royce immediately flicked a knife from his sleeve, but Prescott reacted just as quickly, kicking Royce's legs out from under him and nearly pulling free of the Geek as well. Steen reached into his coat for the small derringer he kept there, weighing the problems of an escaped Prescott against the consequences of killing him so near the site of the chacmool's reanimation.

Steen cursed and cocked the pistol as Prescott took another step, dragging the Geek with him. What sort of misfortune would that bring down, killing Nanahuatzin's father? But then Royce lunged forward and buried his knife in the back of Prescott's left thigh.

Prescott shouted hoarsely and stumbled as his weight landed on the wounded leg. Royce leaped onto his back, another knife conjured from somewhere in his clothes, but Steen stopped him there.

"Enough! Just hold him." Steen repocketed the derringer. "We can't do anything now. Too much has already happened here tonight."

Where else, then? Dockside would be appropriate. At least three establishments in the Fourth Ward featured concealed chutes for the disposal of deceased patrons. In addition, the brackish waters of the river would confuse the old gods' sight.

"Decide, Steen," Royce growled. Prescott cried out again as the Rabbit jerked the knife out of his leg. "Shut up," Royce said, holding the bloody blade alongside Prescott's jaw.

He looked to Steen again. "I want to be elsewhere when the police get a look inside."

"As do I, Mr. McDougall, but some forethought is required here." Steen paused a moment longer, then made his decision. "In the wagon, all of you. We'll take Mr. Prescott to the Old Brewery and conclude our business there."

The Brewery, located in the Five Points scarcely a block from Prescott's former residence, would still be echoing from the events of seven years before. Those echoes, and the fact that it stood on a filled-in swamp, might help to occlude the vision of observers. Steen cast another quick glance at the moon. Certainly the night's activities would be better brought off as secretively as possible, and the fact that the Brewery was home to New York's most desperately wretched citizens would be of assistance as well—their constant misery would swallow Prescott's more acute anguish like a thick fog swallowing the smoke from a gunshot.

Or so he hoped.

The decision made, Steen relaxed enough to unwrap the fresh rosebud again. He pulled it free from the slice of potato he used to keep the stem moist. "Mr. Prescott," he said, affixing the fresh bloom to his lapel and inhaling its sepulchral scent, "kindly indulge my curiosity. Why were you here tonight?"

To his surprise, Prescott laughed shortly. "I heard the mummy was a fraud," he said.

"Well, I hope your doubts have been sufficiently assuaged," Steen said. "With any luck, I won't have to convince everyone in the same fashion."

Royce hauled Prescott upright and shoved him toward the back of the wagon. The Geek was already inside. "I'm still curious," Steen continued. "How does concern over the veracity of Mr. Barnum's exhibit result in your skulking around back doors on a frigid midnight?"

"Look, Steen," Prescott said. "If you're going to have Paddy here stick a knife in me again, I frankly don't see why any of this matters. Why were you here with a dozen Dead Rabbits and a wagonload of dead corn? You know a hell of a lot more about this than I do."

Prescott's bravado drained away as he tried to shift his weight. Grimacing, he said, "But since you ask, Bennett wanted me to have a look around."

"Ah. This is the latest episode in his feud with Mr. Barnum, then?" Steen found the explanation plausible, but the appearance of Archie Prescott of all people on this night was certainly an unlikely coincidence. If coincidence it was. Steen wondered how much, if anything, the man knew about his daughter.

Best, he decided, to render the question irrelevant. "Into the wagon, Mr. Prescott. Bennett will have to wait another day for his scandal."

Royce and the Geek squatted at the back of the wagon, blocking the only exit. Relax, Archie told himself. If Steen really wanted to kill you, he would have.

But was that true? Clearly Steen had planned carefully for this evening, and just as clearly those plans had gone disastrously wrong. Why did Steen seem so certain that Archie knew something about the mummy? And what the hell had happened in there? The thing had been set to gut him like it had the guard; then for some reason it had drawn back. Why?

Archie shifted uncomfortably, wedged in among poles and boxes and bundles, puppets hung from the ceiling knocking against his head. The guard's face, slack and impotent with terror, would not leave his mind. Archie wondered if he had looked the same when the creature had ripped open the front of his shirt and bent over him. The gashes it had left on his chest smarted as he moved around, but the bleeding had stopped. His leg, on the other hand . . .

"Why didn't the booger kill you?" Royce said suddenly.

"I don't know. You nearly did, though. I could be bleeding to death."

"Nah." Royce seemed undisturbed. "Just a poke in the muscle. Perhaps later, though," he said, and Archie heard the smile in the Rabbit's voice.

Later. Why were they waiting? *We can't do it here,* Steen had said. But why—apart from the fact that murders took place there every day—would the Brewery be . . . safer?

That was it. Steen thought Archie posed some danger to his plan. But again, why?

Never mind, Archie decided. If he thinks I'm dangerous, so much the better. Pleading ignorance won't help now.

The knife was buried under belt, shirt, and coat. Royce would surely notice if he tried to reach it. And Archie had no other weapons except surprise.

Acting before he could think better of it, Archie launched himself toward the back of the wagon, plowing into Royce and knocking him half out of the curtained doorway. He cocked his fist to throw a punch—but wait, no, something in that hand, mustn't lose it—

The moment of hesitation cost him. As Royce grappled at the curtains to stop his fall, the Geek caught Archie with a hammering roundhouse, smashing his head into the corner of an ironbound trunk. Pain exploded in Archie's ear and he collapsed across the trunk, his feet scrabbling weakly on the floorboards. *What's in my hand?* he wondered dazedly, his unfocused eyes barely registering the moon outside—

And what fire burned in the moon? It couldn't stay here under that moon; the Rabbit watched, and like an old woman the Rabbit was a gossip. It was weak despite the meal, and needed a place in the womb of earth to rest, away from the fire in the moon, away from the people and the stabbing light that swept across them like the Eye of the Old God itself. It stood and ran as fast as its wasted legs could carry it.

A kick to his punctured thigh shocked Archie awake. "Not dead yet, are you?" Royce's face loomed above him, lit only by gaslight that leaked through the torn curtains.

Seeing Archie's eyes flutter open, Royce nodded. "Just as well. I don't want Steen angry tonight. Although I don't suppose it makes much difference to you, does it? And I'll be frank: I haven't got a desire to kill a man the booger passed over. Still, business is business."

Royce grinned and returned to his station at the rear of the wagon. In the pale wash of gaslight, his shadow swayed back and forth as the wagon rocked on its springs.

"Shouldn't be long in any event," the Geek piped up, quacking a grotesque laugh.

Archie found that he couldn't fathom the joke. The thick cobwebs in his skull cocooned it, hid it away from him. He hurt in more places than he could count, and he had very little doubt that these were the last few minutes of his life—why then was the thing in his hand the only direction his mind would focus? Feathers, he felt feathers, tied together with some kind of cord. Beads bunched at the other end around a flat piece of metal like a coin, and was the coin moving somehow or was that his head?

He was suddenly terribly afraid that he would drop it. *Must hide it*, he thought, knowing it would make no difference if—when—he died tonight. And a pocket wouldn't do; it had to be next to his skin where he could feel it.

Archie rolled over onto his side, bringing down a row of puppets whose strings he had tangled in his escape attempt. He curled into a fetal position and groaned more emphatically than was necessary. Feigning a struggle to disentangle himself from the web of strings, he thrust the beaded feather into his underpants, nestling it securely in his crotch. It might smell when—if—he recovered it, but it would be safe.

"Our boy Archie's feverish, Geek," Royce observed. "Musta cracked him a good one."

"Guess so," the Geek agreed.

"Maybe he'll do us a favor and die before we get there."

The wagon slowed and turned a corner, its springs squeaking as it bounced onto a rougher surface and came to a clattering halt. Not waiting for a command, Royce hauled Archie to the back of the wagon and out onto the street. The Geek hopped down beside them.

They had stopped in a narrow dirt alley behind the Brewery. Archie could see the building itself looming over them, fires flickering behind its rows of grimed windows. A smokestack caught moonlight, throwing a long shadow into the alley where they stood. His head was still reeling from the blow he'd taken; something was funny about the moonlight. He squinted upward, trying to figure out what it was.

Steen said something, Archie couldn't hear what. In response, Royce turned suddenly and drove his fist into the pit of Archie's stomach. Archie *whuff*ed, and his knees hit the ground as Royce sapped him across the bridge of his nose.

He tried to vomit up the crippling pain in his gut, choked instead on the blood flooding from his sinuses into the back of his throat. Bloody vomit sprayed from his mouth and nose. Royce stepped to one side and let go of Archie's collar as he brought the sap down again. A vast distant bell rang in Archie's head; he pitched over onto his side, his stomach heaving again

looking for the stars, but they too were obscured by fires floating over the street, casting strange shadows that merged and split as it ran. Surely it had run afoul of the tzitzimeme, *the spirits of darkness; surely they had built this insane city of tall buildings like teeth to bite down on it as it ran, feeling the blood cool on its mouth, the heart,* yollotl, *beat out the last of its strength to feed limbs that at last were free. Its breath steamed and the air bit at its lungs, stealing already the warm life of the heart within—Toniatuh, the Sun, was very far away, and the rains too. He Who Makes Things Grow was silent, resting, giving his avatar only a few hours' strength; it had to get away from the people staring wide-eyed like pipil turkeys. It stumbled down a narrow alley, seeking the ground, the earth that gave life, searching among mounds of garbage and filthy snow.*

Snow, so close to the sea—

"Ahoy, Archie Prescott." The sap tapped briskly on Archie's forehead. "Look sharp. We've not finished here yet."

Archie opened one eye. The other was stuck shut, whether by mud or blood he didn't know. He saw Royce's boots, the red piping on his trousers. Beyond Royce he could see Riley Steen shrouded in long coat and wide hat, the fresh rose pinned carefully to his lapel. Archie clenched his teeth and tried not to vomit again.

"What's with the crowd, Steen?" said the Geek, from outside Archie's limited field of vision. "You ain't putting on a puppet show, here." Raggedly dressed clusters of people had begun to appear in doorways and windows that opened onto the alley. Other shadows blocked much of the light leaking from the Old Brewery. One group of young men stood close together between the wagon and the rear wall of the Brewery. In front of them stood a young guttersnipe cradling a rabbit in his arms. *I've seen him before*, Archie thought. *God, does he live in the Brewery? Poor little arab; no wonder he never lets that rabbit out of his sight.*

"Point well taken, Mr. Charles," Steen said to the Geek. "At times people need to be reminded that certain transactions should be accorded a measure of privacy."

Steen noticed the boy clutching the rabbit, and Archie saw his composure slip a bit. Had he glanced at the moon just then? "Rabbits are filthy, son," Steen spat. "Misfortune and drunkenness. Let it go."

The boy shook his head and tried to retreat into the

group of men behind him. Archie's groin began to throb as the strange feather token seemed to amplify his heartbeat. In the small of his back, the knife grew uncomfortably warm, and Archie saw with a dazed shock that one of the young men was Mike Dunn. And was he smiling?

Steen looked into the sky again, and whatever he saw shattered his restraint. *"Let it go!"* he roared, four fingers of one hand extended toward the boy. The rabbit exploded into flames, its squeal lost in the *whoosh* of the fire—

and the Eye of the Old One was open now, searching it out in a foreign place to feed its ancient body to the fires. A shock rippled through the night sky, and the winter breeze became more cautious in its flow. In the Moon, the Rabbit was laughing, and the city smelled like the temple atop Mount Tlaloc, when the wind from the sea swirled with smoke rising from the fires waiting to be fed with wailing children—

The boy's thin screams subsided into a series of whooping sobs. Archie blinked and tried to lift his head. The alley had emptied; light shone again from the Brewery, and the moonlight fell squarely on the charred corpse in the filthy snow. For a moment, Archie was sure that the smoke and steam formed a woman's face. Helen's face?

Then the breeze blew it away and the only sounds were the boy's diminishing sniffles and Mike Dunn's ghastly chuckle as he walked over to the dead rabbit.

"You've certainly woken him now, haven't you?" Mike said merrily.

"No," Steen said with difficulty. To Archie he looked terrified, barely able to keep his composure. "No, I believe you did."

"Fair enough." Mike smiled a jaunty farewell and walked slowly away toward the Brewery. "But you should have known better than to do that while I was around."

He strolled around the corner of the building, leaving a clear trail of footprints in the snow.

"God damn it," Steen said, carefully enunciating each syllable. "Royce, listen to me very carefully. Follow my instructions exactly if you wish to avoid the fate of that damned rabbit." He covered his right eye and gazed at the moon for a long moment.

"I'm listening, Steen. What do we do?"

"Mr. Prescott, can you walk?"

In spite of himself, Archie laughed, a short bark that became retching. "Shut up," Royce said, and kicked him in the leg.

All the color bled out of Archie's vision, and the remaining gray pulsed in rhythm with the throbbing in his hamstring and groin. Through the roaring in his ears, he heard Steen say, "The question was rhetorical, Mr. Prescott. Get up."

Archie struggled to his hands and knees but could go no farther. "Assist him, Mr. McDougall," Steen said.

"What?" Royce said. "What did we come down here for?" Even through the aftershocks of the Geek's blow, Archie noticed the whiny tone that crept into Royce's voice. Only a boy, Archie thought. A hard, cold boy, true son of the Five Points.

"Do it. I am leaving very shortly, and your survival will be much more probable if you listen to me until then." Stepping carefully, Steen reached the front of his wagon and climbed into the seat.

"Christ," Royce said. He slipped the leather sap inside his coat and gripped Archie under the arms, hauling him upright. Archie thought he should resist somehow, but he couldn't even raise his arms. He slumped in Royce's grasp like a drunkard.

Steen held up an open palm from the driver's bench of his nightmare wagon. "When I leave here," he said, "I will follow Orange Street to Grand and thence to Broadway. Whichever course you choose after your business here is concluded, do not set foot on any of those streets until the sun is well risen. Is that clear?"

"It is," Royce said.

The Geek gaped silently at the burned rabbit.

"Good. Mr. Prescott is to walk into the Old Brewery

unaided. You will follow him single file, stepping exactly in his tracks."

Even given the night's events thus far, this last struck Archie as ridiculous. "Why—would you rather I waltzed?" He wheezed a laugh. "I haven't—I've got no reason—"

"You have every reason in the world, Mr. Prescott," Steen said. "Think of your friend Michael Dunn. He found himself in a similar situation on a night I think we both remember."

Steen's words pinched off the last of Archie's laughter. God, he thought. Was living like Mike Dunn the only alternative to being murdered by Irish thugs and dumped in the Old Brewery? If it was . . . well, in death there would be Helen. And Jane. Maybe I'll finally see that rabbit in the moon, Archie thought absently. Jane, you can show me.

"I see you take my point," Steen said. He gathered his horses' reins. "Good evening, gentlemen."

"Hold on, Steen. What about in the Brewery? Any instructions there?"

"See that Mr. Prescott remains there." Steen snapped the reins and his wagon creaked and rattled away down the alley toward Orange Street.

"Charlie, Jesus, let's go," Royce said. The hunchback was still staring at the burned carcass lying in the snow. At the sound of his name, he jerked and looked around.

"Where'd Steen go?" he said suspiciously. "And what the hell did he do to this rabbit?"

"Never mind for now, or the same thing's going to happen to us," Royce said. "Now pay attention." He repeated Steen's instructions.

"What makes you think he won't run away?" the Geek wanted to know, indicating Archie.

"Jesus' sake, Charlie, he's stabbed in one leg and can't hardly walk from the clout you gave him. That rabbit could catch him if he decided to run. All right? Go on then, Prescott."

Royce shoved Archie in the back, knocking him off balance. He fell to his hands and knees and remained there, chuckling weakly through the clotted blood in his throat.

"What's so goddamned funny?" demanded the Geek.

"Nothing," Archie said, and coughed. *Just wondering if you need to follow my handprints as well,* he thought. Strange; once death became a foregone conclusion, he could laugh about it. Then he thought of Mike Dunn again, leaving bare footprints in the snow, and stopped laughing.

The nearest door in the Old Brewery's crumbling brick facade hung open a dozen steps away. Archie stood carefully, the effort setting his groin throbbing and his head spinning with strange images of leaping flames and Helen's solemn face. He steadied himself and walked through the doorway.

Once inside, he turned to watch first Royce and then the Geek step carefully in his tracks and over the threshold. Bodies shifted in the darkness behind him, and Archie wondered how many witnesses there would be to his murder. He briefly considered running, realized how much easier it was simply to give up.

Better to face it, he decided. *Think of Helen and Jane.*

"I warned you, didn't I?" Royce said from the doorway. "Bastard, I warned you—did you a fucking favor—and tonight you nearly get me killed. Twice."

The blow came from nowhere, splitting Archie's lips and knocking him over backward. It was funny, really, the way Royce was killing him out of injured pride, to prove he was the meanest b'hoy in Manhattan; *preaching to the choir,* Archie thought, his broken mouth smiling in the darkness as the two Rabbits methodically kicked him in the back and ribs, grunting with the effort and spitting curses between kicks. *You don't have to convince me that this Royce McDougall is one mean son of a bitch. Seems like the mummy could have saved us all a lot of trouble by just taking my heart for dessert.* Archie's mind emptied and blind instinct took over; he rolled away from the Rabbits, coming up short against a wall where he rested for a moment—

feeling the strange texture of burned timbers, breathing the taste of blood and the dead smell of old fires, hearing dim noisy voices outside and unspoken thoughts, wondering at the strange shape of this sanctuary. Here the Eye could not see. Here it would be safe until He Who Makes Things Grow called again. Here it could rest . . .

"Hey, friend." Royce spoke into Archie's ear, breathing heavily. "You're a mess, aren't you? Face is all busted up, you've pissed yourself. . . . God. And that ear is the worst—looks like a bloody carbuncle on your head."

Royce shifted and Archie felt the Geek move closer. His ear was ruined, he supposed, but he couldn't feel it; all of the pain had drained into a tiny pool in the bottom of his mind.

"That ear has to come off, boyo; lucky we have the Geek right to hand. He's been doing this for years, haven't you, Charlie? He's just the man for your situation."

Royce leaned a forearm on Archie's neck. "Hold still for the doctor, now."

The Geek grabbed a fistful of Archie's hair and twisted his head to the right. He clamped his other hand over Archie's mouth and bent closer, moaning like a hungry animal. The moan opened into a throaty growl as he darted forward and bit into Archie's crushed ear. Royce pressed down, choking Archie's scream as the Geek chewed through the cartilage, making noises in his throat like a pig at his trough.

Archie felt his eardrum fill up with blood and saliva; then the Geek whipped his head back and forth three times like a terrier killing rats. After the third jerk, Archie realized that his ear had come free. Like having a tooth extracted, he thought strangely; I should be drunk.

The Geek shook his head back and forth over Archie's face, scattering droplets of blood and growling deep in his throat. Then he screamed and reeled away as Archie's ear exploded into flame—

and it flinched away from the dream of the light, wishing for rain to cool the pain in its head, desperate and weak, praying only for the fire to die down so it could rest and heal and grow.

Atlcahualo, 7–Ocelot—December 25, 1842

❖

The bells of Trinity Church rang Christmas good cheer, echoing off Broadway storefronts and lending a bouncy air of purpose to Jane Prescott's step. She hummed along with the melody as she wove her way through carriages and vendor carts on her way to St. Paul's.

Joyful all ye nations rise, join the triumph of the skies . . .

The last two weeks, Trinity had been ringing that tune three or four times a day; Jane didn't know all the words, but she knew the tune as well as if she'd written the song herself. She'd been dreaming bells.

The past fortnight had also seen the spirit of charity reappear among New York's gentry. Where a quarter-dollar or even a handful of pennies made up a good day's take the rest of the year, she'd cadged as much as a dollar four times in the last ten days alone. Her stomach was full, and the roll of silver coin tightly wrapped around her right ankle meant she wouldn't be hungry again for quite a while. Yuletide was a time of pity for fatherless young girls with scarred faces.

"Merry Christmas, sir and madam!" she cried brightly, swinging up onto the running board of a stopped carriage. Keeping a weather eye out for the coachman's whip, she pressed her face to the passenger window. "Rejoice at our Savior's birth! 'Tis the season, is it not? The season of fellowship and charity?"

The carriage door swung open and a gloved hand appeared, tossing coins onto Broadway's grimed cobblestones. "Merry Christmas, guttersnipe." The voice was lofty and English. "Merry Christmas, and be on your way."

"Bless you, sir!" Jane cried, leaping off the running board and gathering the coins. "Merry Christmas and a joyous New Year!" Clenching the silver, she ran around the back of the carriage and continued up Broadway in the direction of Barnum's museum. Six pennies and a dime; she had nearly six dollars, and it was time to go home and hide it.

"Jane!" She looked around and saw her friend Mitten calling her, his narrow face drawn and tense beneath an enormous fur hat. He beckoned her into the alley next to Segar's Exchange.

She stopped reluctantly, feeling the coins in her palm. There was more to be had and she was impatient to have it, but Mitten looked frightened. "What is it?" she said.

Instead of answering, Mitten grabbed her hand and pulled her down the alley, stopping only when they were out of sight of the street. "Little Bree's been murdered," he said breathlessly.

"Murdered? Who says?" Street arabs often disappeared, for any number of reasons, but everyone always assumed that they'd been killed in some devilish fashion. All too often, it was true. Or so she'd heard.

Little Bree had been Jane's first friend in New York; he'd shared his corner of a basement with her when she'd first fled Riley Steen's traveling carnival in Richmond the year before. The trip to New York had left her starving and feverish, and Little Bree had looked after her until she'd been strong enough to go begging on her own.

If he was dead—Jane calmed herself and repeated her question. "Who says, Mitten?"

"Everybody says. There's a whole lot of children murdered, they say, down under the docks above Battery Place. There'll be an extra coming out—I'm going to the *Herald*. You should come, too."

Jane thought about it. An extra would mean more silver, especially covering a murder. But if Little Bree was really dead . . .

"No," she said. "I've got to go see."

"The papers'll be gone! We have to go to the *Herald*."

"You go." Jane pulled away from Mitten's grasp. "I have to see." Crying now, she ran back out onto Broadway and turned south toward Battery Place.

A crowd had gathered, their Christmas finery bringing bright splashes of color to the gritty dockside. Stacked crates and piles of rope and sail canvas provided the more enterprising onlookers with lookouts, while the rest of the crowd pressed closely against a roped-off area guarded by police, recognizable by the brass or copper stars pinned to their lapels. Jane worked her way toward the ropes, making herself small, practicing the art of invisibility she'd learned in her year of living on New York's streets. She edged her way between two brawny longshoremen and came up short against a policeman, who immediately caught hold of her collar.

"Not so fast, missy," he said.

"I have to see," she pleaded, putting on her best Scared Little Sister face and letting the tears she'd tried to hide from Mitten flow freely. "Please, I have to see if my brother is there. Mum is so afraid, she can't bear to come."

"So she sent you?" The policeman shook his head. "Not too likely, I don't think. Go on, now. Nothing here a young girl needs to see." He turned her around and gave her a gentle push back into the crowd. "Get along. I don't want to run you into the workhouse."

The threat was enough to make Jane abandon Scared Little Sister and put some distance between her and the policeman. She'd been in the workhouse once already, and had escaped after the longest month of her life. Going back there would be worse even than being caught again by Riley Steen.

Moving quickly, invisible again, she skirted the crowd and hopped nimbly into the empty bed of a fish cart. From there she could see that the ropes blocked off one of the docks. Crowds were gathered on the adjacent docks, people pointing occasionally and shaking their heads much as the policeman had. So there was something to see, but how to see it? Jane looked around, kicking the cart in frustration.

There: the docks each had ladders at their sides going down to the water. Jane jumped out of the cart and hurried to the base of the dock that extended White Hart Street. Just to the east, between White Hart and Broad Streets, a cluster of police sat in a small boat, lashed to the pilings of the roped-off dock. She climbed down the slippery ladder and spider-crawled across the struts supporting the White Hart dock on its pilings, a tang in her nostrils that seemed to be more than just rotten seaweed from the brackish water lapping at her feet.

Peering from underneath the dock, Jane saw the policemen in the boat, aided by dockworkers with a block and tackle, raise a long, wide canoe from the waters. One of the ropes caught and the canoe tilted toward her, spilling dirty water and exposing the pale bodies of naked children, packed side to side with bent knees and hands clasped over the ragged wounds in their breasts.

"Oh, Daddy," Jane whispered. "Poor Little Bree." She could see him near the back of the skiff, a trickle of water running from his open mouth. The canoe shifted again, and his dark purple heart fell from his dead hands to splash in the river.

And she could see Deirdre, and Paulo, before the canoe swung back level and was hoisted onto the deck. A wave of gasps and shocked cries swept through the crowd, and the police began shoving people farther away from the horror that sat dripping on the weatherbeaten dock.

Little Bree, and Deirdre and Paulo and all the rest, had

lain dead in the same water that slapped at the pilings just below Jane's feet. Their hearts are still there, she thought. Their hearts are still in the water, beating in time to the dirty waves. Her own heart seemed to stop for a very long time, building a sickening ache in her throat; when it finally beat again, its hammering shook her grip on the slick timbers. She scrambled up underneath the dock and pressed herself into a corner amid spiderwebs, afraid to stay near the water but more terrified still that if she moved she would slip and fall in, to drown in the dark water among the ghosts of dead children.

Stephen stood on the slanting porch of his small cabin, listening to the laughter of the other slaves gathered inside for Christmas supper. It wasn't in him to smile today, and he had come outside to sit and have a pipe and figure out why; but he was neither sitting nor smoking. Instead he was looking to his left at the broad path that sloped down from the hotel's sun porch, crossing the packed earth of the stagecoach turnaround and winding amid debris from the saltpeter mining—old poplar trunks used as piping, mounds of leached earth and sprouting weeds, a broken wheelbarrow—and ending out of his sight, at the rim of the gaping pit that enclosed the cave entrance. Under Stephen's feet lay Houchins Narrows, the stoop that marked the end of the entrance and the beginning of the real cave. After that came the vast Rotunda, which split into the Main Cave and Audobon Avenue. And after that . . . he rubbed his face, trying to get the sand out of his eyes and his head. Sleep had been difficult these last few days, and all of his dreams were of the cave, in particular of the odd square chamber behind Bottomless Pit and the voice he'd heard here. This voice spoke to him, drowning out the other voices in the cave, swelling into a thunder that left him headachy and irritable when he woke. It came not from the mummy, but from the stone face looming over the altar, the face with its ringed eyes and fanged mouth.

Its lips did not move, but the voice was clear, and Stephen feared that he was going insane.

When I return, Stephen, a new world will be born. A new world, and in it you will have all that is forbidden you now. Not a slave, but a man, Stephen.

Would you be a man?

"I am," he said softly, seeing his breath in the afternoon sun and knowing he lied. He was privileged, certainly; perhaps indispensable, even, to Dr. Croghan and his grand plans for "The Mammoth Cave of Kentucky." Stephen's lip curled as he thought of all of the gaudy names Croghan insisted he attach to rooms and rocks in the cave, names like River Styx and Audobon Avenue that bent the cave out of shape, making it a toy for Croghan's self-regard and the wealthy visitors who made Stephen so useful. And Stephen used the names, too, but he knew them for what they were: words that had no real bearing on the places they were supposed to define. This knowledge had come by way of the voice, the silent statue speaking the word *Chicomoztoc* and the syllables reverberating through Stephen's mind. The cave's true name.

Freedom, it promised him, but something was missing. Stephen was canny enough to realize when he was being treated as a resource—which was, in his experience, always—and he instinctively questioned the voice's promises. What was this new world and how would it be different from the one he lived in now?

You will be a man. The simple assertion, confident and infuriating.

I am already.

Stephen's reverie was interrupted by Nick Bransford's arrival on the porch. "Lord help me if Charlotte can't cook," Nick said, patting his lean stomach. He sat on the step, stretching his long legs out onto the ground and contentedly picking his teeth.

"What's on your mind, Stephen?" Nick asked after a silence punctuated by a burst of laughter from the cabin. "It's Christmas, ain't it?"

Stephen didn't answer immediately. When he did, the sound of his voice surprised him; he sounded old. "Sure, Nick, it's Christmas. I'm just not sure what I'm celebrating."

"Charlotte's cooking, for starters." Nick laughed and tossed his toothpick into the grass. Frost was beginning to form in the lengthening afternoon shadows, and those shadows grew in Nick's face as his smile faded. "Your problem is too many ideas. You got to get all them big schemes out of your head. Christmas is just a day when we don't have to work and we can sing around a fire without the white folks bothering us. Don't have to be no more than that."

"Maybe not."

Stephen packed his pipe, feeling the texture of the clay and tobacco, smelling the richness of the weed's smell against the sharp clarity of winter air. He struck a match on the sole of his shoe and sat next to Nick, trying to rid himself of the strange distance he'd been feeling since the dreams began; it wouldn't hurt just to sing around a fire and enjoy a full belly.

But the big ideas wouldn't go away.

"Ever hear of Monrovia, Nick?"

"Town in Illinois, ain't it?"

"No, a place in Africa. Set up by free Negroes who wanted to go back. Feel like I want to go there sometimes, take the boat the other way, see my mother's country. Be free. Be a man." The smoke tasted good on Stephen's tongue. He started to relax the slightest bit.

"Got to get that idea out of your head too." Nick looked troubled, shadows marking creases in his forehead and chin. "Dr. Croghan ain't gonna let you go to Africa. If you left, who'd show off for fancy English doctors? Problem with you, boy, is you learned how to read and got full of ideas that don't have nothing to do with you. We ever get whipped? We ever go without? No. The woods is full of deer, there's fish in the river, and people come from all around the world just to go into the cave with you. Think you'll have it that good in Monrovia?" Nick let the question hang in the air for a while before he went on. "You got to live where you are, not go moonin' around about Africa. Besides, your daddy was a Indian, so you're in his country. Best leave that other alone."

"My daddy wasn't an Indian," Stephen said. "That's just another story for British doctors." His pipe had gone out; he struck another match and gazed into the flame. "My father is a white man," he said, the quiet words ruffling the flame, "and I know who he is. You know him too," Stephen finished, and relit his pipe.

"Hold on." Nick looked away and stood, his hands fluttering like bat's wings, as if to brush away Stephen's words. "I don't know nothing and I don't want to. Your daddy could be Andrew Jackson and it wouldn't make no difference—you'd still be a nigger in Kentucky with a pretty wife inside cutting mince pie. You know what's good for you, you'll go on in and have some of that pie and forget all about Africa and your white daddy. I know that's what I'm going to do."

Stephen smoked the rest of his pipe after Nick went inside, wondering if perhaps the Bransford boy was right. *Boy*, he thought. *When did an eighteen-year-old get to be a boy to you? That's a white man's thought.* Stephen shook his head and tapped out his pipe; his twenty-second birthday was months away yet, but in the last week he'd felt a hundred.

I am a man, he thought, hearing the voice again. It whispered in the leaves of the tulip poplars lining the cave trail. *I am.*

Cries of "Extra!" rang through the crowd as Jane hurried up Pearl Street, nervous because the sun had gone down and she was out of the safety of the gaslit avenues. The stink of the docks followed her, clinging to her clothes and surrounding her in the smells of dead things and fear. She avoided the glance of a staggering Indian, looking down at her battered shoes and seeing the dried river scum streaking them. Again she thought of the hungry water lapping at her feet, the secret sounds of things moving among pilings. All she wanted was to be home, to stash today's silver and hide away.

"Extra! Murdered children! Indian murder on the dockside! Extra!"

Jane quickened her pace to a near run. What sort of person could kill children, Little Bree and Deirdre and all the rest? What had happened to Little Bree's rabbit? Dinner, no doubt, for whoever had found it hopping frightened down an alleyway. Jane wished for a home, a real home with bedsheets and a kitchen table and warm light shining through its windows onto the street. She skirted the edge of Franklin Square, where Cherry, Frankfort, and Dover Streets emptied into an oblong plaza of rutted, snow-covered mud. A few trees straggled up from this mud, having somehow survived the crush of wheels and feet.

Pearl Street came out the other side of the square and curled back north and west until it intersected Broadway across from the hospital. Jane could visualize the whole of New York in her head, and thinking of maps soothed her, drew her mind away from dead friends in sunken canoes. She had an actual map of the city tacked up back in her burrow, one of many maps that helped remind her that there were places where a girl and her Da might go to live other than cold filthy stairwells and tenements.

Jane ducked into the gap between MacGavran's grocery and the meeting hall whose back stair hid her den. The stair rose perhaps four feet from a cobblestone courtyard to a recessed door, with one side of it built against the brick of the grocery's rear wall. Jane didn't know who met in the hall there, but groups of men came and went every Thursday evening. The open side of the stair had been walled off by a row of planks buttressed by a single diagonal board, and the enclosed triangular space was Jane's home. Her burrow.

Pulling aside a loose plank, she crawled under the stair and sat quietly for a moment, letting her eyes adjust to the gloom. She realized that she'd been holding her breath; it came out of her in a long *whoosh* as she saw that nobody had disturbed her home. The pile of blankets, the lamp on the floor, the flat stone in the corner covering her treasure hole—everything was as she'd left it. Hooking a finger through the knothole of the loose plank, she pulled it back to its original position, closing herself off from the alley and the city beyond it.

She took another deep breath, let it out as she dug a match from her pocket and lit the lamp, keeping the flame low even though she'd plugged all the holes in the planking that enclosed her little space. Outside in the square, and on Cherry Street running away from it, nightfall would bring out the roving gangs that frightened even the police, who wouldn't patrol this district in groups of fewer than six. One night in late fall, Jane had peered out her knothole and seen two men hastily burying a dead sailor beneath a pile of rubbish. The dead man hadn't been discovered for nearly two weeks, and then only because a pig had scented him rotting beneath the heap and dragged his body out for a feast. Jane had been more careful coming and going at night since then, and she had doublechecked that all of the chinks in her wall were well filled; but she was still glad to be here because being here meant she was really free of Riley Steen.

Thinking of Steen gave her a chill. She pulled off her shoes and wrapped a blanket around herself, relaxing on her bed. Her eyes went automatically to her favorite map as she settled against the warm bricks of the grocery's wall. It was a complete rendering of the United States, extending all the way from the Florida territory north to Maine and west to the Mississippi River and the Republic of Texas. Jane couldn't read, but she knew her letters and had learned to recognize some of the names on the map. Mississippi was one, with all those s's in it, and the river snaked like an endless series of esses down to the ocean.

Jane imagined it too wide to see across, the buildings of St. Louis barely visible across the expanse of brown water, steamboats blowing their horns up and down, leaving trails like clumsy ducks that couldn't fly.

I will see the Mississippi someday, she swore for the hundredth time. St. Louis, too, and maybe even all the way across the Rocky Mountains to California or Oregon, following Lewis and Clark and looking out for Indians along the way.

She got another chill at the thought of Indians, and snuggled deeper into her bed of rags. People were saying that Indians had murdered Little Bree and the others because the bodies were mutilated and packed in a canoe. Jane had gathered this from eavesdropping on her way back from the docks, and had gathered also that New Yorkers believed it and were angrily ready to do something about it. She thought of the drunken Indian whe'd seen on Pearl Street and wondered if he would end the night buried in a trash heap like that sailor.

Now she was crying again, quietly, a tear itching as it trickled down her scarred cheek. All those children, and how many of their mothers even knew they were gone? And if she'd been among them, her father would not have missed her. She continued to cry, still quiet and mindful of the dangers beyond the loose plank in the wall. Eventually she fell asleep, silently weeping and thinking of her father and brown rivers too wide to cross.

Breaking glass woke her. She scrambled to her feet in the darkness, listening for another sound from outside. Her lamp had burned out, Jane guessed; at least it hadn't fallen over, or she wouldn't have had to worry about her father or her scarred face ever again.

"He came down here. I saw him."

Jane crept to the knothole, unplugged it, and peered out. Two men walked slowly around behind the grocery. They wore heavy boots, and one a long coat and full beard. The other sweated in a thick woolen sweater, his head shaven under a black watch cap.

The bearded one looked directly at her, and she froze perfectly still, not even daring to blink.

"There he is," the man said. He drew a knife from within the folds of his coat, and Jane heard a rustle from just to the right of the loose plank. "Ain't a good time for a redskin to be out alone, friend," the bald sailor said. "Why, you might be a damned murderer."

"Our civic duty," continued the first sailor. "Remove murderers from the streets." Together they stepped forward.

Jane heard the Indian stand up. "You would do well to leave me alone," he said slowly in a strange whisper, a sound that buzzed around in Jane's head after he'd finished speaking. The words sounded odd; she'd never heard an Indian speak before.

They were going to kill him, she knew. It was wrong. They didn't know who had murdered the children.

But what if they did? What if this Indian had? Why was he outside her burrow, today, with her friends killed just yesterday?

"Leave you alone?" The sailor with the knife took another step toward the Indian, who Jane still couldn't see. "Redskin, we're going to get together. We're gonna get real close."

Jane gritted her teeth, wishing she could see more through the knothole. She didn't know what to do; if she made some kind of noise, it might distract the sailors long enough for the Indian to escape, but what if she did that and he turned out to be the murderer? What if he came back for her another time?

"Look here, Dixie," the bald sailor said. "He ain't a redskin, he's a nigger. Look at him."

Dixie shrugged. "He's dressed like a redskin; likely acts like one too, don't you, chief? I'm surprised you didn't scalp them children, chief; but if you're just a nigger trying to act like an Indian, I guess that don't surprise me."

"I want his coat," the bald sailor said. "Always did think feathers were nice."

"Last chance," the Indian said in that same buzzing whisper.

"Your last chance, chief." Dixie lunged forward, out of Jane's field of vision.

She heard a harsh scrape as the knife blade grated across a hard surface, and suddenly the scarred side of her face itched madly. The feeling spread down her arm and across her back until it felt like her skin was trying to fight its way out of her clothes. At the same time, a low growl rose from outside, the sound reminding her of a caged tiger she'd seen once in Battery Park. "Christ, let me go!" Dixie was pleading; then his voice was cut off in a series of sharp cracks.

Something slammed into the loose plank, punching it into Jane's face and knocking her backward. Blood ran from her nose and she screamed as it began crawling sideways, spreading out over her itching scars. Wherever it touched, the itching subsided.

Outside, the second sailor was thrashing against the wall of the stair, gasping thickly and knocking his head against the loosened planks. Blood crawled into Jane's hair, down her collar, across her back and into her sleeve. The dying sailor blocked the knothole, leaving her in complete darkness as the fierce itch in her scars began to recede.

Her face hurt, and blood was creeping in her mouth from loosened teeth and a split lip. *Please let him go away*, she thought. *Please let him just leave. And please let them come soon and take away the dead men and not notice me.*

Moonlight spilled into the knothole as the bald sailor was lifted away from the wall. She heard his body hit the ground a few feet away, and then heard the Indian tapping gently on the loose planks. *Go away*, Jane mouthed, tasting wriggly blood on her tongue and feeling it slick under her shirt.

"Nanahuatzin," the Indian said. The plank was pulled aside with a rusty squeak. "Come outside."

She didn't respond.

"Come outside and I will stop the blood."

"You killed them," Jane said. "You'll just kill me."

"If I wanted you dead, little Nanahuatzin, you would be. Come outside now."

Jane did, slowly, absently scratching at the fading itch and wiping at the blood gluing her shirt and hair to her skin. Once outside she stood. "Why do you call me that?" she said.

"It is your name," the Indian answered simply. "Given long before you were born."

"My name is Jane Prescott." She thought the bald sailor had been right; he did look more Negro than Indian. Blood trickled from one corner of his mouth. Why wasn't she afraid any more?

The Indian nodded. "Your mother gave you that name. This," his fingers traced the broken landscape of Jane's face, "named you again. Nanahuatzin; say it."

"Nanahuatzin," Jane repeated. At the Indian's touch, her nose had stopped bleeding and the itching in her scars had completely gone away. *He killed those two men just to talk to me,* she thought.

"Good." The Indian swiftly licked the traces of her blood from his fingertips, then held the loose plank aside. "Go and sleep now."

Jane yawned, her jaw cracking painfully. "Ouch," she said, and went inside. *Nanahuatzin*: the word fluttered in her head like a moth seeking light. *My name,* she thought. The last thing she heard was the Indian carefully replacing the loose plank.

Atlcahualo, 8–Rabbit—January 8, 1843

❖

The year turned, *and was drawing to a close, but Tlaloc slumbered yet, having woken briefly and seen the distance of the sun. In this time was the cold and the weakness of the sun.*

The Fifth Sun was ending its days, the time approaching when the people would be swallowed by the earth and reborn. Nanahuatzin, the Scabby One, lived; it had touched her and seen the first stirrings of her rejuvenation. As the Fifth Sun set, they would return to Chicomoztoc, the place of origins, and there she would again lie in sacrifice that the world could be born anew. Then would Tlaloc return to claim the new world for his own.

To be within the earth again, beneath the roots to watch the work of He Who Makes Things Grow—soon, soon. First the journey to the west, to Chicomoztoc which lay beneath the skies from whence came the mocihuaquetzqui. Danger there and it did not know why; what had it to fear from the spirits of pregnant women? Still, it stirred and muttered in the depths of its sleep. The West was the place of danger and redemption, the place where it could wrap itself in the earth and wait for the drumming of the rains, wrap itself in the earth and hear the voices of the roots praising Tlaloc—

Archie awoke screaming through a mouthful of mud, the sound muffled by the mud clogging his ears, his arms and legs bound . . . he couldn't breathe. He tried to heave himself upright, but the weight on his chest forced him back down, crushed the air from his lungs. His hands stayed pinned to his sides as he thrashed back and forth, hearing the plangent sucking of the mud over his own gasping screams. The mud was freezing, pressing down on him more with every bit of air he choked out of his panicked lungs, and he was blind. *Not this way*, Archie thought, *please . . .*

Water sluiced across his face, washing away some of the mud. He heard muted voices, realized he was still screaming out the last of his air; then strong hands caught around the back of his neck, holding his head out of the muck. He gasped, inhaling a tiny breath of air along with huge gobs of mud.

There, easy, someone was saying, wiping the mud from his eyes, digging at the mud until Archie could loosen his shoulder and drag his arm free.

He reached out, caught something and pulled on it, choking up mud and sucking it back down with a little air. Rolling out of the shallow pit formed by his torso, he coughed like a consumptive before drawing a huge clear whooping breath. Dim light leaked in through slitted windows high in sooty brick walls, and he focused on it, holding the dusty shaft of sunlight in his mind as a sign that he hadn't gone to hell.

"Breathe slowly, sir. The air will come easier that way and the mud be less apt to follow it." The voice was smooth, cultured, Southern. The man it came from had once been dressed fashionably, but his suit and collar were now drenched and covered with mud. Wavy dark hair hung over a domed forehead, deep-set basset-hound eyes, a neat mustache.

He saved my life, Archie thought, beginning to shiver in the near-freezing mud.

"Is this the Brewery?" Archie hauled on the chopped-off tree root he'd blindly seized before, but the mud still encased his feet and lower legs.

His savior began digging again. "Yes, the cellar. God-forsaken place," he said, freeing Archie's right leg.

As the left pulled free after it, Archie grimaced at a deep ache in his thigh. He suddenly remembered Royce and his knife, and that dwarf—

The man stopped digging when he saw Archie's hand move tentatively toward his left ear. "Not much left there, I'm afraid," he said, shaking his head. "It didn't fester, though; God knows why."

Something about that comment struck Archie unexpectedly. He grappled with it for a moment. "Didn't fester? How long have I been down here?"

"In this cellar? Less than a day, I should think; you don't seem much the worse for your inhumation. Nothing wrong, in any case, that this won't cure." Archie's rescuer offered him an engraved pewter flask, another sign of either wealth or breeding that seemed incongruous given the surroundings. Archie took it and rinsed the mud from his mouth with a draught of strong whiskey.

"In the Old Brewery, though . . ." the man paused. "Twenty days, I think. Yes; it'll be three weeks tomorrow."

Archie swallowed reflexively. "Three weeks!?"

"That's right. Difficult to imagine, isn't it? You were—er, brought here late on the twentieth of December, and—let's see, it's just dawn now—today is the eighth of January. Consider that drink my New Year's toast, Auld lang syne, et cetera."

He smiled briefly, then his expression changed and he leaned forward, regarding Archie intently. "What's your name, my resurrected friend?"

"What?" Three weeks. "Prescott. Archie."

"This is truly a pleasure, Archie. Never before have I encountered a person who has actually undergone this experience. Most, you realize, are not so fortunate as yourself. Something I've only read about before. My name is William Wilson. I edit a magazine. Perhaps you'd be willing to offer an account of your ordeal for publication?"

I'm alive, Archie thought belatedly, surprised both at the fact and at his own surprise, and at the same time it occurred to him how odd it was for this Wilson to solicit him while he was still lying in what should have been his grave. He touched his ear, felt the stubby flap that was all that remained outside the ear canal. The scar tissue was smooth and numb. And his leg—moving it he felt just a faded ghost of agony twitch in the muscles of his thigh. It was nearly healed. Had his ear actually burst into flame after being torn free?

He remembered the feather talisman and dug into his pants, forgetting about Wilson in his sudden panic. Just as quickly he calmed, feeling it still nestled in his groin, quietly keeping time with his heartbeat. It was a real artifact remaining amid nightmarish memories, and it meant that whatever he remembered must really have happened; a surge of relief welled up in Archie's still-heaving chest as he realized that he hadn't lost his mind.

Embarrassed suddenly, Archie noticed Wilson again, but his bedraggled savior hadn't moved his gaze from Archie's face. Wilson's eyes, sunken and glittering in his pallid face, tracked Archie's every motion.

"Why didn't they just kill me?" Archie said. He didn't really expect Wilson to know, but something about the silence was beginning to unnerve him.

"Who, the upstairs denizens?" Wilson laughed, the cultured gentility of the sound jarring in the squalid gloom. "They're mostly born in Old World hamlets, you know, and taboos against interfering with madmen are still very much adhered to there. After seeing what happened with your ear, and watching you thrash about for a few days, they decided that you weren't to be touched. Either you would revive on your own, or God would leave your possessions behind when he finally took your soul.

"On Christmas Day, I'm told, you made quite a display. Actually got up and walked, then settled yourself in a privy trench and made rowing motions as if you were Charon ferrying yourself to see if Cerberus would let you through. All the while you mumbled incoherencies in some foreign tongue." Wilson held up a hand as if in warning. "I repeat this only as hearsay, of course," he continued, "but were it not true, you most likely would have been buried down here shortly after your Dead Rabbit antagonists left you. In any case, your Christmas actions were enough to earn you nearly two weeks of precarious amnesty, despite the fact that you barely breathed during that time. Eventually, however, greed overcame traditional taboos and the rabble approached you again last evening. Holding a mirror to your lips, they shouted at you in a terrible cacophony of languages, but your only response was an indecipherable whisper and a quieting breath that even I initially took to be your last. This I saw happen, having returned from a short holiday, and I stood by as they scooped a shallow pit from the mud softened by our recent thaw; but as they looted your somnolent body I was possessed of an inexplicable intuition that some spark of life in you endured. That is why I kept vigil here tonight; I could not prevent them from interring you, but to be buried alive is the worst fate that can befall a man. It was incumbent upon me as a fellow human being to be absolutely certain that you had departed.

"As, we both now know, you have not," Wilson finished with an odd smile. Archie grew more uncomfortable as the focus of the man's probing gaze. It was bizarre, considering what he'd been through —beaten and mutilated, stabbed and left for dead, buried alive after three weeks feverish in the Old Brewery—but there it was. Something about this Wilson made Archie profoundly uneasy.

Did he do it? Archie thought suddenly, even though he had no earthly reason to suspect such a thing. Did he bury me alive . . . why? Just so he could dig me up again and get a story out of it for his bloody magazine? Even Bennett wouldn't do that.

"Mr. Wilson," Archie began, handing the flask back, "what you did—I am in your debt. Thank you, I can never repay you, but now I've got to go home, I'm starving—"

Wilson cut off Archie's rambling speech with a luminous smile at the word *starving*. "Just as I expected," he said, rummaging in the pockets of his coat. "I've brought a sandwich in anticipation of your appetite."

Archie devoured the still-warm roast beef and bread in four bites, forcing it down faster than he could chew.

"God." Archie swallowed the last mouthful and sucked at his fingers, ignoring the mud that still caked them. "Thank you again."

Wilson nodded, and again offered Archie his flask. "Certainly Archie," he said, hesitating the tiniest bit, "you'll pardon my intrusion, but I'm afraid your home has been colonized by a family of black Irish fresh from the auld sod. I doubt they're inclined to return it at this juncture."

Archie paused to assimilate this news. He should have expected it, if three weeks had actually passed while he was senseless in the brewery. But he hadn't, and strangely it almost seemed as if Wilson had. Archie had the feeling that Wilson was somehow guiding him along, watching his responses to each new bit of information. What else did he know that he wasn't letting on?

"I can do you another favor, Archie," Wilson continued. "Your house belongs to another, and I'm relatively certain given the circumstances that your employment has also passed into other hands."

He paused, wiping distractedly at his jacket; again Archie felt he was being led by the nose. Of course Bennett wouldn't wait three weeks on the off chance that a suddenly unreliable employee would just as suddenly become dependable again. It wasn't strange that it had happened; what was strange was Wilson's seeming anticipation of it, and the methodical way in which he dispensed the news.

Like an experimenter, Archie thought. He considered his situation. Barnum would surely know about his watchman's gruesome murder, and so would Bennett. But if

Archie were suddenly to arrive after three weeks, mutilated and spouting gibberish about living mummies who
swallowed beating hearts . . . the newsman was not known
for his discretion when it came to sources, but he wasn't
likely to believe anything from Archie Prescott at this
point.

And obviously Wilson had known that.

"What do you want?" Archie said.

"I can find you lodging, Archie, and employment suf-
ficient to meet your needs, if slightly sordid. What I want
in return is a simple answer to a simple question." Wilson
leaned forward again, peering at Archie with unnerving
intensity.

"When you were feverish these last three weeks . . . no,
never mind that. While you were interred here, dead by
any known standard, cooling and breathless—" Wilson
began to grow visibly agitated. He calmed himself, placing his hands flat on the ground.

"When you were buried here, *where was your soul?*"

The ants had returned with the brief thaw and were
marching in a strange pattern on Riley Steen's desk blotter. He watched as a silhouette emerged from the pattern,
a reclining figure that stood and moved its arms in a hyp-
notic semaphore. Furious, he pounded a fist into the
middle of the pattern, crushing several of the ants. Their
pattern broken, the remainder milled aimlessly, wandering
eventually over the edges of the oaken desktop and down
to the floor.

He stood and faced his bookshelf, regarding the leather
bindings in hopes that they would inspire him. Tomorrow
it would be three weeks since the chacmool effected its
surprisingly resourceful escape from Barnum's museum,
and in that time Steen's eyes and ears around the city had
reported only two killings that could reasonably be attrib-
uted to the avatar. Other than the children in the canoe,
of course.

That incident disturbed Steen because while the calendar had been properly aligned, the canoe ritual should not have been possible in the chacmool's newly awakened state. All those lives, taken and carefully focused . . . that it had happened at all led Steen to a disturbing conclusion: The avatar was more powerful on its own than he'd expected. It was performing the proper rituals and staying out of sight in a foreign city after more than three hundred years of hibernation. But how was it feeding? Was it able to maintain itself on only two lives in the space of three weeks?

Steen tapped a finger along his bookshelf until he located Bernal Diaz's *Historia Verdadera de la Conquista de la Nuevo Espana*. He returned to his desk with it and paged through it without paying the slightest attention to its contents. Damn Archie Prescott, he thought. If one can damn a man already dead.

It would have been soothing to blame all of his misfortunes on the dear departed, but Steen had only a sporadic talent for self-delusion. The truth was that the chacmool might well have escaped even without Prescott's annoying diversion. The sight of the Rabbit perimeter guard Steen had set up, stumbling into the alley festooned with freshly sprouting corn, was good for a chuckle, but it was also clear evidence that the chacmool was significantly more powerful than he had assumed. But you knew that, he told himself. Stop thinking in circles.

The goal remained the same: with the chacmool harnessed and young Jane Prescott properly sacrificed in her role as Nanahuatzin, Steen could assure himself a powerful position in—what? The Sixth Sun? No; however useful the old gods were, their names and concepts were at bottom pitifully naive. The return of a living Tlaloc would create more than simply another in a series of epochs. It would be a New World, a Kingdom of Earth, and Riley Steen would be kingmaker. It was a position worthy of him.

There were obstacles, of course. The Tammany machine was the most obvious avenue through which to transform Tlaloc's return into real political power, but it had fallen on hard times and withdrawn to consolidate its hold on local politics. This past fall the sachems had been in a fight for their political lives, barely managing to retain their influence in Albany. But that was a quibble, really. With God on their side, as the old saying went . . .

And what a deliciously ironic reversal that would be, to use the society—founded on the ideals of Tamanend himself—to finally strike the decisive blow against the Pathfinders on behalf of the Snake. Aaron Burr would have been proud.

Steen chuckled, but his mind was already moving on to more serious problems. He knew the whereabouts of neither the chacmool nor Jane Prescott, and his inability to locate either had to be a result of his bungling of the operation at Barnum's.

Or, perhaps, Prescott's bungling. None of the old codices offered any insight into the meaning of the fiery, knife-wielding Rabbit that had risen that night. Ometeotl's Eye had been open, that much was certain—an inexplicable occurrence on a night when Tlaloc should have held sway. And to complicate matters further, signs in the Smoke Mirror insisted that the chacmool had been in contact—*actual physical contact*—with Jane Prescott on Christmas Day. Yet she was still alive.

Again, too many variables, too many unanswerable questions. And he hadn't even stopped to wonder about the whereabouts of Tamanend's mask, which John Diamond must have absconded with. Or been killed attempting to acquire.

God damn all dead men, Steen thought. Prescott and Diamond and Burr and all the rest.

A sharp knock on the study door interrupted Steen's train of thought. "Come in," he called irritably, standing to greet the visitor.

Police Lieutenant Ambrose Winkler entered and shut the door. "Afternoon, Steen," he said.

"To what do I owe this pleasure, Lieutenant?" Steen asked, returning the *Historia* to its place on the shelf. He gestured at the lapel of Winkler's coat, where a silver star was usually prominent. "This visit is for reasons other than your law-enforcement responsibilities, I take it."

"Riley, some devilish strange things are happening in my district." Winkler's jurisdiction encompassed the First through Sixth Wards of the city, stretching from City Hall south to Battery Park. He enjoyed close ties with Mayor Morris and therefore Tammany Hall, and was Steen's primary source of information about the Society's activities. Once Steen had occupied a position of considerable power in the Society, but certain events had led to an estrangement.

"New York is a strange city, Ambrose," Steen said. He sat behind his desk and motioned Winkler to the wing-backed chair in front of it. "Why don't you tell me precisely what you mean?"

"All right. Before last night, how long had it been since we had a thaw?"

"Don't pester me with circumlocution, Ambrose. What are you getting at?"

"Almost three weeks," Winkler continued. "A few days before Christmas it warmed right up and I could have sworn I saw buds on some of the trees along Broadway. I remember it because my children were worried there'd be no snow for Christmas. But it's been cold since then."

"Yes. It has," Steen said with exaggerated forbearance.

"Right. Well, last night I was called to the scene of a murder on Front Street. Chilled my very bones, Riley. Four men, all sailors on leave, lined up in a row with their heads crushed flat and the skin peeled from their bodies and hung on them like suits of clothes. Now right away I thought of you, Riley, and I kept it out of the penny sheets. But I can't keep ignoring things like this. You and I go back a long time, and I saw some ungodly strange things during that business with Burr in Kentucky; but this is different. What do you know about it?"

Steen wondered how much he could tell Winkler. He'd anticipated that the chacmool would be more active every twentieth day—that was in accordance with the old calendar, under which every twentieth day was sacred to Tlaloc. But the flaying ceremony was done to propitiate Xipe Totec, the Flayed One, a minor deity whose province seemed to be seeds. Perhaps, Steen thought, the various Aztec gods were simply different names assigned to a very few essential divinities. It was a thought he'd had before. Like Xiuhtecuhtli and the Old God Ometeotl, Tlaloc and Xipe Totec could very well be the same god once the nomenclature was properly dissected.

"You're holding out on me, Steen," Winkler said angrily. "I'm not one to interfere in another man's business, but you had damned well better tell me something so I can protect the people of this city."

"Please, Ambrose. Spare me the platitudes." Steen rose. "If I told everything, it would be much more than you wanted to know. I will, however, tell you this: if you wish to protect your citizenry, you will find some pretext to keep them either locked in their houses or about in large groups twenty days from today."

He guided Winkler to the door. "On the twenty-eighth, very unusual things are likely to happen. It would be best if you remained unaware of them; failing that, avoid them."

"If something like this happens again—" Winkler began to protest.

"I'll talk to you in three weeks, Ambrose. Don't press this."

The lieutenant started to leave, then stopped in the doorway. "One other thing, Riley. One of my sergeants mentioned seeing a young girl with a scarred face on Christmas, gawking at that business down on the docks."

Steen nodded and smiled slightly in spite of himself. Just as he'd thought, she was drawn to the chacmool's activities.

"What does she have to do with this?" Winkler still

looked upset, but a conniving tone was beginning to creep into his voice.

"Just pick her up if you can. Otherwise, three weeks. Happy New Year, Ambrose." Steen shut the door.

He stood in at his study window until Winkler crossed Hudson Street to his waiting carriage. There were plans to be made. If the chacmool kept its schedule, the twenty-eighth would be Steen's next opportunity to capture it and set his plans back on track. But the twenty-eighth would fall under 2-Rabbit, the single most unlucky sign in the old calendar. Trying to get anything done on a day 2-Rabbit would be maddening at best, and possibly fatal if the *Tochtli*'s pranks turned mean-spirited. Perhaps it would be best to wait for a more auspicious signal from the heavens.

Winkler was a bumbler. If he managed to collect the girl, which was unlikely, things would proceed more smoothly on that front, but the lieutenant would be constantly underfoot. It was an exchange Steen wasn't sure he was willing to make, but plans had to be laid for every contingency. Plans were the root of success; history taught that. Improvisers made brief appearances on the pages of history, but careful planning was the stuff of which enduring value was made.

Damn these clouds, Steen thought. The Mirror was blind on cloudy days, and today its vision would have been especially useful. But all things considered, the situation was far from hopeless. He knew when the chacmool would act next, and he had a strong intuition that Jane Prescott would not be far away when it did.

❖

It was Saturday night and Belinda's Bright was filled to the rafters with workingmen drinking themselves into a collective stupor. The steamy heat of the saloon's main room fogged the single window set to the right of the door, and Archie was sweating rivers as he took a short break from hauling kegs out of the storeroom. The Bright featured three-cent drinks, for which price a man could take a tube tapped into a keg and drink until his breath gave out. During busy times, the rubber tubes were passed from hand to hand like a drunk's communion, and the kegs emptied nearly as fast as Archie could roll them out.

Midnight had come and gone, but the banjo-and-fiddle combination still worked steadily through their six-song repertoire. Since nine o'clock, when they'd cleared a corner for themselves and begun playing, they had been through it six times, taking ample breaks to make the best of the free beer that was their only compensation. Fortified by their liquid salary, they showed no signs of tiring. Neither did Belinda's patrons or the two whores who doubled as serving girls.

Archie, on the other hand, was bone tired. He'd never been one for hard physical work—the typesetter's job at the *Herald* had been just a means to an unaccomplished end—and Belinda kept him running, moving casks of beer and whiskey out from the back room and carting crates of iced oysters up from the Bright's cellar. In return, he was allowed to sleep in that same cellar and help himself to the oysters and whatever else Belinda cooked in her "kitchen"—a small hearth behind the bar, hung with a kettle in which she kept a beef stew constantly simmering. Between the food and the work, Archie's body was beginning to recover from its ordeal of the past month or so. He'd gained back some weight and even begun to add a fiber of muscle here and there in his shoulders and back. And his leg had made a nearly complete recovery, although it was inevitably stiff and sore when he got up from his straw bed in the basement chill.

Belinda whistled piercingly from the front end of the bar, near the Bright's entrance. Archie looked up and saw her waving a meaty arm at him as she took an empty glass from a square-jawed black Irishman, who looked carefully in both directions before scurrying out onto the street. She whistled again, and Archie returned her wave, thinking that while her voice wouldn't cut through the din, her whistle could raise the dead. He smiled to himself at the joke.

"Need you to watch the back door the next hour," Belinda shouted in his ear when he'd made his way to her. "My pet copper was in here saying some great fuss is being made at the ward station and patrols being put out all night. It's a raid, is what I'm thinking, and I don't intend to be open for the coppers to bust up my place and pour my liquor down their damned greedy grafting throats. We close early tonight."

"What am I watching for?" Archie asked.

"The only folks I want using that back door are them two niggers," Belinda said, cocking her head toward the musicians. "Bank on it: if a white man tries to leave through the back door, he's either bringing the police or running from them. And if the coppers raid me, and some robber they're lookin' for makes good an escape into that alley, I might as well close up for good. I can't have them thinking I harbor thieves and murderers here."

Belinda turned out toward the chaotic barroom and let loose a whistle that left Archie's ears ringing. She waved at the musical duo, motioning them to wind up; the fiddler noticed and damped his partner's strings with the flat of his hand.

"Closing early tonight!" Belinda bellowed.

A slurred chorus of dismay rose up, and a glass broke near the door. Belinda ignored it. "You've got half an hour to finish what's on your tables and move along. You two," she finished, pointing at the musicians, "one more tune to see everyone off."

She pushed Archie toward the door that gave out on the alley behind the Bright. "Go on, and remember what I told you."

In the half hour that followed, only the two Negroes passed Archie's post at the alley door, nodding and sharing a bottle as they walked out into the chill night. The day had been warmer than usual, but the thaw was fading, and Archie sunk his chin into the knitted scarf Belinda had given him when he started. It had been lost by one of the girls' patrons, as had all of the other clothing Archie was currently wearing; a regular wardrobe was piled on a pallet in one corner of the cellar.

The stairs creaked over his head as either Kate or Lydia ushered a client up to the second-floor rooms. Archie wished he had a drink. He was adult enough to know the difference between sex and love, but every time he heard that creak of foot on stair he nearly drowned in memories of Helen. How many times had he led her across the creaking floor of their bedroom on Orange Street, then laid her on the creaking bed and made delirious creaking love to her?

Not nearly enough.

Archie looked out into the main barroom, saw Belinda with her back to him, scattering handfuls of sawdust on the stinking floor. He went quickly into the back storeroom and brought out a quart of gin, taking a long juniper swallow as he reseated himself and kept watch for thieves and murderers. Bottle in hand, he forgot about Helen, drinking the memory away as Belinda shouted and stomped her booted feet, rousting senseless revelers.

Archie leaned his head against the doorframe and let the gin take his mind where it would. A cool draft dried the sweat from his face, the last memory of the oddly springlike day. It would have been a good night for a long walk, if he'd had the energy, but he'd scarcely left the Bright in the three weeks he'd been there.

A trickle of sweat itched his nose and Archie wiped it away, brushing the lump left by Royce's sap. He hadn't healed badly, considering the punishment he'd taken. Thanks to Wilson, he had food and a bed instead of slow decay in a muddy grave.

"Presto," Archie slurred against the doorframe. "Answer the madman's question and this, too, can be yours." He drank again and repeated, "Presto!" It sounded better when spoken a bit louder.

Although Wilson had saved his life, the situation he offered Archie was like a mean-spirited joke at the expense of Archie's former self. Archie had lost home and employment with a reputable firm, and now he sat drunk on gin, held up by the doorframe of a waterfront saloon he wouldn't have set foot in two months ago.

To his surprise, Archie found his normal resigned bitterness scoured away by a murderous bursting fury directed at Riley Steen and his Dead Rabbit henchmen. Emotion had been rare in the past weeks, when he'd simply been trying to come to terms with being alive, and now it was, well, intoxicating. He enjoyed the anger, reveled in its pure energy. Revenge gave him something to think about other than oysters and barrels of whiskey and the creak of warped floorboards under the feet of whores.

Wilson had asked Archie, as they sat in the Brewery's muddy noisome cellar, if he felt he'd gone insane as a result of his burial. "I certainly would have." Wilson had shuddered before he continued. "Premature inhumation is without doubt the blackest, most horrible fate that can befall a man."

Archie had nodded without understanding; at that point

his mind had been boiling with echoes of the deranged vision that was all he could remember of the previous three weeks. Wilson had listened raptly to Archie's narrative of the dream, nodding now and again as if Archie's recollection confirmed some long-held conviction.

But *dream* wasn't the right word, not really. Archie had felt a constant sense in the vision that he was remembering the incredible events rather than creating or experiencing them. When he told Wilson that, the sad-eyed man had drawn in his breath sharply and looked for a moment as if he couldn't decide whether to dance a jig or run screaming from the room.

"Your soul left you, Archie," Wilson had finally said, terrified wonder quavering in each word. "You must realize that. God! for a mesmerist to draw from you the rest of the tale."

Wilson had made good on his promise, taking Archie to Belinda's Bright ("It used to say 'Belinda's Brighton Tavern' but part of the sign was stolen one night," Wilson explained) and presenting him to Belinda herself. The gray-headed matron had squinted warily at Archie's emaciated frame, looking him up and down as if to assure herself that work wouldn't kill him, but she had taken him in as if the entire arrangement had been made ahead of time.

Archie harbored suspicions that Wilson had taken more than simply altruistic interest in his predicament, but he couldn't fathom why. Once, about a week ago, Wilson had stopped at the Bright and asked Archie if he'd ever had a recurrence of the vision. Archie told him no, he hadn't, and hoped he never would. Wilson had smiled, nodded, and dropped the subject.

"That Wilson's an odd character, isn't he?" Archie had said to Belinda after Wilson had gone.

"Who?"

"Wilson, there. The man who brought me here."

"Archie, that beating must have addled your brains." Belinda held a shot glass up to the light, set it on the counter, and filled it. "His name's Edgar. Edgar Pope or something. An opium-smoking beggar, but folks tell me he's something of a writer."

"Is that so," Archie said. "I'll have to ask him about that the next time he comes in."

But Wilson—or Pope, or whatever his name was—hadn't been back since, and Archie, curious though he was about the man's deception, was perfectly happy not to see him. If Wilson returned, Archie guessed, it would be to ask Archie again for a written account of his Brewery ordeal for the magazines, and Archie had no intention of providing such an account regardless of the incentive. He had poured too much of himself into the writing of other people's misfortunes, and at last, it seemed, he had lost the taste for wallowing in his own.

Thinking of dreams, Archie realized that he hadn't been able to remember a single moment of dream since his arrival at Belinda's. The details of that first vision, though, were still vividly alive in his memory: the city of stone pyramids, shadowed by cloud-wreathed green mountains; the fire, stinking of cooking flesh and roaring like the last breath of a dying soul; the huge fanged face carved from stone in a vast dark room, and the terrifying desperate hope that had come over him upon seeing it.

The feathered token seemed to warm now, radiating a soothing heat against his chest as he let the vision surround him. The small brass medallion had a symbol carved on it, what looked like a crescent moon inside a sun, and three long feathers were attached to a hole punched in the medallion by some sort of beaded string. He'd hung it around his neck on a leather thong, and he kept the knife on him at all times. They kept all of the experience real, somehow, and Archie had found that he couldn't bear to be without either.

He started, realizing that he'd dozed off. Anger and bitterness had both faded away; now he was just tired.

Up front, Belinda was blowing out the last of the barroom lamps. "Go on to bed, Archie," she called. "You can sleep late tomorrow."

That's another thing I've lost, Archie thought as he stumbled down the narrow stair to his pile of straw in the cellar, the gin bottle sloshing in his hand. She decides when I go to bed, when I wake up, when I eat. I might as well be an infant again.

He awoke the next morning with his mouth tasting like a cow's hoof and the odor of gin seeping from his sweaty skin. "God," Archie croaked, sitting up. The motion drove jagged slivers of glass behind his eyes, and he couldn't focus on anything in the room. Objects swam drunkenly within their shapes, and the light was far too bright.

He rubbed at his grainy eyes and someone shifted on the bed beside him. "Helen," Archie murmured. "Can you get me a glass of water, love?"

"Who?"

Archie blinked and squinted; it wasn't Helen in the bed, but Kate, the younger and darker of Belinda's two serving girls. She was naked as a baby under the patched quilt. Helen was dead, and he was . . .

Archie looked around, the sun streaming through the high narrow window immediately telling him that he wasn't in his basement alcove. *Jesus*, he thought. *I don't remember any of this. Was I drunk? When? How did I get here?*

His mind stumbled, as if something kept falling between his questions and their answers like the sick pungency of the gin soaking out of his skin, masking his own smell. Something connected to the fierce pain that stabbed his eyes in the morning sunlight.

He was naked, too, he realized, becoming slowly aware of it as his bare thigh brushed against Kate's ample rear. Too naked, in fact; the talisman was gone from around his neck.

Archie sat up and stripped the quilt from the tick mattress, searching through the rumpled bedsheet. "Archie, sakes, it's cold," Kate grumbled, reaching across him to pull the quilt back over her.

Ignoring her and the vertigo swirling through his head, Archie got to his feet and dug through the pile of his clothes. All of his money was still in his pockets, but no feather token.

"Relax, love, it's early. 'Linda won't need you for hours yet," Kate murmured, turning her face into her pillow.

"Kate, wake up."

"No. What?"

He resisted a powerful urge to shake her. "Where's the pendant I was wearing last night?"

"Dunno, somewhere—" She waved an arm under the quilt.

"Where?" Archie shouted. The effort dimmed his vision, and he felt his knees beginning to buckle.

She sat up abruptly and reached down to the floor on her side of the bed. "Here," she snapped, throwing the talisman at him. "Now stop your yelling and let me sleep."

Archie caught the talisman in both hands, feeling a clarity return as it touched his skin. The blinding pain behind his eyes eased, and the vertigo calmed into a simple hungover daze.

I can think again, he thought, and memories of the night's events flooded back into his mind along with the bludgeoning echo of the realization that Helen was dead and he was a drunk working for board in a sawdust-floored dive.

He crawled onto the bed, struggling to separate the barrage of memories from his present, which seemed suddenly in danger of being swallowed up by his mind's regurgitated past. Last night he had dreamed again, or suffered a nightmare was more like it. The mummy had . . . no, he had *been* the mummy, performing some gruesome ritual among torchlit stone walls with rivulets of mercury coursing down all around him, and watched over by that terrible statue with ringed eyes and some kind of bar splitting its upper lip . . . and Mike Dunn standing at his side, fresh mania burning bright in his eyes even as his lips formed the words *No Archie. . . .*

And the victim of the sacrifice had been Jane.

Kate elbowed him in the back. "Get out of here, Archie, I have to sleep." She burrowed into the bedcovers, pushing him away with her knees.

He stood, his mind full of the image of Jane grown into a beautiful girl, lying silently on the stained altar as he raised a chipped obsidian knife over the pale skin of her belly. *No, Archie*, Mike Dunn had said, his words sparking tiny flames along the scallops in the blade's edge. And Jane had been happy and perfect, a dreamy smile on her face as she echoed the words spilling from Archie's mouth. But Archie hadn't been able to hear those words; they were lost amid the roar of the fire and the rumble of the statue as it said over and over again *mucehuales imacpal iyoloco.*

Archie blinked and tried to knot the leather thong where it had broken, but his hands were shaking too badly. The chacmool had said exactly those words when it stood over Archie with the watchman's heart spurting in its clawed hands.

"Kate," he said softly.

"Go away."

"Kate, please, I'm sorry I woke you. Please—what did I do last night?"

"Ha," she said from under the pillow. "You weren't that drunk."

"Tell me," he pleaded. "Then I'll go away."

She rolled toward him onto her side and pulled the pillow away from her face. "You came in here in the middle of the night blubbering and babbling about some horrible dream, waking me out of a sound sleep. You ripped that trinket from your chest and threw it away, cursing about I don't know what, and then you crawled in next to me.

"That reminds me," she said, fumbling around on the floor again. She came up with the gin bottle and drank off the inch or so left in the bottom, making a face at the taste.

"Next best thing to savin for stopping a brat," Kate said. "It's near my time, and I shouldn't even have let you in. Now go away."

She turned away from him again. "Go somewhere else the next time you're drunk. My sheet stinks like gin."

He wondered what exactly he'd said to her, if perhaps he'd made some strange promise. But instead of asking, Archie dressed silently and went back downstairs.

It was nearly eleven by the time he'd washed and come up for a quick drink at the bar before going off. Some of the resolution he'd felt the night before had stuck, and Archie was determined to see Bennett. The quickest way to anger Riley Steen, Archie had decided, was through the offices of the press, and to use them Archie needed his position back. Bennett hadn't even consented to see him when Archie had gone to the *Herald*'s offices three days after leaving the Brewery, and in retrospect Archie couldn't blame him. His ghastly appearance aside, whatever story Archie came up with—*and Mr. Bennett, have I got a headline*—would have sounded to the publisher like an attempt to excuse three weeks' delinquency with a lurid fantasy. He hoped that by this time Bennett had achieved a more magnanimous state of mind.

Archie felt confident that he could pique Bennett's curiosity even without mentioning Wilson or the exploding rabbit, and his appearance had improved these last weeks, although he was still deathly pale. He'd left Belinda's Bright for only a few minutes at a time since she took him in, wanting instead to rest and also to hide from the Dead Rabbits, one of whom might recognize Archie and inform Steen that he was alive.

He heard Belinda shifting things around in the storeroom. She had come down a few minutes before, assuring him that the price of the night's wanderings would be exacted in labor. "I was about to start you on a small salary, Archie," she said, shaking her head and polishing the bar's surface with the hem of her dress. "But if that's how you'll spend it, it's wasted. I don't waste my money."

Archie knew better than to argue with her. It would be best to just accept whatever penalty she dealt out while he plotted revenge on Steen and Royce McDougall.

He drained his glass of whiskey, feeling his mind clear a bit as the liquor cut through his hangover. "I'll be out for the day, if that's all right," he called.

"If you're back by three, it's all right," Belinda replied, poking her head out into the barroom. Archie left before she could change her mind.

Archie felt like a stranger walking down to Franklin Square, seeing again its smashed teeming mass of dray horses, anxious merchants, sailors at liberty, and the ever-present pigs rutting around the roots of the half-dozen sickly trees some civic-minded individual had planted squarely in the middle of the intersection. His only excursions in the past weeks had been errands to Belinda's brewery and dry-goods supplier. It seemed like ages since he'd walked with a purpose of his own among crowds of people, each with their own purpose and obstacles, running to markets or steering wagons through mad jumbles of people and animals. The city was alive around him, and Archie felt its pulse, felt his long absence.

The day was clear and cold, the late-morning sun reflecting brightly from icicles hanging from eaves and balconies. Archie slowed his pace, enjoying the walk. Let others hurry to where they were going; he had the day, and among those three hundred thousand rushing strangers he was content to saunter past vegetable carts and laugh at frozen laundry strung across alleyways. Where this sudden good humor had come from Archie didn't know, but he was glad to bask in it for now. Revenge could come tomorrow.

He followed Pearl two blocks to Fulton, passing groceries and medical offices while he rehearsed the speech he would make to Bennett. *Sir, my absence has not been without reward*, he would say. *You wanted a story on Barnum's mummy, and I've got one.* Of course the murder of the watchman had been no secret; Barnum had offered a cash reward and lifetime free admission to the American Museum to anyone identifying the killer. Archie's angle for Bennett would be the involvement of Riley Steen, whose association with the Dead Rabbits could only mean he had close ties to Tammany Hall. Bennett wouldn't be able to resist that.

Archie imagined the headline: TAMMANY BRAVE STALKS BARNUM'S MUSEUM. Or something like that. Both names would be in the headline in any case, and the lead article—next to a scathing Bennett editorial—would appear under Archie Prescott's not-so-secret nom de plume. The Eye Peeled on Orange would have uncovered a real story.

That was the crown jewel, the byline. Steen would tear out his hair trying to ascertain the reporter's real identity, and being a meticulous man he would no doubt return to the Brewery to confirm Archie's death. When that happened, any variety of ambush could be laid.

If this is what it's like to be dead to the world, Archie thought, I can accept it. This dead man would have a tale to tell, and Riley Steen would hear it.

A block before the *Herald* building Archie stopped to brush off his clothes and comb his hair back with his fingers. He had a hat, but it was in such miserable condition that he almost thought it would be better to go bareheaded. Too much time would be wasted in buying a hat now, though; at that moment Bennett likely was lunching at his desk, sucking down oysters. Fifteen minutes from now he would be gone on business or sequestered for the composition of tomorrow's editorial. Archie couldn't chance missing him.

He walked briskly the last block, full of determination and optimism, certain that his newfound vigor would persuade Bennett at least to hear him out. What evidence remained of his injuries would serve as testimony that at least part of his story must be true. *One chance*, Archie thought, his eyes on the imposing five-story granite facade of the *Herald* building as he approached the front doors. *One chance.*

"I knew you'd come back, Da."

The voice froze Archie in his tracks. Across the city, church bells began to chime, marking the noon hour. The chimes echoed deep in Archie's floundering mind, shaking him as if he'd been inside the carillon at St. Patrick's itself. The bright sunlight cast strange shadows and the light itself seemed to grow heavy and viscous, as if the passing of noon had aged the sun. *The false sun*, Archie thought, not knowing where the thought came from. It hung in his mind with the weight of certain truth: *In the false sun, men lose their faces and eyes see only lies.*

His eyes were closed, he realized, but he could still see. Faceless people thronged the streets, passing through the strange light as if blind. *I've gone mad*, he thought. The light stank like overripe fruit, like a winter afternoon, like quiet creeping age.

I've been so happy because I've gone insane.

Archie forced his eyes open and saw the ragged urchin squatting against the wall of the *Herald* building. She was scratching absently at the horrible webbing of sores on her face, and the false light clung like fungus to the marks left by her nails.

"I knew you'd come back because of the dream," she said, the words ringing in his head like bells, stirring up the dream until it boiled over into his vision and she was Jane, wearing a cloak of long green feathers and a mask of carved jade. He felt the weight of the knife in his palm, the muted life of her heartbeat beneath smooth skin.

"Jane," he said.

She stopped scratching and looked at him dumb-founded, the false light dripping from her chin and pooling in the shadows under her eyes. "Oh, Da," she said, standing, and she touched him gently on the arm.

At her touch, the bells stopped and the air itself seemed to twist itself into shreds between them. The beautiful false light leaked away, and her face returned, bearing livid scars and a trembling expression of wonder. He cried out and jerked away from her, stumbling into someone behind him. "Nation sakes, look where you're going," a woman said, and shoved him.

So this was madness.

"It's guilt, I know," he said to her, his senses returning. "The guilt has turned my head. I'm sorry, but I'm as mad as you are."

"But you had the dream," she insisted. "Da, you had the *dream*—" Her voice broke and Archie turned away, walking unsteadily in the clear light of afternoon.

As the church bells struck noon, Riley Steen stood in front of his study window covering his right eye with a copy of Bernal Diaz. Behind him, ants crawled in the spaces on his bookshelves, looking for the source of the strange ripeness in the air.

Steen saw the shadow of an eagle pass across the sun. The hour was right; Ometeotl was blinded by the false sun. He uncovered the Smoke Mirror, leaning the obsidian cover against his desk, where it would catch the sun. The mirror sat on a thick pedestal carved from a single piece of milky green jade, with ants covering each of the glyphs adorning the pedestal's squared sides.

Some of the ants left to swarm over the cover, creeping in formation along the scratched pattern of a crescent moon inside a blazing sun. Steen disrupted their patterns by plucking up four of them with tweezers and holding them in his closed fist. He ran his closed fist four times around the chipped rim of the bowl, watching his reflection in the still silver pool of mercury. Raising a spirit from Mictlan, the Place of the Fleshless, was a tricky business, but he could see no other way to gain the information he needed.

"Lupita," he said, and dropped an ant into the quicksilver. It sank without a ripple.

He repeated the action three more times, saying as he dropped the fourth ant, "Lupita, I am who sent you to Mictlan, and I command your attention this hour."

The ant fell onto the mercury, sending a single ripple out the inside edge of the bowl. It stayed on the surface, crawling to the edge of the quicksilver pool and up to the scalloped rim of the bowl, where Steen crushed it under his thumb. As he did, a shadow grew in the pool as if rising from some impossible depth.

"Wide Hat, why do you call me from my journey? The way back is long, across deserts and facing the Wind of Knives, and I have no dog to lead me across the river." Lupita's voice was soft, plaintive, nostalgic for the place she'd been torn from. The shadow of her filled the bowl now, spilling over the rim like smoke.

"Why does Ometeotl watch me, Lupita? *Caninmachiqualtlan nitlapachoa*? Where have I offended him?"

"God's plans and men's plans." The shadow cackled softly. "He watches you because he will; the Fleshless Ones gossip."

"The chacmool has escaped me. With the Old God's Eye so heavy, I dare not even search, lest he destroy it."

"*Otima toyani*, Wide Hat. You threw yourself into waters and only now see that the bottom avoids your feet."

"Parables are of no help now. Swimming lessons are."

"So." Shadow-stuff had pooled at the base of the pedestal. It struggled to find form as Lupita spoke. "The Fleshless Ones laugh at you, Wide Hat, and rattle their bones because you do not think. But your life may yet escape the Old God's anger. *In tlaulli mixpa nicmana*: heed the light I set before you."

"I'm listening."

"Nanahuatzin's father is the fulcrum. Your plans, and your life, tilt as he moves."

"Prescott?" Steen shook his head. "He'd dead, Lupita. His bones moulder in the Brewery."

"*Iztlactli.* You lie, although you do not know it; it is your plan which moulders in the Brewery. Prescott lives, and if you wish to live yourself you will not attempt to run him down."

Steen considered this odd admonition, forcing down his anger at Royce's bungling. Consequences could be meted out later. He'd had an intuition that Prescott had somehow muddied his plans the night of the chacmool's escape; it hardly seemed possible that Nanahuatzin's father would accidentally stumble onto such proceedings.

But if that were the case, logic dictated that he be eliminated, removing any potential for further disruption. Lupita was holding something back.

He forced himself to speak humbly. "I don't understand."

She cackled again. "So the Fleshless Ones say. Hear, then: Prescott wears the marks of both the *huehueteotl* and He Who Makes Things Grow. The gods watch him, save him for a role in their plans. Which of them he serves will depend on your restraint, Wide Hat. You must abide, and know when to act, and only then act without hesitation."

A ripple passed across the Mirror's face as a bird flew in front of the sun. "The chacmool has gone to ground," Lupita continued, "but will soon begin the journey back to Chicomoztoc whether Nanahuatzin accompanies or not. If the Fifth Sun passes away without sacrifice of the *yolteotl*, it will sleep again and rise when the time is right. But Tlaloc's marks are on Prescott, and he is not so patient. He has remembered he wants to live and will seek the chacmool to remove those marks. Nanahuatzin will follow him, Wide Hat, seeking her father as the river seeks the sea. If you would save your *plan*," again she twisted the word scornfully, "you will not intervene until the journey has begun. If you remember nothing else, bear those words in your soul. They are all that stands between you and the Old God's anger."

The shadows began to climb up the pedestal, receding into the depths of the mercury pool. "I tell you this because you command it, *Steen*," Lupita hissed, her voice fading. "But I have not forgotten what passed between us."

The shadow disappeared. One by one, the three ants rose to the surface of the pool and crawled away over the Smoke Mirror's edge. Steen watched them drop to the carpeted floor and lose themselves in the heavy fibers, admonishing himself for his thickheadedness. Of course, he thought. He'd been stupid not to recognize it himself. Of course the girl would follow Prescott when he pursued the chacmool. He'd used the same reasoning when he predicted she would return to New York after escaping him in Richmond.

Everything would work out perfectly. There came a point in the momentum of a man's endeavors when obstacles began to fall away, when the weight of gathering history amassed itself and rolled like a juggernaut over all opposition. Those who marshaled only petty plans, who puttered about the margins of relevance, never experienced that sensation, and in their jealous ignorance they called such momentum luck. But there was no luck; Steen knew that as surely as he understood his destiny. What ineffectual men called luck was in fact history's reward for well-planned audacity and ambitious scope.

And those rewards were beginning to accrue. But enough self-congratulation: the Mirror had to be covered before the hour passed and Ometeotl's Eye blinked open once more. Picking up the obsidian cover, Steen brushed clusters of confused ants from the pattern incised into the glasslike stone. The mirror covered, Steen glanced out the window to see what the sun would tell him, and that was when he saw Michael Dunn gazing steadily at him from across the street.

Snow is falling
& fell on them in those days

& on his companions
who were with him, on
his dwarfs, his clowns
his gimps
          It fell
till they were frozen
lost among the dead

—"The Flight of Quetzalcoatl"

on your way on your way
child be on your way to me here
          you whom I made new

come here child   come be pearl
be beautiful feather

—"Poem to Ease Birth"

Book III

Tozoztontli, 8-Deer—February 16, 1843

❖

A thin skein of ice had glazed the shores of the Green
River the last week or so, retreating on sunny days and
reappearing every morning. Variations in the water level
had left layers of ice on the riverbanks like step fungus
on a tree trunk. Although it was a bit warmer today, Stephen was still glad that he would be spending the day in
the cave, away from the chill winds. The cave's steady
fifty-four degrees was welcome when either heat or cold
got too extreme, but Stephen liked it better in the winter,
when fewer visitors were trooping through and disturbing
it.

Winter itself he could live without, though. Thoughts
of warm climates occupied his mind constantly since he'd
begun thinking of Monrovia: thick, steaming jungles, rain
warm as bathwater, sun that would bake his mulatto skin
to a true dark African hue. The thoughts made him strong,
and angry. He still wasn't sleeping very well, although
the mummy dreams only came every three weeks or so;
he dreamed constantly of a huge city on a broad shallow
lake, ringed by mountainous jungles. In this city Stephen
owned property; men came to him to settle disputes and
seek advice in the shadow of the great mountain to the
east.

That was his dream of Monrovia, his dream of an Africa
that yearned for him the way he burned to return to it. But
every time he had the dream—and it came nearly every
night—he grew more and more certain that the city was not

the capital city Monroeville, and the place was not Africa, and the eyes he looked out of were not his own.

The dream was beginning to frighten him.

"You sure nobody down to Bowling Green gonna talk about this?" Nick Bransford sat in one of Dr. Croghan's buggies, looking toward the hotel as if mentioning Croghan's name would bring the man himself running.

Stephen had made arrangements to travel with Nick to Bowling Green overnight to attend a cousin's jump over the broom, giving him an alibi to cover his solo venture into the cave against Dr. Croghan's orders. Nick was the only person on Croghan's estate who knew what was really going on, and as always he was jittery.

"Everything's gonna be fine," Stephen said. "You just go, and don't talk to anyone you don't know. I'll see you tomorrow."

He slapped the drowsing horse on its flank, and Nick drove the buggy off into the early-morning mist.

Stephen skipped down the trail like a boy, hurrying to be underground before it got too light. Below him gaped the mouth of the cave, its warm breath tickling Stephen's nose with the sweet promise of new discovery. Excitement quivered in the pit of his stomach, as it always did when he had the cave to himself. There would be no visitors today.

The sun was just beginning to sparkle on the frosted bark of the trees as Stephen adjusted his satchel and stepped into the twilight world. He passed quickly through Houchins Narrows and the majestic Rotunda, playing his lamp over the dusty remains of the saltpeter works. The Main Cave curved ahead of him, its gypsum-encrusted roof glittering brightly where smoke had not yet blackened the delicate formation. Stephen wished for a way to touch that ceiling, thirty feet over his head. It would be something no man had ever done.

Half an hour later he reached Giant's Coffin and paused, drinking in the solitude while he decided which way to go. Continuing through the Main Cave would lead eventually to the Temple and after that Ultima Thule, where the cave ended in a gigantic breakdown. There had to be a way through the ancient cave-in, but Stephen hadn't yet been able to find it. And Ultima Thule was a long hike, at least three miles before the real caving would begin.

The other way, beneath Giant's Coffin and across the Bottomless Pit, though, there were more leads than he could count. Open cave gaped there at every turn, and he hadn't returned to his new discoveries since the previous fall.

Stephen waited vainly for the ghosts to offer an opinion. But of course they didn't, and fresher prospects made the decision. Stephen took a nip from his flask and ducked into the steep, twisting drop behind Giant's Coffin.

In the last hour before dawn, the dream returned to Archie.

He lifted his face to the sun, waiting for the moment when it would pass directly overhead into the time of false light, when the Rabbit's antics blinded the searching Eye of the *huehueteotl*. On his left stood the mummy—*chacmool*, it called itself—resplendent in cloak of green quetzal feathers, human except for the golden slitted eyes that tracked Archie's gaze to the sun. On Archie's right stood Mike Dunn, naked and sweating under the flapping shreds of his overcoat. Ghostly flames flickered from his mouth as he said *No, Archie, no*, repeating the words like a psalm. Below, at the base of the terraced stone temple on which they stood, a great fire blazed, the air above it rippling from its heat. Archie looked through those waves at the broad avenue filled with people, the entire throng seeming to dance with one motion in the shimmering air. Riley Steen was there, and Udo, and Bennett and Royce McDougall. Behind Steen stood the portly figure of Phineas T. Barnum, the high dome of his forehead wrinkling as if he was trying to determine his role in the events that would follow.

Jane lay before him on a block of stone, its sides carved

in a tangle of glyphs stained black by crusted blood. Her dress was a mimicry of the chacmool's: painted red rings curved from eyebrow to cheekbone, and a jaguar pelt wrapped like a skirt around her waist. Quiet tears stood in her eyes, but she lay still, looking up into Archie's face.

Toniatuh, the chacmool said: the Sun. Archie looked directly up and saw the change come over the sun, saw its light bend under the weight of He Who Makes Things Grow, saw the ghosts of the *tianquiztli*, the Pleiades, appear as a speckled shadow in the center of the burning hollow sphere.

Tlaloc, in tonan in tota, the chacmool said: our Mother, our Father. It lay down on a lower stone block next to the altar, drawing its knees up and cupping its hands over its stomach. *Imacpal iyoloco*: He holds men in the palm of His hand.

Archie realized he held Helen's old kitchen knife in his hands. Silence spread like a wave over the crowd, and Archie saw Barnum still wearing the determined frown of a man tugging on a memory that will not quite appear.

No, Archie, no, Mike said.

As Archie raised the knife, the chacmool said *Yollotl, eztli; ompa onquiza'n tlalticpac.*

The heart, the blood, the world spills out.

He awoke with the knife in his hands and the quetzal talisman thrumming like a heartbeat in the hollow of his throat. In the subterranean darkness of the Bright's cellar, Archie watched the gleam of the false sun play along the knife's keen edge.

The voices—no, the *voice*—returned as Stephen carefully skirted the edge of Bottomless Pit, the corners of his eyes crinkling in the beginnings of a smile, as they always did now when he thought of that name. The smile faded as he heard the voice.

The cave had stopped whispering when he'd found the mummy. The voices, the ghosts, had gone away. In the few times since then that he'd been able to get in the cave alone, Stephen had realized what it was to be lonely. Solitude by itself was not loneliness; loneliness was when you expected a companion and none appeared. It wasn't a feeling he'd ever thought to experience in the cave. The whispers had always been there to guide him.

Now, Stephen realized, he understood why the cave frightened some people.

Visitors are coming, Stephen. I will return soon.

"Visitors are always coming," Stephen said. "How will I know them?"

You will know me.

Stephen stopped and squatted against the curving wall. Just ahead the passage narrowed into the muddy crawl he'd named Winding Way. After Winding Way came Great Relief Hall, a platter-shaped room barely tall enough to stand erect in. The name was a bit grand, maybe, but it had been perfect when Stephen had stretched his legs there after the first harrowing trip through Winding Way, his mouth and nose caked with mud. He'd had to push the lantern ahead of him, and one of the tight spots had forced him to turn his head sideways in order to get through it. But he'd smelled big cave ahead, just as he had the night he'd found the mummy.

"Yes, I'll know you," he said. "What is it you want from me?"

You will have a task to perform. A new world depends on your task, and when you have completed it you will stand at my left hand a free man. Prepare for visitors, Stephen. I will guide you.

The voice subsided, leaving Stephen very much aware of how alone he was, separated from the sun by a hundred feet and more of solid limestone. And the whispers were still silenced. What was it about that voice that made him fear the cave? What threat hid behind its promise of freedom?

Stephen felt as he had before he'd taught himself to read, when visitors talked about books and goaded him about stories he'd never heard. Angry frustration welled up with those memories, the feeling that just out of earshot scornful laughter was drifting in his direction. The voice was hiding something, lying about something. And if it was lying at all, its promises couldn't be trusted.

"I *will* be free," Stephen growled into the pit. The darkness swallowed his words and kept them.

He needed answers. If the voice was lying, he had to know what it was lying about; otherwise he was no better than a tool, like he was for Dr. Croghan. When the visitors came, they might have information, but in the meantime Stephen resolved to learn as much as he could on his own. And he would start in the room where he'd found the mummy.

In River Hall, Stephen paused beside a large pool called the Dead Sea, to have a drink and consider his options. The River Styx murmured softly from around the next bend in the passage, beckoning him. Down here the cave was different, the passages more secretive. A sense of openness waiting to be revealed hung in the damp air with the smell of the water.

The river had several branches, and Stephen had followed every one until the water rose within inches of the roof and his teeth were chattering with the cold. There was more cave beyond the rivers, he had no doubt about that. He just had to listen to the ghosts and find his way when the water was low. The one way he'd found on the other side of the river had been named Purgatory, a cold and miserable tube that opened out into some magnificent sights after a mile or so. He'd found grand high canyon passages, their walls whipped into strange ridges and scallops by long-gone rushing water, and dozens of tiny cracks and crevices like moleholes. Someday all would bear the names of visitors, Stephen thought bitterly. People who come just to say they've done it.

The other river branches might also lead to big cave, but something about the water made Stephen nervous this day.

The Dead Sea lay still, and Stephen became convinced that the water had somehow silenced the ghosts. *They used to call out when new cave was close*, he thought, *and since they stopped, I've been afraid of water. There's got to be a connection.* And he had to find out what that connection was, had to get the voice out of his head and the cave so the whispering ghosts would come back.

Stephen squeezed into the branch that led to Bottomless Pit, moving at a steady crawl and bearwalking when the ceiling rose enough. Working his way up the corkscrew at the end, he thought he heard someone speaking, and stopped until his own breathing quieted enough to hear; but if there had been a sound, it was gone, and he put it down to a freak echo from a tour in another part of the cave. No tours had been scheduled, but things changed. Perhaps Croghan himself had taken a surprise visitor for a ramble.

Be just my luck, he thought, *if someone dropped a torch into the pit while I was standing at the bottom. Probably scare some eastern dentist half to death, and what would Dr. Croghan say about that?*

He heard no other noises as he worked his way down the rockfall to the bottom of the pit, but Stephen caught himself looking up several times when he should have been paying attention to his feet. He had a prickling sensation on his scalp, like he was expecting to bump his head. Was someone up there?

It was then that Stephen noticed the footprints leading into the Mummy Room. He stopped short, feeling the prickle spread to the nape of his neck and down his arms.

No one else knew about the branch, and he was sure that no other way led to Bottomless Pit. Were the footprints his? It was possible, he guessed; but the pit flooded fairly often when the rivers rose. Who else's would they be, though? Had someone else found the branch and the Mummy Room?

He was surprised at the jealous chill he felt when imagining someone else standing before the great statue. *It's mine*, he thought, *or should be if anything in this cave should. Nobody else has a right to it.*

Holding his lamp closer to one of the tracks, Stephen saw something that sent a chill through him: they were prints of bare feet, each toe clearly outlined by a tiny ridge of sand. And there were no prints leading out, either bare or shod. Whoever had entered the Mummy Room was still there.

The voice had said visitors were coming. Had one of them arrived already? Or was it the mummy itself, already returned from the museum back East where Croghan had sold it?

Neither seemed likely. Whatever the voice had held back, it clearly wanted him to do something before the visitors came. It didn't follow, then, that it would deceive him about the visitors' arrival, and that meant that whoever was in the Mummy Room wasn't on an errand from the mummy itself. There was nothing to do but go on in and see what was what.

Following an old habit, Stephen stepped exactly in the mysterious tracks as he crossed to the triangular portal that led to the Mummy Room. The lamp would give him away to whoever was inside, but that couldn't be helped. Going in without light would be foolish.

He ducked quickly through the quick tight turn between the leaning slabs and the opening into the terraced chamber itself. Standing again, with the altar stone facing the immense carved statue to his right, Stephen was once more overwhelmed by the strangeness of it. The square-cut walls, the stone god's watchful face, the tangled panorama carved into the altar's sides: nothing else in the cave had prepared him for this. And now there was an intruder, a tall lithe black man wearing only shirtsleeves and homespun trousers and carrying a shoulder bag, dripping wet and squinting at the statue like he was in a museum. He was nobody Stephen knew.

"How did you get here?" Stephen asked.

"Same way you did. There's only the one way." The

intruder turned to Stephen, his eyes bulging out of sockets ringed by black dead flesh. A swampy odor rode on his breath, and his skin sagged like a bloodhound's jowls.

"Think, Johnny, introductions." Smiling, the intruder said, "John Diamond. You must be Rebus." He stuck out a skinny hand, the tips of the fingers wrinkled like he'd been too long in his bathwater.

Stephen shook before it occurred to him not to. "Who's Rebus?" he said. "My name is Stephen."

"Oh, *Stephen!* Sorry, Johnny; Christ. Dead man's mistake. They told me you were Rebus." John shook his head and scratched behind one ear, laughing at the joke.

"Dead people?" The swamp smell was coming not from Diamond's breath, Stephen realized, but directly out of his skin.

"They talk to me. I'm one of them, after all. Terrible racket, lucky I don't sleep any more."

Stephen struggled to make sense of what this Diamond was saying. Was he dead? Stephen had heard of haunts and zombies, but never of one who could speak, much less laugh. This man, John, said that the dead spoke to him— was that what Stephen was hearing, voices from the grave?

In any case, Diamond's being in the Mummy Room was no accident. He'd expected Stephen, even if he had a different name in mind.

The realization clicked into place: The mummy wasn't expecting this Diamond. He had come here on his own, or been sent by someone or something else.

"Did the mummy send you?" Stephen asked, to be sure.

"Mummy? Oh, chacmool. No. Chacmool works for Steen, or he thinks it does. Steen's the man drowned me. Hateful thing. Bastard. He wants to be king. Shut up, you." This last was snapped at the air just above Diamond's head. "Sorry, Johnny, not you. My tongue gets loose, too many voices want out."

Steen. The man who'd bought the mummy had been named Steen. "What's this chacmool?" Stephen asked before Diamond started yammering again.

Diamond peered at him as if trying to detect a joke. "You don't know anything, do you?" he said finally, a delighted smile breaking out on his wasted face. "Chacmool's a . . . hm. From the beginning, Johnny.

"Big things afoot. You involved. I wasn't but now I am. Chacmool's a, sort of eyes and ears for him." Diamond pointed at the statue. "He Who Makes Things Grow, Tlaloc, *imacpal iyoloco*."

"Eemac-what?"

"Sorry, Johnny. Nahuatl; his language. I hear him, too. Means he holds us in the palm of his hand. More like a fist for me 'cause I drowned. You he still tries to convince."

You will be a man, Stephen thought, hearing the voice's encouraging echo.

"Right," Diamond nodded, then caught himself. "Sorry, Johnny. Eavesdrop sometimes. Tlaloc in my head, makes me do things, I don't remember all of them.

"But that's his only form now," Diamond said, pointing over his shoulder at the grotesque carving on the cave wall, "that and others like it. All lost in the jungle except this one, and it is trapped in the wall. He can't walk in this world without form. And chacmool isn't strong enough on its own to bring him back. So it plans a sacrifice to feed him, give him strength and form."

Excitement built in Diamond's breathy voice. "That's where this comes in," he continued, pulling a wooden box from his bag and dropping a canvas bundle on the floor. He flinched as he opened the box.

When fully open, the halves of the box met and formed a figure. "Look familiar?" Diamond said.

Stephen nodded. The figure on the box was the mummy. The chacmool.

"Thought so. Now this," Diamond scooped up the canvas bundle, "is for you. I'm not supposed to have it. Maskansisil doesn't want that." He unwrapped a polished wooden mask, featureless except for a lump where a nose might be and a two-inch slit of a mouth.

"Lupita told me to look for this, and—sorry Johnny—I

told Steen about it. Steen killed her too. Bastard. He drowned me—guess I owe him a bad turn or two. I opened the box and now Maskansisil is in my head, too. Tells me to hate Tlaloc, but I can't. Can hate Steen, though. He wouldn't want you to have this."

Diamond held the mask out to Stephen, but Stephen took a step away from him. "Hold on, now," he said. "I'm not in the habit of talking to dead men, and I don't understand half of what you say. Why should I wear this mask? Who's Maskansisil?"

Diamond shrugged, still offering Stephen the mask. "Maybe you won't. Maybe you give it to someone. Maskansisil is in the mask. The Pathfinder."

"Who is Maskansisil?" Stephen said again.

"Sorry, Johnny. Too fast. Beginning again: Tlaloc's people . . . Maskansisil is like the chacmool. He is eyes and ears for a different god, who also has no form. Good and evil is too simple, but . . . He fights Tlaloc, fights the chacmool. For a very long time."

Diamond shrugged again. "All I know. You are a pathfinder, too. Maskansisil says give the mask to you, you'll know what to do."

Stephen reached for the mask, then hesitated. "Maskansisil sent you to me?"

Diamond nodded, grinning.

"Who sent you to get the mask?"

The grin faded and Diamond looked at his feet. "Tlaloc showed me where it was."

"You're serving two masters, dead man. How do I know which one is talking?" He would have to take the mask, Stephen knew that. He was caught too deep already to just step aside. But before he committed, he was damn sure going to know who was pulling Diamond's strings.

Diamond looked at him coldly, and the force of that angry gaze battered Stephen's mind with the realization that he was talking to a dead man. A man who heard the voices of the gods.

"*I* speak," Diamond said, injured fury simmering in his

whispery voice. "I could give the mask to another, could throw it into the sea. I give it to you."

Stephen took the mask. It was heavier than it should have been, and he felt part of its weight settle into him, as if he had betrayed a confidence. Now I'm serving two masters too, he thought, half expecting the voice to return or the featureless mask to suddenly speak; but the only sound in the cave was a hollow click as Diamond shut the carved box.

"I'll keep this," he said. "It should be apart from the mask."

Am I really ready to cross this chacmool? Stephen wasn't sure, but he guessed he already had. Guilt began to gnaw at him as he remembered the city from his dreams, remembered again the feeling of being a citizen rather than a slave.

"Diamond," he blurted, "have you seen the city?"

"Afternoon city?" Diamond said, and Stephen nodded, seeing again the sun reddened by plumes of smoke.

"Ha," Diamond said, his bare feet slapping on the floor as he walked away. "Have I seen it? Rebus, I *live* there."

Archie sat for a long time, the smell of smoke strong in his nose, looking at the knife as the warmth ebbed out of it. He bore small shiny scars on the fingers of his right hand, reminders of the night seven years before when his life had collapsed in a shower of sparks. The blade of this knife had burned him then, and now that he'd finally gone mad, it lay cooling in his upturned palms. Madness was no comfort; even the light of day buckled around him. But what else could be expected? Wife and child dead, job and home lost, reduced to sleeping in a groggery cellar and lugging beer casks for a ration of beef stew. And haunted by macabre visions of pagan sacrifice with his dead daughter as the victim.

This knife is hungry, Archie thought. Not for Riley Steen, or for Jane, but for me. What it wants is to carve out my beating heart and leave it for whatever demons have possessed me. Wilson had been right: Archie's soul had left him. But it hadn't come back.

The knife's edge was sharp enough. If it cut out his heart, who would the sacrifice appease? The suicides Archie had seen had all been desperate—lonely drunks or jilted lovers who stepped off bridges or drank carbolic acid. Knives were too immediate, too close, too active; to kill oneself with a knife took more determination than the average suicide possessed. Suicide by knife was a self-sacrifice, an offering to the swollen hungry god of desperation.

A sacrifice, Archie realized, that he was not yet ready to perform. The point of the knife rested in the hollow below his sternum, twitching in rhythm with his heartbeat. Just above it he could feel the mummy's talisman moving in unison with his breath.

Yollotl, eztli.

The cellar door banged open. "Archie!" Belinda shouted. "Up and about!" The door slammed shut again and floorboards creaked overhead as she moved behind the bar.

The day was beginning without him. If Belinda came downstairs and found him hunched over the knife with his hands full of his own blood, she would shake her head and enlist some other wretch to clean up the mess and take his place. Bennett would hear about it and send someone to write up a paragraph—suicides always sold papers, especially if there was a tragic tale attached—and Archie would be buried under an anonymous cross in the paupers' ground. Helen's parents might read about him in the *Herald*, but they wouldn't come; he hadn't spoken to them in years. Udo would be there, though, to pray over him and then drain a mug in his memory. And that would be all.

I won't be someone else's story, Archie thought. My tale is mine to tell.

And the tale began with the mummy in Barnum's Museum. Archie thought of Barnum's face in his dream, his quizzical expression standing out in a sea of ecstatic worshipers. Steen had taken the mummy to Barnum for a reason, he realized, and if Barnum didn't know what that reason was, Archie was willing to wager that he had ways of finding out.

The clerk at Barnum's Museum, a thin balding man wearing a string tie and a tremendous mustache, steadfastly maintained that the showman couldn't be bothered. "He's attending to important business," he said for the fifth time, looking over his spectacles at Archie's mangled ear. "You must call again at another time."

"Counting figures, is he?" Frustrated, Archie played his trump card. "Well, tell him he'd better count out a thousand dollars for me. I know who killed his watchman last December."

The clerk sighed and sent a long-suffering look upward to the stuffed eagle hanging from the ceiling in the museum's foyer. "You and every other rummy in the Five Points," he said. "Fine."

He gave Archie a sheet of paper and indicated the inkwell on his desk. "Write down what you have to say and your address. You can write?"

Archie bit back a reply. He nodded.

"I'll see that it gets to his attention," the clerk finished.

Archie took the paper and folded it into his coat pocket. "I was born at night, friend, but it wasn't last night. I've got to see him now."

The clerk just looked over Archie's left shoulder.

"All right," Archie said. "In lieu of a note, why don't you take *this* and see that it comes to his damned attention?" He reached into his shirtfront and lifted the feathered medallion over his head. Dangling it in front of the clerk, Archie jerked his head in the direction of the stair. "Go on, take it," he said. "I'll wait."

He might as well have shown the clerk a pistol. The

man's hauteur crumbled immediately and he leaped out of his high chair. "Stay where you are," the clerk said. He took the talisman and held it gingerly at arm's length. "I'll summon the police if you attempt to leave."

Archie had no energy to reply. He stood perfectly still, trying to weather the wave of vertigo that washed through his head as the talisman left his hand. A whine rose in his ears, grew to a deafening roar as he pitched over onto the hardwood floor. *It will subside*, he told himself. *It has to*.

But instead of subsiding, the attack grew worse. Archie's vision narrowed to a dim pinhole and his hands shook as if palsied. He tried to pull himself up using the clerk's chair, but a tremendous weight seemed to be pressing on his chest, squeezing out his breath. He fell again, thinking *I can't live without it*. It connected him somehow; that's what the dreams meant. Without it he was a babe in the womb, umbilicus wrapped around its neck.

In his desperation, a single thought formed: He had to find the mummy, free himself of it before the madness it drove him to became permanent. Kill it if need be.

"Where did you find this?" The voice rammed into Archie's ears and sparked thundering echoes in his head.

Archie looked up, tried to focus on the speaker and couldn't. "Please," he whispered, reaching out, "please give it back."

"Where did you get it?"

"I —I took it from the mummy." Archie began to cry with fear and embarrassment. "Please give it back."

The talisman dropped into his outstretched hands. Archie clutched it fiercely, trembling as the delirium began to fade and things around him took their shapes again. He hitched a great sob, tried to let it out slowly and regain some control over himself.

"Can you walk?" The man in front of Archie came into focus. Thickly built, well dressed, familiar broad features scowling under a receding crop of unruly dark hair.

"I think so." Archie's voice was shaky, but he thought he'd be able to stand.

"Come with me, then," said Phineas Taylor Barnum, indicating the stairs.

Neither of them spoke as Barnum led Archie up four flights of stairs and into a small sunlit study. A desk and two chairs occupied nearly all of the floor space, and all four walls were lined by floor-to-ceiling bookshelves. Sitting on one corner of the desk, Barnum gestured for Archie to sit. Archie did, replacing the medallion around his neck.

"Being deprived of that charm seems to have quite a deleterious effect on you, Mr.—?"

"Prescott."

"Yes. I am Phineas Barnum, although I'm sure you know that. Still, one must observe proprieties. Perhaps you could explain the effect, Mr. Prescott?"

"No, Mr. Barnum, I can't. It's just . . . I need it."

"Hm." Barnum considered this for a moment. "Secondary in any event. Of primary importance here is how you came into possession of part of the Aztec Mummy's regalia, after it disappeared on the same night as the brutal murder of my night man. You realize what you have?"

"I do." Archie was beginning to breathe more easily, and the shaking in his hands had mostly subsided. Seeing that Barnum took him seriously, he began to relax just a fraction.

"How does your possession of this item relate to the murder of my employee?"

How doesn't it? Archie thought. But spinning the entire tale for Barnum would likely get him nowhere, except back on the street no closer either to the chacmool or his sanity.

"I'm a desperate man, Mr. Barnum," Archie said at last. "I used to have a family, a daughter, but now . . . the night your watchman was killed I was planning to break into the museum myself."

Barnum didn't visibly react, but Archie knew that if the rest of his story wasn't believed, he'd see nothing but the inside of the Tombs for the rest of his life. "Go on," the showman said.

"I work—well, did until recently—for the *Herald*, as a typesetter. I've harbored ambitions of being a journalist, though, and Mr. Bennett gave me to understand that an exposé concerning your museum would help realize that goal."

"Do tell," Barnum said, and a broad smile broke across his jowly face. "Pity for both of us it didn't come off. You'd have had your position and I would have gained notice I never could have bought. Bennett has done that for me before, you know, with dear old Joice Heth." Barnum cleared his throat. "But back to your tale."

"Well, when I arrived at the museum I saw a group of Dead Rabbits being ordered around by a man named Riley Steen."

"Steen? You're certain?"

"I am."

Barnum lapsed into thought, and Archie began to feel that he might yet escape this encounter a free man.

"Hm," Barnum grunted at last, rousing himself. "Conduct business with scoundrels, reap the rewards."

Scoundrel doesn't even begin to do Steen justice, Archie thought. But something else was tickling his brain, a connection begging to be made. "What business?" he asked.

"Oh, I've dealt with Steen from time to time these past few years, but his 'discoveries' inevitably turn out to be frauds. That mummy you took your token from was my latest and last purchase from Mr. Steen. I bought it last fall in Philadelphia. He'd brought it from Kentucky expressly to sell it to me, he said, but now I believe he meant the transaction merely as a short-term lease. Steen was at the museum to steal the mummy when you saw him?"

Archie nodded, although *steal* didn't seem quite the right word. Kidnap, perhaps, or capture.

"And how did you come into contact with it?"

Archie paused. If Barnum disbelieved him for any reason, he was in the deepest of deep trouble. Mentioning Steen's name appeared to have divided Barnum's attention, and bought Archie a little credibility, but Archie had no illusions about his own innocence in the showman's eyes. *All I have is the story,* he thought. *And all I can do is tell it.*

"The Rabbits caught me in your main gallery," he said, speaking slowly to keep his voice steady. "They'd posted lookouts, and were using some kind of cornstalk rope that they thought would keep the . . . mummy . . . from escaping. They thought it was going to come back to life, apparently. When Steen saw me, he made it clear that I wouldn't be leaving, but I got free of the Rabbit holding me and the only place I could go was into the museum." Archie continued the story, skipping over Royce's odd threats and his earlier encounter with the Rabbits on Water Celebration Day. "The watchman accosted me in the corner near the chacmool's case—"

"Where did you learn that word?" Barnum barked, levering himself off the desk to stand over Archie.

Flustered, Archie lost his train of thought: "I—in a dream, I think."

"A dream?" Barnum looked out the study's single window and studied the sky for a moment. When he turned back to Archie, his face had settled somewhat. "Look here, Mr. Prescott. When you came in here I was presuming you to be a small-time hoodlum, reporter aspirations or no. But if you continue to bandy about words such as *chacmool,* I will think you something else entirely. There aren't twenty white men on this earth who know that name, and you've got a bit of a task explaining to me how you could have innocently come across it."

"It was a dream, I swear it," Archie insisted. With an effort he remained seated, thinking *Mad or not, I don't want to end my days in the Tombs.*

"More than one dream, they happen all the time," he began to babble, all of his fear and angry frustration channeled into a confessional flood. "Mr. Barnum, that thing leaped out of its case like a damned lion and tried to tear out my heart!"

Archie's voice cracked on the last word, and he swallowed before going on. "I did kill your guard, you know; he tried to save my life and the chacmool tore him to pieces because he distracted it. If I hadn't been there, it would have been out the window before the Rabbits or Steen or anyone else knew what was happening, and your watchman would be alive, and I wouldn't have these horrible . . . these . . ."

Archie ripped open his shirt. "Here!" he shouted, standing and baring his chest for Barnum. "Look at this and tell me what I have to fear from jail."

Barnum's eyes widened at the sight of the four thin white lines hooking from Archie's left collarbone across his chest. They ended in thick apostrophes of scar tissue just below his sternum, at the very point where Archie had held his knife that morning.

"It did this to me, and then it was through the window and gone, but it's still in my head. I dream its dreams, Mister Barnum, because I can't find my own any more. Or maybe they are my own. *I don't know any more.*" Archie grabbed the talisman hanging around his neck. "It all comes from this. The chacmool, it's marked me somehow, left me this token as some kind of window into its mind, and *I can't let it go.*"

His anger spent, Archie's chest began to hitch with racking exhausted sobs. Barnum began to speak, but Archie cut him off, determined to finish whether the showman wanted to hear him or not. "I see—horrible things," he said pleadingly. "I think I'm going mad, and I can't let it go."

He dropped the talisman and wiped tears from his eyes. "You've got to help me, Mr. Barnum. You know something about this. You know what it is.

"Please. Tell me how I can get free."

❖

March had come in like a lion all right, Archie thought as he paged through the day's *Herald*. Nothing but rain and sleet for the past week, driving all but the hardiest vendors under overhangs and into empty storefronts. Belinda's Bright had been full nearly to bursting with grouchy day-laborers, faces red from the stinging ice and hands raw from the cold, when Archie stopped in the night before to thank Belinda for her kindness and let her know he'd found better circumstances.

Better financial circumstances, at least; his mental situation, on the other hand, had deteriorated. With the rain had come the dreams, seemingly refreshed after their three-week absence; each night since the beginning of the month Archie had awakened with his head full of the fluting sounds of the chacmool's language and his hands locked tightly around the hilt of his knife. Had he experienced a week like that before visiting Barnum, Archie was sure, New York's literate citizens would have been glancing at his obituary some weeks past.

The information Barnum had provided him had quite literally saved Archie's life. He was still terrified, but it was peculiar how a little knowledge enabled one to face demons and summon up a certain resolution. All the different elements—the chacmool, Riley Steen, the feathered medallion, Barnum himself—fit together, forming one vast frightening pattern whose edges Archie could not yet discern.

Aaron Burr, as it turned out, had been the first to piece it all together. A Tammany man since youth, he had uncovered in the Society's archives information that nearly made real his dream of forging an empire that would have stretched from the Appalachian Mountains to the western frontier and down into the jungles of Mexico. Archie had been born in the year 1806, when Burr was just beginning to set his plans in motion, with financial backing from the Tammany Society and an Irish businessman named Harman Blennerhassett. He'd read of the Burr Conspiracy in school, where it had been presented as the treasonous, delusional fantasy of a cowardly egomaniac. An aspiring Napoleon, one of Archie's teachers had called Burr. But Phineas Barnum saw things a bit differently.

The American Museum's collection, Barnum told Archie, had been accreting gradually since 1791, when it was first established by none other than the Society of St. Tammany. Like most of the Society's endeavors, the collection was assembled for an ostensible civic purpose that disguised more nefarious aims, and its library, according to Barnum, contained many "extremely interesting and equally scandalous" items. The Society, demonstrating its short attention span, left the collection to molder in a storeroom and eventually sold it to a John Scudder, who included some of the more attention-grabbing pieces in the original American Museum, which he built in 1831. Barnum himself finagled the purchase of the museum building and its collection in 1841, despite shadowy opposition from a group of competitors which, he said, he later determined to have included Riley Steen.

While cataloguing his new assets, Barnum had discovered several books of "arcane scholarship," one of which was an English translation of the *Wallam Olum*, the Red Record of the Lenni Lenape, or Delaware Indians. This tale, of considerable anthropological importance in its own right, was accompanied by an explication written by none other than Aaron Burr.

Archie had held up a hand at this point in Barnum's

narrative, meaning to ask what all of this had to do with the chacmool and Barnum's murdered watchman, but Barnum shushed him as he might have a too-boisterous child in the museum.

"Connections in all of this will become clear, Mr. Prescott," he said. "But you have to think as well as listen."

"Think about what?" Archie had replied.

"The *Wallam Olum* records the migration of the Lenape people from somewhere far to the northwest—Burr believed it to be Asia, but I'm sure you'll agree that's preposterous—to their present location in the Delaware Valley. Along the way, Mr. Prescott, the *Wallam Olum* narrates a series of battles between the Lenape and an enemy tribe called only the Snake, who were eventually driven down into 'the land of swamps.' "

Barnum patted his pockets, then found matches in one of the desk drawers and lit a lamp. Outside, the sun was dropping behind St. Paul's Chapel across Broadway, and the small library had gotten dim. "I don't have all the answers for you, Prescott, but I will tell you this: Burr spent much of his time in Kentucky during the months leading up to the collapse of his plan, and I have it on good authority that he visited the Mammoth Cave there at least once. The mummy, or more properly the chacmool, came from that cave to Philadelphia, where I purchased it from Steen. And Tamanend, the Lenape chief who appears both in the *Wallam Olum* and in the memoirs of William Penn, is the same saintly figure from whom the Tammany Society took its name. Too many connections exist for me to believe them all coincidental."

With that, Barnum had gone to a shelf and removed a slim volume bound in cracked leather. "I have a notion," he said, "that those connections will become considerably clearer once you have had a chance to peruse this."

Archie had spent the last three weeks muddling through Burr's translation of the *Wallam Olum*. Much of the exegesis, scrawled in margins and on facing pages, was beyond him; convoluted mathematics stood side by side with references to wildly deranged Mexican cult rituals and vituperative rants directed at Thomas Jefferson.

The overall shape of things began to come clear, though, as Archie worked his way through the text. The chacmool was one figure in a war that had gone on since the time of the pharaohs, when the Lenni Lenape had first encountered the Snake in—where? Oregon? The Dakota Territories? And now Archie found himself bound up in these events, swept along as they roared toward a critical moment that would come sometime in April. *The Death of the Fifth Sun*, Burr had called it, and dated it April 3, 1807. Seeking to harness the chacmool's power, he had worn ruts in the roads of Kentucky during the years 1805 and 1806 in his efforts to ferret out the avatar's hiding place.

So Riley Steen is following in Burr's footsteps, trying to bring the chacmool to heel, Archie thought, sipping coffee and hearing a shutter somewhere bang in the blustery wind. But what does he expect from it? Why does he think he needs it? He must think it's going to happen this April.

April 3, 1843. Four, three, forty-three. *Dear God*, Archie thought, *what would old apocalyptic William Miller make of that?* And Jane's birthday had been April third. Lately it seemed as if some cruel fate was forcing Archie to be constantly reminded of her, as if every event conspired to thrust her before him.

But despite all of the information he'd gathered, Archie's understanding of the situation came up short against a featureless wall of uncertainty. What was the Fifth Sun, other than a measure of time? And how did its death, or ending, bear on Burr's plans for a western empire?

More important, why had he failed?

What was clear was that Archie had to somehow confront this chacmool, whatever it was, and break the hold it had over him. But Christ in Heaven, if it had fled to Kentucky, how would he ever find it?

Too many questions, and answers would be gained only

by acting. Like getting back on a horse after being thrown, Archie thought, only the horse isn't usually trying to kill you. The chacmool had turned down a chance to kill him once, had even stepped back in a posture that Archie could only describe as deferential—but Archie wasn't at all certain that it would be so respectful now.

The thing to do now was find it, and Archie had tested his newfound resolve to its utmost by enlisting the help of the mad little guttersnipe who thought she was his daughter. The network of urchins and street arabs was keeping a collective sharp eye out for a Negro dressed in green feathers. He hadn't mentioned the canoe full of gutted children found on Christmas Day—or the horror he'd felt when he realized what he must have been mimicking when, in his three-week fugue in the Old Brewery, he'd tried to row himself across a privy trench.

Archie hoped that one of the children would see the beast near its lair—if it hadn't already fled New York—and he was absolutely praying that none of them would be hurt because of his request. But he was getting desperate, and, if Burr was to be believed, for good reason. Burr had flatly stated that the "New Sun" would be ushered in by some sort of ceremony to take place in Kentucky. If the chacmool slipped past the army of children before Archie could locate it, he would have to search an entire western state during the next three and a half weeks. If he wasn't successful, the chacmool would probably disappear into the Mexican jungle after its New Sun was established, and Archie would be left with hallucinatory nightmares for the rest of his life.

Seeing his reflection in the restaurant's front window, Archie considered that despite his persistent confusion, some good had come of meeting Barnum. His hair had sprouted some more gray, and he was still thin, with a crooked nose and a missing ear; but Barnum's thousand-dollar reward had bought him a new suit of clothes, a haircut, and a hotel room with a feather mattress. Most of it, seven hundred dollars, sat in the form of a cashier's check in Archie's breast pocket. The rest he had in bills and gold, jingling pleasantly when he walked.

And Belinda's Bright was a memory now, not entirely unpleasant but certainly nothing to provoke nostalgia. I won't go back there, either, Archie thought. Not even if I spend every dollar of Barnum's reward chasing a murderous half-human priest of some forgotten Mexican god all the way to Kentucky.

Through his reflection and the droplets of water on the window Archie saw a small boy slink through the crowd and peer in the window. Archie waved to him and he beckoned Archie to come outside, holding his hat against the rising wind.

Probably been run out of the place before for being a nuisance, Archie thought. He dropped a coin on the table and went out to meet the boy.

They hunched together under the hotel's front awning. "I'm Lucas," the boy said. "You Jane's dad?"

No, Archie started to say, but he caught himself. Best not to complicate matters. "You have news?" he asked, putting on his hat and turning up his collar against the driven rain.

"Sure do," Lucas said, his eyes dancing with pride and excitement. "Found the nigger myself, on Cherry Street. He's gone from there, though. We're following him."

"It—he's active right now?"

"Oh, I guess he is. I think he's gone to Battery Park. You're supposed to meet Jane there."

"Fine work, Lucas." Archie gave the boy a dollar and told him to buy a scarf. Then he strode into the street, braving the freezing rain to hail a cab.

Royce waited until Archie had gone, then collared the boy. "So this is where you've got to, Allie!" he shouted in the startled boy's face. "Wait'll Mum gets hold of your worthless skin!"

He cuffed the boy on the ear hard enough to cross his

eyes, then dragged him into an alley between Prescott's hotel and the cobbler next door. Pedestrians on Broadway didn't so much as glance up, concentrating instead on protecting their faces from the raw late-winter wind.

Once well into the narrow cut-around, Royce shoved the boy against a wall and flicked his cap off with the point of a short knife. "No monkeyshines, now," he warned. "I'd hate to cut a sprite such as yourself, but just now I'm a desperate man. Where's our man Archie heading?"

"Wh—who's Archie?" the boy stammered, wriggling in Royce's grasp.

Royce flicked his wrist, and an inch-long cut opened on the boy's chin. The boy cried out and Royce clamped a hand over his mouth.

"Hush, now—I warned you," he remarked. "Now what's your name?"

The boy mumbled into his hand. "Lucas," he said when Royce took a step back and dropped the knife to his side.

"All right, Lucas, tell quickly; me knife hand has the shakes."

"Battery Park," the boy blubbered, pressing the heel of one hand against the blood dripping from the point of his chin. "Please, mister, I didn't know his name was Archie—"

"Shut it, sprite. Move along now and spend your dollar." The boy ran for his life back out onto Broadway, swallowed by the crush of traffic and the slashing rain.

Battery Park it was, then. Royce was upset, but not terribly; even though it irked him when men he killed wouldn't stay dead, the second time was always the charm. He slipped his knife back up his sleeve and gave his collar a jaunty turn as he walked briskly to the corner of Fulton, where Charlie waited with a stolen hack.

Jane anxiously scanned the crowd from her perch atop the statue of Patrick Henry that stood at the southeastern edge of Battery Park, near where the passenger-ferry docks began sprouting from the base of Whitehall Street. The wind and rain had nearly frozen her into a sculpted gremlin on Mr. Henry's shoulders, and she'd lost her hat some time ago to a swirling breeze that had whirled it away toward Buttermilk Channel. Now her hair was stuck in wet strings to her face, and her bare face and scalp stung with every fresh gust of sleet.

Despite the weather, the Battery and the docks just east of it were crowded with people waiting to take ship. *Wish I could go somewhere,* Jane thought. *I'll bet it's lovely and warm in New Orleans or St. Louis today.*

Her attention was drawn from the crowds by the sight of a policeman making his way toward her. He had just reached the hedgerow that set off the park from the cobblestoned streets around it, but Jane knew she had a minute at most before she would be run out of the park.

"Come on Da. Damn," she muttered, her lips moving slowly because of the cold. The black man she'd seen outside her burrow had boarded a steamer just fifteen minutes before. He was dressed normally now, in a heavy sweater and cap, but he carried a bag that, Jane was sure, had his strange feather cloak stuffed into it. His boat had been bound for Philadelphia, and Da would have to hurry to get another that would catch him.

She hadn't told Da she'd seen the black man—only she knew he was an Indian—before, and as a daughter she felt guilty about it. It wasn't right to hide things from your Da. But the itching in her scars wasn't something Jane wanted to explain just yet; she had a feeling that she was growing in some way, that something wonderful was happening to her. After whatever it was happened, Da would be able to understand.

Not that it seemed wonderful all the time. Her scars itched constantly, and it always got worse just before sunrise and right around noon. Why, she didn't know.

When she looked at her fingers Jane saw that pieces of flesh had come loose and stuck to her nails. Still the itching continued, but she forced herself to ignore it. If she scratched too much, one of the bloody spots might fester.

There was Da, paying a cab and squinting in the rain. Even wet and disheveled from the storm, he looked better than he had in months. He wore new clothes and his face had lost some of the sickly pallor that had frightened her so when she'd spoken with him a month or so ago.

Jane jumped down from Patrick Henry's shoulders and darted across the lawn toward him, just as the policeman drew near enough to shout out "You, boy, off of there!" Dodging through the hedge, she circled through the crowd before sneaking up behind Da, who was still craning his neck at the crowd.

"You've come. Lucas found you, then?" she said, taking his gloved hand.

He started, nearly pulling his hand free, but caught himself. Jane could see, though, that his face bore the same expression it always did when he looked at her. Disgust and fear; why did he have to react that way?

Well, he wouldn't always. Everything was going to change soon, she could feel it.

"Come on, we've got to hurry," she said, pushing away her resentment one more time.

"Hurry for what? Is it here?" He was looking through the crowd, trying to spot the black man, she was sure. But why had he said *it?*

She stopped and took his hand in both of hers. "He's gone to Philadelphia. You have to follow him, don't you? There's another boat in twenty minutes, over here." She pulled on him, but he held his ground.

"Philadelphia?" Da looked puzzled. He cocked his head as if he was listening to the wind, or voices from the crowd.

"You've got to follow him, don't you?" Jane repeated. "Hurry—the boat's this way."

He pulled his hand from hers and rummaged in his pockets, taking out a scrap of paper and a pencil. He wrote quickly and folded the paper before handing it to Jane.

"You must take this to the *Herald* and give it to Mr. Bennett," he said. "It's absolutely crucial."

"Are you going?" Jane asked, taking the note. Her voice grew small and shy as she continued. "Have I done well?"

"Yes. Yes, I'm going to follow it, and you've done very well. Give that to Bennett, Jane, he has to see it today."

He left her then, running through the throng toward the dock Jane had pointed out, but she didn't see him go. The sound of his voice speaking her name rang in her head, bringing hot tears to her frozen cheeks. He had called her by name. *Jane*, he had said.

"Oh, Da," she whispered, the wind stealing the words from her mouth. "Da, you *know*. You know, don't you?"

She caught herself before she could burst out sobbing in the middle of this crowd of strangers. The policeman would catch her if she wasn't sharp. Where was Walter? He was supposed to be keeping lookout. She'd give the message to him and follow her Da. A daughter could do no less.

From the sheltered doorway of a warehouse shipping office, Royce watched the Bannion steamer idle at the dock, building up a full head of steam for its trip to Philadelphia. Prescott was on the boat, up to God knew what, but his aims didn't matter. What mattered was unfinished business. It didn't matter whether he caught up to good old Archie in Philadelphia or bloody San Francisco. Catch him Royce would.

"Charlie," he said. "Steen's gone to Louisville, right?"

"I told you that."

Louisville. If Prescott was headed there as well, it would be convenient. Royce's orders from Steen were to take care of Prescott with all haste and then go to Steen's safe house in Louisville to locate the booger that had gotten away last December. But they weren't to kill Prescott until they'd got their hands on some girl, who Steen was convinced would be following Archie wherever he went.

That was all fine. If the girl was near when they found Prescott, they'd bring her to Steen. But if not, it was more important to finish what had been started. The booger could do its magic whatever without the girl if it had to, but Royce had a very specific debt to settle with Archie Prescott.

Jane crouched between two stacks of shipping crates, sheltering Da's note from the rain and wanting to scream in frustration because she'd never learned to read properly. She could recognize words if she'd seen them on a map, and knew her letters if she could sing the tune in her head, but the note in her shaking hands might as well have been written in Chinese.

Da was going to Philadelphia, she knew that much. But if he didn't find the black man there, he might go anywhere following him. He might never come back to New York.

The thought made Jane's stomach hurt and nearly started her crying again. She concentrated fiercely on a map pasted to the wall of her burrow, placing first New York, then Philadelphia. The boat would steam through Kill Van Kull and Arthur Kill to the Raritan Canal across New Jersey, then down the Delaware River to Philadelphia.

Picturing her father inching across the map, Jane calmed herself. She couldn't be sure that he would return to New York, but she could follow him wherever he was going. She had to follow him. He'd called her by name. Somewhere inside he must know that she was his daughter. But if she didn't follow him, she might never hear him say it.

She had to get someone to read the note. Who did she know that could read? Elmer, but he was away up Broadway toward Trinity Church, and she didn't have time to go that far. People in the crowd couldn't be trusted; one of them would likely just take the note from her and call the policeman.

Jane walked away from the passenger boats, cutting northward across Battery Park toward the freight docks on the Hudson. She couldn't see anyone she knew and trusted, and Da's steamer would be leaving in ten minutes.

"Shit!" she said, drawing disapproving glances from passing adults. Shouldn't Henry be somewhere around? He was always working the ferries and freighters, selling Top Deck cigars and crowing dire warnings about the quality of tobacco available on the boats. Perhaps he'd been run off, if one of the ferry officers had heard his pitch.

No, there he was, sitting in the lee of a row of whiskey barrels and smoking his wares. Jane realized where she was and had to take a deep breath before she could go on. Just a hundred yards north was the dock where Little Brec and the others had been pulled pale and cold from the water. For Da, she thought.

"Henry!" Jane called, hurrying over to him. "Can you read?"

"The nuns made me," he said. "Cigar?"

She took one from the offered box and stowed it in an inside pocket. "I need a favor, Henry. I'll give you a dollar."

"To read? For a dollar you can choose the language."

"Don't tease, this is important. It's for my father."

She saw the flicker of disbelief in his eyes, but all he said was, "Here, let me see it." He took the note from her and squinted at it, puffing on his cigar.

"Well, what's it say?"

"I'll read it for you," he said around the cigar. " 'Mr. Bennett: Have gone to Philadelphia following 'Aztec mummy' lead. Not sure where this will end up, but have a hunch about Louisville. Will write soonest. Archie.' " Henry looked up, puzzled. "What's an Aztec mummy?"

"Dunno," Jane said, thinking furiously. Louisville; that was all the way down the Ohio River, almost to St. Louis.

She had been there once before, riding in the back of Riley Steen's wagon with one leg chained to the wagon's frame. The thought of traveling so far alone frightened her terribly, but it would be for Da, and she could do anything if it meant he would call her by name.

She held a crumpled paper dollar out to Henry, but snatched it away when he reached for it. "You have to do something else, too," she said.

"What? I already read. That's what you wanted."

She ignored his protests. "Take that note to Mr. Bennett, at the *Herald*. You know where that is?"

"Yeah, Fulton Street," Henry said sullenly. His cigar had gone out.

"Will you do it?" She held the dollar out again and he plucked it from her fingers.

"Yeah, I'll do it. Haven't sold anything today anyway."

"Promise me, Henry. This is," she remembered the word Da had used, "crucial."

"I said I would, didn't I?"

"Promise!"

He stood and dropped the soggy cigar butt. "All right, I promise. Now chase it, will you? I'm busy."

"Thank you, Henry!" Jane called, already running south into the park.

Back down at the ferry slip, she watched as the last of the passengers made their way up the slippery gangplank and either ducked into the shelter of the steamer's cabin or jostled for position at the leeward side of the boiler. She couldn't see Da; he must have paid extra to travel out of the storm.

She waited until the deckhand was ready to cast off, then burst from the crowd shouting "Please, sir! Wait! Please!"

The deckhand, a gangly youth of perhaps fifteen made larger by many layers of clothing, paused as she ran up to the very edge of the dock and looked pleadingly up at

him. "Please sir, my father's in Philadelphia and Mother—"
Jane let her voice break and made a show of trying not
to cry. "Mother's too sick to go herself, and I have to tell
him about her. Please," she said again, digging a handful
of pennies and lint from her trouser pocket. "This is all I
have, but mother is so ill . . ." She stood mutely, letting
tears mix with the rain stinging her face.

Throwing a nervous look over his shoulder, the deckhand hesitated, neither casting off nor moving to help her.

"Please," Jane said again. She didn't have to fake the
tears now.

The steamer's whistle blew, and Jane sent up a fervent
prayer. Then the deckhand bent down, caught her wrist,
and hauled her over the rail.

"Find a hole, little one, and stay there," he said. "If the
captain finds you deadheading, I'll pitch you off myself
to prove I didn't do it." He cast off and disappeared below.

Jane worked her way to the stern and hid herself under
a tarpaulin covering a pile of luggage. The ferry eased
away from the dock, beginning to rock on the windblown
chop. Lifting a corner of the tarp, she watched the dock
fade slowly into the rain, scared but also comforted by
the knowledge that Da was on this same boat. Her scars
itched, and she was cold, but Jane was filled with pride
at the way she'd been able to help him, and she knew that
she would help him again when she got the chance.

At dawn, Riley Steen stopped at a way station just to the
south of Philadelphia. The night's travel in the storm had
lamed one of his horses, and the other was blowing hard,
responding to neither lash nor curse. He bought fresh
horses quickly, with minimum conversation, paying an
exorbitant price for nags he'd likely have to replace by
the time he reached Baltimore. But horses did not matter
and neither did money. The only objective of any impor-

tance was reaching Louisville in time to intercept the chacmool.

It had left New York the previous morning, he was certain of that. The ants that had plagued his office since the night of its reanimation had frozen for a moment at exactly three minutes before eleven o'clock. When they started moving again, their patterns were completely disrupted, and Steen had known immediately that the chacmool had stepped off the island. He'd sent notice to Royce that he was leaving within the hour for Louisville and instructed the Rabbit to follow Prescott and capture the girl if, as Lupita predicted, she followed her father.

If events unfolded the way Steen thought they would, quite a grand reunion would take place at his safe house in Louisville. They would reel in first the chacmool, then Archie, and finally little Nanahuatzin herself. Then, with Prescott disposed of, they could proceed to the cave and get about the business of history-making.

Despite Lupita's derision, Steen felt that his plan was holding together brilliantly. Perhaps his anxiety of the last few months had been unwarranted. Whatever difficulties had been encountered, all of the necessary parties appeared to be on their way to a rendezvous at the proper time. His perseverance over the last thirty years was soon to be rewarded.

And oh, the rewards. With Tlaloc rejuvenated and given form in the world, Maskansisil and his followers would be swatted like mosquitoes. Steen would stand astride an empire that would grow to encompass America, Mexico, even the Floridas. Even Canada.

There was something terribly right, Steen thought, about the ancient Mexican balance of sacrifice and favor. Gods were hungry, and needed to be appeased—as Abraham no doubt had understood in those nervous moments before he'd noticed the ram caught in the thicket. What better sacrifice than to return to the gods the very creatures they had created? Nothing, Steen knew, was ever given without something equal being lost. Human beings had to die in order for the human world to exist. That balance had been ignored for too long, obscured by the absurdities of Christianity. People had flocked like sheep to Gospel platitudes because Jesus promised something for nothing. It was a fool's bargain.

And come April the third, the world would begin to discover just how foolish it had been.

❖

The strange stars were out, and that meant magic was happening. John Diamond shook his head and muttered mournfully into the cold current of the Green River, hearing his voice echo through the water into the cave. "Never wanted no part of no magic."

Sorry, Johnny, he silently answered himself. A chorus of the Micteca, the Fleshless Ones, aroused by the magic in the air, took up the refrain: *Sorry Johnny sorrysorry Johnny sorry.*

He was floating on his back about a foot below the river's surface, watching constellations ripple and allowing the current to carry him along. "Stay off the mountains," he said, and a remnant of air bled from his lungs, the bubbles twisting the stars into vivid streaks. "Mountains belong to Tlaloc, He Who Is Made of Earth. Everybody knows that."

Riley Steen was coming, and soon. The calendar grew ripe and the Fleshless Ones were hysterical for days at a time. In twenty-two days, the sun would rise just as it always had, but if Steen's plan succeeded, the world would be changed. Tlalocan would exist on earth. Somewhere in the hills of Kentucky a strange cult would reappear, growing until it became a fever that would scorch the Americas with sacrificial fires from New York to the City of Mexico and beyond.

And the sun would fill with blood.

In such a world John Diamond would be very lucky if

he could simply die, because he had given Rebus the tool that could foil Steen's plan.

Had he done the right thing? The Micteca laughed.

Jane was as exhausted as she could ever remember being. Even during the time she'd spent as Riley Steen's captive and occasional performer, she'd been able to rest when they traveled; but for the past three days she'd been on the move constantly, hardly daring to close her eyes for fear that Da would board a train or a boat while she slept and be gone from her forever.

She'd spent the first night shivering in a stairwell across from the Philadelphia hotel where Da stayed, waking up every hour or so to see if the sun had come up and scratching at her face and back. Something was happening to her, and it didn't seem so wonderful when she was traveling and hiding alone in strange places. Her scars seemed less lumpy to the touch, but she could feel scabs all over her body raised by her continuous scratching. They cracked painfully when she moved in certain ways. A different itch plagued her scalp; she wasn't sure, but it felt like her hair was actually growing back.

What's happening to me? she thought. The itch had started the night the black Indian had killed those sailors outside her burrow. Lately it had been constant, and she didn't always remember to remind herself not to scratch.

She wished she could ask Da about things. He would know, she was sure. After all, he had to be following the man for a reason. But she had to wait, had to bide her time until she was certain he would accept her.

In Philadelphia, Da had gone shopping, of all things, and then boarded the strangest train Jane had ever seen. It was a series of flatcars that each carried a boat. Da and the other passengers had climbed onto the cars and gone straight into the boats, staying inside when the train started to move. Jane had managed to catch the last car and hide herself from the railworkers, and she had ridden half the day huddled under the slant of the hull of the last boat. The railway ended on the bank of a canal, where the boats were lowered into the water and locked together. She hadn't been able to sneak past the boatmen, and had panicked that she'd be left to make her own way across the Allegheny Mountains to Pittsburgh, where the train was bound.

But the horse-drawn canal boats moved barely faster than she could walk, and Jane had kept just behind the horses, watching the boats carefully lest Da should come out on the deck and see her. Boys called hoggees stood on the decks, using long poles to push the boats off if they drifted too near the canal banks. Even with them poling, the boats often swung near the banks, and Jane was able to make the short jump onto the last boat as night fell. She'd slept gratefully that night on the rear deck, lulled by the boat's gentle rocking and the soft slap of water against its hull.

One of the hoggees woke her at sunrise. "Where's yer ticket?" he'd snapped, whacking her feet with his pole.

"Inside with my Da," she'd answered defiantly. "I like to sleep outside."

"Oh, very likely," he'd said. "Maybe I should get the pilot to roust your Dad and we'll see."

She hadn't said anything to that. After a pause the hoggee had said, "We'll see," again and given her another whack before walking around the side of the cabin.

Jane had stayed on the boat only long enough for it to swing near the bank again. She couldn't risk being caught by the pilot, who would surely ask around about a runaway girl. Better to spend another day walking.

Early in the afternoon, the canal ended at the base of a mountain. The boats were once again loaded onto flatcars, and the cars began to move out of the station house—*up* the side of the mountain. Seeing this mystery, Jane had forgotten her mission for a moment. How were the train cars rolling uphill?

She'd soon discovered that the cars were pulled on

thick ropes by a locomotive engine at the top of the first incline. That solved the mystery, but Jane still felt slightly awed by the whole thing. Nothing like it existed in New York, or anywhere else she'd ever been. And if something like this could be built in the wilderness, what wonders would the cities hold? Pittsburgh, or St. Louis? San Francisco even?

I want to see everything, she'd thought then. *Everything I've never seen.*

There were too many people watching from the engine houses for her to sneak aboard the train, or boat or whatever it was. So Jane spent the afternoon climbing along the tracks, watching the train with Da aboard as it passed other trains being lowered down toward Hollidaysburg, the town at the foot of the mountain. By sundown she was struggling through several inches of heavy, wet snow, and her feet were numb. With every hour she fell further behind the train. *It must stop at the top of the mountain,* she thought—surely they wouldn't try to go down the other side in the dark.

The last length of track was arrow-straight, and she could see the lights of a town perhaps half a mile farther ahead. Jane crouched under a bridge that crossed the track just above the second-to-last engine house, catching her breath before Da's train began its ascent. *What if the rope breaks?* she thought, even though she'd seen the brake attached to the back of each car. It seemed too small to stop anything so huge as a train, and the one trailing Da's car seemed to have a branch caught in one of its wheels.

Jane's face suddenly burned with an itch far worse than anything she'd felt before, and she fought down the urge to scratch. The itch grew, the scarred parts of her skin crawling like they had the night she'd seen the Indian.

"Oh God," she said, understanding. The branch wasn't caught in the brake; it had *grown* there, just as the boards enclosing her burrow had sprouted fresh twigs where the Indian had bumped against them. She could see the rest of the brake's frame bulge and deform, splitting as branches sprouted and grew new green leaves.

With a crack like a gunshot the brake splintered. Its wheels rolled down the track, then bounded away into a ditch. The train had nearly reached the summit, but it slowed and a second later Jane heard the snap of the tow rope breaking. The two cars began to roll back down the incline, picking up speed as they went.

Jane burst out from under the bridge and ran up the incline, veering to the side away from the runaway train. "Jump!" she screamed. "Da, jump! Get off the train!"

The rear car's wheels crunched over the wreckage of the brake. The train shuddered and tilted to one side, jack-knifing as the front car pushed the rear aside, then derailed itself. The boat on the rear car snapped its ties and rolled over into the ditch, landing with a terrific crash and sliding upside down for a hundred feet or so. Wreckage trailed up the mountainside above it.

The second car plowed nearly all the way back to the engine house, finally banging to a halt against a wooden loading platform. Jane heard screams other than her own, from inside the cars and along the side of the tracks where passengers had been thrown from the rear car. Four men ran past Jane toward the upended car, shouting for help. Shortly after, passengers from the waiting cars followed, carrying blankets and lamps. Jane stood frozen. Which car had Da been riding in? She didn't know.

"Da!" she screamed, rooted to the spot by horror and indecision. *"Daaaaaaa!"*

A hand clamped over her mouth. Jane was lifted off her feet thrashing and still screaming into the callused palm.

"Dammit, girlie, hold still!" growled a rough Irish voice. "You've got places to go." The man holding her grunted as he pitched her across the ditch away from the wreck. She crashed into the brush and immediately another pair of hands seized her and dragged her up an embankment into the forest. Twisting around, she caught a glimpse of the man holding her. He was short and blocky, barely taller than she, with a hump bulging under his patchy fur coat. "Da!" she screamed again, her voice nearly gone, and he punched her hard on the scarred side of her head.

Bright sparks burst behind her eyes, and she slumped in his grasp, unable to resist as he dragged her farther into the trees. Through the ringing in her ears Jane heard another man crashing through the brush behind them. They came out onto a level clearing and Jane tumbled to the ground. She tried to get up but her head kept spinning her back to the ground.

"Charlie," the man who'd first grabbed her said, "go around the bend there and see if you can't liberate us a buggy. I've lost my taste for trains."

Good fortune comes when you least expect it, thought Royce. It was lucky enough that he and Charlie had decided to jump off the train as it eased into the engine house, to sneak up to Summitville and surprise Prescott when he put up for the night; but to have the chacmool itself finger the bloody girl was more than an Irishman had any right to expect.

It had walked right up to Royce and caught his arm as he was having a cigar around the back of the platform, and he'd come within a whisker of stubbing the smoke out in its black face before figuring out that it wasn't just a dressed-up nigger who didn't know his place.

"Nanahuatzin is here," it had said.

Before his brain caught up with his mouth, Royce nearly blurted out "Who the hell are you, Bobo?" But he put everything together just as the rope snapped and all hell broke loose on the side of the mountain. Seeing the cars plowing back toward the engine house, he'd jumped across the other track, Charlie hot on his heels, and gotten into the trees a bit. When he'd turned around the chacmool was right there, and it calmly pointed out the girlie, screeching like a banshee in the middle of the incline.

"Bring her to Louisville. I will meet you there," it said. Then it disappeared with unholy speed into the forest.

That had been two hours ago. Since then Charlie had acquired a horse and wagon from some rickety homestead, and they'd made fairly good time along this nameless mountain road. They had the girl, they knew the booger was going to meet Steen, and best of all Archie Prescott was smashed upside down in the wrecked boat. If he survived, he'd come to Louisville following the chacmool, and Royce would take care of him then. If not, well, Royce was a bit put out at the prospect of not being able to slip a blade in Archie himself, but all things considered it was a small disappointment. In two weeks they'd be in Louisville, and then, according to Steen, the real show would begin.

Good fortune all around.

After all he'd been through that evening, the last thing Archie expected was that he'd be unable to sleep. He knew he should be thanking God that he had survived the crash, but his head was still throbbing from the battering he'd absorbed and, all in all, he wasn't feeling very thankful. All he could think about was getting back on the chacmool's trail.

The feather talisman had begun spasming wildly moments before the rope snapped, and if that weren't proof enough, Archie had seen the remains of the derailleur scattered on the tracks. The engineer on duty had simply shaken his head in amazement, crossing himself and ordering his men to clear away the newly grown foliage as quietly as possible.

Well, Archie thought, *at least I know I'm on the scent.* When he'd booked the passage to Pittsburgh, he hadn't been entirely certain that his Louisville hunch was any more than that—just a hunch. But the night's events made it pretty damned certain that his hunch had been on target.

The Pennsylvania Main Line Canal Company had provided lodging for all of the passengers who hadn't needed emergency medical attention, and Archie had been put up in the Lemon House, a square stone inn right alongside the tracks in the center of Summitville. Work at the accident site had stopped several hours ago, after all of the passengers had been accounted for. Now it was after midnight, and the only sound was the rustling of the wind in the forest that fell away into the valley behind Lemon House. Archie's room was at the rear of the inn, on the second floor, and he was glad that he didn't have to look out on the lamplit tracks. Outside his window was nearly absolute darkness; only a patch of sloping lawn, splotched with clumps of wet snow, and the nearest trees were visible under a cloudy sky.

So the chacmool had tried to kill him, and in such a way as to suggest that it didn't want to confront him directly. Was it now afraid of him for some reason, or merely anxious to keep moving and leave him behind? In either case, something fundamental had changed since the December night in Barnum's Museum, when it had backed away instead of gulping down Archie's *yollotl*. But why, that was the question, and Archie couldn't wring an answer from his battered brain. It had recognized him, that seemed certain, but he hadn't changed all that much in the past three months, had he? It must have learned something about him.

If the chacmool thought he was dead, though, he had a slim advantage over it. It wouldn't be expecting him to arrive in Louisville or at the Mammoth Cave, if that was where it was bound.

One way or another, Archie resolved, he would be rid of it. No more grisly dreams, no more attempts on his life, no more horrible afternoons when the sun looked as if it had contracted a wasting disease. If killing was involved, so be it.

And that went for Steen and the Rabbit youth Royce as well. Archie didn't know where Steen was, but he had a strong intuition that a gaudy drummer-wagon was bumping its way toward Louisville. Whatever pagan madness was being planned would surely involve Steen, whether he regained control of the chacmool or not.

Christ, what have I gotten myself into? Archie thought, rolling over on the soft hotel bed and gazing out the window of his room. *I don't even know what's supposed to happen at the cave.*

Again he felt like a walking adage, a sort of object lesson in the dangers of curiosity. After all, it was his inquisitive nature that had cost him his ear, gotten him stabbed and buried alive—generally run him afoul of homicidal madmen. Tonight he'd been lucky, surviving the train crash in fairly good form except for bruises and a twisted ankle. The injuries he'd suffered at the hands of the two Rabbits had been much worse, but it was becoming clear to Archie that no matter how his enemies proliferated, the chacmool was by far the most dangerous.

Which, he thought, *should not surprise me, since it has already murdered two dozen children in cold blood and, like a cat marking its territory, left them to be found in the Hudson.*

Archie sat up in bed and scratched at the stub of his left ear. Someone was pacing the length of the corridor, most likely a fellow insomniac. *A walk might do me some good, too,* he thought, swinging his aching legs off the bed and feeling around for his shoes.

The footsteps outside halted in front of his door. Archie straightened, listening, and the feather talisman swung against his bare chest. It was wriggling just as it had before the crash, and at the first chill touch of brass against his skin, Archie found himself looking out of someone else's eyes.

There was no light, but he could see a door in front of him. The wallpaper border around the frame was an ornate floral pattern, one that had provoked a remote exhausted annoyance when Archie had walked through that door earlier in the night.

Desolate fear rose churning in Archie's gut. *It found*

me somehow, he thought, *and came back to finish the job.*

He swept his hand under the bed, locating his shoes and pulling them on. He was wearing only a woolen johnny, but there was no time to dress, and his coat was hanging on a peg by the door. He had to escape before the chacmool realized that he knew it was there.

Archie almost shouted for help, for whatever passed for a police force in this hamlet. But the memory of Barnum's watchman, his arm torn off and ribs cracked open like an autopsy cadaver, choked off the cry. Whatever happens to me, Archie thought, I'll not kill anyone else through ignorance or cowardice. Stumbling over his untied laces, he fell against the bureau and grabbed the traveling valise he'd purchased in Philadelphia. In it were Helen's knife and some of Barnum's money, both of which were more important than trousers at the moment.

The doorknob turned, first quietly and then with increasing violence as the chacmool jerked against the deadbolt lock. Archie tried to open the window and discovered that it was frozen shut. Behind him the chacmool threw itself against the door, cracking the frame and nearly breaking loose the lock assembly. A strange sound came from the doorframe, a crackling that triggered Archie's memory of Royce McDougall bound by resurrected ropes of cornstalk. The chacmool was *growing* the door off its hinges.

The window wouldn't budge, and drops of rain were beginning to fall from the ceiling. Archie took a step back and swung the valise, aiming for the center of the cross formed by the four panes. The iron-capped corner of the valise shattered the window, leaving the broken sash hanging in the frame. The crackling behind Archie grew in intensity, and a pin from one of the door's hinges sprang loose and pinged on the wooden floor.

Not looking behind him, Archie took two steps back and dove headfirst out the window, carrying with him the remains of the sash and the bits of glass clinging to it. He turned over once in the air before landing heavily on his right hip and skidding on the frosted grass.

Archie gained his feet quickly, his teeth aching from the awkward landing and his ankle shooting sharp pains up into his calf. The sound of splintering wood reached his ears, along with a gathering chorus of angry shouts as the commotion awoke Lemon House's other bruised and irritable guests, but Archie didn't wait to see if the chacmool was pursuing him. He ran, slipping and stumbling on the steep hillside, too terrified even to stop and lace his shoes.

He ran downhill until his lungs were wheezing from the cold night air and the pain in his ankle hobbled him. Then he staggered into a tangle of brush and fell to the ground, listening carefully over the sound of his own ragged panting and feeling the chacmool's feather talisman answer his pounding heart with its own quiet tremors.

Oh God, he thought, *it'll track me by the talisman.* But he couldn't take it off.

The broad valley below Lemon House had narrowed to a steep ravine that swallowed every sound save for the soft rustle of wind and the occasional plop of snow falling from the bare branches of trees. Overhead, the clouds were breaking up, and a half moon peered through the forest canopy. The craters and shadows on the moon's face seemed oddly like a rabbit.

Had that happened before? Steen had been looking at the moon when he killed that boy's rabbit behind the Old Brewery. What, then? Archie couldn't follow the thought. He jumped, hearing voices, but realized the sound was just the ringing in his ears from the blow to the head he'd suffered in the wreck.

Now that he'd stopped, the cold struck forcefully, biting through his johnny. Archie tied his shoes with numb fingers, knotting the laces when he couldn't make the proper bows. *I can't stay out here all night dressed like this,* he thought, fighting to stop his teeth from chattering; *the temperature's below freezing.*

If he didn't keep moving, he would die in this godforsaken ravine. The chacmool, if it even bothered to look, would find him blue and cold, and set about its arcane business without a care in the world. Well, it could go to flaming hell, Archie thought. His days of going passively mad and waiting for his death like a trussed hog for the knife were over.

He took Helen's knife from the muddy valise and stood, chilled muscles groaning. He was soaked to the skin and shivering like a man with St. Vitus's, and his head felt as if it were packed with nails, but his mind was clear. If he didn't find a roof, and soon, he would die. And if the chacmool wanted to get between him and that roof, it would have to tear out his bleeding heart.

Archie began working his way down the ravine, favoring his swelling ankle. If he found a stream, eventually it would lead him to a farm, or even a town—if he wasn't disemboweled first.

At the bottom of the ravine was a faint path, paralleling a rocky streambed swollen with early-spring meltwater. Archie hesitated over the stream, remembering stories of fugitive slaves who hid their scents in water; but he stepped over the narrow brook instead, both in an effort to stay as dry as he could and because of an inexplicable intuition that he should stay clear of running water. When he'd crossed, he looked downstream and noticed the figure straddling the brook.

Archie brandished the knife, resisting the urge to shout a challenge. Instead he waited for the chacmool to make its move. It was bigger and broader than he remembered, likely from all its meals of children's hearts, and Archie stood where he was facing it down. *Come on, you son of a bitch*, he thought. *I'll spill your damned eztli on these stones.*

The wind shifted, blowing up the ravine and lifting long straight hair away from the figure's silhouette. But the mummy's skull in the museum had only a patchy covering of curly hair like a mulatto's, Archie remembered. *Damn;*

if I could see its face I could be sure. But the moon was high and behind the figure, shadowing its features, and even as Archie readied himself to mount a limping charge, it looked up at the moon and disappeared into the cover of trees.

Archie immediately crossed back over the stream, keeping the water between himself and his pursuer. He started moving downstream again, staying clear of the water and looking warily across to the steep rocky slope on the other side of the brook. The chacmool had been looking right at him, or at least he thought it had. Perhaps by some trick of moonlight it had failed to see him.

No, he decided, that couldn't be it. The beast had seen clearly enough in the museum with only the diffused glow of Barnum's spotlight to go by.

A high-pitched yowl ripped through the still night from just upstream. Whirling to face it, Archie lost his balance as he swiped the knife at the air in front of him, expecting to see the chacmool changed into its feline demon-shape and dropping onto him from the trees. Instead he saw an Indian, facing upstream with both feet planted firmly in the center of the stream.

That's who I saw before, Archie realized. God Almighty, he got upstream fast.

The Indian was beckoning to the trees, his long beaver coat waving in the night wind. Archie thought the Indian was speaking, but no sound reached his ears.

Faint shadows cast by the moon twisted and slithered away from the chacmool as it stalked reluctantly out onto the streambed, changed into the horror Archie had seen in Barnum's museum. Its ears lay flat against its feline skull, and its lips, outlined by feathers rather than whiskers, were drawn back in a quavering snarl as it hunched before the Indian, spitting its anger.

The talisman lay cold and inert against Archie's chest. *The Indian's faced it down,* he thought wonderingly. *Somehow he's robbed it of its power.*

A sound like distant thunder vibrated in the talisman as

the chacmool's form rippled, becoming nearly human. "Stand aside, Maskansisil," it hissed, its forked tongue flicking out between jaguar's fangs. "He is mine this night."

The Indian stood his ground. "You own only your skin tonight, blood-drinker, and be grateful of that. These waters are mine, and this mountain. You will not pass."

A long moment passed. Archie stood perfectly still. Finally the chacmool took a step back, the shadows around it shifting as if the moon wished to keep it in sight. "Your heart I will have for this, Maskansisil. I will drain your life and feed it to this mountain and these waters. You and I will not pass one another by again." It spat into the rushing water at the Indian's feet and vanished back into the trees, shambling awkwardly on still-crooked legs.

Archie let out a long shuddering breath and lowered the knife. Was this Indian really Maskansisil, the Pathfinder of Lenape legend? The name had come up in Burr's ravings, but Archie hadn't connected it with any real person. It had seemed more an honorific than a true name, a title given to a series of valiant men in Lenape history. But the chacmool had used the name without hesitation, had recognized the Indian standing before it with his feet anchored in frigid spring runoff.

And it had fled.

And here I am, Archie wondered. He felt foolish in his sodden johnny and muddy brogans, brandishing a kitchen knife and carrying the new leather valise in his other hand. *What is my role in all of this?*

He saw the Indian, Maskansisil, turn toward him and realized he'd spoken the question aloud.

"It is not my place to answer questions," Maskansisil said softly, "only to bring you to the place where they may be answered." He walked down the streambed to the spot where Archie had first seen him. From there he began climbing up the other side of the ravine. "If you seek answers, follow me," he said over his shoulder.

Archie splashed across the stream and paused long

enough to replace the knife in his valise so he would have a free hand. "Follow you where?" he said, working his way up a steep path between bare slabs of snowy granite. They seemed to be moving south, but his flight through the forest had thoroughly scrambled Archie's sense of direction.

The path leveled out and widened as they climbed farther above the stream. Maskansisil moved quietly, visible only when the moonlight caught him through a break in the trees. The moon seemed to follow him, as if it wanted to keep him in sight as it had the chacmool.

He didn't look back, and Archie was rapidly losing what remained of his strength. Toting oyster crates hadn't prepared him for this sort of exertion, and his ankle was about to give way.

At the top of a narrow ridge, Archie realized he'd completely lost sight of the Indian. He turned in a circle, looking for a path and half expecting the chacmool to burst from the trees and gut him where he stood. God in Heaven, I hope I haven't come all this way just to be killed at a more convenient spot, Archie thought. Perhaps I should just take my chances on being able to find my way back to Lemon House.

But his legs wouldn't carry him that far. His ankle was already swelling against the confining shoe, his hands were completely numb, and his thighs trembled just from the effort of standing upright. I could just rest a while, Archie thought.

When Maskansisil reappeared, leading two horses, Archie shook himself out of his stupor. "I—I have to get warm," he said. "I'm freezing."

Wordlessly Maskansisil swept off his long coat and draped it around Archie's shoulders. Thank you, Archie tried to say, but he couldn't make himself understood through his chattering teeth.

"Can you ride?" the Indian asked. Archie shook his head. Growing up in New York, he'd never learned.

"Hm. No time now for lessons." Maskansisil crouched

down and laced his fingers into a stirrup. Archie stepped up, wincing as his ankle nearly buckled, and Maskansisil hoisted him onto the horse's bare back.

As he swung up onto his own mount, Maskansisil said, "Get both hands into her mane and keep your weight forward." With that he wheeled around and spurred his horse into the gap he'd come out of. Archie's horse followed, and Archie did as he'd been told, leaning over the horse's neck and doing his best to hang on.

❖

They flew through the forest at breakneck speed, bounding down precipitous drops and slashing across shallow streams. Hours seemed to pass, but the moon held perfectly still overhead, and Archie realized that either he'd lost his sense of time or time had lost its sense of him. Every impact of the horse's hooves traveled straight up Archie's spine to his head, which seemed about to split; after a time his body, battered and pushed to absolute extremity, simply shut down. His legs grew numb, as his hands had long ago, and the sounds of hooves and wind blended into a soft rush, lulling him into a kind of stupor. Often he felt himself tilting, and righted himself barely in time, keeping his hands tangled in the horse's mane while the beast did its best to keep him mounted. Archie's mind wandered: Wonderful horse, he thought. No glue works for you. Must find an apple for a reward.

They reached the floor of a broad valley and raced across fallow fields, startling a sleeping dog behind a farmhouse. The dog's barking was lost in the rush of wind as the horses unwound into a final sprint, charging up a narrowing dell until sheer granite walls enclosed them and they were forced to slow.

Maskansisil picked out a winding trace where Archie had seen only shadows, and he led the horses through to a clearing sheltered on three sides by towering bluffs. Snow covered the ground completely here, and only a gentle breeze remained of the wind that had gusted around Archie as they galloped.

They'd run straight up the side of a mountain, whose knobby peak loomed just to the north. The rippling shadows of the Alleghenies spread in every direction beneath the frozen, unworldly moon; here and there a cluster of lights glowed. One of them, Archie thought, must be Summitville. But he had no idea which.

He looked up into the cloudless sky, the silence loud in his ears. That's odd, he thought; not only is the moon still exactly where it was when we mounted these horses, but the sky is absolutely clear. He remembered the clouded darkness of the Lemon House's back lawn, and wondered where all of the clouds could have gotten to so quickly.

Maskansisil halted his horse and dismounted. Archie tried to do the same, but couldn't work his fingers free of the horse's mane. It took all the concentration he could muster just to relax his hands so he could pull them free. When at last he untangled himself and stepped down, Archie's legs wouldn't hold him; he sat down hard in the snow, dropping the valise at his side. The horses stood blowing, picking up their feet as if they found it difficult to stand still.

Unshouldering a leather pouch, Maskansisil began pitching small objects from it out across the clearing, murmuring a breathy chant as he did so. When the bag was empty he shook it upside down and held his palms open to the sky, continuing the chant as he turned in a slow circle.

Archie leaned over and picked up the object that had landed nearest him. It was a strip of jerked meat, beef or more likely venison. The sight of it reminded Archie that he hadn't eaten since an early dinner on the packet boat, just after noon. Not even a full day had passed, but the day's travel on the Main Line Canal seemed like a distant memory. And overhead, the bright half-moon hung frozen in place.

Time *has* lost track of me, Archie thought. Somehow it's not passing. He raised the strip of jerky to his mouth.

"Don't eat it," Maskansisil said sharply. Archie started to protest—he'd thrown the stuff away all over the clearing, what did one piece matter?—but when he looked up he saw the Indian pointing away from him, at a brush thicket sprouting from the base of a granite overhang.

An enormous bear ambled through the thicket and out into the clearing, its head sweeping back and forth as it took in the scents of men and horses. It stood on its hind legs, winter fat shrunken to folds of skin hanging from its belly, and grumbled, cocking its head from side to side and baring yellow teeth. Maskansisil stood before the bear, his lips silently moving with the chant. He showed no sign of fear. In fact, he looked expectant, and for some reason a bit sad.

Why haven't the horses run away? Archie thought. He looked and saw that they had gone to sleep, their heads hung down nearly to the ground, the occasional twitch of ear or nose the only sign that they hadn't been turned to stone.

The bear dropped to all fours again and pawed at the grass, tearing huge dark streaks in the thin covering of snow. Maskansisil gave voice to his chant again, and the bear found a piece of jerky and gulped it down.

As it swallowed, Maskansisil shouted "Hey!" and clapped his hands, the sound booming much louder than it should have even in the sheltered space. The bear looked up at him, and Archie held his breath, sure that he was about to see the reverse of the bear-baiting contests that passed for sport in the Five Points.

But instead of charging to tear Maskansisil's limbs from his body, the bear just grumbled again, its tone inquisitive somehow and an expression that Archie could have sworn was confusion in its eyes. Then it padded over to Maskansisil and stood, clapping its paws on his shoulders in an unmistakable greeting.

"Mary, mother of Jesus," Archie said quietly. He

looked at the strip of jerky in his hand and threw it away into the snow.

"I have brought him, *sachem,*" Maskansisil said to the bear.

It swung its ponderous head toward Archie. *You have done well, Pathfinder. Many things might have gone astray this night.*

Archie heard the words clearly though no sound had come from the bear. The voice was that of an old man, gravelly and patient. *Sachem*, Maskansisil had called the bear. That was what the Tammany bigwigs called each other.

He looked questioningly at Maskansisil, who nodded and said, "Repeat your question now." The bear dropped to all fours and came to stand over Archie where he sat in the snow.

Its snout was close enough to touch, its breath smelling of fermented berries and tooth decay. Archie swallowed and said, "What is my role in this?"

We dead cannot read futures, Archie Prescott. Your role is yours to determine.

Perhaps it was disappointed expectation, or just fatigue, or a combination of the two. But for whatever reason, Archie's composure simply snapped. In just the past twenty-four hours he had been nearly murdered twice, and here he was following a strange Indian into the Allegheny wilderness in order to have a possessed bear spin evasions to questions that meant life or death.

"Damn your dithering!" he shouted, standing up despite the pain in his ankle. "What *right* do you have to drag me off to this godforsaken wilderness and feed me bloody politician's drivel? I was nearly killed tonight—*twice* that I know of—because through no fault of my own I've gotten involved in something I don't understand, and you owe me some answers."

The bear stood unmoving before him, and Maskansisil might as well have been a sculpture carved from mountain granite.

I was known as a man of peace, the bear said, *not a weak man. Men did not speak to me in such tones when I was alive.*

"Well, I'm the one who's alive now," Archie said hotly. "And I'd like to remain that way." He pulled the chacmool's talisman from his shirt and shook it under the bear's muzzle.

"You go ahead and kill me—eat me if it satisfies your appetite or your pride—none of that matters to me unless I find a way to be rid of this." He let the token fall back into his johnny. "And to do that I have to be rid of the damned chacmool, don't I?"

You do.

"Then how?"

Save your daughter.

"My daughter died seven years ago," Archie said automatically.

The bear just looked at him.

Slow realization began to seep through Archie's axiomatic denial. Here he was, dressed in undergarments and boots, berating a brown bear in the Pennsylvania mountains while the moon hung like a stopped pendulum in the clear night sky. Did he really think that he'd been brought out here, that he'd been somehow *excused* from *time*, just so a mischievous Indian and a trained circus bear could play an elaborate joke on him?

Wasn't that somehow more insane than the idea that Jane had somehow survived the fire? That the hunched little body burned to a charcoal husk had been another girl?

That he had been seeing his daughter regularly for the past year, and denying what she surely must have known to be true?

When Archie spoke again, he felt as if he was trying to speak around something in his throat that he couldn't quite swallow. "Save her from what? What does Jane have to do with this?"

Your daughter is the fulcrum on which the fate of this

*world balances. In the next twenty-one days you will ei-
ther save her or lose her to the chacmool, which will use
her to give new form to its god. If it succeeds in this, the
fires you have seen in your sleep will darken the skies
over real cities instead of the dead world you dream.*

Archie's brain couldn't assimilate this; the words de-
flected off a vision of Jane plucking pennies from his palm
as he brushed past her on his way to work.

"You must tell him from the beginning, *sachem*," Maskansisil said.

The bear glanced over its shoulder at him, then settled
like a dog onto its haunches. In its eyes Archie thought
he could see ages, all the time that wasn't passing in the
world of the living. *Or do I still walk in that world?*

The old man's voice spoke gently, drawing Archie inward, away from the stinging cold and the guilt that tore
like a hyena at his bowels.

I am Tamanend, *and have been called that name since
before your people learned to make marks on paper. The
Lenape are my people; I led them across the sea of ice
to this land and we settled in the far north, among the
horned whales and the great white bears.*

*But the sun stays away from that place, and again we
moved, following it south until our paths crossed the
Snake. They saddened me even then, white man, because
like the white men, they fed their god with blood. Once
they had been beautiful, but in their debasement they saw
beauty only in death. Their leader came to me with scales
for skin, and told me that the favor of his god came at
the price of our tribe's children. War rose up between our
peoples, and we drove them before us until they fled south
beyond the desert.*

*We heard nothing of them for generations. My people
followed the sun to its beginning in the sea to the east,
and we settled there. We ate well and grew in numbers,
but my mind was heavy with wondering when the Snake*

would return. After many years of peace, I left and walked south and west, crossing mountains and desert until I found the Snake. They had build cities of stone in a swamp ringed with mountains, and their gods had become numberless as the stars. Smoke hung over the cities, carrying aloft the spirits of sacrificed men and feeding them to the hungry gods.

They greeted me with arrow and spear, but seeing that they could not harm me took me before the creature whose voice spoke for their gods. Like me, it had lived many years; like me, it had drawn strength from the lands of its people. Men create gods, Archie Prescott, but those gods are no less real once worship gives them life and form. The chacmool lived because of the hunger of its gods, and drew its form from gods' totems. It still wore scales for skin, but now jaguar's fur sprouted from it as well, and eagle's feathers; the form of a man had become difficult for it to keep. The stories of its people sustained it, as long as those stories and their sacrifices sustained their gods. The sound of their songs, the voices of their poetry hurt my ears because still they murdered, and composed songs to beautify their butchery.

I was saddened by the blood that had been shed between us, but peace can only be made between men; gods and spirits do not bargain with mortals. This creature, chacmool, had lost its humanity before we first warred, and had lost even the memory of being a man by the time I walked south to search out the Snake. It wanted nothing of peace. Go back north, it said to me, before you leave your bones here and your people forget your name.

Still I stood before it. You have power now, I said, but that will not always be. And I, Tamanend, will keep my eye upon you; I will watch as you die and are scattered to the winds, and by the strength of my arm I will keep you scattered until your names and your gods have vanished from the land.

We parted on these words and I turned my face north, even as the white men's sails crawled over the edge of the sea. When the Snake were destroyed, I watched, and wept for the people they might have become. But the white men never set their gaze on the chacmool—they knew it as Nezahualpilli and heard stories of this man who foretold the Spaniards' coming, who was a sorcerer and made pacts with evil spirits. But the chacmool fled its name and its people, and hid itself in the place called Chicomoztoc, and despite my sorrow I remembered my resolve. I have been friend to red man and white, but never again will I be friend to the Snake.

When the chacmool stirred, and remembered the god they named He Who Makes Things Grow, I had gone from the world where this bear walks. But Maskansisil lives, and watches in my stead.

"I watch you, Archie Prescott," Maskansisil said. "I watch because I cannot act. Even if I killed every white man who spoke the word *chacmool*, I could not change the path you must follow. Bringing you here, I hoped the old story would yet hold meaning, and hoped as well that you would understand and act where I cannot."

Maskansisil fell silent, and the bear wandered a short distance away, snuffling in the snow after strips of jerked venison. Archie shivered, bewildered and feeling lonelier than he'd ever been in his life. Had he really just spoken to the Lenape chief Tamanend, the same man who signed a treaty with William Penn and who gave his name to the society that threatened to destroy what he had worked centuries to maintain? It was impossible, surely; but so were talking bears and walking mummies who rejuvenated dead wood and stole daughters for arcane sacrificial ceremonies.

Daughters. He'd spent seven years mourning a daughter who hadn't died, and had denied her when she came to him because self-pity had been too seductive an excuse for self-ruin. Archie thought of the hundred times Jane had begged him for a simple word, for the merest gesture of acknowledgment, thought of the dawning wonder in her face when he'd absently called her by name in front of the *Herald* building a few weeks ago. She'd asked so little, and he had denied her. He had turned away and left her, feeling only pity as her curses and entreaties fell on him like rain on desert sand. He had been a father these last seven years, and had spent them mourning for himself while his daughter had gone freezing in the streets.

Now she was in the hands of madmen ready to spill her blood in the name of a dead Mexican god. The truth of the stories didn't matter; the bear might be a hallucination brought on by fatigue and a blow to the head, and Riley Steen might simply be a lunatic, but none of that mattered. The only important thing left was that he was a father and his daughter was going to die.

"What do I do?" Archie said.

The bear raised its head. *You found the chacmool once when you did not know you sought it,* Tamanend said. *Its token around your neck will guide you to it now. You may yet die, Archie Prescott; or you may live only to see the chacmool swallow your beating heart. But you will find help on your journey as well, if you recognize it.*

I will tell you three things that may assist you.

Travel by water when you can. The chacmool's spirit is in the water, and your token will better guide you if there is water beneath your feet. But stay dry, lest it see you as well as you sense it.

Seek the Mask-bearer and follow in his footsteps. But beware of him as well, for he is torn. You must offer him peace.

Lastly, remember that He Who Makes Things Grow has an enemy, an opposite principle. This enemy is your ally, and you must use his power when the time comes. But again you must be wary. Gods are greedy, and even your ally may seek to turn you to his use.

The bear walked to Archie and stood, placing its paws on his shoulders as it had Maskansisil's. *In twenty-one days*, Tamanend said, *the ceremony will take place. But*

for five days before that the chacmool will not willingly
act, for his people call those days nemontemi *and con-*
sider them unlucky.

I can tell you no more. Too much remains uncertain.
Events draw into focus around you, Archie Prescott, and
I wish you good fortune. Remember what I have said.

A change came over the bear's face, the intent expression in its eyes giving way to sleepy animal confusion. It
dropped to all fours and swung its head back and forth,
grunting and sniffing as it had when it had first wandered
out of the brush.

Maskansisil approached it and laid a hand on its massive head. "Back to sleep, old friend," he said affection-
ately. "We have bothered you enough." The bear shook,
its sharp stink making Archie's eyes water even in the
cold. Then it turned away from them and pushed its way
back into the thicket. Blinking through his tears, Archie
saw that the moon had begun moving again, and streaks
of cloud were beginning to blot out the stars.

Time has found me again, he thought. Twenty-one
days. Twenty-one days until the end of the world.

Maskansisil mounted his horse, pointedly not looking
in the direction the bear had taken. "Have to move," he
said. "Much riding yet to do, and the sun will be up soon."

The cart Charlie had stolen no longer seemed like such
a godsend to Royce as it rattled along the deer-track
mountain road, jolting his lean behind. Not much padding
down there; if the road kept up the way it was, he'd have
to sit on the girl to save his ass. And the road—if it could
be called that—showed no signs of improving. It was a
single track of mud and bare rock, snaking down hills and
valleys with trees leaning over it like a deer's fart might
bring one down. One damned fallen tree, and they'd be
walking to Pittsburgh.

They'd been driving all night, and now the sun was up,
but the terrain still looked the same to Royce. Lumpy hills

rolled away in all directions, the forest broken only by a farmhouse here and there. Damn this wilderness, Royce thought. Without street names and buildings to recognize, how did a man figure out where he was? And despite the bright sunshine, it was cold, maybe not quite so cold as New York but definitely uncomfortable. How far was it to Pittsburgh? There they could get on a boat, get out of the damned weather.

"Charlie," he said over the racket of the wagon's creaking joints. Charlie was older than Royce and had traveled. "You've been to Pittsburgh, right?"

"Twice." Charlie didn't look back from his seat. Probably like sitting on a feather pillow up there, Royce thought. He'd have taken the seat himself, but he didn't trust Charlie to watch the girl. She was bound hand and foot, and buried under a pile of straw to boot, but Royce still worried that she might escape. After all, she'd gotten away from Steen, and that was before she'd learned God knew what sort of tricks living on the streets. Steen had underestimated her, and with all the strange things that had been happening, Royce didn't plan to make the same mistake. It wouldn't pay to be careless.

The girl wriggled under the straw and Royce kicked her, just to remind her that he was there. "Quiet, you," he snapped. "You won't suffocate."

At least he hoped she wouldn't. She could breathe around the gag, he'd made sure of that, and in any case her nose was clear. But the straw dust in the wagon bed bothered him, and he didn't have his face in it. Well, she was still kicking. Best to leave her be. If she was quiet for too long, though, he'd have to dig her out and make sure she was all right. Now that the chacmool knew they had her, they couldn't very well deliver her dead.

He remembered the question he'd been meaning to ask Charlie. "Can you get a boat in Pittsburgh that goes to Louisville?"

Charlie snorted. "Ohio River starts there. Pittsburgh's got more boats than people."

Ohio. That was somewhere near Louisville, wasn't it? Royce had never spent a day in school, either before or after leaving Ireland, and he was lost outside New York. Once he'd been to Boston, but he doubted he could find it on a map. Which way did the Ohio River run?

"Christ," he muttered, not wanting to ask Charlie any more questions.

Ah, well. Devil take it. He didn't need to know geography to take care of his business, and that he would do.

Another hour or so of bone-jarring ruts in the road, and Royce was ready to rest his bruised fundament on anything that didn't buck like a wild horse. He caught himself seriously returning to the idea of sitting on the girl to pad his ass and decided it was time to get out of the wagon for a bit. Stretch his legs. The sun was almost directly overhead, or as close as it got this time of year; a nip and a nap would be just the thing.

The road had dropped out of the hills to wind along the floor of a broad valley. Royce caught the sparkle of water through the trees and called out. "Whoa, Charlie! Dinner break!"

As soon as he said it he realized that they had no dinner. The chacmool had sent them running like passenger pigeons.

What are we supposed to do until Pittsburgh? he thought. *Eat the goddamned grass?*

But Charlie must have known something Royce didn't. After halting the horses, he vaulted over Royce's head into the bed of the cart. He landed near the girl, in the back left corner, and started digging through the straw. For a long, sick moment Royce just gaped at him thinking *Christ, he means to take a bite out of the girl*—and how would he explain *that* to Steen? Or never mind Steen, what would the damned *chacmool* do?

He'd already stood and flicked out his sleeve knife, ready to lance Charlie rather than deliver the girl covered in tooth marks, but at that moment Charlie said, "Aha!" and stood himself. He held up a fat brown chicken in his stubby hands, picking bits of straw from the bloody stump of its neck.

Seeing Royce with the knife, he grinned happily. "Way ahead, ain't you?" he said.

You don't even know, Royce thought. "Where in hell did you get a bird?"

"Old Farmer John who give us this wagon, he didn't have a dog. Farmer should always have a dog, or his chickens learn to fly." Charlie held the carcass out to Royce. "Gut her and let's eat."

Royce shook his head and tucked the knife back into his cuff. "This blade doesn't touch birds," he said.

"Well, why'd you get it out then?" Charlie's bushy eyebrows bunched together. "You weren't gonna stick the girl?"

"Only in the leg, if she tried to run," Royce said smoothly, before Charlie's suspicions could refocus. "Just to slow her down."

"But she's tied up."

"Yeah, well, we're gonna have to untie her so she can piss, aren't we?"

The look on Charlie's face was starting to annoy Royce mightily. He took a deep breath and held up a hand. "No, you're right, bad idea. We'll leave her tied. One of us'll have to hold her up so she can make her water."

"Christ, be careful," Charlie said, still eyeing the cuff where Royce had stashed his knife. "Steen'd have our balls."

With that, he climbed out of the cart and walked off a short distance to where the stream Royce had spotted pooled under a short waterfall. He squatted at the edge of the pool, drew his own knife and swiftly gutted the chicken.

A queasy shiver ran through Royce's own bowels as Charlie tossed a handful of chicken guts into the pool. His head started to swim, and his eyes were having trouble focusing—it was as if he was looking through the sunlight but not seeing what was on the other side. Smelling rain, Royce looked up into a cloudless sky where stars shone alongside the murky sun, and the drumming of rain filled his ears.

Ants were crawling in perfect military single file around the rims of the wagon's wheels, and drops of sap began to squeeze out from the wagon's panels.

Sweet Jesus, Royce thought, remembering the night in Barnum's museum. He turned back to Charlie, meaning to ask him if he could smell the rain as well.

The chacmool exploded from the water amid a froth of bubbles and ropy entrails. It seized Charlie by both wrists and twisted sharply. Charlie dropped the knife and the gutted bird and his mouth dropped open, but whatever sound he might have made was drowned out by the sound of rain.

Digging in his heels, Charlie tried to pull away, but he'd been leaning forward and the chacmool dragged him easily into the pool. He looked oddly like an overgrown infant, flailing in the chacmool's grasp, squalling and wriggling like a muddy babe on the way to his bath.

At its deepest, the pool reached only to the chacmool's shoulders, but Charlie couldn't swim. When the chacmool let him go in the churning water at the base of the waterfall, he sank like a stone. It shrugged off its cloak and laid it flat over the water where Charlie had gone under, and it seemed to Royce that the cloak's feathers were standing straight up and waving as if in a strong wind.

The cloak heaved as Charlie thrashed his way up from the bottom. Like a mother swaddling an infant, the chacmool caught him and wrapped the cloak tightly around him, cocooning him in shiny green feathers. Charlie struggled against the cloak and the strength of the chacmool's grasp, and Royce wondered how the cloak held together; Charlie had once throttled a horse with his bare hands.

But the chacmool held him fast, and Charlie's jerky wriggling became blurred as it carried him under the waterfall. Royce could see it outlined there in the torrent of falling water, standing erect with its ghastly bundle, even rocking it gently back and forth. He imagined he could hear a lullaby over the sound of rain and distant thunder.

A little while later—Royce wasn't sure how long—Charlie's cocooned body drifted out into the pool, looking like a huge obscene waterbug with long green feathers splayed out into the water like waving legs. It turned over once in the quiet eddies, then sank.

The chacmool came out from under the waterfall and climbed up onto the bank, its homespun shirt and trousers clinging to its bony frame. Water ran from it in streams, puddling about its bare feet. Without the cloak, it looked just like Bobo Nigger again, like it had behind the engine house the night before.

Royce sat slumped in the mud at the side of the road, his arms wrapped around his drawn-up knees. He tried not to shiver, tried to get a handle on what had just happened and what it meant, but he was plain scared and feeling much more like a boy than a man. The situation had spun completely out of his control. Charlie was dead, God knew why, and Royce felt that he would be very lucky himself to live out the day. All because of Riley Steen.

Obviously Steen had no control over the chacmool, and that meant a switch of allegiance was in order. If the chacmool didn't kill him in the next few minutes, Royce might be able to make himself useful to it in some way, until it had what it wanted and he could forget he'd ever been to Pennsylvania.

The chacmool walked over to Royce and gazed down on him with its yellow cat's eyes. "It is because of you that I have to do this," it said.

"Me?" Royce said. "Do what?"

The chacmool waved at the pool. "This making. This

chaneque," it said. "Because you did not kill Prescott. Uncover the girl."

Royce smarted a bit at its tone. Magic or no, it rankled him to be talked down to by a nigger. But he swallowed his pride for the moment and leaned into the wagon bed to brush straw away from the girl.

His eyes widened and he swallowed hard when he saw her. She was alive all right, but her face was covered with scabs, as if someone had spent hours carefully peeling away pieces of her skin. Royce looked fearfully at the chacmool, starting to protest that he hadn't done it, she hadn't looked anything like that when he put her in the wagon, but he shut his mouth again when he saw that it was smiling.

Seeing it, the girl started to struggle again, and Royce shuddered, imagining the chacmool smiling down at Charlie the way it now regarded her.

"See, she's all right," he said resentfully.

The chacmool ignored him. *"Nanahuatzin, yolteotl,"* it said—purred, really. "Your time is coming, small one. You can feel it? Your father does, too. His time comes as well."

It turned its attention to Royce. "Her father, Prescott. You must forget him now. The *chaneque* will find him soon enough. Take Nanahuatzin to Wide Hat, to Steen, and I will meet you. That is your only task now."

"Why don't you just take her now?" Royce asked. "God knows I don't want her."

"Too many eyes would be drawn to us if we traveled together. Too many delays, explanations. She goes with you. Make up whatever lie you need, but do not let her out of your sight."

The chacmool looked Royce steadily in the eye. Its slitted pupils narrowed to black lines in its golden irises. "Much more than your life depends on this."

"Right, okay." Royce swallowed again; his throat was dry and his voice sounded like an old man's. "Can we at least take a boat when we get to Pittsburgh?"

"Go quickly. That is all that matters."

Splashing from the pool distracted the chacmool. It turned away from Royce, and he looked over its shoulder. What he saw made him cross himself for the first time since he'd left Galway as a boy of nine. "Mary, mother of Jesus, protect us," he whispered.

The thing crawling out of the icy water was recognizably Charlie. Royce could still see the old Geek in its face, and it was about the same size. But it was Charlie as he might have looked had he come from his mother's womb fully grown, his head huge and bald, his smooth cheeks pouchy around a puckered infant's mouth. It stood naked and completely hairless on the bank, holding the chacmool's cloak in one hand like a babe with its favorite blanket. Its slitted eyes focused on the gutted chicken and it dropped the blanket, scuttling over to the bird carcass and scooping it up in fat greedy fists. Royce saw that its mouth was open, exposing hooked fangs like a snake's, and its chin slick with spittle. It turned the bird over in its hands, pulling at the wings and feet and finally grasping it by the stump of its neck. Staring at the headless chicken, the *chaneque*'s lower lip actually began to tremble.

"Where's the head?" it shrieked, and Royce was chilled to his very soul because it still spoke in Charlie's voice.

In a gruesome parody of a baby's tantrum, the *chaneque* shook the bird at the chacmool and stamped its blocky feet. *"No brains! No brains!"* it howled, and the feathers of the chacmool's cloak rippled at the sound of its voice. *"Where's the heeeeaaaaadd?"*

For this the song rises
                with weeping
The dead take root in the sky
                & the music
sticks in my throat, seeing
them lost in the city of shadows

—"A Song in Praise of the Chiefs"

And the little child, the tot
Still a chick, still a mite, not sensible to anything,
as jade, as turquoise, he shall go to heaven, the House of
                the Sun;
a perfect jade, a perfect turquoise, a smooth and lustrous
                turquoise,
is the heart he shall offer the sun.

—"A Prayer to Tlaloc"

Book IV

Toxcatl, 10-Eagle—March 16, 1843

❖

The bewhiskered proprietor of the dry-goods store hadn't batted an eye when Archie walked in wearing only his sodden johnny and a horse blanket wrapped around his shoulders, and he was immediately solicitous when Archie showed him a handful of Barnum's money and inquired about a suit of clothes for traveling.

"Looks like you done a fair bit of traveling already," was the clerk's only comment as he led Archie to the rear of the store and brought out armloads of trousers and shirts.

After making his clothing purchases, Archie bought a sheath for Helen's knife. "Never sold a sheath for a kitchen knife before," the clerk said, shaking his head. "Sure you don't want a good steel Bowie instead?"

"Call me superstitious," Archie said with a wry smile. "This one's got me this far."

Fully dressed again, with a new hat and coat and good boots to replace his ruined shoes, Archie had gone down to the Allegheny docks wondering if people wandered half-naked out of the wilderness every day in Pittsburgh. He wore the knife on his hip at first, but became uncomfortable with it in view and shifted it around so it rested in the small of his back. It was a bit awkward there, but he felt better having it concealed.

Pittsburgh was nothing like New York, Archie realized as he made his way along the waterfront. It hunched like a sooty dwarf over the confluence of its three rivers, Allegheny and Susquehanna coming together to begin the winding Ohio, which would take Archie to Louisville— and Jane. Thinking of her, he felt a useless guilty urge to bring her some sort of gift, but could think of nothing that would be worth carrying along. Finally he noticed a confectioner's and bought nearly a pound of hard candy, mostly peppermints. Helen had loved peppermints.

Where are you, daughter? Archie wondered as he followed the sloping streets down to the cluster of docks like unfinished bridges pointing at the rivers' western shores. The headwaters of the Ohio were jammed with boats of every description, majestic paddlewheelers standing out among a motley array of flatboats, rafts, keelboats, and even canoes. Smaller than the seagoing vessels that clotted New York Harbor, these agile craft skittered like waterbugs on the swift river currents, their captains bawling curses as they fought for space at the docks. It looked to Archie like all the business of the world was being conducted in Pittsburgh, contracts signed and broken under the pall of smoke from the smelters that grimed the city's brick buildings and billowed over the river valleys. Soot settled quickly into Archie's clothes, and he could feel it on his face.

"Ahoy, traveler." Someone poked Archie in the shoulder, and he turned to face a squat, bearded riverman chewing the stump of a cigar and grinning like a long-lost friend. "Delbert Gatty," the man introduced himself, "merchant captain on the Ohio, Mississippi, Missouri, and every trickle in between. Is it New Orleans you're headed for? Or St. Louis?"

"Louisville," Archie replied. Why had this Gatty singled him out from the crowd?

"Done some riverin' before, Mr.—?"

"Prescott. Archie."

"Archie it is. Yer bulb there marks you a bit among all these Eastern dandies," Gatty said, gesturing at the stub of Archie's left ear. "A man who's seen a scrap, that's what I like, and I'm one man short. One of my niggers caught the complaint and shit out his life down Cairo. Pay's a dollar a day, with three drams and all the bread'n bacon you can choke down."

Gatty stuck out a hand whose last two fingers were a joint short. "Come aboard?"

Archie started to say no, but the thought occurred to him that the anonymity of working passage might not be a bad idea. He'd planned on traveling under a pseudonym the rest of the way, but for all he knew the chacmool could recognize his handwriting. It certainly hadn't had any trouble finding him so far. The talisman must act as some sort of beacon, and if Tamanend was correct, Archie had to be on water to make it work both ways.

"Where are you going?" he asked Gatty.

"Dixieland. New Orleans and octoroon whores for us, and you too."

"Going straight there?"

"River's never straight, friend, but we'll get there fast as anyone. Shake."

Archie did. Working passage it was, then. The more he blended in with the stream of river traffic, the less obvious he'd be to the chacmool and Riley Steen. Or so he hoped.

"Welcome aboard *Maudie*," Gatty cried as they approached a small, boxy single-wheeled steamer. *Maudie* measured perhaps sixty feet in length and thirty across her beam, with a small cabin on the starboard side toward the stern, just behind the boiler. A slanted lean-to roof descended from the base of the rusted stack to the cabin's eaves, sheltering a small group of Negroes asleep on the deck. The center of the boat was taken up by the boiler and several cords of firewood along the port rail, between the boiler and the wheel. Nearly every square foot of deck space was taken up with cargo stacked neck-high under fraying canvas tarpaulins.

Maudie looked tired, Archie thought. Strips of white paint peeled from her hull, and the roof of the cabin was blackened and sagging. At her stern was a manual rudder that wouldn't have looked out of place on a Roman trireme; seeing Archie notice it, Gatty shrugged and said, "Wheel's broke. She's a working boat. Hope you don't mind her paddle's on the left; some men won't sail with me on account of that."

"I'm—not a superstitious man," Archie said, but he remembered what he'd told the dry-goods proprietor about his knife.

"Then I guess old *Maudie*'s name won't bother you, will it, Gator?" Gatty guffawed and slapped Archie on the shoulder.

Unsure how to respond, Archie gave what he hoped was a hearty laugh.

"Rufus!" Gatty shouted as he stepped onto the deck. Archie followed, looking for a place to stow the valise while the crew was otherwise distracted. "Rufus, roust the niggers and let's move!"

The cabin door opened, and a narrow squinting face topped by spiky gray hair peered around it. Rufus came out onto the deck and scratched at his patchy beard, squinting at the late-morning sun. Standing erect, he was a good deal taller than the cabin door, but he appeared to have some difficulty maintaining an upright posture. A brown clay jug dangled from one bony hand; Archie judged it was nearly empty from the way he swung it in small circles. He tipped the jug up and drained it, then flung it into the water.

"Morning, darkies!" he sang, making his unsteady way to the sleeping blacks and prodding each in turn with the toe of his boot. "Time to move along!"

Gatty joined him near the boiler. "Rufus, Archie. He's signed on for this trip." Rufus looked surprised, then shook his head and muttered something about being too far upriver. Gatty laughed and elbowed Archie. "Old Rufus was expecting you to be a nigger, Archie. He done forgot we ain't in Dixie no more.

"Keep your nose clear of the mash until you show Archie around a bit," Gatty said to Rufus. "We got to make time today. MacGruder's cabinets are late, and he ain't a patient man."

As the three blacks stood and stretched, Archie saw that each was shackled about the ankles, forcing them to shuffle as they moved to their stations. They were dressed only in shirtsleeves despite the weather, and holes gaped at the knees of their trousers. Archie had the uncomfortable feeling that when he stepped aboard the *Maudie*, he'd crossed a border of some sort, one that he hadn't really known existed.

Two of the slaves began loading wood into the boiler and shoving it away from the open door with a long poker. At least that should keep them warm, Archie thought. That poor fellow taking hold of the rudder there must have been glad they spent the winter in the South.

Rufus climbed onto the cabin roof, taking care to stay near the edges. "You, Archie, pole from the bow. Keep us clear of the damned rowboats," he called as Gatty settled into the captain's chair, at the front of the boiler behind the useless wheel. Gatty opened the throttle and *Maudie*'s paddle began to churn up the muddied dockside waters, moving the boat slowly out into the current.

Archie hurried to take up the long pole leaning against the bow railing. He dropped the valise between his feet and set the pole against the dock, keeping *Maudie* clear until the dock was too far away to reach. Gatty opened the throttle further, shouting for more steam, and *Maudie* pushed through a gap in the traffic. The rudderman leaned hard to his right, and the boat swung southward into the main channel, picking up speed as pressure mounted in the boiler. Archie kept his pole at the ready, looking out for other craft that might veer too close.

He was weary suddenly. He still hadn't eaten since the packet boat had been loaded onto flatcars in Hollidaysburg, and he'd ridden all night with Maskansisil. When did rivermen sleep? On the cabin roof, Rufus appeared to have fallen into a stupor, but the other four members of

Maudie's crew were still watchful. Archie had always read of rivermen as a lazy, shiftless lot of drunken brawlers, but that had mostly been in the *Herald*. The reality, at least thus far, seemed to be very different.

And that was true not just of river tales. Whatever Archie's basic sympathies toward abolitionists like the earnest pastor bleeding and yolk-smeared on Nassau Street, seeing real living slaves shook him to his soul. Until that moment he had only seen the free blacks who clustered in the Five Points and the Fourth Ward slums, and he had thought of slavery as somehow another, Southern, version of their poverty. A problem, certainly, but just that. Another problem.

Even that perspective put Archie in a minority among his circle of acquaintances. Bennett, like most of New York's newspapermen, tirelessly wrote proslavery editorials excoriating "niggerist" attitudes, and had even gone so far as to brawl with a rival who held the opposite opinion. And Archie's friends, including Udo and poor Mike Dunn, had been adamant in their belief that the "peculiar institution" benefited not only the Southern economy but the slaves themselves.

They never saw shackles on a man who hasn't committed a crime, though, Archie thought. That was real in a way that penny-sheet columns and *biergarten* conversations weren't. Gatty's three slaves were barefoot in March, for God's sake.

Archie raised the pole as a heavily laden flatboat hove near *Maudie* on the port side. "Get your damned raft clear, Hoosier!" Gatty howled from his captain's chair. "Or I'll run you down!"

"Run this down!" cried a man in the rear of the flatboat. He dropped his trousers and slapped his hairy buttocks as *Maudie* drove by. A burst of laughter rose up from the flatboat's crew, and Archie could see the two stokers exchanging glances and suppressing smiles as they shoveled wood into the boiler.

Archie's own surreptitious grin faded as Gatty charged

to the port rail in front of the stacked firewood. "Show me your ass again, Hoosier, and I'll shoot it off!" he screamed, veins bulging in his forehead. Then he drew a revolver and emptied it in the direction of the receding flatboat.

A chunk of the flatboat's rudder burst into splinters, and the laughter of its crew turned to surprised shouts as they dove behind their cargo, leaving their boat to drift in the current. Gatty's antagonist tripped over his trousers and scrambled quickly out of view.

Archie stood dumbfounded, nearly dropping his pole into the river. He didn't think anyone on the flatboat had been hit, but that wasn't really the point; only a madman would react in such a way to an insult he himself had provoked. For a moment he considered jumping into the river and swimming for the nearest bank; enough madness plagued him without the addition of berserk riverboat captains.

But the shore was too distant here, at the confluence of the Three Rivers, and Archie had barely learned to swim as a boy. Being on a boat with a lunatic, as bad as it might be, was certainly better than drowning. There's Jane to think of, he told himself. Remember you're a father still, and do what it takes to avoid antagonizing Gatty.

"Lord, are we attacked by Indians?" Rufus was sitting up, bleary-eyed and confused.

"Rufus, you drunk, we're in Ohio," Gatty snapped. "There's no Indians for two hundred miles." He reloaded his pistol and took his seat in the captain's chair. Suddenly he roared with laughter.

"God Almighty, Rufus, but you missed a funny sight, that nancy Hoosier tripping over his britches!" Gatty slapped his knee. "Ha! He pissed himself for sure."

He lifted a jug from under his chair and took a deep drink. "Archie," he said. "You ever see any such thing?"

Archie shook his head and tried to smile. "Guess not," he said.

" 'Course not! That's because I'm the only man on the

river with balls big enough to give a Hoosier what he deserves. Any son of a bitch who'll show his ass deserves a bullet in it." Gatty waved the jug at Archie. "Stroll back here," he said, "and let's welcome you aboard. How's the water, Rufus?"

"Clear enough."

"Ha!" Gatty roared. "I'll wager it is. Well, let's have us a dram, then, boys. In honor of Hoosiers who can't sit down."

They are coming.

"What?" Stephen rolled over, thinking that Charlotte had mumbled something in her sleep.

"Hmm?" she murmured, feeling sleepily behind her until she caught Stephen's hand and drew it to her breast. He nestled into her, feeling her heart beat, inhaling the warm bed-scent at the back of her neck. Then she was asleep again, her breath settling slow and deep.

The breath of a sleeping woman is one of the things love is made of, Stephen thought. *If I was a poet I'd write that down.*

Moonlight spilled through the window, glazing Charlotte's skin with a drowsy sweetness. To sleep in this bed, to love this woman—that was all a man could do. Stephen slipped back toward sleep.

They are coming.

He blinked and raised his head, and the moonlight was the color of bones turning to dust.

They are coming, and you must prepare.

Stephen squeezed Charlotte's hand and sat up, brushing the balls of his feet on the cold wooden floor. He stepped into his trousers and found his shoes. *Macehuales imacpal iyoloco*, he whispered, and Charlotte made small and frightened noises in her sleep.

———

The cave breathed around him like a sleeping woman, waiting to be awakened by his touch. Stephen ran a hand over the statue's fanged mouth, smelling rain and feeling a tremor in the terraced walls around him.

Why so timid, Stephen?

Stephen tried to lie and found the words caught in his throat. "I'm . . . not sure," he said, feeling each word being siphoned from his mind. "Not sure if this is what I want."

Men waste lives being uncertain. Have you forgotten the promise I made you?

He thought of Charlotte, sleeping in a two-room shack, thought of the months he'd spent with pick and shovel widening the road that led to the hotel whose front door he couldn't walk through. Thought of Dr. Croghan saying *You're too valuable to lose.*

Was he really a man just because he'd jumped the broom with Charlotte, another slave Croghan had bought at the Louisville market?

Again the quiet pressure, forcing words through his throat. "What do I have to do?"

First you have to understand. Lie on the stone.

Stephen sat on the altar stone, facing the dancing statue. He placed his lamp carefully between his feet and lay backward, feeling the chill of the pitted limestone seep through his coat.

Extinguish the light.

Stephen hesitated. Putting out an oil lamp, you ran the risk that it wouldn't light again.

To understand you must trust, Stephen. Extinguish the light.

He did, and lay faceup on the stone as blind as if he'd never had eyes. The darkness had a kind of weight, a presence that Stephen could feel on his skin. It was a feeling of being near something so vast that its true size couldn't really be understood.

He thought he heard the statue chuckle approvingly. *Now you begin to see.*

A delicate scent tickled his nose, and Stephen felt warm sun on his face. He opened his eyes and saw mountains rising around him, green mountains creased by sharp ridges and capped by a dusting of snow. He was standing in a wide valley filled with flowers of every description, flowers he didn't recognize. A broad slow river meandered through the valley, and standing knee-deep in its waters was the most beautiful woman Stephen had ever seen. She wore only a skirt of carved jade, wrapped high around her hips and forming a V beneath her navel. Reflected sun from the water played across her naked skin and burnished the perfect blackness of her hair.

"Walk with me, Stephen," she said, beckoning him into the water. He walked to the river's edge, feeling a gentle breeze on his own naked body. She was magnificent, that was the only word, magnificent like the mountains looming behind her or the grand beauty of a waterfall; so breathtaking and yet so remote that Stephen couldn't imagine touching her like a woman. She seemed like a feature of the landscape, a human form created to match the perfection of the valley.

The water sent a pleasant shock up through his legs as he joined her in the shallows. The woman took his hand and raised her other arm in a sweeping gesture that took in everything around them. "Tlalocan," she said, smiling with pride. "Across the mountains, where the sun hangs low, is the city. This is the land of the dead."

"Are you dead?" Stephen asked. "Am I?"

"No," she replied. "You live, and the question has no meaning for me. I am Chalchihuitlicue. These waters are mine, just as the waters in the sky are Tlaloc's. All names are human names, though, different faces put by men on faceless things. When men wish it, I can be Tlaloc himself."

Stephen pictured the massive bas-relief in the chamber beneath Bottomless Pit, the chamber where he must be sleeping. "The face called Tlaloc . . ." He couldn't find the words.

She smiled. "That is the most ancient face, and it bears the marks of thousands of years of men's fear. But fear is only lack of understanding, Stephen. Walk with me."

They walked together upstream, the smooth stones of the river bottom giving way to larger slabs of bare rock as the current swiftened and the river narrowed to a jubilant mountain stream. They moved easily through the rushing current, and soon came to a spring high in the mountains, on a flat saddle of land between two towering peaks.

"Wait," Stephen said. "Is this a dream?"

"Of a sort." Chalchihuitlicue stood beside him, lifting her face to the wind. She breathed deeply and spread her arms. Stephen imitated her, closing his eyes and letting the clean wind fill his lungs.

He caught the biting scent of smoke and blinked, stepping away from the spring. "The city," Chalchihuitlicue said. "The dead still worship their god."

She led him to the far edge of the grassy saddle, where the land fell away to a forest far below. In the middle of the forest lay a lake like a shining silver coin, and on an island in the center of the lake a huge city stood out like a scar.

Chalchihuitlicue let him gaze down on the city for a moment before she spoke. "Gods exist only as long as men worship, Stephen. And for centuries now, the dead have been our most devout. You find the sacrifices horrible?"

Stephen nodded, unable to look away from the city of the dead.

"Gods hunger, and if they starve the world falls to ashes. What they hunger for is belief. Tlalocan is beautiful because here we are sated—the dead believe."

"What does cutting the hearts out of children have to do with belief?" Stephen said, the words leaping from his mouth before he could stop them.

If Chalchihuitlicue was angered, she gave no sign. "The people who enslave you tell you their stories, Stephen. You have heard of Abraham and Isaac?"

"But God stepped in," Stephen protested. "Abraham only had to be willing. That was enough."

"The lesson was learned, though, was it not? Your king David had that lesson in his heart when he killed those who did not believe. And Cortés, too, ground a civilization to dust because belief was more important than life."

She turned to face Stephen, the blissful smile gone from her face. "Was not your Christ a human sacrifice, Stephen? To die yourself is easy. The thrust of the knife, then paradise. The true believer is that man who will kill another in the name of his God. This is what gods feed on, life spilled in the name of belief. *Yollotl, eztli, ompa onquiza'n tlaticpac*. Cortés, though he murdered our priests and burned our cities, made us stronger. Now it is time for us to return to the world of the living. Now the sun turns, and a new world may be born from the ruins of the old."

Her eyes burned like the fires in the city below. Fire is light as well as heat, Stephen thought. *A new world . . .* "But what will be different?" he whispered.

"What would you kill a man for, Stephen? To save yourself? To save Charlotte?" She stepped closer to him, until her breasts brushed against his skin and passion exploded through his body like an electric shock.

"To be free? Would you kill to be free?"

He thought of the two-room shack, of the bed he'd built himself. Of gypsum flowers, growing beautiful for ages until greedy visitors broke them off for mantelpieces. "Kill who?" he said.

"Answers change," Chalchihuitlicue said. "Questions are what you must remember. Remember, too, that freedom is bought with hearts and blood, and it is kept with hearts and blood." The sun was low over the city now, bloated and reddened by rising smoke from sacrificial fires.

Something tickled Stephen's calf. He looked down to see a black ant working its way up his body. He raised his hand, then let it drop again. Even with the smoke of dead souls smearing the sunset, it seemed wrong to kill anything in a place so beautiful as this. This paradise.

Chalchihuitlicue—Tlaloc, really, Stephen thought; *am I actually speaking to a god?*—had turned away from him. Giving me time to think, like John Diamond did. I took the mask from him, and this woman, this god, must realize that. Why is she showing me all of this? Why doesn't she just force me to do what she wants?

She can't, he realized. They can influence, but they can't command. If they could, Diamond would never have made it to the cave and given me the mask. She wasn't lying when she said that gods feed on belief. Only belief would allow them to return to the world of the living. And in return for that belief, she was offering choices Stephen had never thought he would have.

It was a hard bargain, but a good one. *A new world*, Stephen thought.

Hello, Rebus. Stephen felt a tickle as the ant crawled into his ear canal and settled there. *Taking my name in vain?*

Chalchihuitlicue frowned and looked closely into Stephen's face. "You have much to think about, Stephen Bishop. If you would be citizen rather than slave, you know what you must do. Belief begets enemies. Do not forget that. Other voices will attempt to dissuade you from your cause."

She laid a palm flat over his heart. "Go now, and choose."

The sun dropped below the horizon, and no stars came out in the sky.

Stephen was chilled and stiff when he opened his eyes to the silent blackness of Mammoth Cave. He rolled off the altar stone, smelling the fading odor of strange flowers but hearing no voices. The lamp clinked as his foot brushed against it, and he lit it, grateful for its small illumination.

I'm still in the land of the dead, he thought. Far from the sun and listening for dead voices.

He wanted to breathe a living scent, to see the sun and lay his hand on Charlotte's sleeping body. Hate welled up in him, for gods who needed blood and men who took their living from his body. In Monrovia, would the sun shine as it did in Tlalocan? It didn't matter. Nick had been right all along. Croghan would never free him. Stephen would die in Kentucky, or be sold down the river when he was too old to guide in the cave. He would never see Africa.

Stephen's ear tickled again, and he remembered the ant. *Think on this one question, Rebus*, John Diamond's voice said softly in his mind. *Will things be any better if you let Tlaloc out into the sunlight?*

Not answering, Stephen dug the ant from his ear and crushed it between shaking fingers.

Toxcatl, 2-Flower—March 21, 1843

❖

A **torch burned** along *Maudie*'s starboard rail, illuminating the forward deck and the overgrown shore of the cove where they'd anchored for the night. In the flickering light, the Ohio River gleamed like a pool of oil and the lean-to's shadow blotted out the captain's chair, where Delbert Gatty slumped in a rare good-humored drunk.

"Tell us a tale, Archie Prescott." Gatty's voice wound slowly around the words and drifted out over the river. "Midnight's tale-telling time. How did you come to be divorced from the rest of your ear?"

"Hear, hear. That ought to be good for a bedtime story." Rufus was sprawled on the cabin roof. He lifted his head to drink and let it fall with a *thunk* back to the weathered shingles.

Archie had a jug of his own, nearly empty now. Before boarding *Maudie*, he hadn't imbibed since his last night working for Belinda, but right then he was wondering why he'd bothered with temperance at all. Days on the river quickly lost their novelty, and for long hours corn mash was all that made the boredom bearable. Corn mash, and stories—Gatty and Rufus spent nearly every waking hour swapping improbable tales of their river exploits. "Tapering off," they called it. Whenever the boiler was filled and the two stokers (whom Gatty, for some inscrutable reason, called Punch and Judy) had a free moment, they retired to the stern, where they drank their wages and bantered with Alfonse about Creole women.

After four days aboard *Maudie*, Archie was beginning to understand the Eastern stereotype of the riverman. When they worked, they worked hard, harder than Archie ever had for Bennett—loading and unloading cargo or taking on firewood. And they worked in all conditions, including a driving hailstorm that had come roaring up the river valley the day before. What that had been like for the three slaves, Archie couldn't even begin to imagine. He had made himself look at the welts on their faces and hands, made himself imagine the smack and sting of the hail.

Why do I feel guilty? he wondered. After all, I didn't buy them, or write the slavery laws. Then he thought of Udo, saying *This is what I can do*, and he said to himself Yes, I understand. By not opposing it, I have allowed this to go on.

Maudie made maddeningly slow progress down the river. Four days, and they hadn't yet passed the mouth of the Little Kanawha River in western Virginia. Gatty stopped at every speck of a town peeking from the Appalachian forests, dropping a crate here, a barrel there, and trading when he could. Archie chafed at the pace. For all he knew the chacmool had already hidden Jane where he would never be able to find her in the twelve days remaining. At this rate, he would have been better off on horseback, even if he had to buy a fresh mount at every town.

But Tamanend had said to travel by water. Well, old man, Archie thought irritably, if I'm late to the party because I heeded your advice, I'll be spending the summer bear hunting in western Pennsylvania.

Archie lay back along the port rail near the bow, to block himself off from the torchlight while he watched the stars. That was one of the real prizes of river life, stargazing. The sky blazed with streaks and clouds of light; since seeing the night sky on the river, Archie had understood what Tamanend meant when he said *numberless as the stars*.

Centzon Mimixcoa. The Four Hundred Northerners. It seemed he'd heard someone say that in a dream.

"I seen Mike Fink bite the ear off a Frenchman, once," mused Rufus, snapping Archie out of his tipsy woolgathering.

"That so?" Gatty said. "Was it Mike Fink did your ear? Come on, Archie, out with it." He banged his jug on the deck.

"Not much to it, I guess," Archie said. Not much he wanted to tell, at any rate. Living mummies and Mexican gods weren't exactly standard fare in rivermen's tall tales.

"There was a dwarf named Charlie, but everyone called him the Geek," Archie began. "I had a—a dispute with his friends. Wrong place at the wrong time, really. Three of them caught me where I wasn't supposed to be one night and . . ."

And that was it, really. Those were the facts of the situation. But storytelling wasn't about facts, Archie knew that much. If he was ever going to get Bennett to listen, he would have to do better than that.

"Where you wasn't supposed to be?" The captain's chair creaked as Gatty sat up straighter. "Where was this?"

"New York."

"New York? New *York?* How'd you come to be in New York?"

"Born there," Archie said. He downed the last of the whiskey and tossed the jug over the side. After swallowing, he finished. "This was before I came to the river."

"Well, shit." Gatty sounded disgusted. "You ain't half the alligator-horse I thought you was. Got your ear bit off by a midget in New York."

"I seen a midget in St. Louis once," said Rufus. "Don't remember his name, but I think he was in the circus."

"New York," Gatty snorted. "We got us an Easterner on the boat." He struck a match and lit the stub of a cigar. "I thought you was tough when you didn't blink at *Maudie*'s name, but now I see you're just ignorant. Well, let me tell you something, Easterner. There's three ways to curse a boat: name it for a woman, have six letters in the name, and start with an *M*. This boat's all three. Only white man crazy enough to serve on her is Rufus, and that's only because he's too drunk to be cursed."

And I'm too cursed to get drunk, Archie thought. The jug of mash had just sandpapered his nerves and made him sleepy. Above the river, the *Centzon Mimixcoa* trooped past a gibbous moon hung in the treetops on the Ohio bank.

"You don't believe in curses, Captain?" he said.

" 'Course I believe in 'em. Them niggers at the tiller believe in 'em, too—they'd jump in a minute if I didn't shackle 'em. One of 'em did, shackles and all, just upriver from Cairo. Sank his nappy head like a cannonball. Hell yes, I believe in curses.

"But here's my secret: no damn curse in the world will touch me. I'm crazier than a voodoo man, crazier than the Devil himself. Lady Luck pisses her drawers when she hears my name. That's why I don't fear curses. I could name this boat God and the Old Man himself wouldn't have the balls to strike me down."

Gatty blew the ash off his cigar, the sudden glow of the coal showing Archie that the good humor had completely drained from his face. "You think on that, Eastern man. Think on that before you get ideas about jumping. I'd hate to have to shackle a white man."

A clanging bell woke Archie the next morning. Each peal drove a spike into his head, reminding him of one reason he hadn't missed drinking. There was no bell on *Maudie*'s deck, though. Where was the racket coming from?

He stood, wincing at a deep ache in his thigh from sleeping in the cold. The bell was coming from upstream. Looking in that direction, Archie noticed that the riverbanks had closed in. He could easily have thrown a rock into the brush on either side.

"Man your pole and watch for snags," Rufus called from his rooftop perch.

"Where are we?" Archie took up his position in the bow, wishing death on whoever was ringing the damned bell. He nudged aside the canvas covering a stack of crates and saw that his valise was still where he'd left it. Whether it had been tampered with he couldn't tell, but he would have to wait for a more opportune moment to check.

"Little Kanawha," Gatty said. He looked as if he'd spent the night slouched in the straight-backed captain's chair. "Big river's fifteen miles back."

"Kentucky yet, or still Virginia?" Archie called over the sharp hiss of *Maudie*'s boiler venting steam, but Rufus didn't answer. The boat slowed to ease around a tight bend, Alfonse putting his entire weight into holding the rudder all the way left, and a large whitewashed Colonial house came into view on the right, standing on a hill overlooking the river. An acre or more of lawn had been cleared around it, and a stair cut into the steep slope between the front door and the river. The stair ended in a stubby dock, too short to reach into water *Maudie* could negotiate.

Two boys, both rangy and strapping with white-blond hair, took the stairs three at a time, leaping like goats onto the dock and untying a weatherbeaten rowboat. Above and behind them, a man appeared from the house, obviously the boys' father. He hailed the *Maudie* and Gatty shouted hello in return.

"My cabinetry at last!" the man said, coming down the stairs. He limped as he descended, placing his good leg firmly on each log step before continuing. "I kept my boys home from Sabbath services expecting you."

"Drop anchor, Archie," Gatty said. "We can't get no closer." He cut off the throttle and rummaged through his pockets. "What do you mean, at last, Marlon? It's only the twenty-second. Christ, the river's only been clear two weeks."

"No offense, Delbert," Marlon said. "I'm just eager to furnish my home. Rivermen don't feel that, I suppose."

"Hell, you haven't seen my house in New Orleans. Teak-wood furniture inside and out. I know houses." Gatty stepped up next to Archie in the bow, unfolding a stained sheet of paper. "Says right here 'on or before the twenty-seventh,' " he muttered.

Archie pushed the butterfly anchor off the deck and watched the rope uncoil and stiffen as the anchor bit into the riverbed and brought *Maudie* to a halt. The bell had stopped, but he still had a vengeful headache, and that combined with the pain in his leg put him in a foul mood. Gatty had said nothing about side trips up into the Virginia hills, and this excursion would waste half the day while Jane was taken farther away from him.

And, to top it all off, the chacmool's talisman had been inert since Archie's encounter with Tamanend—ten days now. Either the chacmool was completely inactive, which seemed unlikely, or contact with the Lenape chief had blinded Archie somehow.

Or, he thought, Tamanend was just wrong, and the talisman is simply a bull's-eye for the chacmool to sight in on. But us foot soldiers never find out about things like that until it's too late.

And that was it, really. Archie had been somehow chosen by the Lenape, either because he was Jane's father or for some more incomprehensible reason. He was their latest conscript in their ancient war with the Mexican gods. Well, I never asked to be a soldier, Archie thought. I just want my daughter back. I want off this boat and I want my daughter back.

The rowboat bumped into *Maudie*'s hull and a thrown rope fell across Archie's forearms. "Hold that fast," Gatty said, folding the contract back into his coat pocket.

One of Marlon's boys vaulted onto the deck. "Where's the box with the mirror?" he said, his voice high-pitched and wound tight with anticipation. "I want that one first!"

His brother docked the oars and stood in the boat,

watching as Gatty peeled the canvas back from the bow cargo. "Right here somewhere," Gatty said. "Been carrying your load since Cincinnati, but Little Kanawha was still froze up when I passed on my way east."

"Sure was," the boy in the boat nodded. "First boat of the year was Milt Crowe, and that was just yesterday."

"Milt Crowe?" Gatty jerked as if he'd been shot, and a flush rose from his collar like mercury in a thermometer. "That Hoosier was *here?"*

"Yup. He went on upriver. Said he'd come back through today."

"Jesus bugger his Hoosier head!" Gatty looked as if he wanted to run in several directions at once. He stomped in a tight circle, spitting a string of unintelligible curses.

Coming back around to face Archie, he poked a thick finger into Archie's chest. "Crates are stamped Mac-Gruder. Get 'em off my boat so's we can move. You, Punch and Judy!" he shouted. "Get that boiler hot! Soon as I see that devil Crowe we're gonna race, and I mean *race*."

The stokers jumped to their task, tossing wood into the fire by the armload and working the poker as if they were enraging a bull before letting it into the ring. Gatty stomped back to the starboard rail and leaned out over the water, his bulldog face almost exactly the color of cranberry sauce. "Marlon! What was that damned Hoosier selling?"

Marlon had reached the dock. He stood with his arms folded, his weight shifted away from his bad leg. "Tobacco, mostly. I bought cigars and a dozen tins of pipe leaf."

"From him? We had a damned contract!" Gatty whipped the paper from his pocket again and waved it in the air.

"Only for the furniture, Delbert. I ordered tobacco from you because you said you'd be first through this year." Marlon shrugged. "You weren't."

Gatty stormed into the cabin and slammed the door

behind him. Archie could hear him howling inside, and Rufus dropped down to the deck, shaking his head and laughing as he made his way forward.

Archie found a MacGruder stamp on a flat square crate like a table leaf. He handed it to Marlon's son. "This one ought to be the mirror," he said.

"Boy, I guess," the boy said, taking the crate as if he were cradling an infant. "I'm gonna polish it every morning." He lowered the mirror to his brother, who laid it flat across the rowboat's gunwales. Rufus cast him off and he rowed the few yards to the dock.

Archie pushed the next crate to the rail. "Say, Rufus," he said. "Who is this Crowe?"

Rufus wheezed. "He'n Delbert raced once, out below Cairo, Illinois. Three years ago, I guess. He had Delbert clean beat but hit a snag and sunk his boat. Delbert claimed he'd won, but everybody knew better, and folks let him hear it up and down the river. I reckon Delbert'd sell his mother in Araby to beat Milt Crowe in a race."

Gatty reappeared, snarling smoke from a fresh cigar. "God damn it, Archie," he growled, "I'll pay that midget to chaw off your other damned ear if any of this MacGruder shit is still on board when Crowe comes around that bend. Get to it!" He spat on the deck and climbed onto the cabin roof, glowering out over the Little Kanawha.

With Archie and Rufus loading the skiff, and Marlon's two boys unloading, the transfer was completed in ten minutes. Gatty said not a word, only glared at Archie and then back to the river, as if he expected Milt Crowe to steam by at full speed if he turned his back. "About goddamn time," he said from the cabin roof, as the last MacGruder crate nearly swamped the overloaded rowboat. "Haul anchor and let's turn around. I'll give that bastard Hoosier the surprise of his sonofabitching life." Dropping back down to the deck, he sat in his chair and rammed open the throttle.

Maudie surged forward just as Archie, with Rufus's

help, yanked the anchor free of the bottom. At the same time, a whistle sounded from upstream.

Gatty leaped out of his chair at the sound. "Alfonse," he shouted, "goddamn your nigger hide, *turn this boat around!*"

"Hold a minute, Delbert!" Marlon called from the dock. "I don't have the pegs and nails."

"*What?* Damn you, Archie, get the box of damned pegs!" Gatty flung his cigar at Archie. It missed by feet and flew into the river.

Archie stopped in the middle of recovering the cargo and searched frantically for a last MacGruder box. He found it between the port rail and a row of whiskey barrels and held it up as Milt Crowe's whistle sounded again, much closer this time.

"Throw it over the side!"

Archie turned toward the captain's chair, thinking *He can't be serious*, and looked directly down the barrel of Gatty's revolver. "I mean *now*," Gatty said.

The box weighed at least ten pounds, but Archie heaved it as far as he could in the direction of Marlon's dock. It splashed in the shallows and the two blond boys jumped into the water after it.

"See if I—" Marlon was shouting, but Archie lost the rest of the words and very nearly fell into the river as *Maudie* lurched violently to port. A barrel of whiskey toppled and crashed through the rail on that side, followed by the forward part of the stacked firewood. Logs boomed against *Maudie*'s hull as the boat completed her turn, just as Milt Crowe's own single-wheeler came churning around an upriver bend.

"Ahoy, Delbert!" Crowe gave a great joyous wave as his boat came within shouting distance, a gap-toothed smile splitting the black tangle of his beard. "Care for a jaunt this fine morning? I've got this beautiful new boat, and I haven't yet seen what she can do."

"I'll race you to goddamned Cincinnati, Hoosier!" Gatty's voice cracked with fury. "You'll sink that bastard tub, too, but this time you'll be looking at my hairy backside!"

Crowe's boat was longer and narrower than *Maudie*. It cut through the Little Kanawha's brown water like a shark fin, surging past *Maudie* under a full head of steam. Archie could see the words *Detroit Damsel* painted in bold letters on her port bow.

"I'll just float 'til you catch up, Delbert," Crowe called as he passed. "Hate to take advantage of old *Maudie*." His crew tipped Gatty an ironic salute.

Gatty spat into Crowe's wake. "Watch out for snags, you son of a bitch. No excuses this time!" He cranked the throttle open and jammed it there with the barrel of his gun, then ran up to the bow, shouting curses at Crowe, Punch and Judy, and the state of Indiana. *Maudie* picked up speed, rocking in the *Detroit Damsel*'s wake.

Rufus tapped Archie on the shoulder. "Might as well have us a sit-down," he said over the roar and hiss of the boiler. "Delbert'll either win or he won't. Probably he will, but there ain't nothing for us to do. Can't pole us away from a snag at this speed, and he took me off the rudder when he found out that Alfonse don't drink."

Archie followed Rufus back to the lee of the cabin, where they sat down. Rufus hefted a jug he found next to the railing and grinned. "Must have left this here yesterday," he said. "Bottoms up."

The two boats pulled even as they rounded the bend below the MacGruder house. Even in their sheltered spot, wind whipped in furious eddies, and Archie jammed his hat down over his ears. He'd never moved this fast before, not even on a train, and their speed in the narrow waterway made him nervous. If they crashed, he wasn't at all certain he would be able to fight the swollen spring currents.

"How long will they race?" he asked Rufus.

" 'Til someone runs out of wood or blows the boiler."

"Blows the boiler?" This was a possibility Archie hadn't considered. He upended the jug, drinking until his eyes watered. Rufus watched him quizzically, waiting to speak until Archie set the jug on the deck and gasped for breath.

"You ain't never been on a boat in your life, have you?" Archie shook his head, and Rufus cackled. "I figured. Why'd you git on this godforsaken tub, then?"

Archie looked out over the wakes left by the churning paddlewheels. An odd silence seemed to have fallen, as if the wall of sound created by the race had attuned Archie's hearing to what wasn't there. *Maudie*'s boiler could explode at any moment, leaving him mangled or drowned in the freezing water—he'd read of similar accidents in the *Herald*. There were dozens every year.

And then Jane would be murdered.

What would happen then? Would the war between the chacmool and the Lenape go on, or would some kind of decisive blow have been struck? Archie didn't know, but he also realized that he didn't much care. Whether the world changed or not, Jane would still be dead. None of the rest of it mattered.

"If you don't want to say, it don't sweat me none," Rufus said, but he looked injured despite his words. He looked down between his knees and popped his thumb in and out of the jug's neck.

"No, it's not that. Just woolgathering," Archie said. "My daughter I think she's in Louisville. I'm trying to find her. Her mother's dead, and I," he swallowed hard. "I haven't been much of a father to her."

"Mm," Rufus nodded. "I got a daughter. Two, I think. They're in Vicksburg, though, and I ain't been there in nearly ten years." He glanced off to his right, where the *Detroit Damsel* was beginning to open up a lead. Then he shook his head and sighed. "Reckon I won't never get back there again."

The Kanawha was broadening ahead of them and Archie could see the clustered buildings of Parkersburg, and beyond it the open water of the Ohio perhaps half a mile downstream. He wondered if *Maudie* was running flat out, or if Gatty could coax a bit more out of her once they swung out into the main current. A strange detachment settled over him, all of his anxieties receding into the background like the noise of the race had seemed to before. Almost as if the river itself was singing him a lullaby, relaxing him.

So this was fatalism. His fate was completely out of his hands. Either he would survive Delbert Gatty's mania or he wouldn't. Either he would reclaim Jane from her captors or he wouldn't. Rufus had it exactly right: just take a seat on the deck and watch things unfold. What else was there for a foot soldier to do?

Milt Crowe had pulled a full length ahead, and as the two vessels charged through the mouth of the Little Kanawha, he edged to the left, driving *Maudie* dangerously close to the left bank. Gatty shouted something and flung Archie's pole at the *Detroit Damsel*'s stern.

Maudie steamed nearer the bank, and Gatty suddenly came charging past Rufus and Archie to the stern. He grabbed hold of Alfonse and shoved him to the right.

"Cut the channel! Cut the channel!" he screamed. "You, Punch and Judy, keep stoking!"

Part of what Archie had thought was the Little Kanawha's left bank was actually an island, with a narrow channel separating it from the Virginia mainland. *Oh my God*, Archie thought, *how can we make that turn at this speed? And with a manual rudder?*

"Damn daring move, Delbert," Rufus said appreciatively. "Hope no boat's tied up at old Blennerhassett's dock."

As Crowe's boat steamed out into the Ohio, Gatty shoved Alfonse away from the rudder and hauled on it with all his strength. *Maudie*'s stern came around to the right, and she practically skidded across the river's surface before straightening and plowing toward the channel.

The near bank loomed ominously close, but Archie's mind had fastened on something Rufus had said. "Blennerhassett?" The name was familiar. Something he'd read somewhere?

"Yup, the old man owned this island." Rufus's eyes were fixed on the bank, but his mouth kept moving. "He's gone now since the Burr trial. Don't know who lives there now—*oh my Christ!*"

Gatty had cut the angle perfectly, keeping *Maudie* from running aground while losing a minimum of speed in the turn, but he hadn't noticed the massive dead oak leaning out from the undercut bank just around the bend from the Little Kanawha's mouth. He saw it now, though, and he strained against the rudder, his eyes wide and disbelieving.

Rufus was up and running before it happened. "Into the water!" he cried. "She'll blow sure!" He dove headfirst off the stern and disappeared into *Maudie*'s wake.

As *Maudie* surged under the toppled tree, a hanging branch thick as a man's torso caught the top of her stack, bending it back and crushing it down into the boiler. The branch hung swaying, then broke loose to crash down on *Maudie*'s stern, snapping off the rudder handle and pinning Gatty to the deck.

Maudie shuddered and an ear-piercing whistle drowned out the shouts of Punch and Judy as they stumbled toward the bow, tripping over the shackles binding their feet. The boat drifted into the center of the channel, her wheel slowing and her stern coming farther around until she floated broadside in the slow current. Archie found his feet and scrambled to follow Rufus off the stern; Alfonse had disappeared and Gatty was thrashing under the branch pinning his legs. Archie could see his mouth moving, but the whistle from the boiler had risen to a hurricane scream and Gatty's words were lost.

He had barely made it to the cargo stacked in the stern before the boiler exploded, the blast wave pinwheeling Archie out over the flat brown river.

When he hit the water, Archie sucked in an involuntary breath at the shocking cold. The river flooded his mouth and nose, and he panicked, flailing about in the murky water. Which way was up? Forcing his eyes open, he saw sunlight and kicked toward it, his lungs burning and pulse hammering in his ears.

He broke the surface and gulped a deep breath, immediately choking up a stream of dirty water. Wiping hair from his eyes, Archie saw *Maudie*, burning like tinder as she drifted sternfirst in the mainland side of the channel, her deck barely level with the water. The boiler, stack, and cabin were gone, shattered into bits of flotsam that spotted the water around the wreck. Her cargo, too, was gone, either sunk or drifting away.

Gatty's body hung in the water off *Maudie*'s stern, twisted in the railing and the waving remains of the rudder. His head was underwater. There was no sign of Rufus or the three slaves.

Archie's boots began dragging him down, and awakening pain from his burns made every move excruciating. Water slopped over his chin as he imagined trying to swim with iron manacles about his ankles; any of the three blacks could be gasping out his life from the muddy bottom, eyes fixed on the same sunlight Archie had seen but unable to reach it. A terrible vision of hopeless dark hands grasping at his feet spurred Archie to action; he got his arms moving and began to swim.

A packing crate floated in front of him, burning along the corner farthest above the water. The flame spread and leapt out onto the water, licking along the ripples Archie made as he stopped to tread water. Something about it was soothing, and he forgot his fear of being dragged under.

Just for a moment, and then it was gone; but Archie saw it. He saw the flames resolve themselves into an image, low and shimmering like reflected sunlight on the brown water. Helen's face. He spoke her name, reached toward the flickering image, and then it was gone, extinguished as the crate turned slowly over with a hiss and puff of steam.

"Helen," he said. "Love, what is it?"

The feather talisman floated to the surface, its brass medallion bobbing on the waves created by his awkward strokes. It turned around once, the feathers brushing against Archie's chin, then pointed steadily toward the bank of Blennerhassett's Island.

Archie waited for another sign, some indication of why Helen's face had formed itself from fire and water and death. What kind of magic was this? Was it a warning, come too late, of *Maudie*'s wreck? Dazed and fearing he'd conjured the image out of shock and guilt, Archie followed the talisman and struck out for a sandy strip of beach a few dozen yards distant. The slumping remains of a dock stood out from the beach's downriver edge, just a double row of sunken posts with a few crooked boards clinging to them. Archie's back and shoulders hurt like they were still being steam-cooked; he thought he could feel fresh blisters rising and breaking as he worked across the current, finally catching hold of one of the weathered dock posts and settling his feet on the sandy bottom.

Looking behind him, he saw that *Maudie* was completely gone save for the very tip of her bow, which peeked above the surface in a tangle of brush and fresh debris on the mainland side of the channel. She would lie there caught on a snag until another shortcutting captain either tore out his bottom on her or brought in salvagers to float her down to Cincinnati. Either way, Archie's short career as a riverman was over. There was no sign on the river of the image he'd seen moments before.

"I don't understand," Archie moaned, his teeth beginning to chatter. The soothing lethargy he'd felt just a few minutes before was gone, replaced by a surge of desperate frustrated anger. Jane was in the hands of madmen, and he was stranded on a strip of mud with only the sodden clothes on his back and fleeting visions of his dead wife. He had to find a way to Louisville, and if he were to heed

Tamanend's advice and travel by water he'd have to cross the island and hope that a passing vessel would pick him up. Barnum's money was gone, a windfall for whoever dredged up *Maudie*'s charred bones.

And come to think of it, Tamanend's advice hadn't proved very useful, had it? Archie shivered as he slogged out of the shallows onto the beach, feeling the March wind draw his body heat through the tears in his dripping clothes. *Have to get warm and dry*, he thought. *No inexplicable encounters with Indians this time, just find a roof and get warm. You can't do Jane any good if you catch a fever and die here.*

Helen, what did you want to tell me?

He supposed he was in shock—four men had just died and he'd barely given a thought to finding Rufus. Sorry, old man, he thought. Hope you got clear. Maybe Milt Crowe will come back around and pick you up.

Archie realized he'd spoken aloud, and then that he was deaf. Must have been the explosion, he thought. But his ears didn't hurt, at least not any more than the rest of him. He hoped it was temporary.

A winding, overgrown path snaked back into the trees from the base of the dock. Before following it, Archie stripped and wrung his clothes dry as best he could. Despite the chilly temperatures, the sun was bright, and he actually warmed a bit as his skin dried. The chill settled over him again as he dressed, but it was nothing a brisk walk wouldn't stave off until he could locate a roof and, he hoped, a dry bed and change of clothes.

So this is Blennerhassett's Island, Archie thought as he made his way up a gentle rise and into the denser forest. Harman Blennerhassett had bankrolled much of Aaron Burr's seditious activity and, after Burr's arrest, had fled to Louisiana and died, leaving his island estate to fall into disrepair. The mansion had burned in 1811, and Blennerhassett himself had died in 1831. Archie had never understood Blennerhassett's role, or his interest in the whole affair. Burr's *Wallam Olum* commentary gave no indication that the old Irishman had known of the Tlaloc cult. Perhaps he had simply been hungry for power and had sought to guarantee himself influence by financing Burr's bid to become a western emperor.

It wasn't just Blennerhassett, either. Archie wasn't absolutely certain of the motives of any of the various parties in this endless, invisible war. Tamanend had said that people create gods, but that gods attain a reality of their own as long as they are worshiped. That might explain the conflict between the Lenape and the chacmool's people, but both societies had been practically eradicated by the white man. What was left to fight over? Was it really possible for a handful of fanatics to resurrect a forgotten god?

What did the Lenape really want? Were they really so solicitous of the civilization that had destroyed them, or was Tamanend not telling him something?

And none of those questions, even if they could be concretely answered, explained Riley Steen. He certainly believed that the old gods had power—Archie had no doubt of that after the night at the Museum and outside the Brewery—but he didn't exactly worship, did he? He feared his enemies and used what rituals he could, but Archie couldn't recall seeing him actually *pray*. Perhaps he too was only in it for the power, and thought he could ride the chacmool to some sort of prominence.

At least I know what I want, Archie thought. No one has offered me riches or power, and I don't care. I just want to be a father again.

But was that really true? Would he turn down what Steen sought, if it was offered to him?

The sight of a dilapidated mansion ahead broke Archie's train of thought. Funny, Archie thought. Barnum said it had burned.

He made his way across a muddy field, once a lawn or perhaps vegetable garden but now overgrown with oak and poplar saplings. Archie wished he was better acquainted with edible plants. If this had been a garden,

some of the vegetables might have survived, and ... but
no, it was only March. And unless someone had taken up
residence here when Blennerhassett fled south, it was very
likely that Archie wouldn't eat until he managed to secure
passage farther down the river. How long before hunger
began to seriously debilitate him?

The manor house itself was blocky and squarish, with
most of its paint peeled away by thirty-five winters. The
roof sagged noticeably in several places, and nearly all of
the windows were broken. Off to one side stood a barn,
its roof fallen completely in and its doors standing open.

No wagons or carriages were visible, or any other sign
that the house was occupied. Archie approached the house
and tried the front door. The knob was frozen, no doubt
rusted shut. He debated a moment, then went to the nearest ground-floor window. Peering inside, he saw what
must have been a parlor, dominated by the hulk of a for-
tepiano in the opposite corner from the window. A rotting
divan flanked by Queen Anne chairs had been set up facing a central table. Everything in the room was covered
in leaves and dust.

Archie used his elbow to break out the shards of glass
still clinging to the sash, then climbed through the window. In the front hall a stairway led to the second floor;
a sitting room, dining room and kitchen occupied the remainder of the ground floor. Archie searched the kitchen
and adjoining pantry, but whatever viable foodstuffs Blennerhassett left behind, in this mansion that had supposedly
burned to its foundation thirty years before, had long since
moldered or been ruined by hungry animals.

The talisman began to throb slowly as Archie climbed
the front staircase. He stopped and peered up into the dim
hall at the top of the stairs. Could the chacmool have
somehow known he would be stranded here and set up an
ambush? It seemed absurd, but Tamanend had admon-
ished him to stay dry while traveling by water. Perhaps
as long has he'd had a boat between him and the river,
Archie had been masked, but when *Maudie* had blown

herself to fragments, the chacmool had scented him.

Then what was waiting for him at the top of the stairs?

Archie drew the knife, thanking his lucky stars—if he had any—that it hadn't been torn loose in the explosion, and crept up the stairs. His hearing was beginning to return and he listened as well as he could for any sound other than the creak of his foot on each step.

The upstairs hall was dark enough that the chacmool itself could have crouched invisibly within arm's length, but the talisman's vibration didn't intensify. Holding the knife out in front of him, Archie stepped cautiously ahead. His eyes began to adjust to the dimness and he saw that just ahead and to his right, a door opened off the hall. Another doorway was barely visible directly opposite the first, on the other side of what looked like a drawing room.

A slow pulse like a heartbeat began to throb in it as Archie approached the door nearest him, over the dining hall on the ground floor. He tested the knob and the door clicked open.

Flinging it wide, Archie stood just outside the jamb, brandishing the knife and bracing for an assault. The door banged off the wall and swung halfway back before squeaking to a halt on rusted hinges. Inside the room, light streamed in through a bank of high windows and a breeze swirled fallen leaves around Archie's feet. A large desk stood under the windows, swept clean of debris by the breeze. Floor-to-ceiling bookshelves occupied every wall, mostly empty; what books remained had been ruined by exposure to the elements. Archie pushed the door aside and stepped into the room, his footsteps muffled by a thick rug. Two reading chairs sat across from the desk, flanking a low table. Behind them were more empty bookshelves, interrupted by a humidor and liquor cabinet.

Archie glanced behind the door and then looked the room over more closely, wondering what might have excited the talisman. There were no places for a man-sized creature to hide, and the only other thing Archie could think of to explain the talisman's agitation was some sort of artifact Blennerhassett had left behind. Or had the chacmool itself been here? He scanned the shelves and saw nothing but dust and rotted books, and an empty alcove near the windows that might once have held a sculpture. Examining the alcove more closely, Archie found several blobs of what appeared to be quicksilver. He dabbed at one, wondering what could explain such an oddity; perhaps Blennerhassett had pursued medical interests?

The touch of his fingers smeared one blob over to connect with a second. An electric shudder ran from the talisman down Archie's arm into the liquid, and the blobs rushed together, rippling as if in an earthquake. Several black ants crawled from seams in the woodwork and circled the pulsating blob, marching in exact, almost military, single file.

Ants drawn to quicksilver? Was that something he'd seen before? The light in the room dimmed, curdled as it had on the street in front of the *Herald* that day, and Archie slumped into a sitting position, one finger still thrust into the puddle of mercury.

The light, he thought. Like on the mountain; I'm outside of time again. He felt slow, disconnected.

"Wheeere's the heeaadd? Very close? Wheeeeere?"

Archie twisted out of the alcove, feeling a nearly audible *snap* as his finger pulled free of the quicksilver. He stumbled against the desk and gained his feet, looking wildly around. The room seemed to fall into place around him again, and he wondered what would have happened if he hadn't heard the eerie cry.

Heard? Fifteen minutes ago I was deaf as a post.

His eyes fell on a tiny recess above the lintel of the door through which he'd entered. A small statuette sat there, a jade carving of a crawling infant. Archie stepped closer to the doorway and inspected the carving, queerly certain that it was the source of the voice he'd heard.

It was an infant, but there was something inhuman about it as well. Even for a baby's, its head was huge, and its face was something out of a nightmare. Curled and slitted eyes squinted out over a gaping fanged mouth, and Archie had the unsettling sensation that it was looking at him. The talisman resumed its steady heartbeat throb, and Archie stretched onto tiptoes, reaching for the sculpture.

"Wouldn't do that if I were you."

Still balancing on the balls of his feet, Archie turned and saw a smiling black face hanging upside down in the open window over the desk. *Good God,* he thought, *how did any of them survive the wreck?*

The man hooked his fingers on the inside of the window frame and swung in like a trapeze artist, twisting in midair to land on the desk facing Archie. He wasn't one of the slaves from the *Maudie,* Archie realized, but then who was he?

"Sorry, Johnny," the black man said. One of his eyes was milk-white, with no trace of pupil or iris. "Didn't mean to startle, but you got problems."

"What kind of problems? Who are you?"

"John Diamond, used to be," the man said, bowing grandly. "Used to be an acrobat, dancer. Now just a dead man who can't die."

The talisman had quieted, and Archie wondered if this Diamond person exerted some sort of damping influence on it. "Did you follow me here?" he asked warily.

"Follow, yes; you, no." Diamond stepped gracefully to the floor. "That's the problem I was saying. Thing I'm following is following you. You Presto?"

"Presto?" Archie stared blankly at Diamond for a moment before he understood. "Oh—well, Prescott. My name's Prescott."

Diamond laughed and slapped his forehead comically. Archie noticed that Diamond's hand left a visible impression in the skin of his brow. "Prescott, sorry Johnny. I do that. Must be being dead."

"I suppose so," Archie said cautiously. Nothing Diamond said made any sense. "Who's following me? Is it the chacmool?"

"No, no, chacmool's in Kentucky already. Not exactly

who, more what. *Chaneque*. Statue of it, up there." Diamond pointed at the carving over the lintel.

"You touch that," Diamond continued, "it'll come right to you. Sorry Johnny, if it hasn't already."

"What—" Archie's question was cut off by a bone-chilling wail from the hall.

"Verrryy close, the heeeaad!"

Archie jumped away from the door, spinning to face out into the hall. The thing crouched on the balcony rail, barely six feet away, was the jade carving come to life, only much larger. Its head was twice the size of Archie's own, its infantile body grotesquely bulging with slabs of muscle. Vile breath poured from its pouting mouth between bared fangs. And something about its face was familiar.

Jesus, Archie thought as he caught sight of the hump deforming its naked back, *it's the Geek. What in God's name happened to him?*

Before he could move, the *chaneque* sprang on him, digging long fingernails into Archie's shoulders and knocking him to the floor. Flinging his arms up to ward it off, Archie lost the knife; he grabbed the *chaneque* around the neck with both hands, barely holding its snapping mouth away from his face.

"Oh boy," he heard Diamond say from across the room.

"Head the brains, Archiee," the *chaneque* hissed, its forked tongue flicking across the tip of Archie's nose. *"Bit you once, this time the brain—yum yum yum."*

It locked its fat fingers around Archie's wrists and jerked his hands from its neck, pinning his arms to the floor as easily as he would have a child's.

"Brain—yum yum yum," it giggled, and lunged at his face.

John Diamond's arm shot across Archie's field of vision, blocking the *chaneque*'s snap. Instead of tearing Archie's face from his skull, the *chaneque* buried its fangs in the crook of Diamond's elbow, driving his forearm into Archie's face. A swampy stench choked Archie's nose and mouth; he fought against the weight pinning him to the floor but couldn't get free. Cold stinking blood flooded over his face as the *chaneque* gnawed through Diamond's elbow joint.

Then, suddenly, it released its grip on Archie's arms and bounded away, howling through a ragged mouthful of Diamond's flesh. Archie scrambled backward, coming up short against the bookshelves facing the door. He saw Diamond sitting in the middle of the library floor, shaking his head and saying, "Oh boy," over and over as he poked at his mangled arm.

The *chaneque* fell onto its back, flailing its limbs and gagging. *"Baaad foood,"* it choked, bits of Diamond's skin hanging from its lips. It shook its head violently, spraying gobbets of flesh across the room. *"Didn't bite him, bit* him, *bad, where's the heeeadd . . . ?"*

It rolled over onto its side and vomited up a torrent of black sludge, flecked with red and white bits of bone and tissue. Trying to stand, it slipped on the puddle of vomit and fell back to the floor, where it gnawed at the rug. *"Baaad foood,"* it gasped again. Then it fell still, a trickle of thin black fluid leaking from its open mouth.

"Hoped that would work," Diamond said after a long pause. "Ouch."

His forearm was attached only by the merest strip of tendon. He stood, holding the nearly severed limb by the wrist, and walked over to Archie. "Lend a hand here?" he asked.

"What?" Archie tore his gaze from the dead *chaneque*. Even smeared with blood and vomit, it looked horribly like a sleeping infant.

"Sorry, Johnny. Ha. Bad joke. Pull it off." Diamond nodded at his mutilated arm. When Archie didn't move, he said, "Come on, help us out. It don't do me no good now."

Before he could think about what he was doing, Archie grasped Diamond's right wrist in both hands and jerked his forearm loose with a pop of parting tendons. "Ouch,"

Diamond said again, and Archie flung the limb away toward the *chaneque*'s corpse.

Diamond inspected the naked end of his humerus, picking away a strip of skin. "Wondered about that," he said.

"About what?" Archie said shakily.

"Doesn't bleed."

Another long silence passed. Finally, when Archie was relatively certain that the *chaneque* wouldn't spring up and attack him again, he got to his feet. "I guess I should thank you."

"Guess so."

"You poisoned it?"

Diamond shrugged. "*Chaneque* needs living flesh. I'm not. I was made same way it was, only Steen don't have the chacmool's magic."

"Steen? Riley Steen made you?"

"Drowned me. Bastard. Sorry, Johnny. Didn't know if that would work," Diamond said, gesturing toward the dead *chaneque* and his own severed forearm.

Archie was beginning to regain some composure, enough to realize that John Diamond might have answers to some of the questions that kept him wandering through his quest like a blind man. "Why were you following that—thing, the *chaneque*?"

"Looking more than following," Diamond said. "Forming *chaneque* is damn noisy, if you have ears to hear. I spend lots of time in water, can't abide land for long. Heard *chaneque* far off and old Lupita started me on the trail. Only one reason for *chaneque*, she said, and sorry Johnny, that's to get Presto. Prescott, ha.

"Chacmool set it on you, and I knew it would come here if it could. *Chaneque*'s like me, only worse. Can't much remember what it was and don't know for sure what it is. So that," Diamond pointed his truncated arm at the jade carving over the door, "would draw it. Like looking in a mirror."

"Wait a minute," Archie said. "Lupita?"

Diamond nodded, a sorrowful expression on his face.

"She's sorry, real sorry for what she did, sorry Johnny. Bad act for good reason, way she saw it. But Steen killed her too. Bastard. Drowned me."

Archie felt a pressure in his head, as if the *Maudie* was exploding again all around him. "Lupita did this? The fire, the . . . Helen?" His mouth worked, but he couldn't form any more words.

"Bad act for good reason, she thought. Like I said. Little Jade, she was marked before she was born. Calendar was just right. When she got free of Steen, nearly ruined the whole thing, but now—" Diamond shuffled uncomfortably and looked at his bare feet. "You got to get her, Presto, or bad things gonna happen."

The more the shape of things came clear to Archie, the worse it got. He'd come halfway across the country thinking only that Steen was exacting some incomprehensible revenge on him for mucking up the plan to capture the chacmool. Now, to find out that this plot had been simmering for years . . . *decades* even . . . had killed his wife, disfigured his daughter . . .

He had an overpowering urge to burn Blennerhassett's crumbling mansion to the ground, simply destroy the statue, the books, the memory of the plot hatched by Burr and Blennerhassett that had reached across years to destroy Archie's life.

But wait, Archie thought. The mansion's already burned. Barnum wouldn't be wrong about something like that. Where am I? What kind of a place is this? He remembered the Allegheny mountaintop, the arrested arc of the moon and the stink of the bear that for a moment had been Tamanend. I have to get back to the world, Archie thought, find Riley Steen. No doubt he's been in on this from the beginning.

Archie had let his anger at Steen go in the past two weeks, consumed instead by guilty resolve to rescue Jane and restore what was left of his family; but now he saw that the two goals were the same. He would have to go through Riley Steen to recover his daughter.

And that was just fine. That, in fact, was exactly how he wanted it.

"Look, Diamond," he said, hunger and damp clothes forgotten, "do you have a boat? How did you get here?"

"Sorry, Johnny, no boat. Swam. Can't stay long out of the water now, anyway." Diamond peeled off one of his fingernails and held it up as if in evidence. "Right yonder's the river, though; plenty of boats there."

Archie found his knife and sheathed it. "Can you show me?"

"Right yonder," Diamond said again. He started toward the window.

"The door, could we?" Archie said. "I'm not an acrobat."

As they left the clearing, Archie looked back. The mansion was gone. Only a rough square of stones, a too-regular depression in the ground, hinted at its location. Half an hour later, he and Diamond reached the south bank of the Ohio. The sun was moving again, dropping toward the hills.

"You might see me again, Presto. Guess I owe old Steen a bad turn or two," Diamond said, and slipped out of sight in the shadowy river.

I can hear again, Archie realized, and it must be real. Time seems to be going along again. Barnum had said that travelers called Blennerhassett's wilderness enclave the Enchanted Island, and Archie, thinking of the *chaneque* and the vanished mansion, laughed quietly. If they had only known.

He breathed a sigh of relief that the river had been clear of traffic when Diamond disappeared. Chacmools, *chaneques* and Riley Steen were enough for any fugitive's plate, thank you very much, without worrying about the local sheriff as well. He washed his hands and face, scrubbing the blood of dead man and *chaneque* with river sand and worrying what sort of signal his contact with the river was sending to the chacmool. After that, there was nothing to do but wait.

❖

WHEN HE AWOKE to brilliant midday sun and a warm breeze carrying smells of plants awakening for spring, it took Archie several seconds to arrange everything that had happened to him the day before. The race, the explosion, Blennerhassett's mansion and the thing that had once been the Geek, John Diamond's sacrificial intervention: all of it seemed like a strange fever dream now that Archie was stretched comfortably out on the deck of Peter Daigle's overloaded keelboat.

Archie had nearly resigned himself to spending a cold night on the riverbank when a burst of singing had signaled the approach of a boat. He splashed out into waist-deep water, shouting and waving his arms at the boat when it came casually drifting near the island. The family steering the keelboat picked him up without hesitation, offering him dry clothes and leftover stew after hearing his tale of the wreck of the *Maudie*.

They were the Daigles, of Bangor, Maine, leaving New England's winters and rocky soil for better prospects in the West. "Oregon, I think." Peter Daigle said, and his four children immediately set up a clamor about California and the Pacific Ocean.

"No, children, not California," Daigle said. "Who knows when the Mexicans might claim it again?" Archie had choked a bit on his stew at that point, and then nearly suffered a concussion as Peter pounded him on the back.

"Isn't," he wheezed when he could speak again, "isn't Oregon all British possession?"

"Ah," Peter said. "A man who reads the newspapers. Marie, our guest can read."

"Wonderful," said Marie. "Perhaps he will teach you." She was a few years younger than Peter, with no gray yet showing in her lustrous chestnut hair. Archie could imagine her as a girl; how many hearts had she broken before settling on Peter Daigle? She was the sort of lively woman that Baptists wrote fiery tracts about.

"Peter won't let me teach him to read, Mr. Prescott," Marie said, her French accent thickened by mock indignation. "He says it would be too humiliating to have a woman teach him. So perhaps you can, so I won't have a daydreaming illiterate for a husband."

"My wife exaggerates," Peter said. "I would have a woman teach me, but I don't want it to be common knowledge, you see? Some men are not so enlightened as I." He winked at Archie and leaned forward conspiratorially.

"Right now, Oregon is British, but Americans are settling there. I think the queen would rather be rid of the whole territory than bother with a flood of rabble-rousing Americans, no? Oregon will not be British for long.

"So, children," he proclaimed, thrusting a hand into his coat à la Napoleon, "Oregon it is. We'll farm by a river and smile at the rain because it isn't snow."

The children immediately switched their attention to Archie, barraging him with questions about the explosion: Was he a pirate? Was there treasure to be had, and should they ask Papa to turn around so they could look for it? Was it loud? Was he hurt? How far had he swum?

"Enough," Marie said finally. "Let Mr. Prescott tell his story tomorrow if he will, but let him sleep first."

Archie had accepted this invitation gratefully, stretching out on the deck and asleep almost immediately. Before sleep took him, though, he had a moment to marvel at the Daigle family, laughing and singing after more than a thousand miles of hard travel and with two thousand miles more ahead. *I've made it back to the real world*, he thought as he drifted away. *There are no chacmools here.*

That thought was still in his mind as he sat up and blinked at the colors of the day. The youngest Daigle daughter appeared in front of him. "Are you hungry? Mama said you would be."

"Mama was right," Archie said. He smiled at the little girl, even though he could feel blisters on his back splitting open. Peter was going to regret lending him a shirt.

She offered him a biscuit—Martha, he thought her name was. "Mama's cooking dinner," she said.

"Missed breakfast, did I?" Archie took the biscuit, and the girl looked at him oddly, as if she couldn't decide whether to take him seriously or not.

"Two breakfasts," she finally said.

"Two?" Archie said, sputtering biscuit crumbs. But she hadn't heard him; she was already picking her way among the Daigle family's piled belongings toward the stern. "Papa!" she called. "Mr. Archie's waked up!"

Peter poked his head out from under the canvas stretched across the boat's middle portion. "So he has. Good morning, Mr. Prescott. Afternoon, I should say."

Archie stood up and stretched, grunting at the sting of cloth peeling away from blisters. "Anyone who saves my life gets to call me Archie," he said.

"I am Peter, then," Peter said.

"Great. Ah, your daughter—Martha?"

Daigle nodded.

"Martha said . . . Peter, how long was I asleep?"

"Ah. Hm," Peter said. "It's past noon now, so," he counted briefly on his fingers, "forty hours or so."

"Forty hours?" Nearly two days. The realization brought a fearsome aching pressure to bear on Archie's bladder.

"More or less," Peter shrugged. "We thought you had died for a while, but you kept having nightmares."

"Nightmares?" Archie couldn't remember any. "Did I say anything?"

"Just sleep-talking. In any case, it's Thursday. Come, eat; you must be starving."

Archie worked his way methodically through three bowls of wonderful fish stew, a miraculous change from several days of salt pork and whiskey. "Mrs. Daigle," he finally said, "I could eat this all the way around the world."

She laughed and took his bowl to a washbasin filled with river water. "A starving man will say anything. But thank you."

"No," Archie said. "I should thank you. I haven't yet been—properly grateful to you for picking me up. I'll certainly do whatever I can to make good on your hospitality." He felt stilted and formal, but for some reason it was important to get all of that said.

"Nonsense," Marie said, completely disrupting the gravity of the situation. "It wouldn't be hospitality if you had to work for it."

"I suppose he could fish, couldn't he, Marie?" Peter said. "That is, if he's going to eat like that all the way—"

"Peter, please." Marie glared at him while trying to suppress a smile.

"Or, if he can't *fish*," Peter said, his voice rising, "perhaps he could teach me to *read*, because everyone on this boat now *knows* that Peter Daigle won't listen to a woman." Marie was laughing now, and Peter himself was having trouble keeping a straight face. He stopped in mid-gesticulation. "Where is it you're going, anyway?"

"Only to Louisville," Archie said.

"Well, you'll have all the fish stew you can choke down for the next six days, then."

"Six days," Archie repeated. That put their arrival on the twenty-ninth, the first of the *nemontemi*, the unlucky days. If the chacmool had to be inactive on those days, then it would already be at the cave by then—and would already have ensconced Jane, God knew where. In another six days, Archie's only hope would be to intercept them at the cave itself.

Seeing the look on Archie's face, Peter shrugged apologetically. "We can't travel at night," he said. "And the river only flows so fast. But we could drop you in Maysville, or Cincinnati if you need to hurry . . ." he shrugged again.

"No," Archie said quickly, although Peter's offer made perfect sense. A steamer could carry him from Maysville to Louisville in two days, if he remembered the schedule correctly. But his experience aboard *Maudie* was too fresh in his mind; traveling by keelboat with a migrating family of French-Canadians seemed so much safer, so much more sane.

Deeper fears were at work as well, Archie had to admit. Keelboats could hit snags and sink as easily as steamers could explode. Sitting there with Peter Daigle, surrounded by the happy chaos of his family, Archie realized that despite his single-minded obsession with rescuing Jane from her abductors, the prospect of their reunion terrified him. What would he say to her, this eleven-year-old girl whom he hadn't given a kind word since she was a toddler? Would he be able to face her if she was angry?

Archie watched the three Daigle girls—son Ramon, at two-and-a-half, was too young to work yet, and clung to his mother—go about minor chores, drying dishes or sweeping windblown leaves from the deck. Even in the middle of a months-long journey to an uncertain destination, they had created a home on an Ohio River keelboat. There is something I have to learn from this, Archie thought. Something a father should know.

Thinking back to Jane's infancy, Archie realized that the Prescott household—when there had been one—had never been so calmly cheerful. He had loved Helen as much as he thought it was possible for a man to love a woman, but he had used her death as an excuse to dive headfirst into a morass of self-pity from which he was

only now beginning to emerge. Now he was being offered
an opportunity to redeem himself, and all he could think
was *Do I deserve this? Do I deserve a daughter who has
the faith to pursue me through seven years of abandonment and rejection?*

If I'm doing this just to prove that I'm not the bastard
I thought I was, Archie thought, then I'd just as well not
do it. Good acts for bad reasons aren't any better than bad
ones for good.

"No," he said again suddenly, remembering that he was
in a conversation. "You've been too generous." He managed a weak smile. "I couldn't reject your hospitality at
this point, could I?"

Royce was damned glad that the chacmool hadn't decided
to come along with him. After what it had done to Charlie,
he wasn't sure if he could stand to be near it, wondering
when it would get ideas about changing him into some
kind of baby vampire too. He could still hear the thing
that had been Charlie wailing in its awful old infant voice,
for all the world like a hungry babe. And for the chacmool
to blame it all on him, because Prescott hadn't died when
he was supposed to . . .

God, what sort of mad fairy tale could give rise to
something like that?

He didn't want to know, really. In fact, Royce was
wishing that he knew a great deal less about Riley Steen's
plans, and the chacmool, and wherever it had come from.
And he wanted to know nothing at all about the girl.

He'd had to untie her after being left alone to drive old
Farmer John's wagon. She couldn't lie under the straw in
the back all day, even if she would have, which he
doubted; either she would roll herself to the slats and hop
over them while he wasn't looking, or she'd have some
sort of reaction to all the dust and keel over dead. So he'd
untied her and warned that if she made any trouble, he'd
cut out her tongue and tell anyone who asked that she was

mad. "People are always willing to believe that about little girls, you know," he'd said, "especially with the way you look." She'd nodded and touched one of the thick scabs on her scalp, and Royce had felt a bit low. It wasn't right to hurt a little girl's feelings.

So now she rode next to him on the driver's bench, her feet hobbled by a short length of rope and the knots covered by a blanket that had until recently cushioned the bench for Charlie's delicate bum. Even when I get the driver's seat, Royce thought sourly, my ass still suffers.

Having the girl with him gave him a twenty-four-hour case of the shakes, even though they'd passed through several small villages and she hadn't given a peep. They were making fairly good time, but Royce hadn't really slept since sometime before the train wreck, and he was starting to hear things. Now they were off in the wilderness again, he hadn't any idea where, and every time she had to pee he was afraid she'd go hopping off like a rabbit into the deep woods, and then how would he find her?

I'm a city b'hoy, he thought. Forests and fields aren't for me. He felt out of place in the country. Everything from his soap-locks to the red piping on his pants marked him as an Easterner. Worse, an Irish Easterner. In New York, times could be rough, but an Irishman could always find kin; out here, though, some Nativist sons of bitches could ride up and hang him at any moment. He'd heard stories.

At least then he wouldn't have to think about what would happen to the girl, though. Royce had worked for Riley Steen since he was a boy, but he hadn't killed anyone until he was sixteen, three years ago. He'd been frightened half to death when he volunteered for the job, and nearly pissed himself when he'd actually carried it out, but with time he'd grown fond of his reputation. Killing was probably wrong, he thought, but everyone he'd ever slipped a blade into had known the rules of the game. Even Archie Prescott. Hadn't Royce warned him to stay clear of Tammany business and then found him smack in the middle of the chaos at the museum?

The girl, though, Prescott's daughter, was different. She hadn't crossed a Tammany brave or interfered with Steen's day-to-day operations. She was, so far as Royce could tell, just a little girlie who had the misfortune to be born on a singularly unlucky day. A girl who reminded him uncomfortably of himself seven or eight years before: all toughness and snap on the outside, but on the inside . . . poor creature. Royce had a bit of a chill at the thought. What had seven years done to him?

Well, he thought. I know the rules of the game too, and I've long since gotten in too deep to stop playing now. Royce McDougall still had a reputation to uphold as a man who finished the business that he started. This job he would get over with as soon as possible, handing the girl off in Louisville and getting shut of the whole sordid mess.

That is, as soon as he'd dealt with the elder Prescott. The only thing keeping Royce in the driving seat of the damned wagon, bouncing down nameless ruts until his spine felt like it was made of broken glass, was unfinished business with Prescott. He had known the rules of the game, if not that night at the Brewery then certainly by the time he'd lit out after the chacmool. Royce was man enough to admit his mistakes, and leaving Prescott still breathing in the Brewery had been a big one. Too many insane things had happened that night, and he'd let his fear get the better of him when Prescott's ear had blazed up like a Roman candle between Charlie's teeth. Next time there would be no mistake. Royce would take care of Archie Prescott, like he should have a long time ago, and be on the first boat back to New York. Reputation was all a man had sometimes.

Memories of that night still made him uneasy. Not that he was squeamish when it came to violence, but from first to last Steen hadn't seemed in control of the situation. Royce was beginning to wonder just how much of the chacmool's escape was due to Prescott's meddling and how much could be laid at the feet of Steen's poor planning. He'd thought the cordon of cornstalks was a ridiculous idea from the beginning, and said so, but Steen had insisted that interfering with the chacmool while it was still dormant would queer the whole enterprise. That had seemed reasonable enough at the time—reasonable, at least, as anything else Steen ever cooked up—but now, with the advantage of three months' time to look back on it, Royce doubted that Steen had really known what he was doing. He'd spent enough time with his nose in old books, but books didn't tell the whole story. And even with all his learning, Steen had admitted to Royce later that they'd all nearly been killed by the Old God, whatever that was.

Yes sir, it was clear that Riley Steen had lost whatever control he might once have had over the situation. Some other force was opposing him, or the chacmool, it didn't matter which. And Steen, although he knew his enemy's name, didn't seem able to anticipate it or fight back.

Might be time to look into a different line of work, Royce mused. Steen might not live through his next encounter with the Old God. Hell, he might not survive his next meeting with the chacmool, as birdy as it was acting. Royce had no desire to go down with Steen, but he also didn't want to cut himself off in case the whole mad scheme actually worked. If that happened, the difference between living well and not living at all might be how well Royce could feign loyalty.

If the new world, or Sixth Sun or whatever, didn't happen, then Royce would be needing leverage. Bad things would be coming from the Pathfinders, and a man with the Tammany mark on him would be dodging the executioner's blade for a long time.

Leverage, at least, he thought he had. If something bad happened to Steen, Royce intended to take the girl and run. Probably he would go north, into Canada. Then when the Pathfinders tracked him down, he could point to saving the girl as evidence that his heart had never been in the whole thing from the beginning.

"Pipe up there, damsel," he said to the girl. "The accommodations still to your satisfaction?"

She didn't answer, just sat slumped at the other end of the bench staring straight ahead.

"Look, lass, it's not so bad," Royce said, and realized as he did that for the first time in his American life he was feeling guilty. "Steen'll take care of you."

She glared at him, then looked back out over the road.

"You've been hungry, right? So have I. You've been cold; me, too. I've got no family, and your old man hasn't been a prince to you." Another glare. "I understand a bit more than you think," Royce went on. "For an Irishman I'm not stupid. We find ways to get along, lass. We do what we can. Steen'll keep you warm, he'll feed you. He needs you. Better than begging pennies and stuffing newspaper in your shoes, isn't it?"

Now Jane sat rock-still, her fierce gaze directed over the just-budding forests.

"Ah, well," Royce said. For such a young girl, he thought, she's a sharp one. Doesn't want me talking to her, doesn't want me to get close. Her face and hands were beginning to practically bloom with tiny scabs, each scarcely larger than a fly, but she didn't scratch at them nearly as much as Royce thought he would have. Yes, she was a tough one. He could see her thinking, probably conjuring escape plans from the spring air.

A girl after his own heart, really. Terrible, it was, what was going to happen to her.

It didn't seem fair to Jane that traveling across the country for the second time, they had taken the same road. *I've been to Ohio before,* she thought. *I want to see something different.* But then, nothing else was different. She was still a captive, and the Dead Rabbit driving the wagon had used the same threat on her that Riley Steen had when she was a little girl, and she would have bet everything she had that they would leave the wagon in Aberdeen, across the river from Maysville, and take a boat the rest of the way. Why shouldn't they travel the same road?

She wondered if anyone would believe the Rabbit if he told them that she was mad. Probably; lots of her friends in New York had been locked up in reformatories because people said they were mad. She scratched her scalp, drawing a glance from the Rabbit. Royce was his name. Probably waiting for me to attack him, she thought, scratch out his eyes or something and run away with my feet still bound. That's why he was talking to her, trying to keep her calm. But she hadn't tried that with Steen, and she wouldn't now. It was best just to play passive and wait for the right chance. Jane's scalp still itched, and she scratched again, feeling the fine new hairs growing through the fading scar tissue. If only her skin wasn't so *tender*. Every time she touched herself it seemed like another scab appeared.

The Indian had done this to her, the same black Indian who had done something horrible to the other Rabbit, the smelly dwarf. Jane didn't understand how he could be so cruel when he'd done such a wonderful thing for her. She was still covered in scabs, but the pain from them was good. Scabs healed, while scars just stayed ugly forever. Scabs meant that she was growing new skin again, that someday she wouldn't draw shocked glances from people in the street. She was starting to feel different, not wanting to disappear every time someone looked at her.

Royce and the other Rabbit, Charlie, had called the Indian *chacmool*, but she didn't think that was his name. She wondered if he had a name, and why nobody knew it. Maybe he would tell her, the next time they saw each other. Which would be soon—she visualized Kentucky on her maps, like a thumb extended east from the Mississippi with Louisville at the crook of the big knuckle. That's where she was going, and the chacmool wanted her to do something there. Something important. If he could make her scars go away, Jane thought, she would do anything for him, because with her scars gone, Da would recognize her again.

Thinking of Da, she bit her lip to stop its trembling and turned away from Royce, looking out into the forest. The trees were still naked, but fresh buds were beginning to appear on the sprawling bushes along the roadside. Creeping vines showed bright green against the still-sleeping trees, reminding her of the brake of Da's train, how it had suddenly sprouted and split apart, derailing the car and tipping it into the ditch. The Indian had done that, too, she was sure, but why? Why would it be so kind to her and at the same time wreck Da's train?

She watched as the forest gave way to open fields stubbled with last fall's shorn stalks of corn, spotted here and there by crows pecking at the muddy soil. She didn't know what to think. Da could have been hurt in the wreck, or even killed, and then . . .

Again she bit her lip, harder this time, and fought back tears. She didn't want to cry in front of Royce; she would be passive if she had to, but not weak. Da was alive. He had to be. Because if he wasn't, he would never see her after her scars had faded away.

"Don't cry, lass," Royce said. She looked at him angrily and he reached out to give her shoulder an awkward pat. "Can't bear to see a young girl cry. Would you like to stop for a bit, have a bite to eat? Chacmool'd have my balls, as dear old Charlie used to say—excuse the language—but it's three days off at least, and I know I could use a minute to stretch my legs."

He reined in the swaybacked mule pulling the wagon and hopped to the ground, grunting as he bent to touch his toes. "All this traveling makes me feel older than London Bridge," he grumbled. "Nice day like this, we ought to take a minute to enjoy it."

Jane got down from the wagon too, stepping carefully because of the short length of rope binding her ankles. She was happy to be standing still, even for a moment, but mightily confused as well. Two days before, Royce had threatened to cut out her tongue, and now he was worried when she shed a tear. Perhaps he wasn't the monster she'd thought him to be.

Why was everything so tangled? She couldn't even count on bad men to be bad. It was frightening because if bad men weren't always bad, then good men weren't always good. Her mind raced ahead with that thought before she could stop it, saying—

No. Da would come. He *was* alive, and he *would* come and rescue her.

He had to.

Toxcatl, 8-Skull—March 27, 1843

❖

The locks at the Falls of the Ohio had just been opened two weeks before, and Louisville's waterfront had taken on the appearance of a motley marina. Vessels were lined up four deep, sitting idle in a cold rain while their captains argued with port authorities over tolls and bills of lading. On shore, rivermen fresh from New Orleans, Pittsburgh, and St. Louis prowled gambling halls and grogshops, shouldering past farmers come down from the hills to sell pork, tobacco, and whiskey. The entire scene was given an otherworldly aspect by the rain and the fog of smoke billowing from the ragged flotilla; Louisville's streetlamps diffused into a sickly, mummified luminescence that somehow cast no real light.

Riley Steen maneuvered his wagon past a throng of waistcoated Southern gentlemen gathered for a slave auction. Dusk was falling, and with it the temperature. He'd been thoroughly soaked by the rain and hadn't slept in days, but a steady diet of Traphagen's Balsamic Extract, taken from the box of nostrums in the back of the wagon, had set his brain singing and he didn't mind the wet chill. Traphagen's was a marvelous brew for fending off drowsiness, but Steen hadn't realized its salutary effects on the temperament. He couldn't help grinning as he wove through traffic until he found Third Street and turned south, away from the river and toward a house he owned on Broadway. Harman Blennerhassett had quit-claimed the property to Steen thirty-five years before, when he'd fled in disgrace to the Louisiana bayous. Steen had been there perhaps a dozen times since then, usually to transact some sort of business that would be compromised by public scrutiny.

That wasn't something he would have to worry about if the reenactment of Nanahuatzin's sacrifice worked. Every failed scheme of the last four decades would be forgotten, or perhaps remembered tolerantly as lessons learned toward the greater goal. No longer would Riley Steen be an itinerant doctor, dentist, purveyor of elixirs and small-town puppeteer; after April the third, he'd have every man, woman and child from Canada to the Isthmus of Panama for a puppet. Alexander had never had such power, nor Genghis Khan nor Motecuhzoma himself. With the chacmool as his high priest, Riley Steen would be absolute ruler of one-quarter of the world.

And that was just the beginning. Steen's Traphagen-enhanced good humor threatened to start him actually snickering as he halted the wagon in front of his house. A light burned in the third-floor bedroom window, his caretaker's signal that guests awaited within. Good. Mr. McDougall should have arrived, and if he had the girl with him, the chacmool certainly wouldn't be long in joining the party. Steen had given up trying to monitor its day-to-day movements, trusting instead that its nature would impel it to behave as he predicted. As far as the girl was concerned, he had confidence in Lupita's assessment of the situation. In all likelihood she had followed her father and been captured by Royce exactly as planned.

It would have been much easier simply to travel together, Steen thought. But the *huehueteotl* had been especially watchful these past few weeks, its eye like a weight at the base of Steen's skull. His grin slipped a bit as he looked up into the rain, wishing for clear skies so he could read the signs. The moon would be rising soon.

Steen searched through a ring of keys and let himself in. He lit a lamp on the front table and closed the door on the early-evening din of West Broadway, then stood dripping on the hall carpet until his caretaker Simon appeared from the rear of the house.

"I'll take care of the horses, Mr. Steen," Simon said, taking Steen's coat into the parlor to dry by the fire. "Mr. McDougall and an oddly dressed Negro are waiting for you in the upstairs library."

"Thank you, Simon, but I may be leaving quickly. Best to leave the horses."

A flush of pride nearly set Steen to singing out loud. Everything had fallen perfectly into place. He had successfully controlled all of the difficulties that had arisen, all of the intrusions and irrationalities that would have derailed a man of lesser scope than he. Like a chess master, he had weathered his enemies' forays while consolidating his own attack, had inured himself to the maddening pranks of the *Tochtli*, and all the while he had arranged his own pieces for the mating assault. *Shah mat*, he thought, the king is dead. And that goes for you, President Tyler, and for General Santa Ana as well.

But it wouldn't do to be overconfident just yet. Steen hadn't slept in several days, which was why he'd resorted to Traphagen's in the first place, and he knew that it would take delicate diplomacy to finish what he'd started. He mustn't let the Balsamic Extract run away with his senses. The chacmool had successfully negotiated the problems it had faced after being reawakened, weak and in a strange society. No doubt it felt capable of handling everything itself. But it had never actually governed, never led the people of a state through the day-to-day rigors of taxes and property disputes. It had served admirably in its capacity as divine intermediary, but secular matters were best left to secular people. The Mexican *tlatoani*, philosopher-kings, and *cihuacoatl*, the snakewomen named for the goddess of childbirth, had filled that role in previous centuries. *Render unto Caesar,* Steen thought; Christ had been right on target. Only in the Sixth Sun, the prophets would say render unto Steen.

He rehearsed this argument as he walked up the stairs,

probing it for weaknesses. Everything, he thought again, was falling perfectly into place. He would defeat fatigue just as he had every other opponent.

"Good evening, gentlemen," Steen said upon entering the library. "And you as well, of course, young lady." Mr. McDougall slouched in a chair to his left, warily eyeing the chacmool, which sat behind the desk, near the library's large windows. The girl was curled up on an overstuffed divan, wearing the chacmool's quetzal-feather cloak. Steen noted this with some surprise, and was even more disconcerted to see that the girl's scars were all but gone, grown over by blotchy black scabs. New hair had also grown in over the dead tissue that had covered much of her cranium.

Nanahuatzin, of course—the Scabby One. This was no doubt the chacmool's handiwork. Steen had always looked on the girl's disfigurement as pure evidence of her destiny (and his), but this rejuvenation put the matter beyond all doubt. She was being healed, made whole in order to meet the god who would take her, and in the process she was being fit literally into the role that she had previously filled only through the strange analogy of reincarnation. No longer could he see her as a little girl born under an auspicious sign. She was becoming divine before his very eyes.

"Good you're finally here, Steen," Royce said. He stood and put on his cap. "Means I can leave."

Surprised, Steen stepped back to block the doorway. "One moment, Mr. McDougall. Your part in this isn't quite over."

"Oh, I believe it is. I did what you asked—got the girl and came all the way to bloody Louisville with her. But you and I are finished here. I won't be party to murdering little girls."

Steen shot a nervous glance at the girl, but she looked to be in some sort of stupor. "A conscience, my Rabbit friend?" he said, allowing a note of gleeful sarcasm to color the question.

"Call it what you like. I've always finished my business for you, and I have this time as well." A strange haunted expression carved unfamiliar lines around Royce's eyes and mouth. "But this is where it ends. I might be a killer, Steen, but Christ, she's eleven years old."

"Is her life worth more than a world?" Steen asked jovially. He was enjoying this strange sight; imagine Royce McDougall conflicted by a guilty conscience!

Royce cracked a weary smile, but the haunted expression didn't leave his face. "That's a question *he* would ask," he said, thrusting a finger in the chacmool's direction. "Pardon me, *it*. I don't know if she's worth more than a world. But this I'll tell you: any world built on the blood and bones of little girls is a world I don't want to live in. Now stand aside. I've one more bit of business to finish up, and then I'm out of this madness forever." He stood directly in front of Steen, a tic working at the corner of his mouth and the fingers of his left hand twitching as if palsied.

Steen considered—would McDougall actually assault him?—and then stood aside with a nod and a smile. Best not to take chances with the Rabbit's adolescent bravado, not when everything was so nearly complete.

"By all means, Mr. McDougall. I wish you all the best in future endeavors, provided those endeavors do not require your presence in New York." Steen gestured at the door. "I believe Simon will have your coat."

McDougall brushed past him without another word. A moment later, the front door opened and shut. Strong will for one so young, Steen thought. With luck he would survive to learn discretion.

But never mind; to events at hand.

"So." Steen shut the library door. "Always unfortunate how persons of limited scope interfere with history."

He regarded the chacmool, seeing it hale and hearty for the first time. Extraordinary being—unless one knew what to look for, it would automatically be taken for a normal Negro, just on the threshold of his middle years. Steen was reminded of a story Aaron Burr had told him, of a mysterious black man who appeared periodically to terrorize Mexican tribesmen. They had called it *nahualli*, sorcerer. And the chacmool did bear a striking resemblance to a strange monolith Blennerhassett had brought from the Mexican jungles and kept in his study: strong squarish features dominated by a heavy brow, with just a hint of epicanthic fold about the eyes. Unfortunately, when Burr's plans had fallen apart Blennerhassett had destroyed the monolith in a fit of panic. Steen had barely arrived in time to save the mirror and a few other relics.

He realized he'd lost his train of thought. Fatigue and the Balsamic Extract were combining to make his mind wander. "Introductions are in order," he said, clearing his throat. "I am—"

"Wide Hat," the chacmool finished for him. "You brought me to the city."

"Ah, correct." Steen was slightly put off by its use of the name Lupita had given him, and also by the fact that it had somehow learned English. Its voice, too, had a way of lingering in the mind, disrupting his thoughts. "And you are—?"

"The last name I bore was Nezahualpilli, but it was not mine. Names are of little value here."

"Very well." Nezahualpilli? One of Motecuhzoma's advisers had borne that name and been accused of sorcery. Aztec legend had it that he had foretold the coming of Cortés, then vanished, by some accounts hiding in a cave to avoid the Spaniards' depredations. Steen had never connected the tale with the chacmool, but perhaps he should have. Nezahualpilli was by all accounts considered an extremely skillful politician. Perhaps I've been a bit naive, Steen thought, supposing that a being could live nearly two thousand years without acquiring some insight into human nature.

Nervous, he started to sit in the chair McDougall had recently vacated, but thought better of it. Instead he went through the ritual of replacing his boutonniere, folding the wilted bloom into a handkerchief and dropping it into a wastebasket by the desk. The methodical action calmed him, as it always did; he straightened his tie and took a last moment to prepare his speech.

The chacmool, though, spoke before he could begin. "What are you, Steen?"

Taken aback by the question, Steen paused for several seconds before answering. "I am a man of scope," he said finally. "A man who makes history happen."

The chacmool smiled. "Anyone can insert themselves into history. It records petty murderers as well as prophets."

Was an intellectual discussion what it wanted? Steen supposed it might be; after all, the chacmool hadn't spoken to another human in more than three hundred years. Then again, it wasn't exactly human, was it, and who knew what gods spoke of?

"Granted," he said. "But murders are merely recorded, and commented on. Prophets—visionaries—dictate what will be written."

"Perhaps. How many visionaries, though, have been passed over and forgotten?"

"Some, to be sure. But greatness persists. Ignorance and mediocrity are obstacles to be overcome."

"Ah. And will you persist?"

Steen began to feel as if he were taking part in a Socratic dialogue, in the role of Crito or another of Socrates' willing dupes. *I have to seize the initiative,* he thought; *show it that I am not to be underestimated.*

"I will," he said. "What we are about to do will make the exploits of Caesar look like schoolyard bullying. To reawaken a god, a real living god born from the blood of its people, a being of the world that at the same time transcends it. That has never been done. No one has even understood that it was possible. And we will do it."

The chacmool murmured under its breath and flicked its fingers at the rain outside the window. "Before there were men," it said, "before I was, was Tlaloc. He Who

Makes Things Grow needs no worshipers to live. Men need *him*. He is no infant, to be awakened from a nap by the nipple of your belief."

Anger rose in its whispery voice as it continued. "You think to have power because you feed *yolteotl* to the gods. Power flows to those who believe, Wide Hat, and men, even if they forget for a thousand years, must finally remember that Tlaloc does not live in the smoke from sacrificial fires. He is the wood that burns. He is the earth, he is the water. To know him is to feel the power of earth and water, to cry out for lightning with your feet in the river. Other men have come before you, men who saw power in others' fear of the gods. Tlaloc watches such men, and Tlaloc acts."

"Aye, Tlaloc acts," Steen said hotly. This interrogation was beginning to make him angry. "He was acting when I spent thirty-five years of my life tracking your moldering body to a stinking hole in the ground. He was acting when you reawakened exactly when I'd predicted. He was acting when I chose that girl out of the thousands of girls born the same day. And he was for damned certain acting when we arrived here—again, exactly as I'd planned— with time yet to set fire to the Sixth Sun."

Steen found himself shaking, both with anger and with frustration at losing control of his demeanor. "Look at her!" he snapped, pointing at the girl. "In another week she'll have not a mark left on her. Was that an accident?"

The girl made as if to touch her face when Steen pointed in her direction, but she halted the gesture and clasped her hands in her lap. The chacmool smiled at her self-consciousness.

"A little longer, Nanahuatzin," it said fondly. "Soon, precious jade. Soon you will be whole again, and fit to finish your journey."

Its gaze lingered on her for another moment, then returned to Steen. "As much as you have said is true. But you are like the man who boasts of his fine clothes while his children shiver naked; your words are *pollocotli*, chaff thrown up to hide the harvest of your deeds. It was you who caused all of the obstacles you take such pride in having surmounted. It was you who allowed Prescott to capture a token from my robe and you who let him live long enough to be marked by the Old One's Eye. That mark drew him to Tamanend, and now Prescott wears the Old One's protection like a cloak. And another one, one whom I cannot see, aids him. Why? Out of a desire for revenge on you. Tell me now how majestic, how noble have been your efforts."

The open scorn in the chacmool's tone left Steen completely at a loss. "How many others have tried to do this? How many failed? All of them. You *need* me," he spluttered. "What do you know about government beyond the temple and the fire? What do you know about money? Nothing. You need me to keep the blood flowing on your precious altars. People aren't going to just line up to have their bloody hearts ripped out."

"Again, half-truths," the chacmool said with a dismissive wave. "Someone must govern, yes. But it need not be you."

"Need not, hell. You *owe* me." Too bold, Steen realized as the words spilled from his mouth, but he was beyond caring. To have this, this glorified *medicine man* treat him like a goddamned *servant!* "Yes, Prescott is causing problems and yes, the girl escaped. But I marked her for you. Whatever else has gone wrong, she's still here. And I did that. Without her, you'd have had to crawl back into your hole for another five centuries."

The chacmool nodded as if to placate him. "And for that you will be rewarded. But do not overreach yourself, Wide Hat. Do not ignore the counsel of those you should heed."

Overreach himself? The last fragile strand of Riley Steen's self-control snapped. A man of his scope, a man who saw and understood the sweeping arc of history, didn't have to stand for condescension from a creaking artifact given a semblance of life by the blood of street

children and drunken sailors. "The girl is mine," he
growled. "I offered her as a gift to you, and you treat me
like a dog. Fine. You can shrivel in a hole until the sun
burns down to a bloody cinder, and I'll laugh at you from
my grave." He strode toward the girl.

The chacmool rose easily from its chair and blocked
his path. "Finally you speak an entire truth," it said softly.
"The dead do laugh, and the grave is all about us, although most men cannot see it. Now you will. Now you
will see."

With that, it seized Riley Steen by the skull and gouged
his eyes from his head.

Steen's knees buckled and he folded to the study carpet,
screaming into his hands. Somewhere he'd read that truly
terrible injuries didn't hurt right away, that the shock was
too much for the body to register, but that didn't seem to
be true. This pain left him helpless and howling like a
circumcised babe. It was like an earthquake; it absorbed
everything else; it was . . .

Blinding, one might even say.

Why, there's humor in that, Steen thought, and his
scream modulated into a long, hearty laugh. The sort of
laugh he hadn't enjoyed in years, really; he'd been so
consumed with the whole chacmool business. He laughed
until his stomach ached and he could feel tears pooling in
the sockets recently vacated by his eyeballs. When he
paused long enough to draw a long wheezing breath, another sound distracted him.

There was laughter all around him. Someone else must
have gotten the joke. But wait, he hadn't spoken, had he,
and it would be just too riotously improbable for all of
those other voices to be laughing simultaneously at different jokes.

What were they laughing at?

"Remove your hands and see," the chacmool said.

Steen did the first and was astounded to discover that
he could do the second. The light was odd—the sun
seemed to be shining from somewhere in the wall behind

the chacmool's head. Or perhaps it was the chacmool's head itself that shone—yes, light spilled from its mouth in curdled lumps as it said, "Go now, Wide Hat. Go now, and laugh at what you see."

Jane heard the door click shut behind Steen, and she heard him chuckling to himself as he went down the stairs, but she couldn't take her eyes off the splatters of gore on the Oriental rug. Would they crawl around, like her blood had that night under the stairs? She imagined Steen's eyes itching as blood crawled back up his face into the empty sockets. What would his eyes be like after the healing? Not the same, she was sure. The same thing had happened to her, hadn't it, and afterward she had begun to heal on the outside. But inside, something was different—she wasn't the same as she had been before.

A short scream carried up the stairs, just before the front door slammed shut and someone, it must have been the old man Simon, began rushing around downstairs. *Poor old man,* Jane thought. Steen must have been scary, with stuff from his eyes dribbling into his laughing mouth. She stroked the lovely green feathers of the cloak the chacmool had given her.

She herself hadn't been afraid in ages, it seemed. That had been one of the first things to leave her. A small twinge here and there, when she felt that the chacmool would kill her or when Royce made his nervous threats, but even then the feeling was more a realization that she was in a dangerous situation than an actual fear that something would happen to her.

I'm charmed, she thought. *The chacmool touched me, and it charmed me.*

It had said she would soon be ready to play her role, and she was anxious to find out what that role would be. She was important somehow, and knowing that made her less afraid, too. Riley Steen might have had his eyes thumbed out, but he'd deserved it for all the things he'd done. Jane didn't deserve anything bad, and the chacmool would protect her. Hadn't it already?

After sleeping under staircases and once stealing bits of soggy bread from surprised gulls at Battery Park, it was an odd feeling to be important. Perhaps Da would see something different about her when she arrived. The chacmool had told Steen that Da was alive, and coming.

He must be terribly worried, she thought distantly, wishing he was there in the room so she could soothe him, show him everything was all right. See, Da, she would say. See how I'm healing. See how I'm not afraid.

Only she was, just the tiniest bit. Steen was a cruel man, and he had been cruel to her, but it was still a horrible thing the chacmool had done to him. She wondered again how it could be so vicious to others and so kind to her. Perhaps it was only cruel to men who threatened her, or abused her in some way.

In that case, she would have to make sure and tell it not to hurt Da; it had tried once already, but that was only because it didn't know she didn't want it to. The green feathers under her chin returned her caresses, and she started to lose track of her thoughts, but not before she remembered Royce saying *The blood and bones of little girls.*

What had that meant? Surely he couldn't have meant her, not the way the chacmool was protecting her—as a matter of fact, Royce probably should have been grateful that the chacmool hadn't treated him as it had treated Riley Steen. He had, after all, kicked her and threatened to cut out her tongue. No, she wasn't in any danger. She was safer here than she had been since . . . well, since she could remember. Still, she felt a tremor of unease hearing Royce's words again in her head.

The splatters on the carpet didn't move. The chacmool had been looking at them, too, Jane saw, studying them closely with its cat-eyed gaze. Now it turned and stepped to the window, silently looking out into the rainy night.

"It is now time," the chacmool said, its back still to her.

"You will make two journeys, Nanahuatzin, one with your body and the other in your spirit. Where one ends, the next begins."

"What does that name mean, Nanahuatzin?"

"It means the Scabby One," the chacmool replied. "But when your body has completed its journey, your skin will be whole again and your spirit will fly with the sun."

Not more traveling, Jane thought. *I'm already so tired.* "I've already gone on a journey," she said. "What am I supposed to do?"

"The first journey is not yet over, little jade. We must prepare together if we are to finish it correctly."

The chacmool came to her and ran its long fingers through the green feathers of her cloak. "For many years have I worn these *quetzal* feathers, little Nanahuatzin. Now you must never take them off. You must wear them until your journey ends."

"When will that be?" Jane asked. And when will Da be here, she wanted to add, but the feel of the feathers distracted her. They moved like leaves in a breeze, making a quiet sound like nothing she'd ever heard before. What a wonderful thing this cloak was, and the chacmool had given it to her.

Da had never given her a gift, she thought. She was ashamed of thinking it, but there it was. It was true.

Out of the corner of her eye, Jane saw the chacmool nodding, and the feathers nodded with it. Yes, what had Da given her? Scorn and pity, that's what. She didn't even know if he was coming for her, or just chasing after Steen and the chacmool. He probably wouldn't even recognize her if he did see her, Jane thought bitterly. She wasn't a mutilated waif any more. She was nearly healed, nearly whole, and wrapped in this wonderful cloak she felt like a queen.

The sun's heart
throbs in the cup
His flesh
is the darkness of flowers

Who would not cry for
such flowers, oh
giver of life? who
would not rest in your hands
that hold death?
Opening buds & corollas
an endless thirst in the sun

—"A Song of Chalco"

This is the city of dangers
lost in the dust

The flowering war
will not end
We endure here, trapped
on the banks
of this river
The jaguars' flowers
show their corollas

—"A Song for the Eagles & Jaguars"

Book V

First Nemontemi, 10–Rabbit—March 29, 1843

❖

Predawn breezes were awakening in the trees as Stephen listened to the breath of the cave. He hadn't slept at all. Charlotte had finally banished him to the front porch, where his tossing and turning wouldn't keep her awake too. When he'd seen the sky begin to lighten over the treetops, he'd knocked out his pipe and walked down to the cave entrance, still tense and fidgety with the knowledge that something important would be happening today. The voice had been chattering constantly for nearly three days now, exhorting him to be ready when the time came, as soon it must. Sleep had been far away during that time, making Stephen irritable both from fatigue and from a frustrated desire to see Tlalocan once again. Even when he'd managed to drift off for an hour, he wasn't able to dream, and he was beginning to think that he wouldn't find that dream again unless it was in the cave. Why that should be true, he didn't know, but he'd been afraid to go near the Mummy Room for more than a week, now, lest . . .

Lest what? Stephen didn't know, and the more he thought about the voice in the cave and the chacmool and his own role in whatever was supposed to happen, the less he understood. The voice had made promises, had threatened him, had played on his love for the cave while making him afraid to enter it. *You will be a man*, the voice promised—but what was a man? A man had a family, owned property, a man controlled his destiny. The voice promised him all of that. But at the same time, it played him like a puppet on a string, and where was his control over that?

Again Stephen wondered what it wasn't telling him. *I would give anything—anything—to be a free man,* he thought, *but where is the freedom in being ordered around like . . . well, like a slave?*

All of those questions would be answered soon, he resolved, listening to the cave breathe and half expecting the voice to return at any moment. But when he did hear a voice, it was spoken aloud, from just behind his right shoulder.

"Stephen. There is little time."

He turned and saw the chacmool standing beside him, looking nervously at the brightening sky. It held the hand of a young white girl, her face blotched with scabs like she was weathering a pox, wearing a long black coat with a fringe of green feathers peeking out between tightly buttoned lapels. She looked like she might fall asleep standing there, but Stephen saw no trace of fear on her weary face. This was almost stranger than anything else he'd seen up to this point: how had the chacmool, to all appearances a black man dressed in simple working clothes, managed to travel any distance with a white girl? Stephen had seen men burned alive for less.

His curiosity got the better of him, and he was about to ask that very question, but the chacmool spoke first. "She must sleep, and we have much to discuss. Quickly."

A short path forked away from the main cave trail, skirting the edge of a shallow ravine and terminating at the entrance to Dixon Cave. Like Mammoth Cave, Dixon had been mined for saltpeter during the War of 1812, and several falling-down sheds still remained around the entrance. Dixon was a dead cave, just a few yards of unremarkable passage, and since mining operations had stopped, it had been largely ignored.

Stephen led the chacmool and the girl into an old equipment shed set back from the trail. "Sleep now, little Nanahuatzin," the chacmool said, touching her tenderly on the forehead. The girl lay down on the bare dirt floor and fell instantly asleep.

"You must see to her there," the chacmool said to Stephen, after they had shut the door behind them. "Bring her food, blankets. For the next five days, anything she wants."

"Who is she?" Stephen asked. He knew he'd long since stepped outside formal rules of conduct, but it still made him edgy to be involved in the kidnapping of a white girl.

Although if she was being kidnapped, she was mighty calm about it.

"First, into the cave," the chacmool said, again casting a wary glance at the sky. To the east, bands of yellow and pink were spreading higher. "This day, it is unlucky to speak in sight of the sun."

They ducked through Houchins Narrows as the first rays of real sunlight began to sparkle on dewy leaves outside. Stephen moved by feel along the trail into the Rotunda but stopped when the chacmool moved to the right ahead of him, toward Audobon Avenue instead of the Main Cave. He found a stack of hollowed-out poplar trunks and located a lamp he'd set behind them some months before.

"I don't travel without light," he said, striking a match. "Not everybody can see in the dark, you know."

"Darkness only frightens if you rely on your eyes," the chacmool replied, slowing its pace but not stopping.

"Oh, I see," Stephen said sarcastically. He was fast losing patience with cryptic comments. "Well, I don't need eyes to know that if you're going where I think you're going, that's the wrong way."

The chacmool stopped and looked back at him, impatience clear on its face even in the weak lamplight. "I came to this place when your ancestors still hunted monkeys in Africa," it said. "Follow."

Stephen didn't care much for its tone of voice, and he nearly said so. But again his curiosity got the better of him; he swallowed his pride and followed.

They turned off Audobon Avenue, winding their way down a short passage Stephen called Little Bat Avenue. Near the end of Little Bat was Crevice Pit, a deep crack in the floor that Stephen had never more than looked into. At the end of Little Bat, he knew, was a tremendous domed pit, but there was no way down. Unless the chacmool knew one that he hadn't been able to find? Stephen's pulse quickened a bit at the thought, although he was annoyed that he hadn't found the cutaround himself.

Sure enough, the chacmool lowered itself into Crevice Pit. "Damn, damn, damn," Stephen muttered under his breath. He should have looked into it when he'd had the chance.

"Put out your light." The chacmool's voice floated up from the pit, already sounding far away. "You will need both hands."

Climb down a virgin pit with no light? Stephen wasn't averse to risk, if new cave was to be found, but this was crazy. He hesitated at the edge of the crescent-shaped pit.

"Is this your cave, Stephen?" Echoes muddied the chacmool's words, but Stephen understood it well enough. It sounded as if it must already be near the bottom, pausing to taunt him.

Stephen bit his lip. So he had to prove himself again. It was always the same, people treating him like a trained dog until he passed some test. Well, he'd done it before— hadn't he taught himself to read in Franklin Gorin's library? hadn't he crossed Bottomless Pit on a ladder?— but this was the last time. The chacmool had made him promises, and he was damn well going to collect.

He put out the lamp and took a deep breath, allowing the darkness to settle around him. Sitting on the lip of the narrow pit, he extended a foot and found a toehold on the opposite wall. The pit was a bit less than four feet wide, at least near the top. Narrow enough to chimney, but barely and not for very long. Stephen planted his other foot and lowered himself in, bracing his shoulders against one wall and walking himself slowly down. His eyes were wide open and he began to feel that he could see, that even in the absence of light he could pick out each new foothold before actually putting weight on it. The pit narrowed as he descended, until he could let himself down by working hand to hand, foot to foot—like climbing down two ladders at once. The muscles in his shoulders and thighs began to tremble with the effort of holding his body against both walls at once. *Gonna be a long climb back up*, he thought, *unless I can return by way of Giant's Coffin.*

Below him, the pit narrowed into a glottal opening barely wide enough to squeeze through. He could see the opening, one kind of darkness gaping in the middle of another like the difference between the sun and a star. Rocking back and forth, he worked his hips through, then waved his legs, searching for places to put his feet.

Stephen had heard a story once about a caver who had chimneyed down a pit, only to find that it suddenly belled out below him after a hundred feet or so. The man hadn't been strong enough after that distance to haul himself back up. The only thing to do in that situation was drop your light so you could see where you would land and hope the fall didn't kill you. Or that you didn't fall into water that siphoned into one of the underground rivers that had carved the cave. Or that if the fall only left you trapped with a broken leg, someone would come along before you died of your injuries or thirst or exposure.

As it happened, the bottom of that pit had been only another six feet or so down, and the caver had gotten out unbroken. But if the same thing happened here, Stephen had a feeling he would fall a long way.

He managed to stuff his toe in a crack, and with that leg taking his weight Stephen forced his shoulders down through the squeeze. After that it was easy—he felt like he was climbing down the inside of a tree, the damp stone walls of the pit like rough bark. When his feet touched level ground, Stephen was nearly disappointed.

That one's named after me, he thought, the muscles in his back and legs thrumming. *Bishop's Drop, and it's a bitch. Guess I know why nobody ever tried it before.*

That had been real caving. Everything else he'd ever done, even the daredevil crossing of Bottomless Pit, paled in comparison. The chacmool had been right: Stephen didn't need his eyes, not in *his* cave. It would go on forever, and he would explore it to its very end without light—hell, without water. He could eat and drink this darkness, breathe it inside him and never need air. This was freedom.

"Your first taste, Stephen," the chacmool said. Its voice floated on the darkness and the breath of the cave, coming from everywhere at once.

Stephen smelled the water and knew he was in River Hall. Behind and above him he sensed Crevice Pit, and he could feel the river flowing beneath his feet.

"This is how it feels to know something cannot be taken away from you," the chacmool said. "The senses no longer matter when one is certain. But this feeling does not come without cost."

Stephen blinked and reached out to touch the wall as the darkness closed in around him again. He stood squinting, vainly hoping for some shadow of that—vision wasn't the right word—of that sensation to linger. But he was blind again, blind as the crickets that scampered among the rocks. And his lamp lay by the edge of the pit, far above in Little Bat Avenue.

"Now we must speak of costs, Stephen," the chacmool said, its voice coming closer.

"Tell me," Stephen breathed, pleading against his blindness.

"All deeds have costs, and great deeds exact their toll in lives."

Stephen leaned against the cool stone of River Hall,

knowing what would come next. "You're going to kill that girl," he said.

The chacmool paused before answering. "You had a dream. A dream of paradise, yes? The girl, Nanahuatzin, must be taken to that place if we are to succeed at our task."

In the silence that followed, Stephen heard the faint drip and murmur of water echoing up from the river. The adrenaline rush he'd felt during the chimney down Crevice Pit was still fresh in his mind, the feeling that the moments when he was most alive took place surrounded by limestone walls. Dr. Croghan insisted every day on building roads, improving the hotel, doing everything he could to open the cave to a flood of visitors who would destroy its peace. Many times Stephen had sworn to himself that he would do anything to keep the cave as it was when he'd come five years before. Now here was his chance.

But was it worth a girl's life?

"Far more than this cave is at stake," the chacmool said. Could it read his thoughts? "A new world waits to be born. You are a slave now, and have always been; what price would you put on a world in which you could breathe free? A world in which your children would never know the whip or the auctioneer's bark?

"Greatness exacts its toll in lives. Through the girl Nanahuatzin, a world of men will be born and the world of master and slave will pass into memory."

"I—"

"Decide, Stephen," the chacmool commanded. "Time grows short."

His Christmas talk with Nick Bransford replayed itself in Stephen's mind. *Got to get them big ideas out of your head*, Nick had said. *Best leave that other alone. Dr. Croghan ain't gonna let you go to Africa.*

For you, Nick, Stephen thought, and in that moment he could almost believe himself. *You and all the others like you.*

"What do you want me to do?" he said.

Archie sat in the bow of the Daigles' boat, trying to soak the lingering unease of nightmares out of his mind in the warm morning sun. The sun was well up, but the boat was strangely silent, and when he stood he felt tired, as if the sun was setting rather than rising.

He couldn't remember any of the dreams, which was strange. Lately his problem had been remembering—and experiencing—dreams too much.

"Good morning!" he sang out, trying to banish his willies with forced good cheer. "Made any of that wonderful coffee, Marie?"

For a long time, no one responded. Then, instead of a smiling Marie, it was a solemn Peter Daigle who stepped through the curtain that partitioned off his family's sleeping area. "Good morning, Archie," he said quietly.

"Something the matter, Peter? Where are the girls?"

"Inside. And they'll stay there until you've gotten off."

Peter's voice was barely a shade away from open hostility. Archie couldn't for the life of him understand why, when they'd spent the previous evening laughing and joking around a cooking fire, Marie leading them in choruses of French folk songs. Archie had sung right along with them, although he knew only a few words of French, and the entire time he'd been quietly awestruck. He couldn't remember ever spending such an evening sober. The memory of it amazed him still, seeming at once distant and present—like a comforting vision one could return to for shelter in unpleasant times.

And now Peter, at least, seemed to have forgotten it completely. Archie was struck by a sense of loss, as if Peter's change in attitude had stripped the memory of all of its beauty. "Peter," he began, "what's the—"

"What's the matter?" Peter snapped. "Archie, I swear to you on the Virgin, you nearly ended last night underwater. If I did not believe you were at heart a decent man, I would have—"

He stopped himself, and walked up to where Archie stood in the bow. "I don't want the girls to hear this, especially Sonia."

"What did I do?" Archie asked, hating the pleading tone in his voice. But something much more important than a disagreement between two men was happening. Archie had a terrible intuition that he was being excommunicated from the happiness he'd felt at the memory of the past evening, and he didn't even know what he'd done.

A sudden slippage seemed to fracture everything around him, and dream memories began to slip through the cracks.

"What you did was not so terrible," Daigle said. "My uncle Michel used to walk in his sleep, and I knew you were sleeping even as you spoke. But what you said . . . I have a pistol, Archie, and I tell you again, you nearly did not survive this night."

"I'm sorry, Peter. Christ, whatever it was I did, I'm sorry. Please." Archie felt even more dislocated as he spoke, asking for—begging for—forgiveness when his accuser wouldn't tell him what this was all about. *Don't you realize what this time has meant to me?* he wanted to shout.

But all he could do was repeat himself: "What, Peter? What did I do?"

"You stepped through that curtain last night, flung it aside as if expecting to catch your wife with a lover. Marie and I awoke at once, but the girls, they sleep like the dead. This is God's grace, I think, for they are fond of you, my girls. They don't understand why I keep them inside this morning."

Peter looked out over the river. He started to speak, then shut his mouth. Archie waited him out, desperately anxious but not wanting to hurry him.

Finally Peter turned to look at him. "You have a knife there, in your belt," he said. "You held it last night."

"Peter, in God's name you can't believe I wanted to hurt you," Archie began. Peter shushed him, casting a nervous glance back toward the closed curtain.

"This is not about me," he said. "A fight between you and me, that would be simple. It is Sonia I am concerned for."

A cold lump swelled in the pit of Archie's stomach as a fragment of the night's dream reawakened in his memory. *Jane, dressed as the chacmool, recumbent on a flat stone altar with a blissful smile on her face. Her unmarked face.*

Smiling up at him as he stood over her, watching his own hands raise the knife.

"Never," Archie whispered. "I would never harm Jane."

"Archie!" Peter snapped. "If you do this again—who is Jane?"

"I meant Sonia." Archie's voice trembled, and he could feel the feather talisman coming alive, beating in time with his heart.

"Who is Jane?"

"My daughter. She's about Sonia's age, and I—I haven't seen her in a very long time." Archie sat back down, fearing that the dream-dislocation would unbalance him. His mind teemed with grotesque images—skeletal hands fumbling for life in dark waters, the hungry warmth of blood coursing over his hands.

"Please tell me, Peter," he managed to say. "Did I threaten Sonia?"

Peter sat facing Archie. "No. You held the knife turned inward, toward yourself. But you spoke to her . . . no, that's wrong. You weren't speaking to any of us. You looked at her as you spoke, never taking your eyes from her. And your hands, they looked like you were fighting the knife, forcing it toward yourself instead of someone else. Whoever you were speaking to, you were fighting them too."

Peter's speech slowed as if he were choosing each word with extreme care. "I believe you to be a good man, Archie," he said. "I have intuitions about such things, and follow them. I didn't—I don't believe that you wanted to harm my girls." He took a silver crucifix from his pocket and kissed it, looking again at the curtain before going on.

"My fear was that you would lose your struggle, and whatever possesses you would bend you to its will. You are possessed, Archie. A demon has gotten inside you, and you must cast it out. If I were a priest, perhaps I could help you . . . but perhaps not." Peter lapsed into silence, turning the crucifix over in his hands.

Some of the panicked weight began to lift from Archie's chest as Peter's anger cooled a bit. "Why wouldn't a priest be able to help me?" he asked.

"It is not a Christian demon inside you," Peter said. "You did not appeal to God for help, and the names you spoke are not written in the Scriptures. I cannot say those names, I think, but—who is Nawazee?"

"Nawazee? I don't know." But even as he said it, Archie realized that he did know, and he began to understand what had happened. "Nanahuatzin," he said.

"Yes. You called Sonia by that name. Who is that?"

"That's Jane," Archie said. "I don't call her by that name, but—someone else does." Archie was certain now. The chacmool had been speaking through him during his dream, just as he had taken its role in his vision of the sacrifice. Can it control me now? he wondered. Can it make me see dreaming things as real? And if it can, how can I begin to fight it?

But he had fought it, at least last night. God only knew what would have happened if he hadn't; very likely his body would be snagged like *Maudie*'s wreck on a sunken log in the Ohio. And that, Archie realized, was exactly what the chacmool had wanted. It had tried to kill him again; it feared him for some reason. Why?

Casting about for an answer, Archie remembered something Tamanend had said: *He Who Makes Things Grow has an enemy. This enemy is your ally.* Who is this ally, Archie wondered, and how can I make the alliance work for me?

The answer had to be somewhere in the information he'd gathered since the day in February when he'd spoken to Phineas Barnum. He turned inward to the problem, forgetting Peter Daigle and everything else around him, and there it was: the answer swam up out of the tangled morass of Aaron Burr's *Wallam Olum* commentary.

Xiuhtecuhtli. Lord of Fire and Time. If Tlaloc controlled water and earth, it was only natural that Xiuhtecuhtli should be opposed to him.

Everything began to fall into place for Archie: Steen's fear when the boy's rabbit had burst into flame, the incineration of Archie's ear when the Geek bit it off, the knife. Most of all, the knife. It was a token of Xiuhtecuhtli, just as the feathered medallion was Tlaloc's; Archie couldn't bear to be without either because he stood in some no-man's-land between the two gods. That was why the chacmool had tried to kill him or, failing that, drive him mad. He was a thorn in its side, an unknowing agent of an opposed principle. If it couldn't use him, it wanted him dead.

And it had nearly succeeded the night before.

"Peter," Archie said slowly, "why didn't you just kill me last night?"

"I have never killed a man," Peter said. "Always I hoped I would never have to. Last night it seemed I would, but I could not pull the trigger. If you had moved at one of my children, or Marie or me—then I would have shot you dead. But instead I watched you wrestle your demon. I did not want to send you to hell, Archie. Your demon would have ridden your soul straight into the pit." He laughed without humor. "Perhaps I am simply a coward. But I wanted you to live and free yourself.

"I wish you luck and God's grace, Archie," Peter finished. He stood and offered Archie his hand. "May you find your daughter."

Archie shook Peter's hand, blinking tears out of his eyes. God's grace, he thought. The grace of the Daigles is what will save me, if anything can.

"There is coffee," Peter said as he returned to his family. "Also yesterday's bread, if you would like breakfast."

"Thank you," Archie said, his voice breaking. "I would."

HE SPENT THE day alone on the deck, poling along and trying to fill in the blank spaces in his deductions. He carried two tokens, one from Tlaloc by way of the chacmool and the other marked just as Jane was, by the fire of Xiuhtecuhtli—who seemed to go by several names. Burr had also referred to the god as *huehueteotl*, Ometeotl, and the Old God.

But the knife seemed to have a double valence. If it had been somehow consecrated by fire, that fire had been burning at least nominally in Tlaloc's service. What did that mean?

On the river, traffic grew heavier as they approached Louisville. Even though he knew it was ridiculous, Archie found himself scanning the decks of passing steamers for Rufus. The old sot had been in the water well before the explosion that tore *Maudie* apart; if he was any swimmer at all, he would easily have made the bank and been picked up by a passing vessel or hiked his way back to Marlon MacGruder's.

The three slaves, though, hadn't had any such chance. Archie hoped Gatty was answering for their shackles in whatever forum awaited him in the afterlife.

Strange thought, that. Archie had never considered himself a particularly religious man, but he supposed he'd become a sort of accidental Christian simply by growing up in America. It had never occurred to him to think of things in terms other than heaven and hell, salvation and damnation. Or Purgatory, which was where he'd been since the morning's exchange with Peter. In the last months, though, his experiences had raised uncomfortable questions.

Whatever the truth was, Archie decided, the specter of

Gatty answering to Tlaloc rather than a fatherly Jehovah satisfied his newfound taste for revenge. But on the other hand, Tlaloc might well reward the kind of perversity that defined men like Delbert Gatty. The kind of perversity that led men to buy and sell and shackle one another.

I'm thinking like an abolitionist, Archie thought, and he supposed his experiences aboard *Maudie* had made him one. Certainly watching three men die had forced Archie to take an opinion regarding the shackles that drowned them.

Woolgathering again. What was it about river travel that caused his mind to wander so? It was something he would have to guard against. The chacmool would be only too happy to step into gaps in Archie's awareness, and Archie knew he wouldn't always have the kindness of men like Peter Daigle to rescue him. Something about the slavery question kept drawing his attention, though, but he couldn't quite say what.

It was late afternoon when Peter steered into a side channel of the Ohio and tied up to a short pier on the Louisville waterfront. Marie and the children—even Sonia—came out to bid Archie Godspeed, and Ramon rushed up to give him a quick bashful hug.

Peter shooed the children back into the makeshift cabin, then clapped Archie on the shoulder. "Again," he said, "luck and God's grace."

Marie handed him a small bag. "A bite to eat," she said, "and maybe a little something else as well." Coins clinked as Archie slung the bag over his shoulder and again he found himself brought to the verge of tears by a simple act of kindness. Last night they would have killed me to protect themselves, he thought. And today they've forgiven, and given me food and money.

He made no effort to hide the catch in his voice as he thanked them again. "What can I say?" he stammered.

"Hush," Marie said. "Take it, Archie, and take with you our blessings as well." She straightened a twist in the bag's strap. "Go now. Find your daughter."

Archie stood on the dock and watched Peter and Marie pole through the dead water back into the main channel. He lost sight of them as they joined a line of craft waiting for passage through the locks at the Falls of the Ohio, but he stood watching for a long time anyway.

I never wished them luck, he thought. And they still have the mountains to cross.

A large flatboat laden with tobacco tied up where the Daigles had been, and Archie had to move out of the way of its unloading. He walked along the waterfront looking for stage offices. It was probably too late to leave that night, but he thought he might be able to buy a ticket for the next day's coach to Mammoth Cave.

And what would he do then? Secure a guide and ask to see the chacmool? Strange black fellow, wears green feathers? Changes into a jaguar sometimes?

If I have to, he thought, that's exactly what I'll do. But actually he doubted it would come to that. The chacmool would certainly sense him coming, and the feather token would likewise alert him to its proximity. After that, it would simply be a contest of wills.

But wasn't today the first of the, what, *nemontemi?* The bad-luck days? Archie counted off the days since he'd encountered Tamanend. The ceremony was to take place at midnight on the second of April—the first moments of the third, really. Today was Wednesday the twenty-ninth; yes, it should be the first unlucky day. A tiny bit of good fortune amid all the chaos. The chacmool would be passive these next five days, not wanting to risk queering the conditions for its ritual.

If he could find Jane before Saturday, he might be able to just steal her away. The calendar wouldn't cycle around for another five hundred twenty years, and the chacmool would just have to wait for another little girl born at midnight on April third, what? A.D. two thousand three hundred fifty-one. He and Jane would live out their lives together, and perhaps an earthquake would bury the chacmool so that future Riley Steens could never dig it out.

Thinking of Steen brought out the flaw in Archie's plan. The chacmool might not be able to act during the five *nemontemi,* but its accomplices were under no such restrictions. Or were they? He didn't know. Steen could be keeping Jane hidden away somewhere, or Royce could be waiting along the turnpike to finish the job he'd started in December; Archie no longer held any illusions about being able to surprise the chacmool simply by turning up alive.

I still don't know enough for certain, Archie thought, moving through the crowd toward what appeared to be a ticket office. Have to fly on blind intuition.

Get to the cave, then. That was the first order of business. Everything else would sort itself out once that was accomplished.

The agent at the first window Archie approached sold tickets only for an express to Nashville, but he directed Archie to the offices of the Mammoth Cave line, only a hundred yards or so west. "Believe they're closed up now," he said, "but you might check in the morning."

Archie thanked the agent and walked to the Mammoth Cave stage's office window. The sun was dropping, and so was the temperature. He thought he would see if he could buy a ticket that evening and then hope Marie Daigle's gift was enough to purchase a hotel room for the night. If not, he could sleep outside. He'd grown used to it, and the weather was getting a bit more congenial.

The window was closed, but a schedule posted next to the counter stated that the Mammoth Cave Stage ran daily at eight o'clock in the morning, for a two-dollar fare. Digging in the bag Marie had given him, Archie found that he had nearly ten, most of it in silver.

Again he grew a bit misty at the Daigles' generosity. If everyone emigrating West has that kind of heart, it will be a fine place to live, he thought, and for the first time it occurred to Archie that he could take Jane across the mountains just as Peter and Marie were shepherding their brood. Why stay in New York? His job was certainly lost, and in hindsight it was becoming clearer to Archie that Bennett had never intended to offer him a promotion.

A rush of optimism made Archie giddy and left him wondering why his emotions had been so extreme lately. Western editors wouldn't be so narrowminded. They would need good men with sharp minds and a bit of experience with presses and type.

Well, he thought. Won't Jane be surprised?

He caught himself smiling as he strolled up Third Street in search of lodging, riding a wave of certainty that everything would end well. He discarded his earlier idea of simply stealing Jane away; it was cowardly, for one thing, and in any case it was probable that the chacmool, even if it couldn't pinpoint his location, would know he was coming. There would be no secrets from this point on, no hiding behind proxies and henchmen. Archie meant to end this once and for all. No other father should ever have to endure what he had.

Passing two hotels that looked beyond his means, Archie set his sights on a third, another block away from the waterfront and across the street. Remembering he was in a city again, and not among friends, he reslung his bag underneath his coat and reflexively touched the knife sheathed at the small of his back. He felt strong and focused, prepared for the task at hand; a good night's sleep and then he would be ready to battle the chacmool on its own ground.

The hotel he'd chosen was flanked by saloons, with clusters of revelers blocking their doors and spilling out onto the street. Archie watched the crowds, remembering similar evenings at Belinda's Bright and pitying whatever poor soul had to clean up after Louisville's drunkards. He was smiling a bit, thinking of all the bizarre circumstances that had led him to this place, when one of the figures in the crowd caught his eye.

It was the red piping on the man's trousers that drew Archie's attention. He stopped and retreated into the shadowed doorway of a shuttered milliner's, all of his good cheer flushed away as he recognized Royce McDougall.

His first impulse was simply to keep walking, to find another hotel and disappear early in the morning. Thinking it over quickly, though, Archie realized that if Royce was here, Steen was likely nearby. If his dream was any indication, the chacmool already had Jane, but Steen would know where she was. And Royce would know where Steen was.

What to do, then? He could follow Royce and hope the Rabbit led him to a rendezvous with Steen. But what if he lost track of Royce? Time would be wasted and nothing accomplished.

That settled it. He would have to ambush Royce and just force some answers out of him. The idea seemed foreign, foolhardy even; Royce would be easily Archie's match in a brawl.

But, Archie reminded himself, he was armed. And if ever their was a time for foolhardiness, it was now.

Royce dropped a handful of coins into the palm of an Indian occupying a stool near the hotel door. Then he broke away from the crowd and walked back down Third Street, in the direction of the waterfront. *He's posted his sentries,* Archie thought, *and now he's going to stake out the ticket window himself.*

Or he was paying the Indian for whiskey, or a whore, or any number of other things. *Ease up,* Archie told himself. *You have enough problems in this world without inventing more.*

Archie thought fast. Perhaps he was jumping at moonshadows, but he had a feeling he was down to his last mistake. Best to assume that Royce was going to the ticket window, and better yet to beat him to the spot.

Taking care to avoid the sight of Royce's scout, Archie circled around the few blocks back north and east to the dock where he'd first stepped onto Kentucky soil. The fragrant bales of tobacco were gone, but at the base of the dock a pile of broken lumber and debris offered excellent concealment, with a good view of the entire waterfront.

Archie climbed over it, mindful of protruding nails, and settled behind it in a weedy patch between the paved street and the riverbank.

From there he watched pedestrians spill out onto the waterfront until he saw Royce. The Rabbit paused at the corner, searching up and down the docks. After a moment, he strolled casually past the Mammoth Cave Stage window and took up a position almost directly across the dockside square from Archie's hiding place.

Archie crouched watching him until it was fully dark, shifting often enough to prevent his legs going numb and silently willing Royce to move to a location more vulnerable to surprise attack. Leaning on the front stoop of the Rivermen's Baptist Church, Royce commanded a view of the entire waterfront spreading west to the neck of Shippingport Island. He could even have seen Archie if the night hadn't been cloudy and the docks poorly lit.

A last few boats unloaded their wares on the dock above Archie's head, and he drew a few strange looks from boatmen and shore workers, but no one bothered to roust him. Apparently it wasn't unusual for men to hide behind piles of rubbish here in Louisville, or maybe nobody wanted to provoke a man with no ear and the stink of the river on him.

The later it got, the more raucous were the voices and music from the saloons clustered along Main Street and its side alleys. Archie began to realize that it was only a matter of time before his position was given away by wandering drunks or the local constabulary. He was in a relatively obscure spot, far at the eastern end of the waterfront, but boots still clumped occasionally along the dock above him and enough people were passing that one of them would sooner or later comment on the vagrant peering around the lumber pile by the bank.

Surprise was Archie's only advantage over Royce; all of his plans depended on it. But Royce stood calmly, working on the stub of a cheroot, scanning the docks even though he must have known that only a handful of boats would arrive and moor before morning.

Of course. Archie could have slapped himself for his obtuseness. Obviously Royce had figured out that he'd missed Archie somehow. That was why he'd set up his impromptu sentry network and returned to the docks—he was assuming that Archie had eluded his attention. So he had returned to keep an eye on the one place in Louisville Archie had to visit sooner or later, the Mammoth Cave stage offices.

And Archie, in his efforts to escape Royce's surveillance, had instead trapped himself like a rabbit in tall grass. If he moved, there was no way to hide it.

Wait, though; there might be a way to turn this reversal back around. Royce knew that he didn't know where Archie was, but he didn't know that Archie knew where *he* was. So now the trick was to lure Royce into a trap, rather than spring a stationary ambush. It sounded simple enough, but how to actually do it?

Before he could give it too much thought, Archie stood up, made a great show of looking around, then set off west along the river. He walked briskly in a more-or-less straight line, aiming for the downriver end of the waterfront, where he'd seen narrower streets when wandering earlier. A quick glance back toward the Rivermen's Baptist Church showed that Royce had left his station, but Archie couldn't locate him in the crowd and didn't make much of an effort to; best just to trust that Royce was as good at following as Archie was at leading.

Passing a row of dingy gin mills, Archie saw a narrow space between two of them, too slight even to be called an alley. It looked more like the result of an error in measurement on the part of one of the buildings' architects. He stopped, waiting a beat to make sure Royce would see him, then sidestepped into the space.

It was barely shoulder-wide, and dark enough that Archie couldn't see how far it extended. He pushed on into it, kicking bottles and bits of refuse aside, hoping he could get out of sight before Royce came after him. As his eyes adjusted to the darkness, a wider alley appeared, intersecting this one another thirty or forty feet ahead. Archie broke into a run, half from fear and half hoping that the noise would draw Royce after him before the Rabbit's vision could adjust.

Coming around the corner, Archie slipped on a patch of wet bricks surrounding the base of a rain barrel. His feet went out from under him, and he landed hard on the bare bricks of the alley, jarring his tailbone. He looked up at the sound of crashing from the narrow side-cut and saw a pig standing perhaps ten feet away, a huge sow weighing at least twice what Archie himself did. The pig looked back at him for a long moment as if she was calculating something, then trotted off down the alley, her bulbous body impossibly dainty on tiny feet.

Archie drew the knife and flattened himself against the wall next to the rear door of a groggery. Water dripped into the rain barrel at his left, and his heart slammed against his ribs hard enough that he could actually feel his body moving against the damp wall at his back. *Just like a rabbit,* he thought again, *run to ground not by dogs but by a Rabbit.* Irony followed him everywhere. But this rabbit wouldn't simply die of fright, no.

Then someone stepped into the alley and Archie drove his knife into the man's midsection.

In the split second before the knife struck home, Archie was terrifyingly convinced that this man wasn't Royce at all, but just some beggar or cutpurse seeking an easy mark. *Christ,* he thought. *What if I've killed an innocent man?*

The knife buried itself to the hilt, grating along bone as warm blood surged out over Archie's hands. The man gagged and seized Archie's wrist, dragging Archie with him as he sank to the ground. Once he'd fallen, his grasp weakened and Archie worked the knife free, seeing that his victim was in fact Royce McDougall.

Royce lay on his side, knees drawn up and both hands

clasped to his belly. He gritted his teeth against a series of short wheezing groans. "Nnnggahh," he said. "You've killed me, Archie. Son of a p—" A bubble of saliva broke on his lips. "Bitch."

Archie stood, watching Royce's blood drip from his hands. In his dream, the night before . . .

Everything around him grew clear as if it were noon, and when Archie looked up into the cloudy night, he could see the shadow of a rabbit in the moon, leading the *Centzon Mimixcoa* in a mad dance around the earth. The smell of Royce's blood sparked a hunger in him, and he saw through the dying young man's bones and skin to the heart struggling in his chest.

"*Yollotl, eztli,*" he said. "*Ompa onquiza'n tlalticpac.*"

Fear broke through the sweaty mask of pain on Royce's face. "No," he begged, trying to push himself away from Archie on strengthless legs. "Not like that. Christ, I'm dead already, isn't that enough?"

Archie knelt beside him, smelling blood and seeing it crawl between his fingers, along the tracery of veins beneath the skin. Black ants formed intricate whorls around the splatters of Royce's blood staining the bricks. The knife was hungry, hot in his hands, and Archie was hungry, too.

"Please, Prescott," Royce husked. His hand slipped on his own blood and he fell onto his back, still scraping his heels on the ground. "Please, it was *business*. A man's reputation—"

He broke off and his gaze fixed on something just over Archie's right shoulder. "Steen!" Royce tried to shout, but his voice was barely above a whisper. "Steen, God—!"

The flat crack of a gunshot stopped Royce short. The sound drove like a wedge into Archie's mind, splitting apart the sights and smells, dropping cold reality over him like a sudden rainstorm. He saw the knife, streaked with blood like a dead man's script. A man's life, spilled on his hands, on his coat, on the shrinking voice of his spirit—*and I wanted more than his life. I would have eaten his soul.*

"Corrupts absolutely, doesn't it?" Riley Steen said, and laughed. "Friend, I should know."

He stepped in front of Archie, obscuring Royce's sprawled graceless body, and waved a stubby derringer. "Rabbits," he giggled. "Nothing but misfortune and drunkenness. Not the way you want to go, Mr. Prescott. Not the way I want to go, either. I only learn a lesson once."

Steen ran a finger along the flat of Archie's bloody knife. "Hemoglobin. Corpuscles. Merry little red cells. Or, if your priorities are slightly different, *eztli. Chalchihuitl.* The precious fluid that feeds the gods, makes the world turn. Ridiculous, isn't it? But you and I both know it's true. Look at me, Mr. Prescott."

Archie closed his eyes, breaking the connection between himself and the knife clasped in his hands. When he opened them again, he could look at Riley Steen.

A maniacal grin dominated Steen's face, spreading wide enough that his lips were actually split in several places, smearing perfect white teeth. A single dead incisor stood out, black as a tree stump rotting in spring floods. Steen's cheeks and mouth were caked with streaks of dried gore, which still leaked in slow trails from the springs of his eye sockets.

He shot Royce right through the forehead, Archie thought, *and he doesn't have eyes to see.*

And that gunshot would be drawing attention, even in a rough area like the waterfront. Archie wanted to be gone, and quickly.

"The lesson here, Mr. Prescott," Steen said jovially, tapping at the corner of one empty socket, "is careful what you wish for. A hoary adage, to be sure, but no admonition lives to become hoary unless it has some truth to it."

Archie searched himself for the vengeful rage he'd felt toward Steen. He couldn't find it. Clearly the chacmool had done something horrible to him; the man stood there like a grinning nightmare parody of himself, interposed between a man he'd killed and a man he'd once tried to, and still he acted like a clown. Archie could muster no desire to kill him.

"Why'd you kill Royce, Steen?" he asked. "I can't understand you doing me a favor, and he would have died anyway."

"Certainly he would. But I was doing you a favor, Mr. Prescott. If I hadn't shot that boy, you'd have scooped out his heart and eaten it like a flavored ice. Not—" Steen stifled a sudden guffaw, bending over and covering his mouth. He shook like a consumptive in a coughing fit, a tendril of thick fluid dripping from one eye socket onto the grimy bricks.

"Not," he finished when he'd regained control of himself, "the proper course toward redemption of one's daughter."

"And what's your interest in my saving Jane?" Archie said. He was still shaken by killing Royce, and Steen's glibness was beginning to heat his temper.

"Propriety," Steen said grandly. "Especially now, when I—see—things in a different light, I have a keen sense of propriety. When I allied myself with the chacmool, my reasoning was that it would be improper—unjust, if you prefer—to let pass such an opportunity to rectify the errors of Mr. Burr. To write the history of this nation. Of the world."

"And lives don't factor into this reasoning? My life? Jane's?" Archie's vision actually began to redden around the edges, and he calmed himself. Whatever else Steen said, he was right about one thing: Archie couldn't allow himself to be seduced by the power the chacmool offered. He had to keep a level head.

Steen's face contorted into a sort of gleeful frown. When he spoke, he sounded like a patient teacher educating a simpleton. "Greatness exacts its toll in lives, Mr. Prescott. I heard someone say that once, and I believe it.

Measure your daughter's life against the redirection of history. Surely you see my point?"

"I see that you're a raving madman," Archie growled. He rose to his feet, holding the knife pointed at Steen. "That's the only reason I don't let your guts out on these bricks. Now get out of my way."

"Of course I'm mad, Mr. Prescott. So would you be." Steen leveled the derringer at a point just above Archie's navel. "But I'm a madman with one bullet left. Let's parley."

"If you're going to shoot me, Steen, do it. I don't have time for chatter with lunatics." Archie sloshed the knife around in the rain barrel, then sheathed it and washed his hands. As he walked away, he could feel the gun aimed at the small of his back.

"Wait a moment, Mr. Prescott." Steen ran up beside Archie, and slowed to walk next to him. "Surely you don't think I'd have gone to the trouble of killing Mr. McDougall and saving you from Tlaloc's embrace simply to kill you myself?" He stopped suddenly. "Although the irony— ha! There would be humor in it, would there not?"

"Leave me alone, Steen," Archie said, and kept walking.

He'd gone another ten steps when he heard Steen say, "I know where your daughter is. She's already in the cave, and I can show you where."

It's a trick, Archie thought. Some demented scheme to distract me. But he stopped anyway and turned to face Steen. "And why would you tell me? Another act of generosity?"

"Hardly," Steen chortled. "More along the lines of enlightened self-interest. You're still opposing the chacmool; I find myself wishing to do the same. There's a proverb among the Arabs: 'The enemy of my enemy is my friend.' "

"So it's revenge you're after? Chacmool gouged out your eyes and you want to get back at it?"

Every trace of humor faded from Steen's disfigured

face. "You understand nothing, Prescott," Steen said grimly. "I would give up my eyes all over again, if it meant I would only be blind.

"I'm not *human* any more, don't you understand?" Steen shouted, and then he started to laugh. "My—my heart beats in my body, but I *see*—" Steen's words trailed off into a long screaming laugh and he sank to his knees, fresh tears cutting clean tracks through the gore on his face.

If the shot didn't draw attention, that fit certainly will, Archie thought. He stood watching Steen until the spasm subsided and Steen lay on his side, sweating and gasping for breath.

"I see what the dead see," Steen finished. "And it's all so terribly *ironic*."

That's what I saw when I killed Royce, Archie thought. That's why everything was so bright—what do the dead need of light?

He shuddered a bit, and despite himself felt faint sympathy for Steen. Forcing it down, he prodded the deranged wagoner with the toe of his boot. "Where's Jane?" he demanded.

Steen's head jerked up, puppyish eagerness lighting up the ruin of his face. "Splendid!" he shouted. "Come with me."

"Excuse me, Stephen. What are you doing?"

Stephen dropped the blanket he'd just taken from the shelf in the hotel laundry. He turned around to see Dr. Croghan in the doorway, in pajamas, robe, and a stern expression made grimmer by the gloomy candle in his hand.

"Chill in the air tonight, Dr. Croghan," he said. "Charlotte's got a little cough and I wanted to make sure it didn't get worse." Of all the people who might have noticed his midnight trip to the hotel storerooms, Stephen had thought Dr. Croghan would be the last. He was usually asleep before nine o'clock; what was he doing out in his bedclothes at this hour?

"My sympathies," Croghan said. "I'll look in on her in the morning."

"No," Stephen said quickly. "She just needs to stay warm. She'll be fine."

"Are you now a medical man, Stephen?" Croghan let the question hang in the air for just a moment. "I thought not. The last thing I need is fever spreading around just as the weather begins to warm. The next few weeks will be extremely busy."

Stephen saw that he would have to concede the point. He wondered how Charlotte would react when he asked her to play sick for Dr. Croghan. Her good humor was part of why he'd married her, but she'd want to know what he had been doing in the laundry, and he'd have to tell her some other story. He hadn't lied to her during the course of their young marriage, and he didn't much relish having to start.

But, he reminded himself, bigger things were at stake.

"Yes, sir," Stephen said. "Visitors'll start lining up soon. I'd just as soon not have to worry about her while I'm in the cave."

"Good. I'll be by in the morning." Croghan stepped into the laundry and set his candle on a shelf above an ironing board. "Empty your pockets now and then you can go."

Stephen had already taken a step toward the door before all of the doctor's words registered. "My pockets?" he said dumbly.

"If you would," Croghan said, his tone of voice leaving no doubt that the phrase was just a formality. He pushed aside a pile of sheets and tapped the cleared space on the ironing board. "Here. Someone's been stealing small items from the hotel. I didn't think you were the type, but then here you are skulking in the middle of the night. Blood is thicker than water, I suppose."

Fury struck Stephen so heavily that he nearly choked on his own heartbeat. A vivid fantasy streaked through his mind—Croghan strangled on the laundry floor, he and Charlotte running for their lives. But where would they run? The cave had made Stephen slightly notorious. And Croghan's life was not worth having to leave it.

Silently he emptied his pockets, placing each item carefully on the smooth cotton draping the ironing board. Pipe, tobacco pouch, pocketknife, matches, candle, a handful of coins.

Croghan poked among Stephen's possessions, lingering over the gold piece Stephen still carried from his trip with old Professor Tattersfield. "Fine," he said eventually. "Go ahead with the blanket, Stephen. I'll look in on Charlotte tomorrow."

He paused in the doorway to give Stephen a wink. "Give her my best, will you?" he said, and left Stephen alone in the laundry.

Stephen replaced his pipe and pocketknife and other things in his pockets, smoldering with a rage that was all the more focused because of its impotence. He picked up the blanket and rolled it under his arm, then stood for a long time turning the gold piece over in his fingers. He wanted to throw it away, fling it into the river just because Croghan's attention had fallen on it. But it reminded Stephen of other things as well: in his mind he saw it glinting on the floor of Bottomless Pit, and he thought again of promises made to him.

Come Monday morning, Dr. Croghan, he thought as he slipped the coin into his pocket, *you'll see just how thick blood really is.*

The girl was awake when Stephen entered the abandoned supply hut, and stroking the feathered cloak as if it were a purring cat. She looked up at him long enough to see the blanket and say, "I'm not cold."

"Well, that's fine," Stephen said. "But you must be hungry." He placed a small leather bag in front of her. "Bread, cheese, jerky, and some apples Charlotte—that's my wife—dried last fall."

"Yum, apples." She opened the bag and started in on the dried fruit, chewing happily while her fingers played amid green feathers. "Don't like jerky; it's too salty," she said between bites.

Well, isn't she the little princess? Stephen thought. Not scared a bit. Treated him like he was a servant come into her bedroom with the royal supper. Either she was crazy or she knew something he didn't.

"All the same, you better eat it," he said, because it seemed like the right thing to say.

"That's what my Da would say," she said, screwing up her face. "I don't have to listen to him. Or you."

Definitely addled, Stephen decided. But the chacmool had been very clear: she was to be treated like royalty, given whatever she wanted, but under no circumstances could she leave the hut until after sunset Saturday, when Stephen was to take her down to the Mummy Room and wait for the chacmool's appearance. It all sounded like mumbo-jumbo to Stephen, but he had seen enough strangeness to take it seriously. And she certainly looked the part of a princess, even sitting amid dry-rotted mining implements with her mouth full of dried apple and scabs cracking as she chewed. She wasn't pretty, no, but there was something important and striking about her. A sense that she was the pivot point for everything that was supposed to happen.

Does she know she's going to die? he thought. She must, even if she wouldn't say it. I knew when I laid eyes on her—she's marked somehow.

I wonder if I am too.

He put that thought out of his mind. "Anything else you want?" he asked, hoping she wouldn't name something he'd have to sneak around Croghan to get. Anger started frothing inside him again, but he quashed it. It wouldn't help anything if he was sullen all week. Croghan had always kept a close eye on him, and after tonight

Stephen thought he'd be lucky to get a moment alone, without either the doctor or one of his tattles snooping around.

All that would change on Monday morning. Everything would change Monday morning, and this little white girl would make it all happen.

She hadn't answered his question. A dreamy expression dulled her features as she took to stroking the cloak again, and Stephen grew uncomfortable. She looked like she was listening to someone, maybe the same voice that spoke to Stephen; she cocked her head to the side and nodded slowly at the air in front of her.

"What's your name?" Stephen said suddenly, spurred by jealousy. The voice had been silent since the chacmool's arrival, and even though he knew it was because of the unlucky time, it still rankled him that she could hear *something*.

"Da named me Jane," she said sleepily. "But the chacmool—his name was Nezahualpilli once, did you know that? The chacmool calls me Nanahuatzin, and that's my real name."

"Oh." The chacmool had warned Stephen that the girl's father would be pursuing them. He wondered when the man would arrive, and if he would be marked, too, marked to die like his daughter was. Stephen didn't know his name, and didn't want to ask. He would find out soon enough.

The girl fell asleep, lying on her side with her hands pillowing her head. Feathers rustled as the cloak seemed to draw itself in, settling protectively around her sleeping body. *Like it was around the chacmool when I found it,* Stephen thought. He left the blanket where it was and went to the door.

Maybe tonight he would sleep. Maybe he could just slip into bed next to Charlotte, make sleepy moonlit love to her, then sleep until the sun rose and Dr. Croghan came around to bother them. To pass a night without stretches of wakeful anxiety—Stephen couldn't think of anything he wanted more at the moment, except maybe for all of it to be over. A troubled conscience could not rest, he'd once heard a preacher say, and some of the things the chacmool wanted him to do definitely had Stephen troubled.

Then he remembered Croghan saying *Blood is thicker than water, I suppose,* and his conscience retreated to a place in his mind where he could barely hear it calling.

❖

When Archie spotted a billboard advertising Bell's Tavern at the side of the turnpike, he could scarcely restrain a cheer. The cave was only fifteen miles away. It was just before dawn, meaning they'd been on the road more than thirty hours, and even though the road was better than anything Archie had seen in Pennsylvania, he still felt like he'd been over Niagara Falls in a barrel. His ankle throbbed, and his back stung as the old blisters dried out and tightened.

THE MAMMOTH CAVE OF KENTUCKY, blared another sign, at the intersection of the turnpike and the road to the cave. LARGEST CAVE IN THE WORLD. FINE HOTEL. OPEN EVERY DAY OF THE YEAR.

"We should arrive in time for lunch," Steen said merrily, turning the wagon onto the macadam of the cave road. "Although, if you're unbearably hungry, we could continue on to Bell's and enjoy a fine breakfast there."

Steen's relentless morbid good cheer drove Archie to the brink of mania himself, but he continued humoring the madman as he had the entire trip. After all, Steen had the gun.

"No, let's go on," he said, as if he had really considered Steen's offer. "I can eat there." In fact, he was hungry, ravenous even; the last of Marie's edibles had run out the day before.

"As you wish," Steen said. "But nothing will happen until Sunday night. What a shame it will be if, after all of your travails, you find these next two days *boring*." He snickered.

Αfɪɛr σnly ɪwσ hours in the wagon, Archie had already begun wondering how he would get to Mammoth Cave without either killing Steen or going mad himself. Steen babbled incessantly about the chacmool, the cave, Aaron Burr, Herodotus, his previous trips to Kentucky—anything that percolated up from the crumbling ruin of his mind. Most of it Archie didn't understand.

Sometime late on the first night, after a rain shower had passed and the moon had risen, Steen had shouted "Of course!" and he made a circle in the air with two fingers, pointing them at the passenger-side horse.

"*Mictlan,*" he said, and the horse dropped dead in its harness. "Haha!" Steen cried happily. "I knew it would work!"

He turned to Archie. "There were never any horses in Mictlan, you know," he said. "Wonder what the people there think of them. I'll have to ask old Lupita, next time I *see* her." He burst out laughing as Archie clambered down to cut the dead horse free so they could go on.

It had been like that ever since. Archie began to believe that Steen had been possessed by the maddened spirit of a court jester; one moment the wagoner shouted ribald limericks at the top of his lungs, the next he misquoted Shakespeare and Ben Franklin.

At one point the previous morning, just after they'd crossed the Salt River ferry with the ferryman spitting between his fingers onto the wagon's wheels, Steen had stood bolt upright. Throwing his head back he howled, "*I am the Rabbit!*"

Misunderstanding, Archie said, "I thought they worked for you."

The wagon rocked as Steen dropped back onto the driver's bench. "No, you sot," he said. "Not a Dead Rabbit. The *Tochtli,* the Rabbit in the Moon." He pointed up, and Archie could have sworn that there *was* a rabbit in the setting moon.

Jane had said "Rabbit" once, while looking at the moon. Archie wondered if she still could see it. If she could still see anything.

"What's the *Tochtli?*" he asked Steen.

"Trickster figure. God of chaos, of drunkenness and random action. The dead, I can tell you, are always happy to see the Rabbit; things in Mictlan can be monotonous."

Bell's Tavern began to obsess Steen sometime after midnight, and Archie had been subjected to endless praise of the Tavern's food and accommodations. Now he seemed to remember that obsession. "Roast pig they have there, it would make a man forget heaven!" Steen roared at the sunrise.

"Of course," he added more soberly, "it's difficult for me to eat meat now, particularly if the cut has a bone in it." He dabbed at the corner of one of his oozing eye sockets. "Dead things seem a bit like family. Funny, isn't it?"

"Oh yes," Archie agreed, and then they turned off the turnpike, onto the road that Dr. Croghan had built to the cave.

The day warmed as they plodded along the winding dirt road. On their right rose a lumpy ridge of hills, cut through by a number of streams swollen by spring runoff and the previous day's storm. These hills gave way on the left to a grassy plain pocked by shallow conical depressions.

"Sinkholes, they call those," Steen said suddenly. "Like hourglasses, aren't they? Water seeps through them like time, dripping into the cave. We're over the cave now, you know. It's in those hills, it's under the grass, it's everywhere. Can you hear it?" He started to whistle a marching tune, then modulated it into "Onward, Christian Soldiers."

Almost there, Archie thought. He'd been able to glean some useful information from Steen's raving. Now he knew who to look for when they arrived at the cave, hopefully around noon; the man who discovered the chacmool was a mulatto slave named Stephen.

But he didn't know where the chacmool had hidden Jane, and that was the only topic Steen wouldn't touch. "You'll see her when we arrive," was the only answer he would make to Archie's repeated questions.

If she was in the cave, Archie gathered that Stephen would be able to find her. If not, he would at least be able to lead Archie to the cavern where the chacmool had been resting for three hundred years. The ceremony would take place there, Archie was sure; and one way or another, he had to be there before it happened.

And what would he do then? A direct assault would end with him gutted like a fish, probably in front of Jane. He wouldn't be able to do this by himself, not against an adversary who could change shape and work magic and God only knew what else. How could Archie even the odds?

He Who Makes Things Grow has an enemy, Tamanend had said. *This enemy is your ally.* And Steen had said something very similar: *The enemy of my enemy is my friend.* But Archie still didn't understand how to tap the power of Xiuhtecuhtli. If that was what he was supposed to do.

Again he felt caught in the middle of a struggle between forces he couldn't begin to comprehend. He knew more about what was at stake, but he still had no idea how to use what power he had. And he did have some power; the diabolical hunger that had possessed him when he'd buried the knife in Royce's gut proved that much. Unfortunately, it also proved that whatever power he had could easily turn him into the very thing he was trying to defeat.

And wouldn't that be ironic, he thought grimly. Yes sir, Steen would enjoy that.

He had to know where Jane was. Without that information, everything else he knew was like a map with no compass points on it.

"We're nearly there, Steen," Archie said wearily, trying one more time. "Where's Jane?"

"Getting nearer all the time," Steen said. "Really, Mr. Prescott, your single-mindedness is tedious."

"I thought that's why you wanted me to come with you," Archie grumbled. "Someone who's just a bit put out wouldn't further your plan very much, now would he?"

"Touché. But if you must know, I don't have any plan. Plans are only useful to those who think time is important. The rest of us simply do what is called for at any given moment. Our interests coincide at the moment; tomorrow or next Thursday, who knows? Time is odd that way. Relief from it is the chief joy of madness."

"Well, time is important to me at this moment, and I need a plan. What do you propose we do when we get to the cave?"

"We? Nothing. I suppose you'll speed off in search of your little girl. As for me, I'll take the appropriate action when the moment arrives." Steen snickered and started whistling again. He would say nothing else to Archie after that, interrupting his whistling only to point and cackle at some feature of the landscape that caught his attention.

THE PLAIN WAS soon swallowed by forest again, oak and cedar and maple, and shortly before noon they pulled to a creaking halt in front of the Mammoth Cave Hotel. The hotel was perhaps two hundred feet long, with broad porches extending its entire length. Four coaches were parked in front of the stable attached to the south end of the building. Across a graded turning circle stood a loose cluster of shacks, perched along the edge of a steep hillside. Black women hung laundry and hoed small garden patches, and the men were at work shingling the roof of one of the nearer shacks. From the turning circle a trail led below the slave quarters, dropping out of sight under tall straight trees.

Archie just had time to register all of this before the sun reached its zenith and Riley Steen let out a joyous shout. "There!" he cried. "There it is! Murmuring before, now I hear it perfectly!"

Archie saw heads turn in their direction, but he couldn't react. A tremor raced through his mind, setting off a deluge of sounds and smells. Smoke and muttering voices, dripping water and a chill damp musk.

When his senses cleared, Archie saw Steen shambling toward the trailhead. "Yes!" he was screaming, pure mad ecstasy in his voice. "There it is! There, I hear it!"

Steen broke into a run, gathering momentum until he was moving at a dead sprint. Two of the slaves shouted at him to stop and chased after him, but he had too great a lead. He sprinted down the trail and out of sight, and a few seconds later Archie felt a sound like a huge sigh ripple up from the ground.

He's gone home, Archie thought irrationally. But before he could grasp hold of the thought, force it to yield up some sort of meaning, it was chased away by the sound of angry voices.

Blinking, he saw a stout man in a formal morning suit staring at him. It came to Archie that the man was expecting some sort of response.

"I'm sorry?" he said.

"I said where does he think he's going?" the man demanded, his genteel Southern accent sharpened by indignation. "Visitors can't go into the cave without a guide. This isn't a charity exhibit."

"I don't know," Archie said, confused. "He just jumped up and ran."

"What was he shouting about? Damn." The man—he must be Dr. Croghan, Archie realized—turned to shout at the slaves who stood looking down the trail where Steen had disappeared. "Don't gawk, get aftcr him! Bring him out of there!"

Returning his attention to Archie, Dr. Croghan noticed the wagon. "Was that Steen?" he asked. "What got into him?"

"You know him?"

"He was here last autumn. Bought a mummy we brought out of the cave. Didn't seem quite right to sell it, but he offered a very handsome price. Who are you?" Croghan looked at Archie suspiciously. "If you want to see the cave, you'll have to hire a guide. Imbecilic visitors who get themselves killed are singularly ineffective as advertisement."

"That's what I've come to do. Hire a guide, I mean. My name is Archie Prescott," Archie said, climbing down from the driver's bench. He offered his hand to Croghan, who shook it once and let it drop.

"Dr. John Croghan. What got into Steen?" he asked again.

"Honestly, I have no idea," Archie said, and he didn't. How much did Croghan know about the chacmool? Not much, Archie decided; judging from his comments, he'd sold the mummy as just another museum attraction.

"Is Stephen available?" Archie asked. "I only have a short time, and—well, I was told not to go with anyone else."

"Were you? Well, notwithstanding Stephen's reputation, all of our guides do a superb job here." Croghan looked annoyed that Archie had mentioned Stephen by name. "He's already leading a tour today, but perhaps tomorrow or Sunday. Take a room and I'll send him to see you. Now, if you'll excuse me, I need to see about your addled friend Steen. Good day, Mr. Prescott." Croghan stalked off toward the trail.

Archie checked into the hotel and made arrangements to stable the exhausted horse. He made a mental note to search Steen's wagon.

Standing in his room, Archie felt at a loss for what to do next. He wanted to act, to force the chacmool's hand somehow, most of all to find Jane. *Where are you, daughter?* he thought. *Do you know I've come for you?* But he couldn't very well set off into the woods searching for her, or just wander into the cave. He had to wait for Stephen. And nothing would happen until Sunday night, anyway. Well, at least I survived the trip, Archie consoled himself. After everything he'd been through, he was finally at Mammoth Cave. Now he would just have to wait.

The one thing he could do was take a bath, and that he did, scrubbing himself clean of three weeks' traveling grime and soaking his weary bones until the water cooled and he started to get a chill. When he returned to his room, he felt incredibly refreshed. Even his thigh felt better; the scarred-over wound had stopped aching for the first time in months.

Archie didn't realize he'd fallen asleep until a knock at the door woke him. "Just a minute," he called, groggy from his nap and surprised to see that darkness had fallen. It took him a moment to find his trousers and get to the door.

A young mulatto, in his early twenties perhaps, tipped his dusty hat and said, "Mr. Archie Prescott?" His clothes were grimed with reddish-brown mud, and so was his hair, which ran in unruly waves down over his collar. *My God,* Archie thought. *He looks like the very double of Frederick Douglass.*

"Yes. You're Stephen?" The mulatto nodded. "Ah. Wonderful." Archie realized that he'd forgotten to eat earlier in the day, what with all the chaos Steen had caused. His stomach rumbled loud enough for both of them to hear. "Excuse me," Archie said sheepishly. "I'm—could we talk over supper?"

A shadow passed across Stephen's face, but his voice

stayed level. "If you want to take your supper on the back porch."

"Oh, God," Archie said, terribly embarrassed. "I'm sorry; I wasn't thinking."

"Never mind," Stephen said. He smiled broadly, and Archie found the sudden mood shift somehow unsettling. "You go on and get dressed. I'll meet you on the porch."

"Dr. Croghan said you were a bit pressed for time," Stephen said, after Archie was settled on the hotel's expansive porch with a meal and a full mug of beer.

"I am." Archie chose his words carefully, unsure how much he should give away in a public setting.

At this late hour, the porch was deserted except for the occasional house servant banging through the kitchen door. Still, Archie had an odd feeling that someone could easily eavesdrop on their conversation. "I only have until Sunday night."

"Well," Stephen said, "I reckon you won't have to wait that long." He took a swallow from a pocket flask and offered it to Archie, who declined even though the smell of liquor drew him powerfully. In hindsight, it was clear that his heavy drinking had contributed to the creeping resigned comfort he'd felt while traveling aboard *Maudie*, and he couldn't afford any such laxity now.

"How's tomorrow morning sound?" Stephen winked, and drank again.

"Tomorrow? Excellent, but aren't you already engaged?"

"Nothing that Mat or Nick can't handle. There's times they go by my name just so a visitor can say Stephen took him through the cave." Stephen laughed at this, as if he found the idea of his fame ludicrous.

Archie couldn't quite believe this sudden good fortune. "Well," he said, toasting Stephen with his mug. "Tomorrow then."

"If you want the whole-day tour, we'll have to leave

by seven o'clock. I'll meet you in the hotel lobby."

At that moment the kitchen door swung open and Dr. Croghan stepped out onto the porch. "Mr. Prescott!" he said heartily, catching Archie, who had been expecting Croghan to question him again about Steen's bizarre behavior, off balance. *Lucky no one saw him up close,* Archie thought, *or I'd be answering questions about how a blind man managed to make a beeline for the cave like that.*

Apparently Croghan had decided that a paying customer could be forgiven unfortunate traveling companions, though. Looking every inch the wealthy burgher in formal evening dress, he strode beaming to the table where Stephen and Archie sat. Archie conceived an instant dislike for the man.

"None of my guides have been able to track down Mr. Steen," Croghan said. "I'm afraid I'm beginning to be concerned. Are you sure, Mr. Prescott, that you can shed no more light on his actions?"

"I just traveled with the man," Archie said apologetically. "I didn't know him very well."

"Ah. Unfortunate." Croghan shook his head. "Well. Have you made arrangements?" He inclined his head toward Stephen. "My apologies for the dining accommodations. If it were up to me, why, I've broken bread with Stephen many times, isn't that right, Stephen?"

Stephen appeared preoccupied with filling the bowl of his pipe. "Yes, sir," he said.

"Still, certain proprieties must be observed. I'll tell you the oddest thing." Croghan hooked his thumbs in his cummerbund and chuckled to himself. "That mummy, the one I sold to Mr. Steen," his eyes flicked toward Stephen, who didn't look up, "well, I dreamed about it last night. Dreamed it was back in the cave, of all things, resting in the chamber where Stephen found it. And then Mr. Steen arrives this afternoon, dashing into the cave like an impetuous boy! I suppose old Pharaoh wouldn't have stumped Joseph with that one, eh, gentlemen?"

Croghan laughed, and Archie joined in, although the doctor's story gave him a chill. The dream explained Croghan's lack of interest in pursuing Steen's disappearance; apparently the chacmool exerted influence even while it was dormant.

It wants me in the cave, Archie thought. *It's removing all the obstacles.*

What sort of ambush was it planning?

"Or perhaps it's just an unsettled conscience," Croghan went on. "I didn't feel altogether at ease selling the remains of a human being, but Mr. Steen's offer was extremely persuasive." Again he looked at Stephen, who lit his pipe and gazed back at Croghan through a cloud of cherry-scented smoke. After a long moment, Stephen shrugged and looked away.

Croghan turned his attention to Archie. "I've heard that Steen sold the mummy to Mr. Barnum," he said, "in New York. True, Mr. Prescott?"

"That's right," Archie said. "Barnum had it on display in his museum. I saw it there." *Saw it bite the arm off a man and rip out his heart while making dead plants grow again.*

"Well," Croghan said. "Perhaps some scientific good will come of it. Good night, Mr. Prescott; Stephen." He strolled down the porch and turned the corner.

Unnerved by Croghan's dream, Archie considered again what he could tell Stephen. Stephen seemed lost in thought, puffing absently at his pipe while he toyed with a gold coin, flipping it through his fingers.

"Ah, Stephen," Archie finally ventured, "there's something I'd like to ask you, but . . . is there somewhere a bit more secluded?"

A thin, somehow knowing smile cracked Stephen's studied indifference. "Come on," he said. "Let's walk a bit."

From the rear of the hotel, a path led into the woods, skirting the edge of a valley that fell away on their right. "There's a spring down there," Stephen said, pointing into the darkness. "Comes from the cave. I call it the River Styx Spring, 'cause . . ."

He looked at Archie, his face unreadable in the dim glow from his pipe. "Well, we'll just wait until you see River Styx tomorrow."

After a few minutes the trail ended in a grassy clearing. Perhaps a dozen tombstones were scattered about, simple block headstones bearing dates Archie couldn't make out. "Supposed to be the guides' cemetery, but enough of us ain't died yet," Stephen said. "Right now it's slaves, plus consumptives from the sanitorium Dr. Croghan had in the cave."

"People lived in the cave?"

Stephen snorted. "Not for long." He struck a match, its tiny flame making the surrounding darkness seem deeper, and puffed at his pipe.

When it became clear that Stephen was waiting for him to speak, Archie cleared his throat. "There's something in the cave I'd particularly like to see," he said.

"And what would that be?"

"The place where you found the—the mummy." Archie watched to see if the guide had reacted to his slip, but he couldn't discern Stephen's expression.

"Hmm," Stephen said. "Ain't an easy trip."

"Well, I think I'm fit enough, if that's what concerns you." *I wish I could see his face,* Archie thought. *Like talking to a cipher when you can't read expressions.*

"That's not it," Stephen said. "River might be too high."

"It's important," Archie said. "It's vitally important; I have to see that room."

"Depends on the river, Mr. Prescott. Some things I can't do anything about. Why do you want to go there, anyway?"

Because my daughter's going to die there and some vast incomprehensible evil be loosed upon the world, Archie wanted to say. *Because I want to touch my daughter again, be a father again.*

Instead, knowing that Stephen would detect the lie even as he spoke it, Archie said, "Scientific interest. The mummy hasn't been studied, really, and—"

"You a scientist, Mr. Prescott?"

Tell him yes, Archie thought. *How will he know, a backwoods Kentucky slave?*

Except he thought Stephen would know.

"Didn't think so," Stephen said after a pause.

He knocked out his pipe on the nearest tombstone. "Time to turn in, Mr. Prescott. Seven o'clock comes early this time of year."

"I have to see that cavern, Stephen. Please."

"Depends on the river," Stephen replied, and walked away toward the hotel.

John Diamond badly wanted to be back in the water again. He felt the cold without really being affected by it, but it still made him uneasy, like a fish must feel when it poked its bony mouth through the surface into naked air. "More fish than man, sorry Johnny. More dead than alive," he moaned softly. When he said *fish*, a tiny piece of his lower lip came loose and stuck to his front teeth.

From the bottom of the hill, the still waters of the spring called out. "In a minute," Diamond said. "Got to look after Rebus."

Rebus was worried, Diamond could see that. He walked away from Presto, making straight for the hotel, but fifty yards before he reached the lamplight flooding the hotel grounds, he doubled back into the woods. Diamond shivered, but he couldn't go back to the water just yet. He had to see what Rebus was up to.

Presto went on back to the hotel, and Diamond absently touched the stump of his right arm. Seems silly to collect debts from the other side, he thought, but still . . . you owe me one, Presto. My body's still mine, and I miss the parts that are missing. The arm didn't hurt any more—it hadn't hurt much to begin with—but Diamond had noticed that he was leaving little bits of himself all over Kentucky. Especially when he'd been dry for too long.

Quiet as a ghost—ha-ha—Diamond followed Rebus back to the small cemetery, then around a side trail that wound down into the valley. He could sense the cave, breathing softly from the bottom of a sinkhole as they moved along its edge. Rebus walked slowly, hands in his pockets; Diamond was glad that he wouldn't have to hurry. Haste made him fall apart faster.

The trail looped around and climbed a hill, then began to slope back down. Somewhere up ahead, the mouth of the cave breathed out the chacmool's stink. Rebus stopped in front of a smaller cave and looked around, sneaking up to a rickety old shack after he'd satisfied himself that he was alone.

Diamond stayed well back, nestling under an overhanging rock. He watched closely and tried to keep thoughts of water from distracting him. The trees, too, drew his mind away from Rebus. They hung over him full of dormant life, muttering in sleepy voices that made Diamond want to yawn. *Under my dead feet,* he thought, *life is stirring out of a long sleep. Wish I could sleep.*

He realized he'd started whispering, carried away by the torrent of voices from the trees, the ground, from his head where Lupita yammered like a parrot. Shushing himself, he tried to concentrate on Rebus, who took a last look around and opened the shack's squeaking door. He disappeared inside, shutting the door behind him, and Diamond crept closer, cursing the roaring of watery voices that drowned out the soft words coming from inside the shed.

One of the voices in the shed belonged to a little girl. *She's here,* Diamond thought. *Nanahuatzin is here. What can I do now?*

Batting at the air around his head to shoo the voices floating there, Diamond turned and stole back down the path, eagerly answering the insistent call of the water.

"Your father is here." Stephen had to force the words out.
The girl's presence seemed to have grown somehow.
There was a fineness about her that made him feel clumsy,
as if he should only speak when spoken to. And it shone
through despite the scabs caking her face and curling under her jaw. They were growing like some sort of fungus,
even beginning to cover areas that Stephen would have
sworn were unscarred when she arrived.

This is how it feels to speak to a queen, he thought.
Even a disfigured wretch of a queen who won't see another sunrise.

"I don't care," Jane said. "I'm nobody's daughter any
more. You never saw me before." She smiled, and her lip
cracked and began to bleed. "I was ugly and unwanted.
Now I'm important, do you see? Something's going to
happen very soon, something important, and it can't happen without me. Da could have helped, but he didn't want
to. He didn't care."

Her smile slipped a bit. "He would rather I was dead."

"Harsh words, girl," Stephen said. "Why would he
come all this way if he didn't want to help?" *And why,*
Stephen asked himself, *are you asking these questions?
You've chosen your side already—are you going back on
it now?*

No, it wasn't that. He didn't like one bit what was
going to happen to Jane, but there was more at stake than
one girl's life. Did she know what she was looking forward to? Stephen didn't think she did. But it would be
useless to tell her now. The chacmool had charmed her
somehow with the gift of its cloak.

Would it? His conscience piped up, a mocking echo
forcing him to face questions he'd just as soon have left
alone. At least until Monday.

If she doesn't know, his conscience said in John Diamond's voice, *you know what you'll have to do, don't
you?*

He did. And that was why he couldn't ask her.

If what you're doing is right, you should be able to face it. Sorry, Johnny, it said, *I think you're just afraid of her answer. That's why you took the mask, isn't it?*

"Shut up," Stephen muttered.

Ask her, then, if you're not afraid of her answer.

"Fine." Stephen took a deep breath. "Jane, do you—"

"My name," she said, lifting her chin primly and drawing the cloak about her narrow shoulders, "is Nanahuatzin."

Stephen started over. "Nanahuatzin." He didn't like the feel of the word in his mouth. It felt *potent*, as if he were making something real by saying it out loud. "Do you know what's going to happen Sunday night?"

"I'm going to leave my body," she replied promptly. Feathers rustled approvingly and stroked her cheeks. "I'll miss it, I know. Especially since it's been healed. I'm pretty again, can you see? But I'm going to the valley, where it's always warm and always sunny and I'll be important there. You've seen the valley—it's like heaven, isn't it?"

She touched her face where the feathers had caressed her, and Stephen saw scabs growing in thick slabs on the backs of her hands. "I'll never be cold, never have to beg," she said slowly, as if chanting a litany. "I'll never be alone again." A deep yawn swallowed her last words, and her eyelids began to droop.

It's lulling her to sleep, Stephen thought, not knowing whether he meant the chacmool or the cloak itself, or whether the distinction mattered. *This happened when I tried to talk to her before.*

But she'd said she knew. She'd seen the valley. Stephen thought again of the dream he'd had—if it had been a dream—and thought of the woman, Chalchihuitlicue, saying *The smoke grows to have its own beauty, the beauty of fresh life bought at the cost of death.* If the girl had seen the valley, she must have seen the smoke. She must know.

Stephen's conscience started to say something, but he forced the words away before they could band together and make meaning. The girl had fallen asleep, and things had come too far.

"Greatness exacts its toll in lives," he whispered. Wedging the door shut behind him, he hurried through the awakened night, wanting only to hide in Charlotte's sleeping embrace.

Fourth Nemontemi, 13-Monkey—April 1, 1843

❖

Archie was in the hotel lobby before six-thirty, when the western sky was still blazing with stars and a faint smear of dawn was just visible in the east. He hadn't slept for hours after returning to his room around ten o'clock, and then had started awake shortly after five, edgy and dull from the combination of fatigue and excited dread. He hadn't the slightest idea what he would do once he was in the cave, and conjuring half-baked schemes in the pre-dawn darkness had done nothing but exacerbate his tension.

The most obvious course of action would be to simply tell Stephen everything. If Stephen was able to believe even half of it, he might be persuaded to help; if not, nothing would have been lost, and at least Archie would have seen the parts of the cave he would need to get through later. Yet, if Stephen didn't believe Archie's story, Archie realized he would have to find some way to sneak back in, with enough time before the ceremony that he could set up some sort of surprise attack. The trouble with that alternative plan was that the chacmool would see him coming as soon as he entered the cave, if not before. But it couldn't do anything until Sunday midnight, when—unless Archie came up with a plan a good deal better than what he had so far—it would end Jane's life with a stroke of a sacrificial knife.

I will not live to see that, Archie swore to himself. If the chacmool doesn't kill me, I will kill it. I can't sneak up on it—all I have left is the force of my will. And the mysterious ally, whoever that was. *Seek the Mask-bearer:* what did that mean?

Stephen came in through the swinging doors between the lobby and the ballroom, startling Archie, who had been watching for him through the front windows. Archie stood, reaching for his coat before he remembered that he'd left it in his room. He thought it would be too bulky for some of the narrower passages. Actually he thought *he* might be too bulky for those passages; he was broader than Stephen through the shoulders and hips. I'll get where I have to go, he thought, his resolve bolstered by Stephen's appearance. It won't kill me to leave a bit of skin on a rock somewhere, not after what I've been through to get here.

"Bad news," Stephen said solemnly. "Can't go to the cave today."

"What? But you said—"

"April Fools', Mr. Prescott." Stephen smiled broadly and nodded toward the front doors. "Come on. Let's get you a coverall, and then we'll go."

"I didn't find that humorous, you know," Archie said as they walked down the sloping trail to the mouth of the cave. He pulled and twisted at his mustard-colored canvas coverall, trying to adjust his clothes underneath it.

"You're too fidgety, Mr. Prescott," Stephen said without stopping. "Tense people freeze up in caves, the small parts in particular."

"Oh, so that was your idea of an icebreaker? Well, let me tell you something—" Archie broke off as they rounded a sharp bend in the trail and he saw the mouth of Mammoth Cave.

The trail ended in a series of rough stone steps that dropped perhaps thirty feet into a steep-walled depression in the earth. A broken pipeline made from hollowed-out tree trunks paralleled the stairs and was swallowed by the cave.

"God," Archie said, awed not because it was big—though it certainly was, gaping from beneath a protruding slab of limestone like the half-lidded eye of the earth itself—but because he could feel it breathing. A whispering breeze, warm compared to the predawn chill of the surface, touched his face like the finger of a curious spirit, and Archie had the strange feeling that his own shallow breathing was being taken for some sort of answer to a question he hadn't heard. Archie's mouth dried up and he could feel his pulse pounding in his throat; the talisman against his chest took up a steady, slow counterpoint.

He took a deep breath, held it, then let it slowly out, forcing his attention back to the task at hand. If Jane was in there, he had to go and get her, if he had to crawl to the very gates of hell to do it.

"Come on, Mr. Prescott," Stephen said. He was already at the bottom of the crude stairway, leaning casually on the trunk of a fallen tree that lay roots upward against the rocky wall of the pit. "It's easier once you get inside and see how big it is." Somewhere above Archie's head, the stuttering clatter of a woodpecker echoed through the trees. Archie took it as a signal, a farewell from the world of light and air.

Stephen was right. Once Archie actually entered the cave and ducked through the flattened tube Stephen called Houchins Narrows, his fear began to melt away. Stephen's rambling guide patter took them through the first tremendous room, the Rotunda, and a mile or so down a gently curving passage called the Main Cave. Archie nodded and made the appropriate noises at the appropriate times, responding automatically to Stephen's prompts while he gave himself time to get used to the enormity of the cave and the furtive sound of dripping water.

He couldn't shake the feeling that all of this had been *made,* consciously constructed by some forgotten agency of incredible power. The Main Cave was perhaps thirty feet high and forty wide, and it went on seemingly forever like an abandoned hall through which majestic processions must once have moved. The Rotunda was larger still, far larger than any room Archie had ever been in. He thought it would have comfortably fitted a country estate within its pocked limestone walls.

Stephen pointed out branching passages as they appeared: Gothic Avenue, Kentucky Cliffs, Cyclops' Gateway. Just after the arched entrance to Gothic Avenue, Stephen held his lamp up to illuminate two stones, each taller than a man.

Looking closely, Archie could see the remains of a pattern scratched into the stones. "What does it mean?" he asked Stephen. "Some sort of gateway?"

"What do *you* think?" Stephen answered, and led Archie on.

Each dark space seemed to call to Archie the way he imagined the words *terra incognita* must have called to Marco Polo or Vasco da Gama, an irresistible seduction spiced with unknown dangers. Several times he nearly called out to Stephen, wanting to ask about the room where the chacmool had been discovered, but each time he stopped himself. Stephen knew what Archie had come to see, and he'd closed off completely the night before when Archie had pressed the issue. Best to wait until Stephen brought it up himself.

Archie had the feeling that rules of conduct between free man and slave didn't apply here. They were artifacts of the surface world, like the picks and shovels scattered about from the long-abandoned mining operations in the cave. *I don't belong here,* Archie thought. *But somehow Stephen does, and that gives him power.*

"Giant's Coffin," Stephen announced, holding up his lamp to illuminate a huge block of stone, fully thirty feet long, resting on the right side of the hall. It was indeed shaped like a coffin, precisely enough that it might have been carved that way. A visible crack ran the length of it, separating a three-foot thickness at the top of the formation that gave the appearance of a lid.

"Does a vampire come out of it at sunset?" Archie asked. His voice sounded strange to him—not muffled, exactly, but strengthless. He laughed shakily, trying to dismiss the nervousness that had crept up inside him again.

Stephen smiled at him and nodded, as if to say *Now you're getting the idea.* "I always wanted to take a peek inside myself," he said.

A trough in the cave floor separated Giant's Coffin from the cleared trail. Stephen clambered down into it, motioning Archie to follow. At what would have been the foot of the coffin he stopped. "If I fell down a hole right now, Mr. Prescott," he said, "you think you could find your way out?"

"Of course," Archie said immediately, though he wasn't at all sure. "Just stay on the trail and then stay to the right in the—Rotunda, right?"

Stephen nodded. "But you'd be in the dark. How's your sense of direction with your eyes closed?"

Archie understood suddenly. He'd been right: down here Stephen wasn't a slave anymore. He quite literally held Archie's life in his hands, and this little interlude was a performance carried out to make that point clear.

How many times has Stephen acted out this drama? Archie wondered. *He doesn't need to tell me to be careful.* But this was more about power than safety. A slave on the surface, Stephen was in total control once daylight faded around the first bend in the Main Cave. And he wanted Archie to know that.

Quite a presence he has, Archie thought, and was reminded again of Frederick Douglass. Something about Stephen's hair, the shape of his jaw; and they were both mulatto . . . He didn't say anything. Stephen looked into his eyes for a long moment, then broke into a broad grin. "Now things get interesting," he said. "Down this way."

Doubling back behind Giant's Coffin, Stephen led the

way down a steeply descending tunnel into a low-ceilinged room. "Used to be a wooden bowl here, right on the floor. Think we'll wait a bit before lunch, though. That is, unless you're hungry now."

"No, let's go on." Let him have his game, Archie decided. "What's down this way?" he asked, pointing into an opening on his left.

"Oh, nothing so much. This is the way to go," Stephen said. Archie followed him into a narrow passage just tall enough to stand in. They followed its sharper curves for several minutes, the silence broken only by Stephen saying at one point, "Careful here." He held his lamp out to the right. "Sidesaddle Pit."

The trail around the pit looked perilously narrow to Archie. He could feel faint stirrings of vertigo as he stepped carefully past the yawning hole, and along with the vertigo came the uncomfortable realization that he had completely lost his sense of direction. Could I find my way out now? he thought. Not bloody likely. Probably I'd find my way to the bottom of that pit, or another one Stephen hasn't seen fit to mention.

"That's just a little one," Stephen said as they approached a four-way intersection. "Forty feet or so. Big one's up here."

Turning left, Archie saw that just ahead the trail narrowed to a muddy trace with a sharp dropoff on the right and absolute blackness on the left. A few wooden posts were set at the lip of the pit, a sort of gesture at the idea of a railing.

My God, Archie thought. Who was foolish enough to cross that first? At the same time, the feather talisman began to quiver excitedly against his chest.

Is this where the chacmool was? Or is? Archie strained to see beyond the limits of Stephen's lamp, but his gaze was drawn back to the pit on his left. "When did you first come down here?" he asked.

"Two years ago. Hadn't found this path yet, so I went across the pit on a ladder."

"On a ladder? Christ, how deep is it?" Archie could feel himself edging dangerously close to babble, but God, to cross that chasm on a ladder—he couldn't even imagine it, and the feather token kept jittering, distracting him when he needed all of his attention just to stay on level ground.

Stephen appeared not to notice Archie's anxiety. "It's hard to plumb," he said, shrugging. "But this'll give you an idea." From his bag Stephen took a twist of cotton. He struck a match to it and beckoned Archie closer. "Watch it fall."

Archie stepped as close as he dared to the edge of the pit and looked down into it, gripping a rail post so tightly his fingers ached. Stephen dropped the torch and it fell in a lazy spiral, throwing light on the grooved walls of the pit. After an impossibly long time, the torch hit bottom, a flurry of sparks bursting from it as it landed among a jumble of rocks.

"Might be only a hundred twenty feet or so on that far edge," Stephen said. "But that rockpile slants down under this crossing. I don't know how deep it is there."

"Have you been to the bottom?" Archie watched the torch burn itself out, swallowed by darkness returning to the bottom of the pit.

"Nope. Don't even know if there's a way. Think there is, but the lead's a long way from here. This is the deepest pit I've found; it could run across all kinds of other cave down there."

"What's it called?"

"Bottomless Pit." Stephen chuckled. "Used to think it was true."

Leaving Bottomless Pit, they wound through a sharp S-curve, the roof of the cave dropping continuously toward the muddy floor. The mud was deeper here as well; Archie sank in over his ankles at every step and still didn't feel solid rock. He wondered if quicksand was a feature of the cave. At the end of the S-curve, the talisman had quieted somewhat, leaving Archie certain that Bottomless Pit was, if not the chacmool's lair, certainly some kind of focus for its activity. He made up his mind to ask Stephen about the possible way to the bottom of the pit; Riley Steen had babbled something about Stephen often taking his charges into previously unexplored portions of the cave. Maybe he would do that for Archie.

Soon I'll have to ask him again about where he found the chacmool, Archie thought. And what can I say about Jane that won't make him think I'm a lunatic? Then he lost his train of thought completely as he saw where they were going next.

"Welcome to Winding Way," Stephen said with a wicked grin. "It's bigger now than it used to be. Everyone who goes through takes a bit of the mud out with them."

The hole in the wall ahead of them was perhaps four feet wide, but Archie doubted it was more than eighteen or twenty inches high. "Keep your nose up," Stephen said, "and watch out, under the mud there's a crack that can catch your foot."

"Thanks for the warning," Archie said. His throat had gone dry again, and he was very much aware that more than a hundred feet of limestone hung inches over his head.

Stephen saw Archie's apprehension, and his expression grew serious. "Just keep moving," he said. "Follow my light. This only goes a couple hundred feet and then there's big cave after that.

"Follow my light," he repeated. Then he pushed the lantern ahead of him and wriggled into the hole.

I could just stay here, Archie thought. He'd have to come back for me. The cave felt cold to him for the first time.

If Jane's here, she's cold, too. And she doesn't have Stephen to guide her.

"She . . ." Archie swallowed the rest of what he was

going to say. Who was he answering, anyway? No one had really spoken.

No time to start hearing voices, Prescott, he told himself. And certainly no time to start answering them.

"You say something, Mr. Prescott?" Stephen's voice was muffled in the narrow crawlway. Archie could see his feet in what little lamplight showed between his body and the walls.

"Right behind you," Archie said through gritted teeth. He leaned into the hole, found handholds on the muddy walls, and hauled himself toward the glow of Stephen's lamp.

Prescott came out of Winding Way looking like there were demons on his tail, breathing fast and shallow. Quite a few visitors reacted to their first crawl like that, but there was something different about Prescott's fear. He'd carried an edge of desperation with him into the cave, and Stephen had seen it creep closer to the surface when Prescott had looked down into Bottomless Pit. He's come this far on sheer force of will, Stephen thought, to find his daughter. How long is that will going to hold out?

"Let's go a little ways up ahead, then we'll stop for a bite," Stephen said. Prescott nodded, and they walked through the arched passage called Great Relief Hall. The name seemed appropriate now. Prescott relaxed visibly now that he could stand upright.

Following a bend to the left, Stephen led Archie into River Hall. The floor sloped away to the left, down to Echo River. But Stephen pointed the other way, upward and off to the right. "Big dome up that way, if you want to see it," he said.

"No," Prescott said. "Is that water I smell?"

"Echo River," Stephen said. "We should have a look down there, see if it's flooded bad."

"Is that where you found that mummy?"

"Not right there. Sometimes the river blocks off the

way to get there. It's a good place to stop for lunch, too."

At the bottom of the slope, Stephen stopped, looking at the still black pool they called the Dead Sea. *Why am I leading him on like this?* he thought. *Whatever I'm going to do I should just do it.*

The chacmool wanted Prescott dead. It had made that very clear, and Stephen could have killed him a half-dozen times already. A little shove on the edge of Bottomless Pit would have done the trick. Or Sidesaddle.

So why hadn't he done it? Hiding the girl had been a hell of a lot more dangerous. If discovered, that would have earned Stephen a quick trip to the nearest tree branch—if he was lucky enough not to be burned alive instead. But if Prescott had taken a misstep over a pit, no one would have thought anything was amiss; Stephen didn't know of anyone who had recently died in the cave, but it was always a possibility. The simple truth of it was that he couldn't kill Prescott. The man didn't deserve to die.

Not even for a new world? the chacmool's voice asked him. *Is his life worth slavery for your children's children?*

Stephen smelled the smoke of Tlalocan. Men in chains or dead men feeding altar fires, are those my only choices? he thought. Murderer or slave? No. Prescott didn't need to be dead, just out of the way. The cave was huge. A man could easily be lost in it for days, going in circles even if he had light to guide him.

Prescott called out, interrupting Stephen's reverie. "What's down here?" he said, dropping to his knees in front of the branch passage that led to the bottom of Bottomless Pit.

Damn, Stephen thought. Why'd I bring him this way? But he knew the answer to that question. *Because you needed a reason, that's why.*

Stephen had hoped that the chacmool's fears about Prescott were groundless, but now Prescott had perked up like a dog seeing a squirrel both times he'd passed a direct path to the Mummy Room. He could sense the chacmool somehow, and it knew that. More than knew: the chac-mool feared Prescott.

"That hole, I'm not sure where it goes," Stephen lied. "It's a big cave. Lot more passages I haven't been through than ones I have."

Something odd struck him then, as he walked back to where Prescott crouched. The front of Prescott's coverall was moving. It twitched as if something alive was inside, trying to get out. Had that been happening when he'd looked down into Bottomless Pit? Stephen was certain he would have noticed if it had, but then again it was awful hard to not look at one of those torches, throwing light on walls no man had ever touched.

That's how he does it, how he senses the chacmool. Some kind of charm around his neck.

"Is this where you found it?" Prescott asked, like he hadn't heard Stephen before.

"No, like I said, I've never been down there. Come on, Mr. Prescott. The place you want to see is farther ahead." *And please don't you call this bluff. Don't make me do something I don't want to do.*

Prescott looked up at him then, saw Stephen's gaze focused on the front of his shirt, and clapped a hand over whatever was wriggling inside. "It's a—a magnet," he stammered. "Must be some strange metals near here. The mummy, it reacted strangely to magnetism, so I thought . . ." His voice trailed off.

Sure, we're under three hundred feet of limestone, and he's got a magnet that jitters like water on a hot griddle, Stephen thought. "Come on, Mr. Prescott, what you want to see is up here," he said, trying to keep the urgency from his voice. He reached out and laid a hand on Archie's shoulder.

A dam broke in Stephen's mind, and a torrent of voices exploded into his head. All of them, laughing and yelling like they hadn't spoken in years, their words flying by too fast to catch. Stephen reeled away from Prescott, numbed by the endless clamor in his mind and one single thought cutting through: *He brought them back. The chacmool hushed them, but Prescott brought them back.*

The rush of voices faded to a murmur as Stephen broke contact with Prescott, but they didn't go away completely. Like they had from the moment he'd first stepped into the cave as a seventeen-year-old boy, the voices flowed in a steady undercurrent through Stephen's mind, a muttered chaos of languages that made him feel at home again.

How can I kill him now?

He realized he was staring at Prescott, and fumbled for something to cover up his strange behavior. "Lost my balance there."

"Ah," Prescott said, his face giving nothing away. "Right. Well, let's go see the ch—"

"This way," Stephen said. He helped Archie to his feet and led him deeper into the cave.

Stephen continued pointing out and naming the cave's prominent features, but he seemed distracted, performing the role of guide almost as an afterthought. And the names began to sound like grim jokes: River Styx, Lake Lethe, Purgatory.

Even the boat ride along the River Styx and Lethe gave Archie a chill, with Stephen rowing quietly and the water like liquid night. *I'm so glad he isn't poling,* Archie thought. *I don't think I could take it.*

After they had left the river complex behind them and begun a gentle ascent, Archie asked Stephen how much farther they had to go.

"Oh, I imagine it's another four miles yet. You tired, Mr. Prescott?"

"No, just curious. How long will it take to get there and back?"

Stephen appeared to consider the question. "Should be out right around sunset," he said finally.

Archie was glad that the river had proved low enough that they could continue past it, but he wasn't fool enough to think that he could retrace the route they'd taken without Stephen's help. I'm going to have to tell him soon, Archie thought. He saw the talisman moving on my chest—he must know something out of the ordinary is going on. Probably I should have told him right away, and just taken my chances. It was too late for that, though; there would be quite an interesting conversation whenever they did stop for lunch.

The aspect of the cave began to change around them as the riverine passages dropped away behind. The spacious, ovoid passages that made up the greater part of the Main Cave had given way to narrower, high-ceilinged canyons. In crevices, Stephen pointed out gypsum flowers, tiny delicate tendrils of stone that looked like a million snowflakes all in a row. At times Stephen and Archie straddled protruding shelves on either side of such a passage and made their way ahead with the floor lost to sight below.

Archie had a growing sense that while the halls nearer the entrance were laid out in some kind of comprehensible pattern, these winding canyons formed a many-leveled maze. Several times he thought they passed a section of cave that he'd seen before, only to have it dip or curve in an unexpected way. The floor grew muddy again, and small pools gleamed occasionally in the light of Stephen's lamp.

Abruptly the passage they were following doubled back and shrunk into a crawl. Archie hesitated, feeling panic begin to nibble at his composure again, but Stephen reassured him. "This one's quite a bit longer than Winding Way," he said, "but it's not so tight. And what's on the other end makes it worth your while." With that he scrambled in, pushing the lamp ahead of him.

Archie followed, his knees already raw, locking his gaze onto Stephen's light so he wouldn't freeze at the thought of the ceiling an inch above his head. There was plenty of lateral room, though, unlike Winding Way, and he fell into a rhythm—elbow, knee, elbow, knee, and don't look up.

Standing again, Archie found himself smiling. His fear had broken, or been transformed into exhilaration. After all, how many people had done what he was doing? Some, to be sure, but crawling through miles of muddy cave was hardly a commonplace activity. And the subterranean beauty was growing on him, seducing him by its stark, gloomy grandeur. "There's no other place on earth like this, is there?" he said.

Stephen grinned. "You think that now, wait another few minutes."

Over the next mile or so, they passed three giant domes, each one causing Archie to stop dead and gape at the sheer size of them. They towered farther than the lights could reach, and dropped away below the rocky lip Archie and Stephen traversed, their far walls barely shadowed. "Good place for a bite to eat, don't you think?" Stephen said at the last dome. They had climbed down into it, stopping at a level place with tremendous stone blocks standing like monuments around them.

"Oh, yes," Archie breathed, and Stephen unshouldered his bag, taking out paper-wrapped roasted chicken and a block of cheese. He nipped at his flask and offered it to Archie, who again declined. There was something about this place that made him want to experience it without the filter of spirits.

Now I'm beginning to understand how a man could spend so much time down here, Archie thought. Perhaps I'm beginning to understand Stephen a bit. This hint of common ground cheered Archie, giving him a feeling of camaraderie. It was time to explain a few things; Stephen would understand.

"Have any . . . well, strange things been happening near here recently?" he asked.

"Cave's always full of strangeness," Stephen replied between bites of chicken. "Get people under the ground, away from light, it's like sailors alone at sea. They start seeing things. People tell me all the time they can see in the dark when I put out the light. Maybe they can. I can't, but there's times in the dark when I feel like a bat must feel, making pictures in its head when it can't use its eyes. You ever been in absolute dark, Mr. Prescott? Dark with no glow from a star or gaslight or anything else? Five-miles-deep-in-a-cave dark?"

Archie shook his head.

"Tell you this, you can feel it. Feel it touching your skin. Even the tiniest light takes all the weight from darkness, but down here it's *heavy*. Pushes in from every direction. I read Plato once, you know that? The allegory of the cave." He savored each syllable. "Bet you didn't think slaves could read."

"I know quite a few whites who can't," Archie said, but Stephen didn't seem to hear him.

"Plato said that the people chained in the cave saw only shadows of the real things outside. Well, I been chained to this cave since I was a boy, and I get the feeling sometimes that the shadows down here *are* what's real. All that up there," he said, waving at the darkness over their heads, "they're the shadows. They hide what's real. It stays buried down here like it's waiting to be born."

Archie began to feel that Stephen was playing a game with him again, that he was intoxicated by the reversal of power that had taken place sometime since they'd left the surface. *What has he seen? What does he know?* Archie wanted to stand up and shout, "Where's the chacmool, Stephen? What has it done with my daughter?" But he was helpless, completely at the mercy of Stephen's knowledge of the cave, and all he could do was nod silently and wait to see what Stephen would do next.

"I'm not a scientist," Archie said.

"I know. What are you, Mr. Prescott?"

"I'm looking for my daughter," Archie said in a rush. "She's been—stolen away, and I think she's here. I know she's here."

The words hung in the air for a long time. Archie

waited for Stephen to react, certain now that he knew something. But how much? What was his role in all of this? He fell back on Tamanend's words again, picking them apart in the hope that they would offer some guidance.

Seek the Mask-bearer. He is torn, and you must give him peace.

Give him peace. Why was he torn? What could Archie do to give him peace? Stephen remained silent, brooding over the struggling glow of his lamp.

Now or never, Archie thought. "Stephen, I need to see the room where you found the chacmool. It has my daughter, and I mean to have her back."

Seconds passed, stretched into the sort of moment in time that could only occur when important words hung unspoken: a moment pregnant with an awful imminence. Archie was conscious of everything around him: the invisible vastness of the dome over their heads, the smell of smoke from Stephen's lamp, the chill of the rocks on which he sat, the sound of his own voice in his head saying again *I mean to have her back.* Still Stephen sat, as if he had become mummified himself, rooted to the cave floor by the passage of that endless moment.

Finally he stood and shouldered his satchel. Gesturing with the lamp, he said, "Up here. There's something up here I think you should see."

A few minutes later, Stephen halted Archie. "This is what darkness is," he said, and put out his lamp.

Archie closed his eyes, heard the sound of water falling, opened them again. All he could see were bright images of the lamp flame, and those faded in a few seconds, leaving him in a darkness more absolute than he could have imagined. He could feel it, just as Stephen had said he would, a gentle weight resting against his skin, reminding him of the way the breath of the cave had seemed like ghostly, inquisitive fingers. But this darkness asked no questions. It knew the answers already.

He felt in the midst of an immense space, supported by the press of the dark. He couldn't feel his own weight, couldn't tell where his feet ended and the floor began. This is the darkness of a child in the womb, he thought, or of a soul loosed from its body. He thought that if a light were suddenly to return, he would see himself exhaling darkness, watch it trail away into the shadows. Light was an absence of dark, he realized, not the other way around.

Stephen lit a match, its eager flame like a hummingbird sun. He lit three cotton torches and used a stick to fling them away onto ledges high up on the walls of a mammoth series of domes. Five, Archie counted, forming a semicircle each higher than light from a torch could reach. He saw the stream of water he'd heard, separating into jeweled drops as it fell through the light to patter on the rocky floor.

"I've never been here before," Stephen said. "Heard it. Knew it had to be big, but never came this far."

The torches burned low, bringing the dark out to reclaim the majesty of the domes. "I like to show visitors a little virgin cave," Stephen said. "You got a feel for the cave, Mr. Prescott. You've done better than most."

"It's like a cathedral," Archie breathed, as the torches faded to afterimages in his blind eyes. "If this is where you found the chacmool, I understand why it chose this place."

"Chacmool's all through the cave, Mr. Prescott. Everywhere. It's in the darkness you feel and the peculiar grand gloom you see. This is the chacmool's place." Stephen's voice floated into the space, coming from no fixed point.

"It can have this place," Archie said. "But it can't have my daughter."

After a pause, Stephen answered. "No, it can't have this place, Mr. Prescott. Your chacmool is all through this place, but it's my place, too. The world, up there, doesn't know that. Nothing up there is mine. But there's a new world, waiting to be born." Archie heard his feet scuff on the dusty stone floor.

"You brought the voices back, Mr. Prescott, and for that I know you're a good man. And you're trying to save your daughter cause she's all you have, isn't she? Well, this new world is all I have, and your daughter's only one girl."

The darkness folded around Archie as he realized what was happening. He'd been right yesterday. The chacmool had laid a trap for him in the cave, and he'd walked right into it. "Stephen, please . . ."

"No, Mr. Prescott. I can't give this up."

Something clattered hollowly against the rocks near where Stephen stood. "If you are what I think you are, that'll lead you out. I was supposed to kill you, but I can't do that."

"My *daughter,* Stephen. Please." Archie held out his hands and found nothing to support him. "Please don't leave me here."

Stephen made no reply. The quiet crunch of his footsteps faded away.

"Don't leave me, Stephen! *Stephen!*" Archie's voice rose to a broken scream. He kept screaming Stephen's name, paralyzed by the crushing darkness all around.

Fifth Nemontemi, 1-Grass—April 2, 1843

❖

Stephen felt like he was sleepwalking as he passed the mouth of the cave on his way to the toolshed. Ground fog lay heavily among the trees and obscured the path, but his feet seemed to know their own way. The sun had just risen, but the dawn had no freshness. Its light seemed like another strange kind of fog, clinging to things, dripping from branches and twisting birdsongs into unrecognizable murmurs. He hadn't slept again, lying awake next to Charlotte with his mind cluttered by gabbling voices. Twice during the night she had rolled against him and begun stroking his stomach, trailing her fingers through the curly hairs that grew there. Both times he had stopped her before she went any further, emasculated by the tumult in his head and his conflicted conscience. He had felt like warning her away, saying *I'm one small step from a murderer, blossom. One very small step.* And then he had burned with desire to make love, crush her to him, and when she had fallen back to the edge of sleep, speak to her. Justify himself: *If it's not just for me? If it's for our children, for every black child who could be born and live and be able to say* I am free?

Would that make it all right?

Maybe he had slept. In the darkest hours, anyway, he hadn't exactly been awake. At times the voices had subsided into a quiet rushing noise like faraway rapids; at other moments he'd had to hold the blankets tightly to remind himself where he was. Fires had sprung up in the corners of the room, then faded out, leaving a stinking roasted odor behind. Charlotte muttered sleepy complaints and tossed on the bed, uneasy but not alarmed enough to wake up.

It had not been sleep, Stephen decided, but he hadn't been awake. He'd passed the night somewhere in between, in a place where he could see and smell dreams that weren't his own. And somewhere deep inside he was certain that no living man had dreamed those dreams.

He hadn't been able to return from the place, either; it was still all around him as he popped the shack's door open. The chirp of warped wood set off a fresh flurry of voices, but he couldn't pin any of them down. Prescott brought the voices back, Stephen thought, but I can't understand them anymore. Was that because of Prescott or something in Stephen himself?

I am not a murderer. I do this for the Bishops and Bransfords who aren't yet born. Her life is not worth all of theirs.

Jane's appearance shocked him. Her skin had grown nearly transparent from days without sun and her eyes blinked feverishly deep in their sockets. She was so thin that Stephen could see the pulse under her jaw. The blanket he'd brought her lay flung in a corner, wrapped partly around a rusting shovel, and she hadn't touched any food in at least two days, since the dried apples. The rest of the food he'd brought her lay exactly where he'd left it.

Worst of all were the scabs. Stephen had seen fading scars on her face and hands when the chacmool brought her, and even then she had been picking at the scabs, but they had been few and small—just normal from the itch of a healing burn. Now the scabs had grown to cover one entire side of her face, nearly closing one eye and pulling the right corner of her mouth into a smirk. They covered her hands as well, fusing the fingers together into single crooked hooks. Still she stroked the green quetzal feathers, and the feathers stroked her back, leaving fresh lumps of scab wherever they grazed unblemished skin.

"Is it time now? I think I'll miss this body, now that it's been healed. But is it time?" Scabs cracked as she spoke, and when she smiled her bottom lip split open and began to bleed. Stephen could see her nearly hidden eye rolling under a crust of dried blood, peering past him in hopes that the chacmool had come with him. When that shattered gaze returned to him, Stephen had to force himself not to run.

"Yes, it's time," he said. "Time to finish your travels."

She stood, keeping the feather cloak wrapped tightly about her. "Hooray, it's time," she said, and all of the voices in Stephen's head echoed her.

Archie had no idea how long he screamed for Stephen before his voice gave out and he sank to the floor, still choking out wordless guttural whispers. There was no time where there was no light. He lay on his side, feeling carefully about him to make sure he wasn't on the lip of some invisible abyss, and gave up.

I will die here, he thought, the chill of the cave seeping into him. *If I stay here, I'll go mad and die of thirst. If I move, the rock will open under my feet and my body will lie in a hole, decaying into a stringy curiosity for some scientist a hundred years from now.*

I'm buried alive again.

He couldn't move. If he explored the floor around him, he would find that there was no floor, that Stephen had led him onto a narrow spire with nothing but emptiness all around, burying him in space, in a bubble encased in stone.

Ridiculous, of course; he'd seen the cavern in the light of Stephen's own lamp, and knew that he was near a wall, a solid wall that curved into a solid floor that extended beneath the domes towering over him.

But it was cold like his grave in the Brewery, and where there was darkness, there was no knowledge. Outside the sun might be shining, but here the only real thing was the dark.

If the sun is shining, it's Sunday. And if it's Sunday, Jane's going to die tonight.

The thought came unbidden, and Archie tried to reason it away. She'll die quickly, he answered. That's more than I can hope for. He shivered, feeling the cold settle deeper into his body.

You want to die quick? Get up and walk. Fall down a hole. Shrivel up like the chacmool did, waiting for someone to find it.

"Don't make me do that," Archie moaned hoarsely. "I don't want to know if there's nothing there."

What did Stephen say?

"Nothing."

What did Stephen say before he left?

"What does it matter? He left."

You want to go crazy before you die, Presto? Do you want to die shivering and sobbing in the dark?

Do you?

"Don't," Archie said.

Do you?

"He—he dropped something."

What did he say?

The words ground out between Archie's teeth. "He said, 'If you are what I think you are, this'll lead you out.' But he lied about everything else—why should that be true?"

He also said he could have killed you. Was that true?

"Don't make me do this. I've done enough."

When the chacmool cuts out your daughter's heart, will she think so?

"She'll die quickly."

She'll still die. What if Stephen was telling the truth? What if you could have gotten out? You've spoken to the dead, Presto. What will you say to Jane when she's one of them?

"Don't make me do this," Archie moaned again, but he

was already crawling across the floor, feeling ahead inch by invisible inch.

Stephen didn't light his lamp as he led Jane into the cave. The blindsight the chacmool had granted him a taste of had returned the day before, when he'd put out the lamp and left Prescott. It was a gift, he knew, a reward for the work he'd done so far. He served the master, and the master granted his favor. It was the kind of thing Dr. Croghan would do.

Thinking of Croghan, Stephen wondered how he would explain his absence. He hadn't specifically committed to giving any tours today, but even if no visitors had requested him, Stephen knew there would be trouble. If nothing else, Croghan would be angry that he'd missed Sunday service at the church across the river. The doctor liked to have his slaves in church.

Well, I will be in church, Stephen thought, watching Jane—he still couldn't call her Nanahuatzin—step eagerly ahead of him. It seemed she could see in the cave too. Different church, and I've got my very own Messiah walking next to me.

Besides, Croghan's bluster wouldn't matter come morning, would it?

He led Jane along the route her father had taken the day before, around Giant's Coffin and past Bottomless Pit, where she stopped and looked longingly down. "We're very close now, aren't we?" she said eagerly. Her scabs had begun to bleed a faint light, a sickly glow that reminded Stephen of the decayed gleam that morning's dawn had brought.

"Very close," he agreed, and they went on.

The mud from the Winding Way didn't stick to the feathers of her cloak, and she came out into Great Relief looking like she'd been freshly bathed. She stared to chatter, prattling constantly about missing her body but looking forward to the next part of her journey. Half of what she said was unintelligible, muffled by the scabs that limited how far she could open her mouth. She didn't seem to notice, and Stephen stopped listening—the voices were growing louder, and some of them were mimicking everything she said.

She pushed ahead of him, leading the way up the branch from River Hall to Bottomless Pit. By the time he reached the pit she had already gone into the Mummy Room. She fell silent, and he had to stop and take a deep breath before he ducked through the triangular opening after her.

Real light burned in the Mummy Room, illuminating the massive carving on the wall, the altar stone before it. Jane stood facing the chacmool, her disfigured face transformed by an expression Stephen had seen on voodoo women when the *loas* started talking.

The chacmool stroked her scabbed-over cheek, strings of light dripping from its clawed fingers. It didn't look human. Tufts of fur sprouted from its pointed ears, and its skull had lengthened, growing a thick feline muzzle. Its cloak twitched, the feathers hardening briefly into scales, then fluttering like feathers again.

It turned to Stephen. Jane stayed where she was, half of her face smiling broadly. Her eyes were closed. She swayed slightly, in time with the ripples in her own cloak.

"Stephen," it hissed. A forked snake's tongue flicked out between feline fangs. "You have done well."

It touched him lightly on the forehead and Stephen gasped as the voices in his head fell silent. "But not all is well," the chacmool purred. "Prescott lives."

Stephen felt like his mind had been laid bare by the chacmool's touch. "He's—he can't get here," Stephen stammered. "He's lost. I'm the only one who could find him again."

The chacmool growled and pressed its claws into Stephen's brow. "Find him then," it rasped. "And this time do as I told you." Its claws withdrew, leaving trickles of blood from four shallow punctures.

"Do not fail me, Stephen," it said. "Your dreams are not yet secure."

Thᴇ ʙlindsiɢht had left him. No: it had been taken away, by the same touch that had blown the voices away like leaves before a strong wind. Stephen stood among the breakdown rocks on the floor of Bottomless Pit, remembering the flush of excitement he'd felt when he'd first stood there. Before he'd discovered the Mummy Room, before he'd somehow brought the mummified chacmool to the surface, before he'd delivered a little white girl into the hands of her killer. And now he had to find Prescott and kill him. The chacmool would know if he didn't.

Stephen wiped at the blood on his forehead. When was it too late to turn back? Now, he decided. The chacmool's claws could as easily have torn out his throat, and they definitely would if he didn't do as it said. *So now,* he thought, *I will be a murderer. Take that last small step.*

He lit his lamp and made his way back to River Hall, wondering how he would face Charlotte. Wondering if she would know. *Will I lose my love for this?*

The chacmool was testing his loyalty. After he killed Prescott, it would find another test. When would it end?

Near the Dead Sea, Stephen saw something on the floor. He picked it up and saw that it was half of a raw potato. How had it gotten there? A strange smell hung about it, one he remembered but couldn't place.

He sniffed at the potato and the smell came to him, among a flood of associations from a Christmas pageant Dr. Croghan had put on the year before. It was myrrh.

"Chacmool giveth and the chacmool taketh away, eh, Rebus?"

Stephen saw John Diamond's head poking from the Dead Sea. "I gave Prescott the mask, dead man," he said. "It's not my fault if he doesn't take it."

"Hedging your bets? Sorry, Johnny, that's no good." Diamond climbed out of the pool and stood dripping. Stephen saw that he was missing most of one arm and part of the other hand. He stood awkwardly, as if one of his legs was shorter than the other, and strips of skin had peeled away from his bald skull.

"Better find your tomb, dead man," Stephen said. "Before you can't get there."

"Oh, I'm not worried about that. Tomb's all around. *You* worry me, Rebus." Diamond grimaced, working at a loose tooth with his tongue.

"Why's that?"

"You going to kill Presto? You are. Why?"

"You know why. You knew what this was all about before I did, and you just played games." Stephen remembered the potato and tossed it away.

"No games. Dead man do what he can. You playing games with yourself. Why you going to kill Prescott?"

Stephen paused. "Were you a slave, Diamond?"

"Nope. Born free. Not that way now, though."

"Then you don't know. A man, a man just like me, *owns* me. Owns my wife. If I have to kill a man to change that, I'd be a coward not to." Stephen's voice began to rise.

Diamond raised one of his truncated arms, then chuckled. "Sorry Johnny—Rebus—can't shush you proper. But you don't want the chacmool to hear us." Diamond worked the tooth free and spat it into the Dead Sea. "New world, eh?" he finished.

Stephen nodded. "That's what's at stake."

"Got it. Question you haven't asked yourself, Rebus. Chacmool makes promises, then it's gonna kill you if you don't do what it says. How's that different from your master now?"

"It's not about me, dead man. It's about my children, every other Negro child that hasn't been born."

"Hm. You think that little girl's the only one going into the fire? Who the rest gonna be, Rebus? You think He Who Makes Things Grow won't want *your* daughter's heart?"

"That—"

"I asked you this before. Listen this time. What makes you think its world," Diamond waved toward the passage leading to Bottomless Pit, "gonna be any different than the one you got?"

Stephen couldn't answer.

"You think on that, Rebus. You think on that while you go to kill that Presto."

Diamond walked away down River Hall, leaving Stephen alone staring into the water of the Dead Sea.

Each rock Archie grasped seemed a small miracle to him, a solid bit of certainty holding firm against the void around him. He belly-crawled slowly, painfully, in what he hoped was the right direction, shying away from slight dips in the floor that might suddenly drop away. The knowledge that he could be moving deeper into the cave ate at his fragile will, but he forced himself to keep moving. If he was going to die, he was going to die moving.

His left shoulder brushed a solid vertical surface and he laid both hands on it, reaching up and out to both sides. It was a wall, thank God. If he had set off in the right direction, it would lead him to the entrance, where Stephen had dropped the wooden object before abandoning him. A new world, Stephen had said as he left. Archie wondered if Stephen had seen this new world, had heard the meaty crackle of burning hearts and seen the pillar of smoke from the sacrificial fires. What had the chacmool shown him?

"If I see him again, I'll ask," Archie croaked. He was terribly thirsty. His tongue felt swollen and it stuck to the roof of his mouth. "When I see him."

Archie stood, hunching against the wall. He reached over his head and felt only emptiness. He was still in the main domes, then; the passage leading to them narrowed toward the ceiling, and he thought he could have found the sloping roof without jumping. Not that he had any intention of leaving his feet.

His control slowly returning, Archie began to look at the darkness as a problem to be solved. *I've been buried alive,* he thought. *What do I have to fear from being lost in a cave?*

The thing Stephen had dropped had to be near the entrance, but not against the walls; Stephen had been coming back from throwing torches when he put out the light. Archie would have to leave the wall to find it.

Slowly expanding vertigo twisted in his stomach at the thought. But what was the alternative? He couldn't just follow this left-hand wall all the way back to the river. Far too many intersections and slippery slopes lay between here and there. The only way he was going to survive was if he found the thing Stephen had left for him.

Archie supposed that he owed Stephen a certain amount of gratitude. After all, Stephen could certainly have killed him any time. Stranding him in these remote domes had been an act of direct defiance, particularly since Stephen had left a way out. And why had he done that, if the chacmool's promised new world was all he had to believe in?

He has doubts, Archie realized. *He's torn between the chacmool's promises and its cruelty. After all, he must know it's going to kill Jane. He said as much.*

This is a test, isn't it? He wants something else to believe in. Seek the Mask-bearer, *Tamanend said.* He is torn, and you must give him peace. *Solve the problem,* Archie thought. If he was going to find the Mask-bearer, it had better be soon. And he would need the mask to do it. So he was looking for a mask. Good. The idea of searching for an object—a mask, wooden to judge by the sound it made hitting the ground, probably near the way out of the domes—focused Archie, made it a little easier to hold blind terror at bay. *I can do this,* he thought.

But giving the Mask-bearer peace . . . how can I give Stephen peace?

"Don't be stupid, Archie," he said aloud. "The man's a slave, and the chacmool's a Negro, isn't it?" But if freedom was the chacmool's promise, what could Archie offer in this world?

Archie remembered the clergyman's speech, back in New York the previous fall. Blackbirders stealing children. Ironic. He'd had his own daughter stolen and hadn't even known it then, hadn't known how much he had in common with the Negro father chasing through the Five Points after his vanished daughter. How very much he hadn't known about himself. He thought of the three slaves aboard the *Maudie*, drowned by their shackles. I never knew their names, Archie thought. Alfonse, Punch, Judy: those aren't real names. No one should have to die that way, and each of us is a little bit to blame.

"All right, Stephen," Archie promised, his voice fading into the domes. "If that's your peace, I'll do what I can to give it to you."

And if I don't get out of here, that will be exactly nothing.

So there was a mask lying among the rocks somewhere on the floor. Archie placed his back squarely against the wall and took two shuffling steps away from it. He did an about-face and took the same two steps, finding the wall exactly where he had left it.

"Here we go." This time he took four steps, then turned to his left and counted five steps before the floor began to rise. The passage out must be dead ahead, he thought, unless he'd gone in the wrong direction. But that didn't really bear thinking about, not at this point. Archie turned left again, took a step, and went sprawling as his foot caught a rock protruding from the floor. He stayed where he'd fallen, getting his bearings as best he could. The floor under him sloped slightly down to his left; the wall should still be in front of him, then. Not wanting to stand for fear of knocking himself unconscious on an overhang from the entry passage, he raised himself to hands and knees and began a slow crawl toward where the wall should have been.

His hand fell on something smooth, and his heart skipped a beat. He felt the object with both hands, picking it up and turning it this way and that. It was a mask, of polished wood; he could feel the grain under his fingers.

If you are what I think you are, this'll lead you out, Stephen had said. Archie assumed that meant he had to put it on, but it had no straps, or even eyeholes. It was simply a convex piece of wood, with a protrusion where a nose would be and a narrow slit of a mouth. Well, he could always hold it to his face; it was heavier than he thought it should be, but not so heavy that he couldn't hold it up to save his life and Jane's. And God knew how many others as well, he thought, remembering a sky stained brown by smoke from the chacmool's fires.

The mask fit snugly over Archie's face, and he held it there, waiting for something to happen. After a moment he realized he'd closed his eyes when he put it on; he opened them, feeling his eyelashes brush against its inner surface.

Shock blasted through him as the feather talisman froze to his chest. Shriveling cold spread into his chest and a terrible squeezing sensation settled around his heart, cutting off his breath. Archie ripped open his coverall and seized the talisman, his fingers instantly numbed by the contact. He cried out as he tore it loose, feeling a patch of skin come with it. It stuck to his hands, sending waves of freezing pain up his arms to his laboring heart.

He tried to fling it away, couldn't. His head began to swim and he pitched forward, breaking his fall with his frozen hands. The impact tore the talisman partly loose, and Archie scraped it frantically along the floor. The back of one hand banged against a rock; Archie raked the talisman along the rock's edge, bloodying his hands as each pass loosened it a bit more. His labored breathing whistled through the mask's mouth slit, and he could hear his heart, slow and ponderous like the drumbeat of a military funeral.

Last resort, he thought, getting to one knee. He laid his hands flat on the cave floor, the talisman frozen crookedly between them. Placing one foot squarely on the brass medallion, Archie lunged to his feet.

The talisman came loose, tearing long shreds of skin from Archie's hands. He scrambled away from it, then lost his balance and fell, remembering not to break the fall with his hands this time. Pain rolled his stomach into a somersault as Archie watched the bits of his skin stuck to the talisman shrivel like green leaves in a fire. His breath returned and he sucked in huge grateful breaths, the cold fading from his hands. The pressure lifted from his chest and his heart began to beat again, erratically at first but settling in a moment to a fast, excited hammering in his aching chest.

He could see. The talisman lay before him, its quetzal feathers gummed with blood and bits of wrinkled skin. Above and behind it Archie could clearly make out the passage leading out of the domes. He looked from it to his hands, which throbbed with pain far worse than what he'd felt when Royce had stabbed him, months ago now; his palms and fingers looked as if they'd been clumsily butchered. Touching bloody fingers to his face, Archie found that he was still wearing the mask. It had no weight now that it rested securely on his face, covering his eyes, and he was confused enough to wonder how it stayed attached.

I'm the Mask-bearer now, he thought, wondering if that was what Tamanend had meant all along. *And it's time to seek my peace.*

As soon as he thought of Tamanend, something in the air shifted, as if an unthinkably vast face had swung toward him and begun watching him. Archie stood and looked around, but the presence—if there was any real presence—stayed just outside his field of vision. Its attention was hungry somehow, neither hostile nor encouraging but uncomfortably curious. Using the mask attracted its attention, Archie thought. It's waiting to see what I'm going to do next, watching me like that man Wilson did in the Brewery basement. He repressed a shudder at the thought that Wilson—no, Pope—had been somehow an agent of Ometeotl.

Steen must have felt the same gaze when the rabbit exploded in that boy's hands. He had said as much, warning Royce that the *huehueteotl* was watching and going to bizarre lengths to escape the Old God's attention. Of course, Steen had reason to avoid the Old God—he was working in Tlaloc's service.

This enemy is your ally, Tamanend had said. But he had also warned Archie that this ally was not entirely to be trusted. The knife in Archie's belt grew warm, and he decided that the less attention he drew at the moment, the better.

If he was lucky, removing the feather talisman had blinded the chacmool to his whereabouts. But he had, in essence, traded the talisman for the mask, and given up some of his own flesh and blood to do it, and Archie had no idea what sort of allegiance that exchange had committed him to.

Outside the Old Brewery, Archie remembered, Steen had insisted that Royce and the Geek follow directly in Archie's footsteps. The two Rabbits had lived long enough afterward that Archie decided to give the same tactic a try now.

Ally or not, he thought, I believe I'd rather proceed without anyone watching, just for now. He searched the floor and caught the trail of Stephen's footprints leading out of the domes. Perhaps the *huehueteotl* would see Stephen instead of him, Archie thought. He fell into Stephen's trail and followed it into the maze separating him from the chacmool and Jane.

The feeling of being watched fell away as Archie retraced Stephen's path through the nameless canyon passages. The trail persisted even over bare rock, and Archie realized that he wasn't seeing actual track, but presences. Stephen's prints took the shape of bare feet, recording the passage of the man rather than the impact of his bootsoles.

I'm still blind, Archie thought. *It's not my eyes I'm seeing through.*

Whose, then?

He felt the Old God's attention return as he worked his way through the long crawl back to the junction Stephen had called the Pass of El Ghor. Every time his flayed palms touched the damp gravelly floor, Archie's stomach flipped and pain rose up like a roaring in his ears, but behind the stabbing agony he could feel the patient gaze of the *huehueteotl*, like a weight on the back of his neck. Would this happen every time he wasn't able to follow Stephen exactly? What if Stephen hadn't gone back to the chacmool, how could Archie escape the Old God's Eye then?

And why did he want to? *This enemy is your ally.* Tamanend had been maddeningly obscure, but he had never lied. Somehow the Old God's attention could be turned to Archie's advantage.

None of that matters, Archie thought. He paused to pick a triangular pebble from the base of his thumb. *If I have to carry the Old God on my back, I will.*

But as soon as he came out of the crawl and picked up Stephen's trail again, the presence faded, and Archie made his way laboriously along, passing through Purgatory with the quiet rippling of Echo River sounding all around him. *God, I'm thirsty*, he thought, but he didn't dare stop. He had no idea how long he'd been cowering under the domes—for all he knew, the ceremony could already have taken place.

No, the Old God would have given up on him then; there must still be some time. But even if Archie had time for a leisurely lunch on the riverbank, he thought that the chacmool—talisman or no—would notice the moment he came into contact with the river.

Archie pressed ahead, cursing at the knot of pain tightening at the base of his spine. Stephen's stride was shorter than his, and following the tracks forced Archie to take toddler steps even when the path was broad and level. His ankle was throbbing again, threatening to buckle with each step, and as fatigue slowed his reactions, he stumbled more often, once nearly slipping into the river. *Would have solved my thirst problem,* he thought, but through the mask he could see things moving in the river, things that took the shape of its spidery currents and waited for a certain interloper to make a misstep. Archie thought of the *chaneque* and wondered whose bodies and souls had been conscripted to watch for him from the water.

After the torturous trip through Purgatory, Archie was stunned to see the rowboat still tied up to its post on the rocky beach of Lake Lethe. It hadn't yet occurred to him to worry about it; getting even this far had seemed impossible.

Stephen, he thought. *But then how did he get back?*

Even this good fortune, though, left Archie having to row back using his flayed hands. Quickly he tore strips from his shirt and bound his hands as best he could. Then he untied the boat and pushed off into the river.

It was only a short distance to the end of Lethe, and thence to the River Side-cut that led around most of River Styx, ending in a natural bridge. Archie worked into a steady rhythm after a few minutes, doing his best to ignore the ragged pain in his hands and chest.

Something tugged suddenly at his right hand, and he nearly dropped the oar on that side. He looked down and stifled a scream.

Maudie's rudderman Alfonse was there, his bloated hands clamped on the oar and his teeth clenched on the bloody trailing edge of Archie's bandage. Vacuous hunger animated Alfonse's face as he chewed away at the bandage, pulling Archie's arm toward the water. Below Alfonse drifted Punch and Judy, floating along in tandem, their legs dragged down by rusty shackles with chains that trailed away to invisibility.

Blood in the water, Archie realized. I can't touch the water, especially not here.

He let go of the oar and swiftly unwrapped the bandage, then threw it as far as he could back the way he'd come. The bloody strip of cloth unwound over the river, landing like a clumsily cast fishing line.

Around it the water surged as the dead rose from the river and fought over this offering. Alfonse lost his grip on the oar and was dragged away by his clenched teeth, his eyes rolling back to stare at Archie as he faded into the dark water.

BEFORE HE GOT to the Side-cut, Archie thought he'd have one last try at coming up with a plan, or at least isolate some things he *didn't* want to do. Bleed in the river, was one. Kill anyone, another. He looked over the side and saw that the shapes in the river were again dispersed by its currents. His blood had given them form. That was important somehow.

But there was simply too much he didn't know. If Stephen had somehow resolved his doubts, Archie would likely have to kill him to get to the chacmool. He had the knife, but the experience with Royce, the ghastly seduction of the man's dying heartbeats reverberating in his mind . . . he wasn't sure he could use it on Stephen, not knowing what he did now. If he had to become something like the chacmool to defeat it, the real battle would be lost.

The only person Archie hadn't been afraid to threaten with the knife was himself. He remembered awakening with it in his hands at least twice, knowing that he could find his own heart and end his struggles. The incident aboard the Daigles' keelboat seemed to confirm it: the knife could only be a defensive weapon. Archie had killed a man with it, and had nearly lost his soul as a result, but he had also used it to stave off what Peter Daigle had called his demon.

What can I gain by turning the knife on myself? Archie wondered. The question gnawed at his mind as he grounded the boat on Lethe's muddy banks, watching carefully to make sure he wasn't bleeding into the river.

At last Archie crossed the natural bridge over River Styx and began working his way toward the Dead Sea and the crevice he was sure led to the chacmool's lair. He picked up his pace, hopscotching along Stephen's track, then stopped dead when he heard the whistled strains of "Onward, Christian Soldiers" carrying lightly down the hall ahead of him.

Riley Steen sat on a ledge over the emerging River Styx, dangling his booted feet in the water. He stopped whistling and inclined his head at Archie, smiling from behind a near-mask of mud and gore. "Good trick, Mr. Prescott," he said with the air of a hunter complimenting his companion's last shot. "I see you learned something the night of our Five Points excursion. Did you take the boat ride on this lovely river? Matchless experience, but too little light to gamble properly."

"I thought you were dead, Steen." Archie remained where he was. Steen's derringer nestled in one meaty fist, not pointing at Archie but not aimed away either. Archie couldn't understand why Steen was here waiting for him, or why the chacmool had allowed him to traipse through the cave all this time.

"Oh, in every way that matters, I am, Mr. Prescott. I see what the dead see, hear them speak. Quite a lively bout of wagering has sprung up regarding the odds of your success."

"It has? What do dead people bet?" Keep him talking, Archie thought. Keep asking questions.

"Poems and songs, sometimes, but primarily jokes." Steen chuckled. "The dead are tremendous pranksters. I've placed my own bet, of course, which is why I've dallied here so long."

Steen splashed his feet in the river, shredding a delicate shape that had begun to coalesce around them, and shifted the derringer so it pointed more directly at Archie. "I'll tell you a little tale, Mr. Prescott. When Beethoven premiered his Ninth Symphony, the *Chorale*, he was completely deaf and couldn't hear the musicians. But he conducted grandly, even if his motions didn't have much to do with what was actually happening onstage because his musicians were following the first-chair violin, and when the music had ended he kept right on conducting until that same first-chair violin got up and turned him around so he could see the ovation he was receiving from the crowd.

"Well, that's exactly what has happened to me, Mr. Prescott. The musicians play my tune but ignore my conducting. Beethoven composed music he couldn't hear, I've made possible a world that I never could have seen. But, even though Beethoven was ignored at the premiere, no one now forgets that it was he who composed the Ninth—and history will give me my due as well. Seeing as the dead see offers one a certain perspective. From that perspective I see that my importance to these proceedings is undiminished, even if I myself do not exist to enjoy the temporal fruits of their success."

Lost in his own story now, Steen hadn't noticed that the shape in the river had reformed. Archie could see it, though, a ragged human shape with one arm truncated at the elbow. John Diamond.

But Diamond has a body, Archie thought, or at least did a week ago. Was Steen bleeding into the water, and *his* nightmares taking form around his feet?

"If I allow you to disrupt the ceremony, and by some

stroke of fortune you defeat the chacmool, no history will
ever record what I have done. You will move on and
forget this as best you can, and the nigger Stephen will
keep all of these marvelous events a secret. I can't allow
that to happen, Mr. Prescott. I cannot allow these proceedings to fade unrecorded, and I cannot allow myself
to disappear into the anonymity reserved for wandering
madmen. I am dead, and history is all I have.

. "Surely you understand." Steen raised the derringer.

At the same time, John Diamond rose out of the River
Styx and dug the fingers of his remaining hand into the
fleshy wattle under Steen's jaw. Diamond started to fall
back into the water, and Steen was dragged along with
him, flailing his arms for balance as he pulled the trigger
of the tiny gun.

The shot hit Archie squarely in the forehead, knocking
him over backward. He lay blind on his back, thinking
Stephen wasn't the trap, Steen *was the trap*. Trying to sit
up, Archie couldn't find his balance and succeeded only
in rolling onto his side, where he reached out for something to hold onto. Something to keep him from drifting
away. Spasms shook his legs, and he flipped onto his back
again.

Someone was shouting, the voices coming in a rush that
mingled with violent splashes from the river. One sen-
tence rose clearly out of the muddle, sticking in Archie's
mind: *Guess I owe you a bad turn or two, Steen.*

So it had been John Diamond. An image arose in Archie's mind: Diamond's puzzled glance at his mutilated
arm, as the *chaneque* vomited out its life in Blennerhassett's abandoned study.

How did Steen get to Blennerhassett's? Archie thought.
I have to get to Kentucky. But don't touch the river.

"Ahh, God," he cried out, seeing again the explosion
that destroyed *Maudie*, thinking of the three slaves grasping vainly at the sunlight just beyond their reach. He lost
consciousness then, slipping into the waters with dying

slaves clutching at his ankles and Helen's ghostly face riding in pale flame on the receding surface.

Light awoke him, real light that stabbed into his ringing head. Archie flinched away from it, clutching at his forehead. His hands stung as they touched his face, joining a chorus of agony from his face, his chest ... his entire body hurt.

"Mr. Prescott." The voice was Stephen's. Archie couldn't help but smile, even though the movement ground his broken nose painfully. Blood trickled onto his lips.

"Come to finish me off, Stephen?"

"Get up, Mr. Prescott. No time for you to be hurt." Stephen dangled a watch in front of Archie's face. He couldn't focus on it. Reflected light from its case dazzled him.

Stephen put away the watch and took hold of Archie's shoulders. "Twenty minutes before midnight, Mr. Prescott. Got to go." He hauled Archie to his feet and held him upright until Archie could stand shakily on his own.

"I've been shot, Stephen. In the head."

Stephen bent down and picked something up off the cave floor. Archie saw that it was the mask, or rather half of it. It was cracked cleanly down the middle, the broken edge marred by a hemispherical gouge. "Never seen a man so lucky to be shot in the head," Stephen said. "Now come on."

"Steen shot me," Archie said as Stephen led him around the Dead Sea. "Where's Steen?"

"Gone down River Styx," Stephen answered. "John Diamond too."

They stopped in front of the Bottomless Pit branch. Archie recognized it; his wits were beginning to return. "Reckon we've seen the last of them both," Stephen said. "Now follow me. You hear, Mr. Prescott? Follow my light."

————

Follow the light, Archie repeated to himself. Steen was dead, Royce and the Geek as well. Three men on whom he had sworn mortal revenge, but he'd actually killed none of them. Royce would surely have died from the wound Archie had given him, but it had been Steen who actually finished him. Archie supposed he should feel cheated, but he didn't. Revenge seemed irrelevant when one's head still rang from the impact of a bullet that should have been fatal. He was lucky to be alive. But then, how often had that been the case during the past few months?

He followed Stephen automatically, wincing whenever he had to use his hands to negotiate the cramped passage. Ometeotl's Eye returned then—or Archie noticed it again, he wasn't sure which. The light, inquisitive pressure on the back of his neck seemed to lessen the pain from his hands and chest, but his nose was still bleeding freely. Blood dripped from the end of his chin, spotting the muddy floor as Archie focused on the one task remaining before him. One last adversary to overcome, and then . . .

Then would take care of itself. Jane was all that mattered now.

Stephen clambered out into an open space, then turned to wait for Archie. Reaching the end of the branch passage, Archie saw that it emerged well above the bottom of the pit. A rough hill of breakdown sloped away into darkness to Archie's left, reaching as high as the passage mouth only at the near wall. Stephen crouched under a leaning block of stone as large as Riley Steen's wagon. He held a finger to his lips, then helped Archie climb down next to him.

"You have to take it from here, Mr. Prescott," he said, just above a whisper. "I'm sorry for what I did, but I did it for the same reasons you're doing this."

Stephen lay on his stomach and set his lamp on a level space a few feet below. "Stay to the left. The light'll give

out before you get there, but you won't miss the way in."
Archie nodded, imagining the hungry glow of the sacrificial fire set to consume his daughter's life. He stepped
down next to the light, then picked his way slowly down
the ancient rockslide, leaving the light entirely behind.

Dangling his feet from a canted ledge, Archie found a
level sandy floor. He looked up and behind him: the
faintest glow from Stephen's lamp shone far above, but
Archie was in complete darkness. He paused, his progress
interrupted by a powerful feeling that his success very
much depended on his reasons for entering the cavern that
lay hidden ahead of him. Were his reasons so similar to
Stephen's? The chacmool had promised Stephen freedom,
but it had done its best to kill Archie after their first brief
encounter in Barnum's Museum. Why it had let him live
that night was a mystery to Archie, unless it was out of
some bizarre deference to his being Jane's father. Or perhaps that idea wasn't so bizarre. Even with his connection
to the chacmool severed, Archie knew he had some sort
of power. Stephen had recognized it, and given him the
mask because of it. I'm still suspended between the two,
Archie thought. Tlaloc and Ometeotl. I have to throw in
with one or the other.

But he'd done exactly that, he realized, when he put on
the mask. Tlaloc had rejected him them, and the talisman
had nearly killed him. And with Tlaloc against him, Archie had no choice but to turn toward the Old God. But
beware, Tamanend had warned: Ometeotl was as hungry
as Tlaloc, for he had been as long without sacrifice.

Archie stood, realizing what he had to do. Tamanend
was right. Events had drawn into focus around him, and
if he didn't act, Ometeotl's Eye would burn him like an
ant under a magnifying glass. He drew the knife and held
it in front of him, feeling with his other hand for invisible
protrusions in the walls or ceiling. His hand found a triangular opening in the wall and he ducked though it, holding his breath as he followed the faint glimmer of firelight
that began to light the way.

"Nanahuatzin, precious jade, it is time." The chacmool plucked a feather from its cloak and laid it in a bowl-shaped depression in the floor between the feet of the fanged statue. Reaching into the statue's mouth, it removed a small green stone and set it on the feather. A bright flame sprang up and grew to fill the bowl, burning soundlessly and without smoke. "Now you begin the next journey, to Tlalocan."

"I'm ready," Jane murmured. She lay on the square stone, feet toward the flame, her head slightly raised by the stone's angle. "I'll miss my body, I suppose."

"Much more awaits you, Nanahuatzin. He Who Makes Things Grow calls to you, and you must leave your body behind."

Reaching again into the statue's mouth, the chacmool found a wide-bladed stone knife. It passed the blade four times through the flame, and with each pass its form changed a little, became less human and more like the thing she'd imagined the night the two sailors had died outside her door.

That was also the night it had begun to heal her. The night it had chosen her. A flush of gratitude brought happy tears to Jane's eyes. She smiled as they trickled across her smooth cheeks; oh, how she wanted the journey to begin. She thought of the maps in her little den, of all the places she'd determined to go. Now she would be going someplace grander than New Orleans or San Francisco, or even Zanzibar. No map could ever show it, and she had been chosen to go there. Her cloak rustled, feathers lifting to brush at her tears.

The chacmool came to her side and raised its cupped hand over her. The tip of the stone blade pointed out past its clawed fingers. "Nanahuatzin, you go now to He Who Makes Things Grow, and a new world will rise in the wake of your journey. You go to Tlaloc, *macehuales im-*

acpal iyoloco," it purred, so very like a cat. She'd always
wanted a cat.

"*Macehuales imacpal iyoloco*," she repeated, resting in
the sounds the words made.

"*Yollotl, eztli; ompa onquiza'n tlalticpac*," the chacmool purred. It raised the knife over her breast.

"Jane."

It was her father's voice, and Jane felt a surge of impatience that he had come just now, to interrupt the start
of her journey. He hadn't wanted her when she was ugly;
did he think he could just be nice when she was healed
and whole again? "My name is Nanahuatzin," she said
crossly, turning her head toward him so he would see she
was angry. He stood before the entrance holding a knife,
and she felt a twinge of pity at the stricken look twisting
his face. *Poor Da*, she thought, *someone's broken his
nose. Look at it bleeding.*

"You can do nothing, Prescott," the chacmool said, its
words distorted by its feline muzzle and forked tongue. It
lowered the point of the knife until it pricked Jane's skin,
and she gasped a little. It was *cold*. "She goes to Tlaloc."

"She comes to me," Da said, and despite being cross
with him, Jane cried out when he turned the knife inward
and plunged it into his own chest.

So you have come to me at last.

I had no other choice, Archie said. The knife shifted in
his grasp, sliding deeper until he could feel its point prick-
ing into the wall of his heart. He tightened his grip, but
his hands were already slick with blood.

You've been watching me, Archie said. I didn't go anywhere; I brought you here.

Look around you.

Archie did, and could make no sense of what he saw.
The cavern still enclosed him, the chacmool and Jane held
their tableau in front of the bas-relief of Tlaloc on one
wall, the fire still blazed up from the floor, but behind that

scene was something else. A dark sun cast the fire's shadow on a floor of patterned sand, throwing a blackness so intense it hurt Archie's eyes. Behind the blackness a jungle grew from the sands, its breezes heavy with the smells of earth and decay.

Sharing space with Jane on the altar was Archie himself, naked save for a green quetzal feather cloak thrown back to expose his breast. Over him stood a woman, her colorless skin shining in the black light of the sun. She held an obsidian knife against his breast; its tip pushed ever so slightly into the hollow beneath his sternum. Looking down, Archie saw nothing, despite the growing ache in his shoulders as he struggled to hold the knife in place.

Where is this place? Where am I? he said.

Omeyocan, the woman said, only she had become a man, his hair long and straight and blacker than the impossible light. *The Place of Duality. You are in my place, Archie Prescott, where everything is at once itself and what it is not.*

At her words, the objects in the room became indistinct, fading to outlines, and stars appeared where the roof of the cavern had been.

All except Ometeotl, who stood at the center of a reality that shifted faster than Archie could blink. *See, you have come to me*, Ometeotl said, and the god's words wrapped themselves around a shape that coalesced into a stone altar bearing Archie's spread-eagled body. *You have offered yourself to me.*

I have offered you something much larger than myself, Archie said. On the altar he could see his lips moving. You've been kept from the world because your worshipers died away.

I am kept from nothing, Ometeotl replied. Leaning over the altar, he pushed on the knife.

Archie grunted as his hands slipped another fraction. The smell of his own sweat rose into his nostrils, lingering for a moment before sharpening into the pungent odor of woodsmoke.

You will slip, Archie Prescott, and then I will have eztli *to drink. You have a strong heart,* yolteotl, *strong nourishment.* Ometeotl smiled.

If you drink from me, you lose the chacmool. Tlaloc will have this world, and you will have only my life.

I am Lord of Time, Ometeotl growled. *If this new sun is born under Tlaloc, I will wait for the next.*

And what if no man like me waits for you there? Archie's arms began to go numb. Lord of Time or not, he thought, time was passing in his body, and he didn't have much longer.

Then I will wait yet another sun.

With no one to sacrifice to you, no one to remember you. You'll grow very hungry. Have you ever been so hungry? Only half a sun has passed, and you are already starved. You ignore your enemy of ages to toy with my one life. After I am dead, Tlaloc will eat well; will you feed on your own heart? You'll certainly taste the smoke from Tlaloc's fires.

Ometeotl's anger drained all the light from the stars. *I will taste your life.*

Archie cried out as the knife slipped deeper into his chest. Fresh pain pierced him with every heartbeat, and the trickle of blood over his hands grew into a steady stream. Only the last two fingers of his left hand held the knife back from burrowing into his heart, and the smell of the rotting jungle choked off his breath.

Is my sacrifice worth so little? he cried. I offer you my life and you won't even kill your worst enemy to save my daughter.

Is that your boon, Archie Prescott? Ometeotl lilted, like a young woman teasing a suitor. *You would have the chacmool destroyed and your daughter saved from the knife?*

Yes, Archie sobbed. In return for my life, that's what I ask.

That has already been done, Ometeotl said. *Did you think I would shrink from my rival? You know little for one who speaks so well, and your time for speech is past. Even at your end, you know so little of yourself.*

Archie felt the knife begin to sink still deeper, working itself free from his bloody grasp. Sold my soul to the devil, he thought dully. Tricked into a bargain, and now he's come to collect.

As soon as Da stabbed himself, everything changed. The fire blazed up and turned dark, spilling shadows into every crevice of the cave. At the same time, the chacmool looked up from Jane to the statue carved into the wall.

Flames scoured the statue, burning away the rings around its eyes, its feathered headdress, the skulls dangling from its hand. Another shape began to emerge, without decoration, a giant shape of a man.

The statue stood, towering above the chacmool, and the cave groaned as the wall behind the figure stretched. It stepped through the fire, and the flames leaped onto it, clinging to it and giving off that awful shadowed light as they ate through the ropy strands of molten rock attaching the statue to the wall.

"Ometeotl, Tezcatlanextia, in teyocoyani," the statue grated. It began to grow, splitting as it did. Flames filled the cracks like mortar.

A wave of heat washed over Jane, sucking away her breath, and the feathers of her cloak sprang into a thousand individual flames. She rolled off the altar stone, landing heavily on her side, shrieking and beating at the fire. Her lovely cloak was thrashing about her, raging in every direction away from the burning statue as each of its feathers exploded in tiny puffs of smoke.

Jane's eyebrows singed away as the flames leaped from the feathers to the scaly clumps of scab that covered her hands. *No, I was healed*, she thought. *The chacmool healed me, and the journey . . .* But the scabs stayed, blackening under the flames that leaped among them and crawled under the cloak to sear the hard shell of scab covering her back.

Then her face caught fire, and through the flames in her eyes she watched as the statue caught hold of the chacmool and tore out its shriveled heart.

Do you feel the knife moving closer? As you move closer to me. Ometeotl was losing shape. All Archie could see was a burning curiosity, like William Wilson's when he'd said *Where was your soul?*

The knife dug into the wall of his heart.

Archie's vision slipped and he felt a blast of heat on his face, carrying the sharp stink of burning hair and flesh. *Jane*, he howled, and on the altar his body arched, the obsidian blade sunk nearly to the hilt in his chest. *Helen*, he thought. *I tried.*

Would you see your daughter a final time? Ometeotl asked, and Archie did—she rolled on the cave floor, wreathed in shadowy flames. Behind her stood a burning colossus, the wall of the cave stretched and buckled behind it like a molten stone umbilicus. Flames licked at the chacmool, and Archie's ears ached with the sizzle of rain falling into fire. His vision misted over, as if steam had filled the cave, and through the blinding fog Archie caught a momentary glimpse of Jane, standing whole and unscarred as the dark light blew about her like wind.

You see she lives, Ometeotl said. *Few last visions are so kind.*

The chacmool squalled in the statue's grip, dangling by its throat from one burning stone hand. A blaze of burning light gouted from the statue's mouth as it gulped down the chacmool's heart, and as the burst of fire rose to the cavern's ceiling, Archie saw Helen's face.

The stone tendrils holding it to the wall snapped, and a hole appeared, opening on a tunnel that led straight to hell. Or Mictlan—he could see deserts, and mountains that clashed together, and a little red dog waiting patiently to show him the way.

Archie began stumbling toward Jane, each step jarring the blade sunk in his breast. *Jane*, he tried to shout, but the only sound he could make was a wheezing moan. Shadows grew and hid Jane from him, closing him off with the presence of the *huehueteotl*.

Now you come to me. Omeyocan will be your home. The darkness closed around Archie, and he heard Wilson say *Easy, now, easy*. The chacmool's dying feline screams became the sound of rain falling on fire.

Oh, I'm burning, I'm burning, I don't want to die this way.

Jane watched the chacmool struggle, watched its limbs curl like a dying spider's around the crater torn in its chest. And she was dying, too, she must be. When she breathed fire came out, like fog would on a cold night.

But it didn't hurt, and it seemed that through her right eye she could see herself being scrubbed clean of some filth, something that had been clinging to her and that she hadn't been able to see.

The floor shook as one of the statue's arm broke off in a burst of molten droplets. It began to fragment, the fiery cracks in its form yawning wider and brighter. Behind it she could see a hole in the wall, and in the hole the faces of the dead crowded to watch her.

"Jane," Da said. His voice was barely a whisper, but it cut into her through the deafening roar of the statue's collapse. He staggered toward her, both hands clasped desperately around the hilt of the knife in his chest.

I'm sorry, Da. I'm sorry for how I thought about you before, she wanted to say. I knew you'd come for me, I did.

But there wasn't any time.

"Da, don't touch me—you'll burn," she said. But she ran to him anyway, then shrank back as tongues of fire leaped from her to play about the knife and curl under his clenched jaw.

"Slipping . . . soon," he gasped, but the voice came from behind Jane. She looked over her shoulder and saw him lying on the altar, his chest gouged and bleeding. The statue bent over him, bits of itself falling onto his body, the chacmool dangling like a broken doll from its remaining arm.

And in the flames rolling from the gateway to hell Jane saw her mother's face.

She looked back and Da was still standing before her, dying even as he tried to step closer. Blood, black in the awful light streaming from the hole, soaked the entire front of his coverall and pooled about his feet.

A strange calm settled over her and she said, "No, Da. You're not slipping. Let go and let me help you."

He didn't appear to hear her, but his hands dropped limply to his sides. His body jerked as the knife sank all the way in, and an anguished wail rose behind her.

Don't look at him there, she told herself. *He's not there. He's right in front of you.* But he was fading before her, being taken away to that other place where he lay on an altar with his beating heart exposed to the hungry god.

"I'll help you, Da," Jane said gently. She took hold of the knife in both hands and pulled it from his breast.

Omeyocan drained into itself like a whirlpool, crushing Archie into himself again as his double was swept away with the jungle and the patterns in the sand. He felt cold stone under his feet as things took their shapes again, and gratefully he fell onto that stone.

He felt the Old God slipping away, sliding free of his mind as the knife had from his chest. *Another Sun will rise, Prescott,* a fading voice warned. *Another Sun, and I will drink from the skulls of your descendants.*

Archie's ears roared. No, the roar came from outside, from the bas-relief of Tlaloc as it crumbled outward from the wall, burying the altar and the body of the chacmool that lay draped over it. All of this he saw in a flash, then the fire was extinguished and the last of its light siphoned away by the wind of Omeyocan's passing.

The floor shifted, then heaved as huge rocks crashed invisibly down from the shuddering ceiling. *Have to get out*, Archie thought, but he didn't think he could stand. Each breath he drew felt as if the knife was being thrust back into his heart.

"Light, Da!" Jane shouted in his ear. "Light over here!" She hauled on him, and with her help he was barely able to stand. Now he could see the light as well, the faintest glimmer showing in the low arch that led out.

Another rockslide roared behind them, raising an invisible cloud of choking dust. Jane pulled him toward the light and he stumbled after, wincing every time a falling slab of limestone crashed around them. Larger blocks were falling now, heavy enough that Archie's ears rang with echoes of each impact. He held blindly onto Jane's tiny hand, marveling at its strength. She led him as she would a child, once jerking him aside as a fragment of the ceiling smashed itself to pebbles where he'd been standing the moment before, stinging him with flying shards. They crouched to enter the passage out, and Archie saw Stephen waiting for them at the bottom of Bottomless Pit.

The entire cave shuddered around them, shadows dancing crazily from Stephen's lamp, and a blast of wind from the collapsing cavern behind them threw Archie off balance. He fell against the wall and felt it shift under his weight. A broad section tilted against him, forcing him backward as it fell slowly over to jam itself diagonally across the passage. A vast echoing groan rolled through the cave, and with it a shower of small stones.

A narrow crevice was all that remained of the exit to Bottomless Pit. Archie dropped to his hands and knees to see if they could squeeze through, and light from Stephen's lamp caught him full in the face. He heard Stephen shouting, "The girl! Mr. Prescott, give me Jane!"

No, Archie thought, reason choked off by panic and the thickening cloud of dust that gritted in his eyes. *It's one last deception, one last trick.*

But Jane scrambled ahead without looking at him, catching Stephen's hand and pushing herself through with froglike kicks at the enclosing rock. Archie tried to follow her and found himself caught, his head and one arm through the crack but his progress arrested by a sharp ridge that pressed down on his other shoulder. "Stephen!" he shouted. "I can't get through!"

For a single heart-stopping moment Stephen didn't turn around, and memories of the tomblike blackness in the domes closed in around Archie. But no, he saw Stephen had just been hoisting Jane to safety on the same fallen chunk of rock that Archie himself had paused on before entering the chacmool's sanctuary. That done, Stephen turned and dropped to his knees in front of Archie.

"Breathe out, Mr. Prescott," Stephen commanded. Behind him, the lamp's dancing shadows reminded Archie of shapes he'd seen in River Styx, less than an hour before. "Breathe out and push with your legs. Your chest is too big."

He seized Archie's flailing arm with both hands and set his feet against rocks on either side of the slowly closing crack.

A booming rumble like a peal of thunder sounded from behind Archie, and dust blew through the tiny space between Archie's back and the leaning slab. Small rocks and gravel were beginning to pile around his feet.

"Breathe *out*, Mr. Prescott!" Stephen said again. "If the dust can get out, you can too! Come on now, set your feet and count three. One! Two!"

Archie kicked his legs, finding no purchase on the dusty floor.

"Three!"

Stephen hauled on Archie's arm hard enough that something popped audibly in his shoulder. Archie expelled all the air from his lungs, feeling the crack press tighter around him and scrabbling madly for a toehold to push against. He squeezed forward a bit and grunted with pain and effort as the buttons popped off his blood-soaked coverall. His flayed chest scraped agonizingly on the rock.

"Da, *please!*" Jane cried. Another tremor shook the cave and the slab pinning him shifted the tiniest bit. Stephen hauled again, lifting himself off the ground and moving Archie another inch forward, and then Archie's shoulder scraped through.

Stephen fell backward, losing his grip on Archie's wrist and striking his head on a spur of rock between Jane's feet. Jane leaped down and took his place, helping Archie wriggle forward until his other arm worked free and he pulled himself out of the tiny crack.

The cave continued to shift and heave, loosing cascades of rock and gravel from the walls and the dome over Bottomless Pit, out of sight far above. A single oblong boulder larger than a man's head bounded down the breakdown pile and hit the wall over their heads. Stephen scrambled to his feet and caught hold of his lamp, then led the way up the breakdown. Archie pushed Jane ahead of him, staying close behind her to lift her over ledges she couldn't easily scale herself.

Climbing the breakdown was like trying to dance in an earthquake, keeping time to each surge of the angry earth. The number of falling rocks increased, each one flashing suddenly through the hazy sphere of lamplight and booming away into the darkness below. What if the branch above had collapsed? The walls of the pit rose sheer from the top of the breakdown another hundred feet or more. If they couldn't duck into the shelter of the branch passage, falling rocks would crush them sooner or later.

But the branch was there, and they ducked into it gratefully. Archie kept one hand on Jane almost continually as they crawled and squeezed their way back to River Hall, listening to the roar and rumble of the cave-in fade behind them. By the time they were able to stand, on the gentle slope above the Dead Sea, the cave was quiet. Archie looked at Stephen, rimed with gray dust, and wondered what to say. Something unresolved hung between them.

Jane broke the moment by stepping close to Archie and slowly, hesitantly, putting her arms around him. "I knew you'd come, Da," she murmured into his chest.

Archie tried to answer her, and couldn't. He stroked her dusty hair instead, feeling awkward and out of practice. A father again, he thought. It was going to take some getting used to.

As was being alive. Archie's body still held the memory of the knife cleaving his heart, and even though he knew where he was, who he was with, nerve and muscle let go their belief in death only reluctantly. He worked a hand inside his torn coverall and found, next to the patch of missing skin from the talisman, a knobby scar about an inch under his left nipple. Omeyocan, he thought: I was and was not there, was and was not pierced, was and was not dead. The smell of his daughter filled his lungs, and he exhaled, finding that he could speak again. "As soon as I could, Jane. Soon as I could."

She held him tighter, her arms trembling with exhaustion. He could see smooth skin in the meandering part of her hair, and her ear was whole again—more than his would ever be. The pressure of her face stung his raw chest, and his hands gave off jagged waves of pain each time he touched her, and he thought he would never again feel quite so much at peace.

After a long while, Stephen gave an embarrassed cough. "Reck on the pit isn't quite so bottomless anymore," he said. "Hope that trace still goes."

He unscrewed the cap from his flask and offered it to Archie. "No, thanks," Archie said.

"Bottoms up, then," Stephen said, and drained the flask. "Come on," he said. "If Dr. Croghan catches us coming out, we gonna have some fancy explaining to do."

No one so strong, no one
so lovely
in all the things of this world

As the eagle
ready for flight
& the jaguar
whose heart
is a mountain

See how they carry
my shield now
These slaves

—"The Eagle and the Jaguar"

Epilogue

Coda—May 1, 1843

❖

The Mississippi River gleamed broad and bright under a warm cloudless sky, as wide as a lake but moving slowly south, building islands and erasing others in its patient journey to New Orleans. Life was everywhere. Weeds grew on waterlogged snags that accumulated silt from the river, and frogs rested on the snags, and herons hunted for frogs among the weeds. Archie was beginning to breathe a little easier.

There had been times in the past three weeks when he'd started awake in the middle of the night, wondering *How will things grow now? Will the rain still fall or will the rivers dry up?*

What have I done?

But men create gods, he reminded himself. And he added something that Tamanend hadn't said: Men create gods, but life—the world—creates itself.

Archie leaned on the railing of the steamer *St. Louis,* watching Jane as she gazed out over the water with an expression of pure joy on her face. She'd done nothing but talk about the river since they'd boarded the *St. Louis* in Louisville, besieging him with facts about its breadth and length and notoriety as a Waterloo for careless navigators.

He'd been happy to see her react that way to the prospect of a trip. They'd stayed two weeks at the Mammoth Cave Hotel, recovering from their ordeal, and during that time Jane had been moody and prone to nightmares, clinging to Archie wherever he went. Of course he couldn't blame her. The wounds of abandonment she had suffered would take years to heal. The scars on her body, though, had faded to light pink tracings on one side of her face and her arms. The chacmool had done that much for her.

The one place she had refused to follow him was into the hotel's barn, part of which was used to store carriages. Riley Steen's yellow drummer-wagon sat under a film of dust, looking strangely like an archaeological find amid the tack and farming implements hanging from the walls. Archie had gone through it, looking for anything he could sell or barter; he found a bizarre assortment of potions and elixirs, a collection of puppets, books in several languages, and a lockbox that when broken open proved to contain nearly three hundred dollars in various currencies. Not a fortune by any means, but enough of a stake to get him and Jane settled wherever they decided to go.

That night he'd asked her if she wanted to return to New York. "Eww, no," she said, screwing up her face in such a delightfully childish expression that Archie had nearly broken down in tears at the sight of it. He did that fairly often, whenever some action or speech of hers struck him or reminded him of Helen. He supposed that, like her nightmares, this lachrymose tendency would pass, but for now it was good to be reminded of Helen, reminded of what it had been like to be a part of a family.

Like almost everyone else they spoke to, Jane wanted to go West. "San Francisco," she said, her face alight with fantasy, and he'd agreed. But he thought perhaps Oregon would be a better place for them. Like Peter Daigle, Archie found himself suddenly averse to large cities.

West, in any case. If it was already too late in the year to join a wagon train, Archie figured he could find some sort of work until next spring; after all, he'd acquired a few skills in the course of his travels. Also he would have to see about getting Jane into school.

Archie had given the wagon to Stephen, who had set about whitewashing it and trading its contents for a down payment on two horses. He meant to buy his freedom, he said, and go to Monrovia in Africa. Acquiring whatever property he could was the first step. Archie wished him luck and wondered if he had discharged his oath. Was it peace to have a goal in sight, and believe you had the means to achieve it?

"I ought to thank you, Stephen," Archie had said, standing by as Stephen scraped the painted slogans away from the drummer-wagon's sideboards.

"You're welcome, Mr. Prescott." Stephen paused long enough to nod at Archie.

"You didn't have to do that for me. I know—" Archie's throat dried up as he thought of Alfonse in the waters of the Dead Sea, somewhere beneath their feet. "I mean, I think I know the promises the chacmool made you. It spoke to me as well."

"Mr. Prescott," Stephen said, laying the scraper down on a worktable, "I didn't do it for you."

Then he had walked out behind the barn. They had parted amicably, Archie supposed, with a kind of unspoken agreement to let sleeping dogs lie. Fair enough.

A May Day festival was taking place on Laclede's Landing, with crowds of people and a fiddle-and-banjo group whose sprightly music drifted across the expanse of brown water. Jane rushed up to Archie, pointing at the gaily dressed crowd. "Can we go to the festival, Da?" she asked, tugging at his hand.

"Of course we can," he replied. "It wouldn't be a holiday if we didn't see a festival."

She smiled at him, and he felt another sudden urge to weep with joy at the sight of her. Then a shadow passed over her face, and she said, "Oh."

"What is it?" he said, fearing she was about to lapse back into her melancholia.

She opened the small handbag he'd bought her in Louisville to go with a new dress and shoes. "I kept this, I don't know why," she said, and brought out a triangular-bladed knife of chipped obsidian.

Archie took it from her and turned it over in his hands, feeling a tightening in his chest around the scar below his left nipple. He had felt this knife biting into the heart of his other self, the one splayed on the altar in Jane's place.

Or had Jane been there in his place?

He didn't know. But Helen's knife was gone, and this relic was what remained.

"No, that's exactly right," he said to Jane, keeping his voice steady. "When we cross the Mississippi, we should say goodbye to everything on the other side."

He drew back his arm and threw the knife far out over the water, drawing the attention of some of the other passengers gathered on the deck. It sparkled in a high arc before skipping once and splashing into the river.

Jane watched the spot where it had fallen for a moment, her face troubled. Then she nestled against his side. "Nobody'll ever find it there," she said firmly.

"No, they won't," Archie agreed. He put his arm around her, and they listened to the floating strains of fiddle music as the *St. Louis* steamed toward the festival throng celebrating May Day on Laclede's Landing.